Vanishing Raven

D1519710

Also by Stephen B. Smart

Whispers of The Greybull

Vanishing Raven

Stephen B. Smart

High Mule Publishing

ISBN: 978-1-5059-0663-9

High Mule Publishing
www.highmulepublishing.com

First Edition – Trade Paperback

Printed in the United States of America

Dedication

This book is dedicated to George and Marlene Knight, who invited me to be a part of their family and introduced a young teenager to life on a ranch. Thank you for helping to sculpt my life in such a positive way.

Vanishing Raven

Prelude

The silence was deafening as she cautiously walked down the rocky, tree-covered ridge through two inches of fresh powder snow. She looked down at her wrists scarred by the heavy shackles she had been forced to wear. Realizing she had really escaped and that freedom might be as close as the valley below, was almost more than she could handle.

The snow had stopped but a thick fog had crept in making the best route off the mountain difficult to find. Never had she felt so alone, as she questioned her decision to split up from the other two fugitives hoping one of them might make it to safety. The three of them had parted ways at least three hours ago and now she hoped and prayed that somewhere down in the valley she would find help.

She worked her way down through a leafless patch of aspen with branches coated with frost. Stopping for a moment, she savored the surrounding beauty, something she hadn't done for a long time. The sun was trying to filter through the fog, and in spots, the ice crystals sparkled like rays off a sunny lake. Her fur-lined moccasins generously coated with bear grease and the long march down the ridge kept her warm. The old burlap she had found at the cabin had slipped. Stopping under the protection of a downed tree, she lowered her baggy pants and carefully removed the rawhide strips holding the burlap in place. After rewrapping her legs to just above her thighs, she snuggly secured the strips. The burlap was old and dirty but at least it would help keep her legs warm when the temperatures began to drop.

The sun began to shine brightly and the warmth felt almost reassuring but as quickly as it appeared, a dark, puffy cloud rolled over the mountain ridge dropping the temperature. Pulling her blue scarf tighter around her neck, she used her pointed walking stick as she carefully chose each step.

There were large rocks and unseen drop offs and she had come too far to be lost to one of them now. It would be very dangerous for her to travel at night and the sun was already low in the sky. With the short days of late fall there wouldn't be enough daylight for her to make it down to the valley. Soon she would need to find shelter for the night.

It was getting dark quickly and the wind picked up as she came to a large, snow covered rock slide. There was no direct route down through the boulders so she was forced to detour over to a steep treed hillside. In places it was so steep that she needed to hold on to branches to help navigate her way down the ridge. At the bottom she stopped and took a moment to catch her breath. Taking off her pack, she set it down beside one of the many moss-covered boulders partially buried by snow and noticed a hole almost two feet in diameter between two large rocks and partially hidden by a fallen snag.

It was pure luck that she saw the opening as she dropped to her knees, crawled to the entrance and cautiously peered inside. Several cracks in the ceiling of the cave allowed just enough light inside that she could see the majority of the small enclosure, and to her relief it was empty. Pushing her pointed stick ahead of her, the strong, pungent scent of animal dung stung her nostrils as she crawled inside. The uneven floor of the small cave was littered with small, dry twigs that probably came from the shattered snag that help conceal the opening.

Going back outside, she grabbed her pack and shoved it through the entrance and then crawled inside behind it. Quickly she opened the pack, pulling out a small flint that she set on a convenient rock shelf. Gathering dry needles and leaves from the floor she built a small mound and topped it with a few twigs. The leaves, needles and twigs were dry and made for perfect kindling. Picking up a dry chunk of wood, she smashed it over a pointed rock to create small wood fibers. She cradled the small mound in her hands and moved it directly under a tiny crack in the rock ceiling.

For the next ten minutes she worked at getting a spark to ignite from her small flint. Finally a small flume of smoke arose from the pile as she knelt down and gently blew on it. There wasn't enough wood to last longer than a few hours but while it did the small fire warmed both her and the rock.

Her stomach rumbled. Placing a piece of dried grouse on a stick, she held it over the fire until it was warm and then quickly devoured it. She had tried to drink at every creek crossing but there hadn't been many. Turning to the pack made of deer hide, she removed a small tin cup and filled it with snow and set it beside the fire to heat. Next she unfolded the light wool blanket, pulling it tight around her shoulders as it would be her only protection against the cold long night.

It had been a week now since they had seen the campfire high on a ridge to the east and she hoped that hiding for almost a week had thrown the Indians off their trail. The ability of the Indian trackers was well known. Even though she tried to convince herself that she was safe, her mind just wouldn't let her accept it. There had been talk in camp about people who had tried to escape but to her knowledge no one had ever accomplished it. Normally escaped prisoners were hunted down within a day and brought back dead over a saddle.

She vividly remembered watching the Indians bring in a young man in his late teens that had lasted several days on the run before capture. He was more dead than alive when they brought him in and tied him to the Devil's Cross. For two days they beat him and then cut the tendons on one leg just above his ankle. For some strange reason they respected this man. Eventually he healed, but after that, he was little more than a pitiful cripple that limped about the compound.

The wind had picked up and the hole she had crawled through was filling with snow. She prayed that the blowing snow would erase any of the tracks she had made that day, and with luck, the Indians were no longer on the mountain.

It was still dark when she opened her eyes to the pitch-black darkness. She didn't panic as her eyes adjusted. Somehow she had slept through most of the night but now she shivered from the cold. After she ate some food from her pack, she reached for the small tin cup from beside the dead coals of her fire. The half cup of water was almost frozen solid. For the last three weeks she had tried to sleep in camp without her buffalo robe covering her body, trying to get her body adjusted to the cold before the escape. She knew the plan had little chance of succeeding but she had nothing to lose. The rumors lately of shutting the camp down had slowly spread even to the prisoners.

It was still dark outside but she thought she heard something, not much but almost like someone was moving slowly through the snow. The sound was so faint and muffled that she held her breath so she could hear it. Then there was total silence.

Several hours later, she crammed everything back into her meager pack and used it to push the snow from the entrance. Overnight it had snowed over a foot and now the going would be even tougher. She shook the loose snow off the wool blanket that covered her shoulders before picking up her pointed walking stick and starting down the ridge. Within thirty feet of the small cave, she found what she thought were the tracks of a single elk making its way down the hill. She followed its tracks down the crest of the ridge for close to an hour before the animal changed direction and headed back up. Too tired to follow his path she continued working her way down the ridge. The deep snow slowed her descent as she leaned heavily on her stick for balance.

Finally, she came out on a rocky ledge on the side of the mountain and noticed a pattern of holes in the snow. She followed the tracks a short distance until they went under a large Douglas fir. Panic rose in the back of her throat as she recognized the tracks were from a large mountain lion. The soft, deep snow made it difficult to identify the source previously but now under the tree they were very clear and large. A sharpened stick would be no match for a hungry mountain lion and she knew it. If the cat caught her scent she would probably have both the Indians and the mountain lion hunting her.

Quickly she headed down the mountain at a steeper angle, hoping to put as much distance as possible between her and the large cat. From the occasional views through the trees she knew she was close to where the thick forest transitioned to the sagebrush prairie. Pausing a moment to figure out the best way to proceed, she heard a branch crack in the forest above her. She couldn't see anything but then she heard a low guttural growl. Terrified she plunged down the steep slope, bouncing off trees and throwing herself over deadfalls. Her only goal was to make it to the tree line before the mountain lion caught her. Hopefully the cougar wouldn't follow her into the open prairie.

All of the sudden she could see an opening through the branches where the timber thinned. Stopping for a moment, she looked back up the hill. A large flash of brown bounded between two trees and then was gone. Turning she slipped and stumbled over a snow-covered log and then regained her footing, before pushing herself down the hill once again. With a quick glance over her shoulder, she saw the mountain lion charging down the path she had just made through the snow. The opening was only twenty yards further and there was no other choice but to run.

She hurled herself forward and moments later landed in the clearing, caking her face with snow. Whirling around, she pointed her spear uphill ready to face her pursuer. To her amazement, the large cat had vanished. Her eyes quickly scanned the forest for movement but there was none. For some reason the big cat had stopped in the middle of its attack. Bending over she put her hands on her knees, her lungs screaming for oxygen.

Finally after a few minutes, she felt the danger had passed and turned to start walking down the hill. Looking up, she stifled a scream, in front of her stood a stocky Indian. Everything went black.

Chapter 1

Greybull River Country, Wyoming

1866

A drop of sweat trickled over Chance Creager's eyebrow as he lifted his dirty, stained hat and wiped his forehead. He could hear the sound of a creek far below, hidden in a valley of brightly colored aspens. His cotton shirt was moist from the long, hurried pursuit of a wounded mule deer. Normally the maxi ball from his forty-five caliber Hawkens was deadly, but the gusting winds had altered the long shot, leaving the wounded deer trying to lose its pursuer on the steep shale slides of a timbered ridge. The weather, warm for the middle of October, could cause the meat to spoil if he didn't find the body soon. The bullet would eventually kill his prey even though he'd hit the deer low and too far back.

Usually he was capable of finding a deer, elk, or antelope closer to the cabin. On really good days, he was lucky enough to shoot a buffalo within a day's ride, but in the last two weeks, something had changed. Game was scarce. He'd made the shot at about eight that morning, and now it was close to ten-thirty and the buck, almost the size of a small elk, showed no signs of slowing down. It continued to travel up the ridge and farther from his family's isolated cabin. Torn ground, an occasional spot of blood, bent grass, or a dislodged rock, were all signs that helped Chance in his pursuit.

His frustration deepened the more he thought of the missed shot. There was a lot of work to be done back at their homestead. Soon the snows of winter would come and they were low on meat. The brothers could spare only one man from the tasks at home, and Chance was the most experienced and best hunter of the three. More often than not, he was the one sent hunting because he knew the lay of the land for miles in most directions. His brothers, Virgil and Vern, had named this drainage, Canvas Creek, for no particular reason that Chance knew. Unlike most wounded animals, this deer was headed up the ridge away from the creek bottom and that bothered Chance. This certainly wasn't normal for a deer of the area. The massive rack and size of its tracks spoke to its cunning and many years of survival.

The narrow trail was littered with debris. Chance climbed over another fallen log and stopped in his tracks, surprised by what lay ahead. It was a rock shelf, the size of a narrow road, tucked into the steep hillside. In one direction, the shelf sloped down towards the valley, and in the other, it seemed to gently work its way up the ridge. The country around their homestead was littered with interesting rock formations but Chance had never seen a ledge such as this. He stood for a moment and examined it. There were no pick marks, piles of waste rocks, or any other sign of man's influence. To find a continuous ledge the width of a road was something Chance had never seen before. This had to be a unique act of nature.

Something else caught his eye. In the middle of the narrow shelf stood a short rotting stump perforated by small insect holes. By the look of the wood, it had to be at least ten years old. What puzzled him was that the stump showed the rough chop marks of an ax. Why would anyone in his right mind cut down a tree on this rocky shelf nearly fifty miles from the nearest wagon road?

The thought faded as he finally noticed another crimson-stained rock amongst the grass. For some reason the deer had almost quit bleeding, but this new sign of blood gave him hope that he would still find this deer. Stealthily he continued up the ridge, rifle in both hands, focused on finding more signs. With the exception of some fallen debris, scattered sagebrush and a sprinkling of small trees, the shelf was mainly low grass. He followed the trail as it meandered up the mountain through a small stand of spruce and then broke into another clearing.

In front of him stood an even larger stump, measuring almost eighteen inches wide, cut smooth just above the ground – the work of a crosscut saw. Up until this time, he and his brothers had believed that they were the first white men to settle in the valley. Now he wasn't so certain.

Chance kept moving and found a bed where the buck had laid down, leaving blood-soaked grass. It won't be long now, he thought.

He carefully placed his heavy, worn boots on the ground, trying to make as little noise as possible. In front of him lay a narrow, babbling creek that sprang from the hillside. The water flowed down onto the bench, saturating a large area. He scanned the ground in front of him and then knelt, cupping his hand to drink. His throat was parched, and he scolded himself for his carelessness in forgetting his canteen. The water tasted cold and sweet.

Chance continued on but he didn't go far before being jerked to attention. In front of him stood two strange monuments built of native stone in a tight pyramid. Protruding from the two high stacks of rocks were weathered gray poles that rose another two feet into the air. On top were the grisly remains of an impaled skull, sun bleached and aged by time and weather. Chance's focus on the tracks had brought him to within a few feet of this bizarre scene before he realized the monuments' presence.

The gruesome sight shocked Chance, and for a moment he stared nervously scratching the stubble on his chin. Slowly kneeling down beside a small spruce, he carefully scanned the shadows on the ground in front of him. What type of man would make such a gruesome shrine? He noticed deep brown grooves in the skulls. They'd most likely been scalped. Chance prided himself on being a skilled woodsman, aware of his surroundings, and he didn't like that he had unknowingly walked right into the middle of this hideous place.

He stood up and cautiously raised his rifle as he scanned the trees in search of movement. His first thought was that he had stumbled upon some type of Indian burial ground. He had heard a few horror stories about what Indians did to white men who violated their sacred places, but something just didn't fit. He found himself quietly muttering, "Get hold of yourself, we need this meat." Chance had always been a courageous man, but what he had just experienced had shaken him.

Standing a well-muscled six foot two, Chance stood far larger than most men, and had never been beaten in a fair fight. Now he felt nervous, sweaty, and wary. He continued looking for sign and saw a large track in the dirt. He would continue on.

Chance had spent time hunting within a few miles of here, but because of the ridge's steepness and noisy loose shale, he had avoided it. This was new terrain and he didn't know the lay of the land or its shortcuts. Chance guessed he was a good five-hour walk from the cabin. He prayed he would see the deer any second as he poked his rifle around the thick needles of a small spruce. What he saw only added to the mystery.

Embedded in the hardened clay were the graying remains of a wagon. It wasn't a large wagon, much smaller than a Conestoga wagon. He scrutinized his surroundings and moved closer. With the exception of one broken sideboard, the wagon appeared reasonably intact and in good shape for having been left to rot for who knows how long. He rested his hand on the broken sideboard and closely examined the graying wood. The thick oak planks of the wagon's floor were still fairly solid. The wagon's spokes disappeared into the clay showing signs of rot several inches above the ground. Had it gotten stuck or just settled into the mud over time? That was a small mystery compared to everything else. The metal frame that had once supported the canvas cover stood rusting above the wagon.

Chance took a step back and sat down on a boulder to one side of the wagon. Bewildered, he said aloud, "Why in tarnation would anyone in their right mind drag a wagon up this steep ridge? The whole thing makes no sense."

The sounds of birds chirping in the forest reassured him as he nervously looked around. Small pieces of brown, decomposing canvas littered the ground. Dozens of pieces of wood that could have once been shipping crates were scattered here and there. A large piece of bleached thigh bone lay partially buried close to one of the wagon's wheels, a black arrowhead deeply imbedded in it.

Chance's gaze came to rest on what looked like a large box or chest lying beneath the wagon. The chest was protected by the solid wagon bed above and camouflaged by thick grass. He bent down and with both hands pulled the aged chest from beneath the wagon. It was solidly built with a liberal use of brass adornments and fancy buckles engraved with flowers and leaves. This chest must have been an item of great value, probably someone's prized possession. Chance took his knife and carefully removed the dried moss that had filled the grooves of the metal hinges. When he opened it, he found it empty.

Chance suddenly stopped and looked around. The eerie feeling of being watched came over him. I can't let my imagination run away with me, he thought. Right now, he needed to focus on the wounded deer. It was past noon and still he had no meat to show for his efforts.

It wasn't more than five minutes later when he came upon the horns of the huge deer rising above the grass. A sense of relief flowed through him.

He would need to work fast and drag the body down to the coolness of the creek bottom. The shade of a thick stand of aspen and the cold night would cool the meat.

It took Chance over an hour to drag the deer down through the loose shale and scattered brush to the creek bed. At times he released the deer and watched it tumble and slide only to hang up on a patch of sage or a protruding rock. Once at the creek bottom, he cut the deer into four manageable quarters and removed the two thick back straps. He lashed two heavy branches horizontally between two sturdy aspens with leather straps. He hung the quarters slightly apart so air could freely circulate around them and draped the back straps over the limbs. If the night was cold enough, the meat would be ready for the mules to pack back to the ranch in the morning. He dragged the hide and the rest of the remains up the creek a ways and washed the blood from his hands.

It was almost four o'clock when he picked up his rifle and started walking home. It would be dark within an hour, so he planned to drop down into the open prairie to make the traveling easier. It concerned him that he knew little of where the strange shelf began or ended. How had those people gotten so far up the mountain? He picked up the pace, glad to be off the ridge and headed home.

It was dark with only a sliver of moon visible amongst the clouds. Chance tramped for almost five hours before he saw the flicker of a candle in the cabin's only window. The two dogs barked wildly, letting Vern and Virgil know someone was coming.

"Red fox a riding," yelled Chance when he was a hundred yards out, the brothers' signal that everything was okay. Inside, Vern lit the kerosene lantern and headed towards the porch as Virgil stood looking into the darkness. Sadie and Three Dot, brother and sister Heeler-Dingo crosses, rushed into the darkness, their barks now ones of welcome.

Vern raised the lantern and smiled approvingly. "A little late, but I see blood on your pants, so you must have shot something."

Chance walked through the door and flopped into a handmade spruce chair. He sighed with relief. "Strangest day I ever had is what it was."

"What do you mean?" Virgil frowned with one eye lifted. He walked over to the wooden bucket of water by the stove, dipped the ladle, and filled a tin cup.

Chance reached eagerly for it. "Well I shot a deer, a real hat rack, but wait till you hear the rest of the story. I don't think we are the first people to settle this valley. I found an old wagon and two skulls mounted on poles up near that ridge you two call Canvas Creek."

"What the hell? Are you pulling our leg?"

"I said you wouldn't believe it. I think it might be some type of Indian burial ground."

"A wagon?" Vern shook his head as though he didn't believe his brother. "That's thick country, and steep. How could anyone possibly get a wagon up through that country? Are you sure you didn't take a little of that bad moonshine with you?"

"I didn't figure you would take to the story immediately, but it's the truth." Chance paused and took another drink of water. "I'll show you tomorrow. We need to pack out the deer anyway."

"We believe you, but how'd they get up there? There ain't no road."

"Well there's at least part of what looks like one. I don't know where it begins or ends, but I know where to find the middle," replied Chance. "Heck, I'm still questioning myself about what I saw. It makes no sense. You'll see the wagon is in decent shape, though it's weathered a mite. I bet it's been there at least eight to ten years."

"What do you think happened to the people?" asked Vern.

"Darn if I know, but I did find an arrowhead stuck in a horse's thigh bone. There were pieces of bone and wood strewn about. I didn't waste much time looking around. Thought it was more important to get the deer. I figured I'd come back with you two tomorrow anyway."

Vern slowly nodded his head. "Even with as much work as we have stacked up, I think the three of us need to figure out what's going on. If it's an Indian burial ground, we need to know."

Virgil nodded and tossed another stick of wood on the dying coals inside the stone fireplace. Vern pulled up a chair and sat beside Chance. "With the exception of those few homes that are being built down on Meeteetse Creek, I always thought we were the only white men in these parts. A man has to wonder who those folks were and why the heck they were halfway up that ridge."

Chance straightened up in his chair. "There's a whole lot of country we still haven't seen, and I think we might be in for a few more surprises," he paused shaking his head, "and not all of them good."

Chapter 2

Chance lay awake, too tired to sleep. A lot had happened over the last two and a half years. He thought about how hard it had been to say goodbye to their family, his brothers' young brides crying as they rode away with their one small wagon. It had taken several years but they had successfully made the journey and built their small stout cabin and barn in this vast land called Wyoming.

In all that time, they hadn't seen or heard anything that would lead them to believe they weren't the first white men in the valley. Maybe years ago a fur trapper had traveled through the valley and for some reason made his way up that ridge, Chance thought. But would he have taken the time to cut trees and pull a wagon up into such a difficult location? His mind raced back to conversations with the settlers at Meeteetse Creek about what they knew about the valley known as the Greybull. They'd settled a year after the Creagers.

He rolled over and pulled his blanket over his shoulders. His mind wandered back to thoughts of Iowa, of his family and his mother sitting by the fireplace, needlepoint in hand. As a boy, stories of adventure and this vast new land had enticed him, a land where a man could chase rainbows and perhaps find his pot of gold. He missed his family. He and his rebellious brothers had used their shares of their grandfather's inheritance to travel west. It took three months with their small wagon, two mules, and three saddle horses to make the journey from their Iowa farm to Independence, Missouri, the starting point for their journey over the Oregon Trail.

After they had arrived, they met a man who went by the single name of Hamilton. In his mid-forties, Hamilton was short, thin, and extremely quick in his movements. He ran a large ranch just outside town that sold stock and wagons to settlers headed west. He was not a man given to loose talk. He wore neatly pressed, tight-fitting clothing and appeared very successful.

Hamilton's beard and mustache were neatly trimmed and almost hid his gold front tooth. The man rode an exceptional paint horse, by which you could tell he knew his stock. It was Hamilton who sold them the additional stock and wagons needed for their journey.

They had found a small cabin just outside of Independence with a barn, corrals, and hay for the winter. If everything went right, they planned to find a wagon train leaving for Oregon in the spring. Once settled, the two brothers would figure out how to bring their wives.

Hamilton had numerous men working for him, and on one bitterly cold spring evening, an older man with a gray beard showed up at the cabin. He drove a fine team of mules pulling a wagon with a horse tied to the back.

"Whoa," he yelled, as he pulled back on the long reins of the mules. "Here's your boys' team and wagon. It's a good one."

Virgil looked angrily at the man, "We aren't boys!"

"Hell, son, anyone under forty is a boy to me. Anyway, here's your wagon," said the man as he flapped his arms trying to get some circulation going.

"You might as well come in for a minute and get warm by the fire. It's going to get colder on the trip back," said Chance with a smile.

The man looked hard at Chance through his weathered face. "Well, I guess it probably wouldn't hurt, at least for a few minutes."

Nimble for his years, the man hopped down from the wagon and followed Chance inside where a crackling fire warmed the room.

"Would you like a small drink to heat your innards?"

"Well, usually not. The boss is a hard man, and we don't get paid to drink."

"I doubt one for the road will hurt anything. Back home my brothers and I are known for our smooth whiskey, a skill we plan to use in Oregon," Chance said handing the man a shot.

The man quickly drank and put down the shot glass, "That is mighty fine whiskey."

"Would you like another?"

The old man just stared at them for a moment, "I guess I would. Best damn whiskey I had in years. So, you say you're headed for Oregon?"

"We hear there's land for the taking, real beautiful with elbow room."

"Beautiful place that Oregon; been there a time or two trapping," he said, as he moved his empty glass towards Chance to signal he would like another. "Yes, sir, she's beautiful, one of the prettiest places I have ever been."

"Have you been a lot of places?"

"Oh yeah, trapping took me a whole lot of places."

Vern looked at the man credulous of his comment. "Well, of all these places you have been what's your favorite?"

"Well, my favorite – I think it's different with each man, but to me, the Greybull country fits me the finest. There is lush grass and game is surely plentiful. The water from those mountains is the best a man can drink."

"Would it make a good place to start a sheep or cattle ranch?"

"If I wasn't so old, I'd probably do that myself."

The brothers seemed interested and continued to ask questions, and the old man continued to drink.

"So how do you find this Greybull Valley?"

The man looked sternly at Vern, "It's in the Wyoming Territory, but that's all I'm going to tell you."

Vern reached for the bottle and poured the man another drink. "Don't worry, we are just making conversation. Is there a wagon trail near it?"

"Even if I did tell you some directions, you farm boys wouldn't ever find it. It's too well-hidden."

With that, he staggered to his feet. "Thanks for the drink I need to be headed back to the ranch now. Don't want the boss on my hide," he said, as he untied his horse from the back of the wagon and with great effort swung his leg over the saddle horn.

For the next two weeks, one of the dominant subjects of conversation amongst the Creager men was Greybull Valley and where it might be. The wagon trains wouldn't start heading west for at least another month, and during that time they started buying the sheep and cattle they would need to start the ranch. The brothers never missed an opportunity to ask folks if they knew of a river named the Greybull, and the answer was always the same, no. Two weeks later, another ranch hand from Hamilton's spread delivered their second wagon, but this time a new man drove the wagon, and he wasted no time visiting before he mounted his horse and headed back.

A month later the three brothers sat around the table, slowly sipping a little of their homemade shine and talking. "You think that old trapper was just making up the story about that Greybull country? I haven't found a single person that has even heard of the river much less knows anything about that country. I sure hate the idea of passing good ranch country like that trapper described to go hundreds of miles farther. He sure described it beautiful like."

"It may or may not exist, but if no one knows how to get there we can't waste the time looking any more. Tomorrow we got the meeting with the wagon train master and we need to get signed on. With the train leaving in three weeks, we need to get focused on the journey." Chance smiled. "Anyway I hear Oregon is real beautiful."

The stocky older man who was the wagon master welcomed the three brothers into his drafty wood-plank office. "So you three have read the contract and understand what's at stake?"

"Yes, sir," answered Chance.

"Well you three will have two wagons and livestock. Are you going to be able to keep up with the group with your cattle and sheep?"

"We have done plenty of herding in our day and think we will be good."

"Well, I got your money. We leave in about twenty days, so get all your affairs in order, and welcome aboard."

Vern stopped at the door and turned back to the wagon master, "By chance have you ever heard of a river in Wyoming called the Greybull?"

The man looked Vern in the eye and hesitated for a moment, "It's been a long time, but I have heard of it. Somewhere around ten years ago I was taking a wagon train of folks to Oregon and about halfway there I got into a pissing match with this settler named Walsh, big-mouth fellow, and we had words, and he left the train in the middle of Wyoming. Took his wife and two kids and headed north by themselves. Damn fool was what he was, being Injun country and all. There was no talking to him, thought I was one poor leader and just took off headed north. I asked our scout if he knew that country and he said he had traveled it once, called it the Greybull. I will never forget the name. He took what looked like an old trail that kind of branched off to the north, but it wasn't much."

"Do you remember where this trail was?"

"Oh yeah, every time I take a train past that spot I relive that experience. I am sure that thick head of his cost him and his family their lives. Never did hear anything again about the whole deal."

"Is the scout still around?"

"No, he was killed the next year by Indians while he was riding point. Damn heathens bushwhacked him." He paused for a moment, "I do remember him saying that Greybull was mighty fine country, but that's about all I recall."

"So if we were to choose to leave the train, you could show us that spot."

"That's not my normal policy. I don't make no guarantees on what you will find and I won't give you any refund on your money. You would still be taking up a spot on the wagon train. You leaving early might rub some of the folks wrong."

"Well, we haven't decided for sure, but we could do that with you?"

"Yeah, I guess I would be okay with it, knowing in advance."

* * *

What they found in Wyoming was exactly what the old trapper had described —snowcapped mountains, meadows full of tall, lush grass, and a sparkling Greybull river. They chose a spot for the cabin near a wide stream that descended from a thick grove of aspens with plenty of grass for the livestock. It was picturesque and defensible, the perfect place to raise a family and start a ranch. They worked hard, and within a month, they had cleared enough land to build a small cabin. For the first couple of years they were prepared to live mainly off their hunting skills, but the future looked bright with all the many varieties of seeds they'd brought to plant their orchard and garden. There had been a lot of urgency in getting the ranch functioning. Sufficient crops were needed to support themselves as well as their families back home, which they hoped would eventually join them. Now the small herds of cattle and sheep were doing well, and they hoped that time was near.

* * *

The next morning, the three men were up early doing their chores while Vern saddled their two horses, their pack mules, Jasper and Dolly, as well as Dixie, Chance's saddle mule. Chance opened the corrals to let the sheep and cattle out and opened the chicken cages while Virgil started breakfast.

About an hour later, Chance led the group out of the yard followed by Vern. Virgil followed leading the two larger mules with their packs. One mule would have been plenty to pack out the deer but the brothers weren't sure what else they might find at the old campsite, so they decided to take two.

Overnight the weather had changed and the windy morning was downright bitter. Each man wore a heavy sheepskin coat as the group rode through the frozen, dew-laden grass towards Canvas Creek. They made good time on the horses and mules, and four hours later, they were close to where Chance had hung his deer.

"It's sure colder today than it was yesterday," said Chance as he slowly rode up to the hanging deer. He carefully scanned the area for unwanted critters before walking up to the deer quarters. The meat hung firmly from the horizontal poles latched tightly to the stout aspen.

"Well, here's the deer, probably none the worse for the chase. The meat smells good, I was a mite worried."

"That's a big-un," said Vern with a smile, "I can see why one shot from over a hundred yards wouldn't take him down."

Chance stopped for a moment. "The two back straps are gone. I hung them right beside the quarters and they're gone."

"Must have been a bobcat or coon or something. The ground is frozen enough that I don't see any tracks."

"At least it didn't take a quarter."

"We can live with losing a little meat. Where's that wagon and those skulls?" asked Virgil.

"They are straight up the hill probably four or five hundred yards and its hell for steep. It's nasty with all that shale." He pointed up the ridge, "I wish I knew where that ledge starts; it would be nice to know how that wagon got there."

"You don't have any idea where it starts?" questioned Vern.

"Not really, I walked around the point of that ridge once and there are some good game trails but I surely didn't see anything that looked wide enough for a wagon to pass."

"With this amount of horses and mules, I think it's safe to tie up and leave the stock. Let's just follow your drag marks," suggested Vern.

They took their time finding the best route as they ascended the ridge weaving between the boulders and treacherous rockslides. After thirty minutes of climbing, Chance crested the ledge and carefully inspected the kill site before moving closer. They had been talking and making a lot of noise as they approached the kill site. With the exception of a few birds, they saw nothing.

"That was a fair drag down to the creek," said Vern, "no wonder it took you a while. Where's the wagon?"

"See that game trail? The wagon is down there about twenty yards," answered Chance. The three carefully spread out to allow enough room to quickly raise their muskets, if needed, and started walking.

"Wow," said Virgil as he stared at the ledge. "The only way they could have gotten a wagon up here is if this ledge goes all the way to the bottom."

"I told you," said Chance, "it weighs on your mind, don't it? This ledge is a little steep in places but it runs down this ridge at least a couple of hundred yards farther. That's where I found the old cut stumps, but from there, I have no idea where it goes."

"Maybe it's some kind of cutoff road or shortcut," said Virgil.

"We are at a pretty high elevation, and if it is a cutoff road, then it sure wasn't used much. No, I believe there's got to be another reason. Maybe they were hiding from Indians or something like that," Chance answered.

"No matter how you slice it, it makes no sense," said Vern. "Keep a good watch while we look around, I'm none too comfortable with this place."

The three men walked up to the skull monuments and then onto the wagon. For the next hour they explored and searched the site for any clues or anything of value, but the only thing they found was a rotting lean-to tucked back into the rock cliff. The site was void of shovels, pots, house wares, any of the normal supplies a wagon would usually carry headed west. Pieces of wooden boxes were scattered on the ground and only the old chest lay beside the wagon mostly intact.

"Not much here," said Chance in a disgusted voice. Virgil and Vern knelt down close together near the wagon. To a person unfamiliar with them, they looked like twins. Both wore black canvas pants, plaid shirts and hats with round, flat brims. Their thick black beards were trimmed alike, and even their mannerisms were similar.

"We didn't find any answers to anything," said Vern, "frustrating is what this whole thing is."

Chance walked over to the wagon and knelt down by the chest.

"In its time this chest was real expensive, a true thing of beauty, all these brass buckles and all. Even these decorative metal accents must have cost a sight." The chest's reinforced corners and strapping remained in place as Chance lifted the chest.

"The main part of this chest is in pretty good shape. I was kind of thinking I would take it back to the cabin and see if I could fix her up."

"I can see taking the hardware, but are you really going to pack that piece of junk all the way to the bottom of this mountain?" asked Vern.

"Yeah, it will be my back that does the sweating." Chance turned to Virgil. "Would you follow that ledge out? I would really like to know where it starts."

"I can do that. As soon as I find where it comes out, I will head over to the stock."

Chance lifted the three-foot-long chest onto his back and gave Vern his rifle to carry. The two half slid, half walked down the steep shale slide towards the creek bottom.

"You really think you can rebuild that chest?" asked Vern.

"The way I see it, we got one heck of a long winter in front of us and it should keep me busy."

The stock quietly watched them as they made their way out of the aspens. "I can't get it out of my head how strange this whole thing is. I wonder if we will ever figure it out?" pondered Chance, as he untied Jasper and led him over to the deer. "Let's just tie the deer on Jasper and use Dolly for the chest. No use bloodying all the manties. It's a nice sized deer, but Jasper can handle the load, no sweat."

"I'll tie the horns on top; they will make a good hat rack for the cabin," said Vern as he cut down one of the quarters and wrapped it in clean cotton cloth. Chance mantied up the chest and secured it to the sawbuck. On the opposite pannier, he placed a couple of round rocks and a small chunk of log nearly equal to the chest's weight and tied them in the other manty.

Just as they got the mule loaded, Virgil hurriedly burst into the clearing. "Well, did you find where that shelf starts?" asked Vern, noticing the flushed look on Virgil's face. "What's the matter, are you all right?"

"Yeah, I'm all right, but I wasn't sure I was going to be. I found where the ledge comes down. Something followed me all the way down that ridge. I heard it several times and it broke enough branches that the hair on the back of my neck stood up."

"What do you think it was?" asked Chance.

"Heck if I know. I never saw it, just heard it," said Virgil.

"Did you see any tracks?"

"I turned and backtracked once, but I didn't see anything, no tracks, nothing."

On the ride back, Virgil rode up beside his two brothers and cleared his throat, "I've hunted and tracked a lot of animals over the years, but this one seemed to be tracking me." He paused for a moment. "Anyway, that trail down the ridge, it's old and rough, but passable. Someone put a lot of effort into getting that wagon up there. On the way down, I stopped periodically to clear a few deadfalls off the trail and that's when I got the feeling I was being watched. It took me longer than I thought because I kept stopping and listening to my back trail. Darn if whatever it was stayed back just out of sight and then followed me all the way to the bottom. Anyway, the start of that ledge is well hidden by a rockslide. I can see why you would have walked past it with that rockslide and all those young trees. If you didn't know it was there, you would probably miss it."

It was not quite four hours later when the group rode into the ranch, the two dogs greeted them with joyful barking and stubby tails wagging.

The area around the cabin had been cleared of sagebrush and small trees and now was mainly dirt and new grass. It had taken awhile, but the men had been meticulous in their task. With the exception of a couple of partially burned stumps, which they would finish burning next spring, the field of view was totally clear. For protection, they had built a small viewing tower that stood about twenty feet tall at one end of the cabin opposite the chimney. The tower gave them an excellent view of at least several hundred yards in each direction. The lookout allowed two men protection and room enough to shoot and reload their rifles.

Chance and Vern dismounted and tied up the stock. Once finished, he led Jasper towards the barn. Virgil removed the manty containing the chest and balancing rocks from Dolly. The small cabin and barn were separated by a little more than fifty yards of cleared ground. The barn had been the last building built after the privy and the cabin. They had built the barn with a large spruce log across several of the barn's main support beams, which they had carefully shaped with their crosscut saws and axes. Tying a small pulley in the middle of the log beam, they intended to hang their meat high enough to be out of the reach of the dogs or any other varmint.

Virgil walked up to the cabin's heavy door and removed the plank that held it firmly in place. They had built strong bars with a lock to secure the cabin at night. He lit the kerosene lantern that hung by a nail on the porch and with his gun in hand, opened the door slowly. He carefully surveyed the cabin. The brothers had not made it this far by being reckless; they were careful men by nature. The cabin felt warm, and although the fire had gone out hours before, the warmth from the massive stone fireplace remained.

Virgil began making a small fire in the cast iron stove so he could prepare a dinner of brown beans, potatoes, and the last of their elk meat. It would be good to have fresh deer for a change. The interior of the cabin was not big or fancy, but they intended to add several new rooms in the spring, in preparation for Virgil and Vern's new wives joining them. The summer before they left for Independence, they'd traveled to Chicago and bought a heavy cast iron stove, and now it stood prominently in their new cabin. The stove had many different compartments, one for boiling water, another for baking bread, making several of the women at the settlement openly jealous.

"I don't think I ever want to go back up to that place," said Virgil between chews as the three brothers sat together for dinner. "I don't know if it was the skulls or the sound of something following me, but whatever it was it sure spooked me." He took a long drink of water and just stared at his food not wanting to make eye contact.

"I know just what you need," said Chance with a smile. "We finished that batch of Hooch a couple of weeks ago and well, we sure don't have anyone to sell it to or trade with, so why don't we have a glass?"

"That sounds great," replied Vern, "it's been a while."

Chance smiled and spit a little chew into the small tin can that had once been the home of some brown beans. "After all, we did brew it."

"I guess if you put it that way," Virgil responded, as he turned with a smile and got a small, brown and gray jug that sat to the left of the fireplace. They had recently finished building three chairs from willows and spruce on which each man sat down and sipped his whiskey. The small copper still they had built would provide them a marketable product to sell or trade later.

"I think I will take a closer look at the chest and see what kind of a job it's going to be to restore it," said Chance, as he set his drink down, got up and opened the front door. The chest sat on one side of the front porch, and when he went to pick it up, his hand slipped and the chest dropped several feet to the thick wood planking.

"One drink and I am already dropping things," he laughed as he looked over his shoulder towards his brothers. He picked the chest up a second time, moved it to the kitchen table, and gently set it down.

"Packed it all the way down that mountain without dropping it and now on my front porch I lose my grip. Heck of a deal, if you ask me," laughed Chance again, as he stood back and admired the beat-up, weathered chest. He reached for the brass buckle that secured the lid and opened it, then stared for a moment. The soft lining of the chest's top had torn. "Look here, something tore loose from the lining, must have ripped when I dropped it."

Even in the dim light they could see a small tear in the chest's lining revealing a hidden pocket.

Both Vern and Virgil jumped to their feet and joined Chance as he slowly and carefully removed the small leather packet from the chest's lid. Chance carefully removed a jacket of brittle leather and exposed what looked like a small brown book. Delicately he opened the book's cover exposing a moldy, water-damaged first page. He glanced at his two brothers in disappointment as he turned to the next page. "Hope it isn't all ruined."

It was dimly lit in the small cabin as Chance struggled to turn the pages of the damaged book, often using his knife to keep from ripping them. He was almost halfway through the book when he came to a few pages stuck together. Slowly peeling apart the pages, he noticed that he could read at least some of the words. Chance looked up at his brothers, "I think some of the last part might be readable."

The size of the handwriting was small, which made reading even more difficult. Chance stared at the page for a moment and then spoke, "I can't make out everything, but it appears this is a diary, not just a book. It says something about getting in an argument with the wagon master and then heading out on their own."

Chance turned the page. "Shoot, I thought we got past the water damage," he said. "I can kind of read this, but in other parts, it's more like guessing. From what I can read it says, *After two weeks away from the wagon train, we found an old road. We followed that for a week or so before it seemed to peter out, and then we became lost. The following day, we came upon an old Indian camped in a small meadow. He was alone and had little food. He was badly crippled and abandoned. We knew he was dying. Quinten gave him some food, but he died that night.*"

"Who's Quinten?" asked Vern.

"Well I would guess he is the husband," answered Chance before beginning again. "'*We buried him beneath the prairie. Later we found a small leather pouch amongst his belongings. Inside the pouch was a map.*'" Chance paused.

"So where's the map?" Virgil asked.

"It doesn't say; there is a large stain and I can't read it," responded Chance.

"That's a heck of a deal. It doesn't tell you where the map is or what's on it?"

"Nope, it don't," replied Chance as he reached back up into the small, hidden pocket. "I can feel something else," he said as he pulled a small, neatly folded piece of hard leather from the chest's hidden pocket. He set the package on the table and took a deep breath. Slowly he unfolded the stiff leather. In front of them lay an old but well-preserved map. The thin sheet of leather measured no more than nine inches square and was well oiled on the outside. The map side had four dashed lines that likely represented trails. Colorful symbols painted in different colors began and ended with the dashed lines. There was what looked like the head of an old man staring at the sky and a symbol that reminded them of an Indian war club covered with pointy spikes. But what was most shocking was the small figure-eight-shaped nugget that was tightly bound with thread in the center of the map. It was definitely gold.

Chapter 3

"That's gold for sure," said Vern, in an excited voice. "This has to be a map to where they mined it."

"This is gold, but how do you know this is a map to a gold mine?" replied Chance in a skeptical voice. "Indians use gold in their ceremonies and decorations, and who's to say how it got in that chest or how far it came to get here."

Chance took another sip from his tin cup of moonshine and looked at the leather map again like there was something he'd missed. "Put some coffee on, Virgil; I think we need to put a little more thought into this."

For the next couple of hours, they sipped their coffee and discussed theories until they found themselves covering the same ground. "It's pretty clear we are only guessing. Until we can find a few more clues, I don't think we can go any further," Vern said, as he lit a rolled cigarette and glanced out their only window.

"No stars out there and it's really getting dark, feels a whole lot colder, too. We might be in for some snow by morning."

"I sure hope not; I was hoping to travel back up to the wagon tomorrow and look a mite more. I want to know where that trail goes and maybe find these people's main camp; Indians don't take crosscut saws and the like. I really don't believe they intended to spend the winter there, not on that little shelf," said Chance as he took another sip of spiked coffee.

"Yes, sir, I believe somewhere farther up that trail we're going to find their main camp and a whole lot of answers."

"You better hope it don't snow too much. If it does, Virgil and I will need to stay here and cut up some more firewood. If you want to take another look at that wagon, it probably needs to be done before the snow really sets in," replied Vern.

About an hour later the sound of the cabin's small, crackling fire mixed with heavy snoring. The cold air and the long trip took the steam out of a man. They were ready for a good night's sleep.

It was nearly midnight when the sound of the two dogs' frantic barks and deep growls awoke the brothers. Vern jumped to his feet and began lighting the candle beside his bed as Virgil growled, "What the hell is going on? " By the time the three of them made it to the porch, Sadie and Three Dot had retreated to the front door. The dogs' thick winter neck hair stood straight up as they shook and growled between barks.

"What in tarnation is going on with these two? Light the lantern and get the guns. Let's see what's going on."

Chance struggled to balance himself against the porch as he yanked his boots on over his thick long johns. With the aid of a candle, he stared out into the cleared ground surrounding the cabin. "Hurry up you two, there may be Indians and I don't want to be shot."

Moments later, Vern came outside with the lit lantern just as Chance's candle blew out in the wind. Vern handed Chance his Hawkens and the three men together scanned the grounds. The dogs had not let up on their barking. Vern looked at Chance and then Virgil. "What do you think?"

"Must be something more than a coyote to get these two dogs riled up this way. Why don't you check the corrals while Virgil and I check the barn?"

The dogs paused in their barking, but their slow, deep guttural growls continued. Large flakes of snow began to accumulate on the ground as the three men split up and cautiously walked from the cabin in separate directions while the dogs followed.

Vern looked over towards his brothers, "Be careful, no telling what we got here." Vern walked around by the corral and checked the cattle first. They were bunched together and nervously staring at him from the other side of the corral, but even with the dim light of his candle he was able to count them, and none were missing. Vern was continuing towards the sheep corral when he froze.

"Oh my God," he muttered to himself. Then he hollered, "Something got the sheep!" As he leaned over the corral poles, he focused on the small flock of sheep tightly bunched in one corner. He stared at the spattering of blood that stained the snow. It looked like a sheep had been killed in the center of the corral and then dragged to the fence.

"Did you get a count?" hollered Chance as he hurried to the corral.

"My guess is there is only one missing, but they're so bunched up I ain't sure. We will need to separate them and get some light back here. It's too dang dark to see with just one lantern," shouted Vern. He followed the blood trail with his eyes as he scanned the area outside the corral. With what little light there was, he could see bloody drag marks in the light snow disappearing into the darkness.

"Whatever it was, it was hell on strong. I can tell you that. To take a grown sheep and hop this fence takes a big critter."

Virgil came running from the back of the barn with another lantern and froze when the second lantern's light illuminated the corral area. It began snowing harder as the three brothers moved around the corral to better investigate the back area.

"Look for tracks. I want to know what caused this! I'm going back to the cabin for pants and a coat," said Chance as he brushed some of the snow off his shoulders and his long johns.

Vern and Virgil moved the lanterns over to where they hoped to find tracks. At first it seemed like they suddenly disappeared, but then Vern spotted blood on the top of some tall bunch grass. "I think whatever it was jumped the corral fence and landed out here. It's capable of jumping at least a good ten feet so let's make a wider circle and see if we can pick up anything."

Within minutes, they found the tracks. They were huge, almost eight inches long. The heavy flakes of snow made things difficult and were rapidly covering what few tracks they had found. "If'n I was to guess, I think we got a mountain lion problem and a darn big one at that," said Vern.

Chance turned the corner, now fully dressed. "Did you find the tracks?"

"Sure did. I was just saying to Virgil that I think we have a mountain lion problem. There's probably sixteen feet between indentations in the snow. No good track to look at, just indentations, but by the size and shape it has to be a mountain lion. We should take the dogs in the morning and see if we can catch up to it. I seriously doubt it will be back again tonight."

The next day the men awoke an hour before sunrise and Vern was the first to walk outside as he made his way to the privy. At least a full foot of snow covered the ground, and the bright stars in the clear sky illuminated the path, which sparkled in the cold, crisp air. Even without the sun, a sliver of moon and clear sky allowed a man to see for miles across the dimly lit landscape. Vern looked down. The snow came close to the top of his high boots. The door to the outhouse had a thin crust of ice over the handmade handle, which was firmly stuck. Only with some forceful hits did it open.

He swore as he entered the small drafty building and sat down on the frigid pine boards to relieve himself. A small pile of dry tall fescue was stacked in the corner and he used some of it to clean himself while Three Dot whined outside the door. They had been wise enough to build a small box house for the dogs and had lined it with thick buffalo hides. On really cold nights they would set a large rock near the fire and, just before going to bed, put it inside the small house. The dogs' job was to watch and protect the ranch, and taking them inside the cabin at night would not allow their coats and skin to thicken.

As he sat there, Vern thought of the old book that his grandfather had read him, talking about a general in France named Napoleon who had led his armies against Russia only to lose most of them to the cruel Russian winter. Some of the soldiers had huddled around large fires at night, never allowing their skin to thicken against the cold. Those soldiers were the ones who became most vulnerable and died first when the conditions worsened on their long cold march home.

Vern heard Three Dot and Sadie barking and then the sound of the cabin door going shut as he finished his duties and walked back to the cabin. The dogs were having a hard time working their way through the snow and had to go to more of a jumping motion to make any real progress. Vern opened the door and brought out some scraps from the night before to feed them. He walked to the stone-lined well and brought up a bucket of water. The well was good and deep and they weren't worried that it would freeze. Vern knocked the ice out of the dogs' bowl and poured in some fresh water. Then he took the bucket in and set it next to the fire to stay warm for their daily use.

"There's way too much snow for me to take the dogs," said Chance, "I'm just going to take Dixie."

"The mule, why don't you just take one of the horses? Why take that wide back canary? Who knows how she will react to that mountain lion?" warned Vern.

"I've always felt comfortable with Dixie. I like how those big ears of hers seem to always be perked, her eyes always scanning the horizon for trouble. I have gotten a lot of game over the last two years because of those ears. She always tells me when there's something out there."

"I'm going to take a couple of days' rations just in case this turns into more of an ordeal than I'm thinking. I'm sure I can find those tracks in the snow. With some luck, I'll get that cat by nightfall."

Vern spilled a small amount of water on the hot stove as he tried to move the coffee pot. The water sizzled and hissed as it burned off. "I can't seem to get my mind off that wagon and those skulls, but I think this snow has wiped out any chance of us getting up there and investigating any more until spring. You know it always seems to work that way for me."

"What way is that, Vern?" asked Virgil.

"One part of me is just like you, Virgil. I really didn't like that place, too many weird things, kind of spooky. Maybe it was that mountain lion that was watching you up there or maybe it wasn't, but just when I got myself all worked up to go back, I can't."

"Well I guess we won't have to worry about it for a while. Anyway, Chance, do you need any help getting ready?"

"No, I'm good."

After breakfast, Chance saddled Dixie and loaded his supplies into his saddlebags. He put his Hawkens musket in his scabbard and tied a piece of rolled buffalo hide on top of his saddlebags. He picked up his fancy canteen and hung it over his saddle horn. There was close to forty pounds of gear besides his saddle, but the load would be no problem for the stout sixteen-hand mule. One of the ranch hands on Hamilton's place had told Chance that his chestnut mule was eight years old. Chance guessed her at closer to ten. Dixie was well-built but still narrow enough to ride comfortably. Her gait was smooth and even. Chance had ridden the mule a lot during the trip from Independence to their valley. At night, they would unbridle the horses and mules from the wagons and picket them out. At those times, he would often take Dixie on short hunting trips to find game. She didn't seem to need near the grazing time the horses did and was able to grab plenty of mouthfuls of grass as they rode.

The cold leather of the saddle creaked as he launched himself up into it. Chance felt stiff and uncomfortable in his layering of clothes. He took a drink. His fancy canteen, which he had won five years earlier in a shooting match at the fair, was from Australia, and someone had done a beautiful job of covering it with stretched ostrich hide. The hide gave it a warm yellowish brown color that could easily be seen from a distance. He circled the corral and then rode off into the sagebrush following the faint dents in the snow. Chance wrapped one of his thick wool scarves around his neck and pulled it tight. He then tied a second, smaller scarf over his hat and around his chin to protect his face from the cold wind. Dixie must have known what he wanted, as she followed the slight imprints in the snow at a fast trot.

It was a half an hour later when Chance came over a small rise and a crow flew from the sagebrush. Then other birds began launching themselves into the air. He rode closer and saw what remained of the sheep. The snow was worn and crimson stained, and only the head and rib cage of the sheep remained intact. Chance was sure the mountain lion had feasted most of the night as he stepped down from his mule and tied her reins to a thick branch of close sagebrush. The mule's eyes were exceptionally wide as Chance patted her neck. "Easy girl, that cat is long gone," he said in a soft voice.

He turned to the mule, untied her, and in one fluid motion stepped back into the stirrup and mounted. Lightly pulling back on the reins, he removed his tobacco pouch from his pocket. He rolled a cigarette, sealing it with his chapped lips, and then continued following the tracks.

Three hours later, Chance was squinting against the morning's brassy sunlight when something caught his eye – the silhouette of a huge cat up against a patch of juniper bushes nearly three hundred yards away. "That didn't take long," Chance smirked. He scanned the ground for an unseen approach, but the high rock on which the cat sat gave it a panoramic view of most of the area. Finally he nudged the mule ahead, hoping the mule wouldn't scare the large cat. He was out of range and needed to close the gap to less than two hundred yards for his muzzle-loader.

He was sure the cat was watching his every move as he inched the mule closer. Maybe he hadn't ever seen a person before and was more curious than afraid. Chance hoped that was the case. The large cat had perched itself on a high rock to watch the prairie, but to Chance that was his mistake. The small patch of rocks and the juniper bushes that were growing amongst them were like an island on the prairie and Chance could see that the next patch of timber was more than a half a mile away at the base of a distant ridge.

As Chance rode closer, the mountain lion continued watching his approach with no signs of urgency or need to escape. Over the years Chance had killed at least four mountain lions, but all had been treed by dogs. One shot to the back of the head had dispatched them. This is going to be easy, he thought as he rode into range and slid silently from the mule, tying her reins to another thick branch of sagebrush. He pulled his musket from the scabbard and untied two willow shooting sticks from his saddlebag.

Crouching in the snow, he shoved his pointed shooting sticks into the moist, unfrozen soil. The cat never moved, staring unconcerned in his direction. Chance reached into his pocket, removed a primer for the gun's percussion nipple, and felt it slip between his fingers. He cursed to himself as he looked down in search of the primer then reached for another and placed it on the gun's nipple under the hammer. When he looked down the long metal sights, the large cat had disappeared.

Chance jumped to his feet and started running towards a high piece of ground where he could see the backside of the pine and juniper patch and the distant timbered ridge. It would be a harder shot, but it wouldn't be the first long-range shot he'd made. It was hard running in the snow, but in the open grass areas where the snow was not as deep, he was doing a good job of covering more ground. He felt he had a good chance of getting the cat, for the terrain was open and the cat's head, shoulders, and tail should stand out above most of the snow-covered sagebrush.

By the time he had gotten to his ambush spot, he was out of breath and worried that he might not be able to shoot straight because of his heavy breathing. Scanning the terrain, he saw no movement. Maybe the large cat was hunkered down and Chance just needed to flush him out. He took a step forward, gun ready, and for the first time he noticed the moist feeling of sweat on his body. In these conditions sweat could kill you. It wouldn't take long for a man to go into chills and lose body heat, if his undergarments weren't dry. He needed to slow his pace and examine the terrain around him.

Slowly walking to the east in a straight line, he hoped to intercept his prey between the junipers and the timbered ridge. Having chased a lot of animals, he knew they usually took the quickest route to escape. When Chance reached the area in the sagebrush where he thought he would find the cat's tracks, he found nothing, and that puzzled him.

"Where in the heck did he go?" he muttered to himself, as he turned and headed towards the small island of rocks and junipers. "I should be able to see him."

It was then he heard the terrified braying of his mule. He had made a mistake and hopefully he wouldn't lose his best mule learning this lesson. Sweaty or not, he broke into a run to find the mule. In the chilled air, his chest felt like it was going to explode, and he hopped sagebrush after sagebrush as he sprinted towards the sound of Dixie's terrified bawls.

Chapter 4

In one quick motion, he jumped to a stop and squarely planted his feet; raising his rifle he came to a spot overlooking the area where he'd tied Dixie. All that greeted him was the quiet, pristine landscape covered in a thick blanket of sparkling snow. Dixie was gone and he saw no movement in the prairie below. Somehow both the mule and mountain lion had now disappeared. He began walking towards the spot where he'd tied the mule, and several minutes later he stood looking at the scene.

The area told a story. Both mule and mountain lion tracks covered the torn up ground, mixed with the occasional stains from droplets of blood. He stood staring at the mixture of dirt and snow and realized why he hadn't seen their departure. Following their tracks only a few yards, he could see a small gulley that seemed to come out of nowhere and drop off over the hill. The tracks of the mule and the mountain lion led into the bottom of the gulley where the smooth carpet of snow outlines their path. The deep holes in the snow were easy to follow, accented by drops of crimson every couple of yards. He felt sick to his stomach. He cared a lot for that darn mule and they had put in many a mile on the trail together. Who would have guessed that a mountain lion would actually double back and attack? Did it have no fear of man? He swore and tried to figure out his next move. Dressed in a heavy coat, he could feel the damp sweat on his body. With the exception of his flint, all his supplies were on the mule. It would take most of a day to hike back to the cabin. By then he would have no chance to rescue Dixie, if she was still alive. He immediately started following the trail as it continued down the snowy gulley.

The ravine was similar to hundreds he had seen over the last couple of years. The prairie seemed to gently flow for miles without a break, but then suddenly, without warning would dive into a deep gulley that hadn't been visible moments before. Most of these gullies had small trails in the bottom that usually led to water or the safety of thicker brush. He didn't miss the fact that their course led him farther away from the cabin and the warmth of its evening fire. The brown stained snow of the path was easy to follow. Both mountain lion and mule were still running. In places, the animals had leaped across large stretches of ground leaving only the drag marks of the mule's reins. He continued on at a steady trot. At some point he would need to find a place to stop and dry his undergarments, but for now he was focused on finding Dixie.

A little more than thirty minutes later he noticed the mountain lion was now walking but Dixie was still loping in an easterly direction. The mule's chance of survival had greatly increased. It was interesting how the mountain lion tracks would suddenly leave the mule's trail and then several hundred yards later show up again. After observing this several times, Chance followed the big cat tracks as the mountain lion traveled to the top of the gulley and seemed to check his back trail and then returned to the tracks of his prey. This cat was smart.

An hour later, Chance came around a small bend in the trail and saw his buffalo hide lying beside the trail. It wasn't a complete hide, but it was big enough for a man to wrap himself at night and keep warm. He had taken care to securely tie it to the back of the mule and was surprised to see it lying in the snow. Had the mountain lion torn the straps he had used to tie it or had the amount of running somehow loosened the knots? He picked up the bundle of hide lying in the snow and noticed that only one of his original straps remained. The attack had probably ripped one side of the bundled hide from his saddle. The thick buffalo hide had saved the mule's life.

Later the gulley converged with another gulley and he found a small creek at its bottom, outlined in thin ice. Kneeling, he removed his thick leather gloves and cupped his hand for a drink. The icy water tasted good and he knew he needed to drink enough to keep from getting dehydrated. From the tracks he understood the mule was out ahead of the mountain lion and felt comfortable enough to take the time to make a fire and dry his clothes. He leaned his Hawkens against a small juniper tree and then unrolled the buffalo hide. Reaching inside his coat, he removed a small leather pouch; inside it were his flint and the dry, crumpled remains of a bird's nest, which he set upon the buffalo hide.

He walked to the top of the ravine where a lone dead pine tree silhouetted itself against the skyline. The sky was full of fast-moving thick, white clouds that raced across the sky with the strong wind. Removing his ten-inch Bowie knife from its sheath, he began to strip dry bark and pitch from the dead pine tree. He then walked back to the hide and cleared a small area of snow down to the dirt. The spot was protected for what he had in mind. He mixed some of the bird's nest with pitch and the dried bark from the tree and molded it into a small cone shape.

Removing his flint, he flicked sparks into the small, dense cone until it ignited, and he blew on it until a small column of smoke rose from the tiny pile. He rubbed his hands over the small fire for a few minutes, his hands still cold from the icy creek water. After several minutes he walked back up to the dead pine tree and began removing larger branches until he felt comfortable he had enough. He used some of the light leather strapping from the buffalo hide to tie together some branches to form a small, branched structure above the fire. Then he stripped naked, pulled the thick buffalo hide around himself, and carefully placed his undergarments above the frame of his tiny fire. Moving a flap of the hide to sit down on, for the next hour he vigilantly maintained the fire and tended it to dry his clothes.

It was early afternoon before everything was completely dry and he was dressed. Chance repacked the hide into a tight bundle, which he tied in such a way as to sling it over his shoulder for easier travel. Going back to where he had veered from the trail, he had only gone a short distance when he noticed the mule's tracks had turned from the smooth, snowy trail of the gulley floor up the steep sides towards the sagebrush flat above. Slipping several times as he used sagebrush branches for balance, he climbed until he reached the crest of the ravine. Chance stood for a moment and inspected the tracks. The mule was no longer trotting and there were still mountain lion tracks mingled with the mule's tracks. After only a few yards the mountain lion tracks turned abruptly and began paralleling the gulley where he had just dried his clothes. Chance stopped and then decided to follow the cat's tracks. He could see where the cat had stopped in the thick cover of some juniper bushes and he knelt down and looked under the branches. It was a straight line of sight to his smoldering fire.

"That damn cat was watching me," he swore to himself, "lucky for me he didn't just come down and join me." Chance was not mad at himself, but he was extremely frustrated that this mountain lion had somehow outsmarted him at every turn.

He returned to Dixie's tracks and after about twenty yards, once again, found the mountain lion tracks on the trail. From the distance between tracks, he could tell the big cat had picked up the pace.

Even though there was a blue sky, the temperature was no more than thirty degrees, but he could feel the temperature rising. The trail was leading away from the cabin and towards a distant set of hills unfamiliar to Chance. This was big country, rough with lots of steep rocky cliffs.

For the next hour, he followed the tracks up through the sagebrush as the trail seemed to make a beeline towards a particular hook-nosed ridge. He could feel the warm breeze beginning to blow on the back of his neck, and after about twenty minutes, he reached the base of the ridge where the sagebrush hill began turning to grass and small, scattered trees. That was when he heard it, the loud scream of a mountain lion farther up the hill. Chance looked down and made sure the primer was securely on the nipple of his gun and began walking faster as he climbed the snowy hillside. By the look of the tracks, the mule must have felt the big cat's presence and begun to trot. The screams continued as he worked his way closer, and then, as quickly as the screams had started, there was silence when he was less than one hundred yards from the source.

He crept forward in the snow until the tracks led into the timber. He hadn't walked far when he saw the reason for the screams. At the base of a large, heavily branched, limber pine, tracks of wolves covered the ground. It was pretty clear to Chance that the wolves had come upon the mountain lion, run it up into the tree, and then waited at the base. A mountain lion this size could have probably held its ground against just a couple of wolves, but by the abundance of tracks, it appeared to have been a small pack. He heard several branches break farther up the ridge and assumed the wolves had caught his scent. He was pretty sure that in the past the pack had either had a run-in with man or was just uncomfortable with this new, unidentified smell.

Chance made a wide circle around the tree, examining the tracks, and found where the pack had made its exit up the ridge and where the mountain lion had made a huge jump and landed almost on top of the snowy tracks of the mule. He walked over to the mule's tracks and saw a small crimson spot staining the snow. The mule was still bleeding, but as he walked, the bloodstains became farther apart. This was a good sign.

Standing for a minute to scan the area, Chance caught his breath before resuming the task of trailing his mule. The weather was changing fast, like it did in Wyoming, and a persistently warm breeze had the snow melting even faster, making his footing even more precarious. Several times he almost slipped as he worked his way higher toward the small pass at the ridge's crest. He removed the scarves from his neck and hat as he climbed. The rocky pass was at least four hundred yards above him, and the hillside had turned to mostly yellowed grass sticking above the snow with an accent of small boulders and random aspen. In some places, the boulders helped define the trail and created steps that aided him with firm traction.

Twenty minutes later he began to walk through the pass, which was lined with large, mature aspen. Most of the aspen carried the blackened scars from elk and other animals that had used them for winter food, but for the most part, the trees seemed healthy as they rose above the snow. He stopped and visually followed both sets of tracks as they continued up through the aspens and then vanished over the crest. Walking towards a large boulder, he stopped and knocked the snow off its surface and then laid the buffalo hide down upon it. He needed a break, and the hide would keep his butt from getting wet as he rested.

The site was eerily quiet with only the rustle of the gentle wind and his heavy breathing breaking the silence. He scanned his surroundings, appreciating the beauty of this small pass and its majestic stand of large aspens. Half daydreaming, his eye caught something that brought him back to the present. There, ten feet up on one of the wider aspen was something carved into the tree. He stood up and approached it. The initials QW and date 1853 were clearly carved into the white, leathery bark. Chance often carved his own initials into trees when he found a special spot that made him want to tell the world he'd been the first to explore it or that he, too, had made this journey. He sure hadn't expected to see someone's initials here on this isolated ridge in the middle of nowhere.

Almost daily he was questioning if he and his brothers were the first people to live in the valley, but he wasn't totally sure one way or the other. They had found graves and an old wagon, and now a carving on a distant ridge, but certainly no real signs that someone had built a home or had a long-term camp, nothing that was solid evidence that someone had not just passed through years ago to trap or prospect, or maybe die.

It was sunny now and the warmth of the sun felt good on his bronzed, weathered face that came from the Wyoming wind. In a couple of hours it would be getting dark and his stomach reminded him several times with loud growls, that he still needed to find some food. He started down the other side of the pass and soon found a game trail in the snow that gently meandered down the hill, a path the mountain lion and mule had also found. As he descended the open, grassy hillside, the terrain became thickly timbered. Shortly after, the tracks of the mountain lion turned from the trail and headed uphill and deeper into the timber. Chance followed the mountain lion's tracks for about fifty yards as they continued away and then returned to following the mule's tracks. Maybe the mountain lion had given up, but the mule seemed to have been content to continue down the hill using the trail Chance had found. Several times he saw where the mule had stopped and grazed on scattered clumps of grass that lined the trail, and he could also see sign of elk that he assumed had been spooked by the mule. Chance was impressed by the amount of game sign he saw and how well developed the trails were, but he didn't seem to be gaining any ground on Dixie.

Close to an hour later, he came to a small opening at the bottom of the ridge. It wasn't large, but it had ample grass for horse or mule, a small creek, and the protection of thick timber on one side. Leaning his Hawkens against a tree, he pulled his long Bowie knife from its sheath and began hacking densely needled branches for his shelter underneath an old spruce tree with high, heavy branching. The warm wind had taken the majority of the snow off the trees, and only the constant drips of icy water remained.

It didn't take him long to build a tight little shelter with the opening facing the meadow. With several large, fallen trees behind him in the timber, the little spot was almost impenetrable from any direction except the front. Several more dead trees littered the meadow. He broke off a handful of small branches that were slightly damp but burnable. Next he removed close to a dozen rocks from beside the creek and placed them in a circle in front of his shelter. Scanning the meadow again, Chance walked up to a lone snag standing at the edge of the timber and removed a large section of bark from its south side, and then, using his knife, he dug out strips of dry wood from its side. The bark he stacked with the branches, and the small wood splinters he stuck in the dry inside pocket of his coat.

He paused again for a moment and scanned his surroundings before lifting his gun and vanishing into the forest. It didn't take long before he saw rabbit tracks. Within twenty minutes, he was carrying a fat snowshoe rabbit back to the little meadow he would call home for the night. With the aid of the bird's nest and a handful of wood splinters, he began coaxing the small fire until it was capable of absorbing the larger branches he had collected earlier. Using a thick, straight stick he removed the bark from one end with his knife and slid it into the rabbit. There was something about having a fire that just seemed to make everything more comfortable and friendly. Chance thought about the many nights he had slept alone beside one.

With nothing left of the rabbit besides the bones, using his gloves, he carefully moved some of the hot rocks inside his buffalo hide to warm it before he lay down for the night. The warm breeze had raised the temperature considerably and he appreciated his luck as he rolled up in the warm buffalo hide and fell into a deep sleep.

It was fully daylight when Chance awoke, slowly opening his eyes. His eye caught movement. After several minutes, he saw another rabbit. It was taking its paws and bending over the long stems of grass to eat the kernels of seeds from the grass's crown. His eyes moved from the rabbit to his gun. He slowly reached out from under his heavy hide blanket and raised his rifle to his shoulder. It is a good morning, he thought to himself as he filled his stomach with another meal of cooked rabbit and cold water from the creek.

An hour later, he was following the small meadow down to where it broke with the forest into another grassy valley. The center of the valley was mainly sagebrush and grass, but where he stood it was mostly a mixture of small juniper bushes and native fescue. He had left the trail the previous night to find a campsite and now he needed to pick up Dixie's trail again. Certainly the mule had gone this way and he hoped to find her tracks somewhere close to where the timber met the prairie. Soon he saw traces of the mule's track in a small area of snow and mud; and beside them, the mountain lion's tracks as well.

"This cat doesn't give up," he muttered to himself, as he began following the straight trail out into the prairie. "I hope I find Dixie before that cat does." He was getting angry with this demon cat and he swore to himself that he would track it down.

For the next hour, he jogged as he relentlessly followed their tracks. Most of the snow was gone now, and in places the trail was difficult to follow. He had just made it to the top of a small rise when the mountain lion tracks stopped and took a ninety-degree turn up the small ridge. Chance wondered if the big cat was trying to get ahead of the mule by circling or if it had finally decided to give up. He paused for several minutes to survey the surrounding terrain to determine if he was missing something, and then returned to trailing his mule.

In a small meadow at the bottom of a draw was where he found it, an old trail that at one time many years ago had seen a fair amount of traffic. His mule Dixie had led him there, and now both of them were following it up the ridge. According to the tracks, the mule hadn't stopped for any length of time to eat much more than an occasional bite as it walked along. Chance stood for a second and surveyed the trail ahead. It just didn't look right. It wasn't like an old buffalo trail, or a trail made by elk and deer, somehow it was different. This new trail impressed him with how well it followed the grades and made for good traveling. Several times the trail entered some scattered timber where an occasional fallen tree blocked his way and he worked around it. He wasn't sure if he was following a game trail or one built long ago by Indians or trappers.

It was in one of these timber patches that he saw something that made him stop and stare. Another old stump with ax marks at its base, here in the middle of nowhere. Who had done this, he asked himself, as he stared at the rotted remains of the stump and snag that lay on the downhill side of the trail. Someone years ago cut this tree down, but why? They probably could have easily worked their way around it. He was certainly in the middle of nowhere, and to his knowledge the nearest cabin was at least thirty miles away. This would have been a lot of work for a man who was just passing through. There seemed to be only one tree that had been cut, but that was enough to fuel his curiosity. He wondered if these tree remains and the insect-infested stumps he had found up Canvas Creek might have something in common.

The snow was now almost completely gone with the exception of some of the shadiest areas, and the warm wind had begun working on those. At the top of the small rise, the trail veered to the right and its grade increased as it headed into another patch of heavy timber. His stomach was growling again. Chance wished he had saved just a little of his rabbit for lunch, but in his hunger, he hadn't thought of that.

For only a brief moment he thought he smelled smoke. Taking another deep breath through his nose, he couldn't smell anything. Maybe it was just his imagination, but he would keep his Hawkens ready. He had no desire to be surprised by man or beast. Chance was worried the mountain lion might double back, knowing it wouldn't hesitate to strike if it sensed the advantage. Close to half a mile later, the trail opened into a large meadow carpeted with yellow grass. What really caught Chance's eye was the blackened, skeletal remnants of what once had been a cabin, now nothing more remained than a few old burnt logs and the stoic rock column that had been a chimney.

"So that's why there was such a good trail, it leads to this cabin," he muttered. His mind was racing with who these people were and what had happened to them. From a distance the damage sure looked like the work of hostile Indians, but there were others in this country who at times could be every bit as vicious and cruel. The charred remains of the cabin were surrounded by decaying stumps of various sizes with a few close to three feet wide. Whoever built this place had worked hard to carve out a new life, and now all that remained of their existence were these blackened ashes of a forgotten time.

He leaned against a large Douglas fir, one of many that seemed to grow in the protection of this secluded valley. A small babbling brook ran through the small dip that occurred between the trees and the remains of the old cabin and from what he could see, everything seemed quiet and peaceful. The sun's rays reflected off the frost-laden rocks of the old chimney directly into Chance's eyes. He squinted and shifted out of the sun.

The cabin was of common size, around fourteen by sixteen feet square, and he noticed that several of the scarred corner logs had escaped the fire by falling and rolling away. The building must have collapsed upon itself, but what caught Chance's eye were the tight square cuts of a craftsman. Most of the trapper cabins he had seen were of far lower quality due to the fact that a trapper might only use one for a winter and move on. This fire had burned hot, and not much remained of the cabin's interior except a few burnt spikes and rusty traps that lay amongst the blackened earth and ashes. Chance chose not to explore any further as he cautiously moved farther into the meadow.

The cabin sat amongst the stumps on a raised bench of ground, which gave it an excellent view of the valley below; and it had been cleverly built into the trees so as to not be sky lined. As he turned he noticed a blackened wooden wall of another building, a much larger building almost completely hidden in a thicket of spruce about sixty yards away. He walked closer, and to his surprise there stood a large barn almost fifty feet long by forty feet wide and mostly intact. The aged, lichen covered logs were well camouflaged with dangling clumps of moss growing in spots where the chalking was missing. Chance smiled at how well it was hidden and the fact that he had not seen it at first glance.

He walked to the large barn door and gave it a tug, and that's when he heard it, the bray of a mule somewhere behind the structure. He froze for a moment. Had he finally found his mule? He excitedly and warily turned and entered a small opening in the thick spruce trees that seemed to lead to the back of the barn. The small opening was just wide enough for either a man or mule to walk through comfortably, but it was dark and littered with brown spruce needles. The path led to a small open area containing an old, sagging corral. There in a corner stood the mule eating at an old manger. Dixie turned her head, and with a grass sticking out both sides of her mouth walked across the corral and stood beside Chance, allowing him to pet her neck.

"That a girl, I thought I would never find you," he whispered into her ear, as he gently rubbed her neck. "How did you find this place, girl?"

He continued scratching and petting her head as he worked his way towards her bloodstained hip. A shallow nine-inch cut was covered with dried blood and a little dirt from the corral. It didn't look good, but it would have been far worse if it hadn't been for the buffalo hide. He would need to boil some water to clean the wound, but that wasn't going to happen here unless he could find something to boil water in. Dixie turned and walked back to the manger where she began eating again.

He moved farther around the corral to where the gate stood and found it partially open, but only by a foot. In front of the gate were the muddy tracks of the mule, which made it look like she had stood there a while before figuring out how to get in. It was strange that somehow Dixie had opened the gate by herself, but Chance dismissed it as one of the tricks she was known for back at their cabin. Where did she get the grass from? Chance wondered, as he walked over to her and peered into the manger. There was a small pile of relatively fresh cut grass lying in the bottom.

Chapter 5

"What the hell!" Chance said loud enough that if someone were near they would have heard. He stood there for a couple of minutes petting Dixie as he tried to figure out what to do next and asking the mule questions that he knew she wouldn't answer. He reached up and loosened the saddle's cinch before carefully removing the crooked saddle and blanket, making sure nothing rubbed against the nasty wound in the process. He set the saddle down and leaned it up against one of the rotting corral posts, never allowing his rifle to be more than a quick step away at any time. He had no idea how long the mule had been there, but Dixie seemed totally comfortable in her new surroundings; her coat was dry and she was calmly eating the last of the grass. The bit hung a little unnaturally to one side of her mouth with one rein still tied to the saddle and the remains of the other dangling several inches below the bit.

Chance was surprised the saddlebags had stayed on, but there they were and still buckled down with his gear and provisions inside. The saddle was missing a tie strap, one of the two that Chance had found and used to tie the buffalo hide to the back of his saddle. He couldn't tell the age of the grass in the manger, but he knew it hadn't been there for too long, and he was pretty sure it was from this year's cuttings. Was this left over grass from someone else passing through or was there someone watching him? He slowly turned and visually scanned the forest for danger or movement, but there was none.

His mind was full of questions with few answers. Had someone found his mule? But if so, who? And where were they now? He wasn't sure of anything. He scanned the ground for tracks and other clues, but found none except those of the mule and his own. With gun in hand he walked to the gate and shut it securely. He was worried that this was a setup and there could be an Indian out there hiding in wait, but the mule was calm and that told him a lot. He wanted to leave this place, but he was exhausted, and from what he could tell, so was the mule.

To make matters worse, it would be dark in another hour and this was unfamiliar ground. His movements slowed and his caution rose as he made his way to the barn door and slowly opened it, extending the gun's muzzle in first as the door creaked loudly. Inside the barn the rays from the setting sun filtered through numerous small holes created by missing chinking and a large hole in one end of the barn's roof provided enough light to examine the barn's shady interior.

The building contained five nice-sized stalls as well as a numerous old tools, several wooden barrels, and other materials common to a barn. Whoever had burned the cabin down had for some reason decided to spare this barn. His eyes went to one of the horse stalls where he found a pile of grass nearly three feet high that had been harvested and dried that year. Maybe someone is using this place as a stopping point when they go hunting, he thought. Yeah, probably just one of those people who live down at Meeteetse Creek, Chance thought, as he subconsciously nodded his head as if in agreement with himself.

An old metal tub with several small rust spots hung from a rusted square nail on one of the many peeled logs that acted as supports for the barn, and he reached up and removed it. If I tip this to one side to avoid the hole in the side, this may work well enough to boil some water, he reasoned. He turned and cautiously walked down to the stream that he had crossed entering the meadow, his rifle never leaving his shoulder. Using fine sand and small gravel he washed the tub out several times, removing dust and other gunk that had built up in its bottom over time. He laid his gun down beside him and put a little less than half a gallon of water in the tub, then slung his gun back over his shoulder and, with both hands, carefully carried the tub back into the barn.

In the one corner of the building where a section of the roof was missing, he found the signs of a campfire complete with a circle of rocks and blackened ashes. He couldn't tell how old the remains of the fire were, but no volunteer grass was growing up through the ashes. With the help of some dry grass from one of the stalls, some small sticks, and old dry shakes from the collapsed section of the roof, Chance started a fire and carefully tilted the tub on its side using rocks to balance and secure it. It was a small fire by design, and he purposely made it just large enough to heat the tub, but not enough to illuminate the whole area. More than one man had been killed from a well-placed bullet shot through a hole in the wall created by missing chinking and he didn't plan on repeating their mistake.

After Chance was sure the fire was well started and had some decent coals, he walked back out the barn door and through the small passage beneath the trees to the corral. He knew this was no time to let his guard down and he was sure if something was lurking out there, they were just waiting for an opportunity. Walking over to the tired, quiet mule he talked to her and then led her into the barn and over to one of the stalls where he placed a small pile of grass. Next he went back out and got his saddle, saddlebags, and what remained of his headstall and moved them inside the barn and against a post close to the fire.

Leaning back against the smooth, peeled support post of the building, Chance removed some dry biscuits and jerky from his saddlebags. He was impressed that his saddlebags had survived the ride and that his knots hadn't come loose on the mule's panicked journey. The two days of rabbit had been good, but he was happy to make the change to biscuits and salted jerky, at least for one night.

After an hour of careful tending, the water began to boil, and Chance removed his shirt and dipped it into the hot water. Slowly he walked back over to the mule and tried to clean the wound the best he could. Dixie laid her ears back, but she stood still and let him gently work on the gash. It took a bit of soaking to loosen the dried blood, but he was pleased to see the wound wasn't any more severe than he had feared. Finishing the task, he walked back over to the fire and sat down and stretched his back once again against the post. He knew staying in the barn was dangerous, but it offered more protection than being outside and was probably his safest bet. Securing both the front and back doors with old boards from a stack in one of the stalls, he laid some grass from the pile down in one of the shadows close to the fire before lying down for the night.

Chance tried to make himself comfortable on the pile of grass, rolling around in several different positions until he found just the right one. He stretched his hand out towards one of the old boards that made up one side of a stall and was surprised to feel something soft against the tips of his fingers. His first impression was that it probably was just a piece of an old burlap grain sack, but the material felt different. He picked the soft object up, and in the dim light of the small fire, he could tell it was a small leather pouch not six inches long. He could feel at least a couple of small objects inside as he tried to open the pouch.

Quickly he loosened the leather strap that tied it shut and poured the objects into his hands. There was a small metal cross, the inexpensive type that a lot of young ladies wore as jewelry, a statue of an angel not more than an inch high, two snake-eyed marbles, and a small colorful stone decorated by small rings of red and what looked like a valuable piece of jewelry. It appeared to be a lady's brooch, the type you only saw on high society ladies in the big cities. Moving it around in his hand, he could feel a small latch on one side and soon was able to open it, revealing a water-stained picture of what looked to be a woman with long hair. From what he could tell, the piece wasn't real old, but it was worn and showed the signs of heavy wear by its smooth edges.

He moved closer to the fire so he could better examine it. It was certainly a lady's brooch, silver and ivory and accented with four small rubies embedded in its silver edge. How did this valuable brooch get here, he pondered. Did the past lady of the house lose it or did someone hide it? They looked more like the treasures of a young child than those of a lady. How the brooch got in the pouch, he had no clue. After a couple of minutes, he put the items back into the leather pouch and tied the top before rolling it up into his handkerchief and stuffing it into his shirt pocket.

He didn't sleep well that night, even though he was tired and enjoyed the warmth of the buffalo hide and small fire. Several times he awoke to the howl of a distant coyote, but his nightmare was always of a huge cat with bright yellow eyes.

The next morning Chance awoke to a beam of light piercing through a hole in the old barn's shake roof. His mule was lying down and appeared to be asleep until he moved and she opened her eyes and struggled to her feet. She was a good-looking, chestnut-colored mule with trusting eyes and a muzzle slightly lighter in color than the rest of her thick coat. He gave her some more grass and then led her to the small creek down by the cabin where she drank for an extended period. While she drank, he refilled the small water tub and set it to one side. Next he leaned his rifle against one of the many old stumps that littered the area and cupped his hand to drink.

He had just swallowed his first mouthful of water when he heard a small branch break about sixty yards away at the edge of the forest. Grabbing his Hawkens, he rose and in one quick movement raised the gun to his shoulder, ready for whatever was to happen, but there was only silence. He knelt back down beside a stump and waited for a full five minutes, his gun in his lap facing the noise that had alerted him. His father had taught him to hunt and had told him that silently waiting was his best defense if someone or something was out there. A person was always safer to just quietly kneel and scan the area for movement, listening for another crack of a twig or swish of a tree branch. Maybe it was a squirrel or some other varmint, but he was a cautious man and only cautious men survived in this country.

It was a while later when he slowly stood up, walked over to the mule, and picked up her lead rope. She had stood perfectly still, her long ears pointed in the direction of the sound. Chance was wary, and his intuition told him he was not alone. He tied Dixie to a small tree and, with Hawkens in hand, quietly snuck towards the source of the sound. After a couple of minutes he reached the edge of the forest and stopped and listened again. It was quiet except for the slight breeze high in the trees and a few birds flittering from branch to branch in another tree. Whatever or whoever had been there was gone, and still he wasn't certain that it wasn't just because he was tired and his imagination working overtime.

Chance walked back to the mule, untied her, and led her back inside the barn. Examining her wound, he was impressed with how well it looked in good light. Many times back in Iowa, he had helped his family doctor with farm animals, and he had a pretty good idea how long the healing process would take. Within a month she should be fully recovered, he thought. The night before he was sure he was in for a long walk back to the cabin, but today he wasn't so sure. Dixie seemed to be doing fine, and he wondered if he took the thick buffalo hide and tied it to the front of the saddle instead of on the back, maybe it would be possible to ride her. Chance had a little catgut that he kept in the bottom of the saddlebags that he could use to do stitches, but he felt the wound would do better to breathe in the open air. He also kept a small currycomb in the bottom of his saddlebags and used it to rub and comb the mule.

Several minutes later he tenderly placed the blanket and saddle on her back. He was very careful with the wound, but he knew how tough mules were and he felt pretty comfortable that she would be okay. He cut off the last two long pieces of leather straps from the back of the saddle and made them into a short set of reins. They weren't great, but Chance hoped they would at least last until he got back to the cabin. He then double-checked the barn to make sure he hadn't forgotten anything as he opened the door and led his mule down the trail and through the creek.

As he entered the small meadow where the trail had started, he noticed numerous stumps; this had not been a lazy man that had intended to clear this much land high up on this protected little valley. He had picked his site well. It was protected from most of the hard winds and snowdrifts, and he'd surely intended to stay there for a long time.

Leading the mule down the trail, he carried his Hawkens over his right shoulder as he went. If someone were to set up an ambush, he felt it would be soon. When another trail branched off the main trail and headed in the direction of his cabin, he took it. Chance wasn't sure if the new trail was just a heavily used game trail or one the previous owner had created. Quietly he continued on the new trail for about a hundred yards before climbing up through the sagebrush as the trail descended below him. Slowing his pace, he cautiously watched the country below him as he began paralleling the slope. He could just see the trail in the distance and it was his plan to watch the route long enough that he felt that he wasn't being followed or this wasn't a trap.

The mule was quiet as she picked her footing and seemed ready to head in the direction of home. Chance walked for another ten minutes before finding a good vantage point and a place to tie up the mule where she wouldn't be easily seen. He sat on a flat rock buffered by a large juniper bush for the better part of ten minutes as he carefully scanned his back trail and as much of the country in front of him as possible. He was pretty positive nothing was following him and if there had been an ambush, he was now far past it.

He walked for another thirty minutes, breaking trail along the steep hillside scattered with small pine, spruce trees, and clump fescue grass. He was pleased that the saddle seemed to be holding its position on his mule's back and not causing her any issues. The hillside was still damp and slick in places where the sun didn't hit, and he finally decided to work his way back down to the trail several hundred yards below. Chance led the mule down the hill, zigzagging through the trees and rocks until they came out on the path he had originally taken. He felt that he could now make good time getting home and was happy to know the hidden location of these two trails for future journeys.

For the next twenty or thirty minutes he made good time, as the mostly level path paralleled the grade in a direction towards home. He wondered how he could have possibly missed these two great trails leading to the burnt cabin. Surely he must have crossed at least one of them but maybe in the excitement of following the mule he had just not seen it. At the top of a ridge, in fairly dense spruce, he found out part of the mystery of why he didn't remember crossing the trail – it stopped there in a maze of smaller trails, all leading in different directions over hard and rocky ground.

Whoever had built this trail had cleverly disguised its entrance, and Chance could see at least a dozen ways a man or animal could exit without leaving a trace. The man who had built this trail and cabin was cautious, and from within the trees a person could see at least five miles down into the valley in one direction. The way the land lay, the view was only to the northeast and not west towards his cabin, but it made him comfortable that he couldn't be seen by anyone or anything moving in the valley below.

Chance felt a sense of confidence and security now and decided it was time to ride and make up a little time. With Dixie tied to a tree, he tightened her cinch with one good tug and then crammed three fingers under the cinch to make sure it wasn't too tight. Untying the mule he threw the makeshift reins over the saddle horn and launched himself into the saddle. He intended to ride out across the open slope where he could make good time and maybe get home sometime late that night. With a gentle nudge from the heel of his boot, Dixie took several steps towards one of the openings in the trees. He knew it would be a long ride back, but he began to relax as he thought of finally heading home and spending the night in the protection and warmth of the cabin.

Suddenly a pinecone the size of a large fist landed several feet ahead of him in the path and rolled to a stop. He yanked back on the reins and looked up the hill, wondering what had just happened, but after several minutes he decided it was just a random pinecone cut lose by the constant wind. What a coincidence, he thought, that big pinecone landing in my path just as I started out. The mule had reacted calmly and he gave her another gentle nudge just as another pinecone landed ten feet above them, then rolled down and came to rest in the trail beside the mule. This time he jumped from the mule, rifle in hand, and slid behind a tree for cover. This was no random occurrence and he knew it. He scoured the hillside for a presence. Who or whatever had thrown the pinecone was not revealing itself. Dixie stood still for a moment, her ears and head pointed uphill. Finally she lowered her head and commenced eating from an old stand of tall fescue that grew beside the trail. Usually when there was an issue she was all ears, but now she seemed relaxed and calm.

Chance began working his way cautiously up the hill until he came to a spot where someone had stood. It was difficult at best to see any tracks in the thick pine needles that cluttered the ground, but he could see where someone's foot had turned in one spot, probably when they were in the act of throwing. Who in the heck would be throwing pinecones at him and then running away, he was at a loss to answer. He hiked farther up the hill and then looked back. There was another view of the valley, and this time it was towards his cabin and an area he couldn't see from the lower spot on the trail. Sitting down on a large rock, he took in the large expanse of scenery for a moment, wondering what just happened, and questioning his own woodmen's skills.

It was then that he saw movement deep in the canyon before him. It was at least six hundred yards away, but he could make out what he thought were the head and shoulders of a trapper riding a stout black horse. He was working his way up the valley, and then another person came out of the gulley behind him. It looked like an Indian on a white horse with what appeared to be a musket lying on his lap as he rode. Next came another white man, who, from his colorful clothing, looked French, but there was no way of knowing for sure from this distance.

As the group closed the gap to about two hundred yards, Chance saw his distinctive canteen tied to one of their saddles and almost fell backwards. Somehow they must have happened upon it as they crossed the valley, and now he was sure they knew they weren't alone. His gut told him that this wasn't just a hunting party, that there was something wrong, but he didn't know what.

By the time the party had cleared the gulley, Chance had counted two white men and five Indians, and they seemed to be headed up and to the south. He sat and watched, glad that he hadn't ridden out only seconds before and exposed himself to their view. It was then that another rider rode out of the gulley far behind the others, leading a packhorse with what looked like a woman riding on it. They would get as close as a hundred and fifty yards of his position. His first thought was to head back to the mule and make sure she didn't do her mountain canary imitation and alert the party of his presence.

Keeping low, he crawled back behind the rock he had been sitting on, and in a crouched position, headed down the hill to the mule. He untied Dixie and led her deeper into the canyon he had just traveled and tied her to another juniper bush. Ripping several large handfuls of long dry grass from along the trail, he placed the grass at the mule's feet, hoping to keep her occupied and quiet while he snuck back around and took a second look.

Chance moved back to his saddlebags and dug down until he found his collapsible telescope, removed it from its soft cotton sack, and then scrambled back up the hill, Hawkens in hand. He slid behind the boulder he had been sitting on and extended his telescope, making sure the sun wouldn't reflect off the metal or glass. On closer examination, it appeared the six Indians were Blackfoot from their clothing. The last horse carried a woman, wrapped in what looked like a faded red blanket. She wore a blue scarf tied tightly around her face and neck. Her long brown hair and what he could see of her pale complexion were definitely those of a white woman. She looked cold and miserable, and appeared to be tied to the saddle horn. Her head bounced unnaturally as the horse struggled up the hill; something was definitely wrong here.

He clenched his fist and ground the eyeglass. His anger grew into frustration. One against eight was odds that only a fool would take. They were headed high, and Chance was sure there must be a pass somewhere up amongst the jagged rocks, but he didn't know where; this was unfamiliar country. The party continued up almost to the tree line where they entered the last of the snow that had fallen two days earlier. He wasn't about to follow them without the mule, especially with some unknown presence lurking somewhere in the bushes around him. There were stories he had heard about captured white women and what the young bucks did to them, and if he could help her, he would. He watched as they disappeared into the trees and then waited several minutes before moving.

As long as the group stayed to the snow, he knew following at a distance would be fairly easy, but if they were to stop and backtrack, the mule's smaller tracks would be a dead giveaway that they were being followed. Whoever the captive was, Chance probably wasn't going to be able to help her, but at least he might figure out where they were going before the snow and rain erased any trace of their tracks. His thought was to parallel their trail and keep at least twenty yards between him and the broken snow of their trail. He would pick his steps carefully and quietly, walking under trees whenever possible. The group appeared to be following a faint trail outlined by a shallow dip in the snow, and within a half an hour they had worked themselves up and over a small hidden pass in the rocks.

Chance was amazed at how hidden the trail was, and yet it was smooth and not too steep. He felt comfortable with his plan of skirting the perimeter and felt fairly certain that he wouldn't be detected. Every few steps he would stop and listen for either voices or the sound of crunchy snow breaking, for now he heard neither. He knew the group on horses would be making good time on this trail and his caution and lack of clear travel would increase the gap of time between them. He had worked his way up through the pass, but it had been difficult, and in a couple of places he had to turn back and find a better way so the mule could follow.

The other side of the ridge was much more open and gentler; he had increased his pace when all of the sudden he realized he was about to step onto the trail. The sharp switchback surprised Chance, and he paused and looked around for movement. He felt fortunate that he wasn't moving faster or his tracks would be easily visible and give his presence away. Cutting a few clippings from a juniper, he stuck them in his track to camouflage the only visible footprint and then backed farther into the brush and away from the trail. Minutes later he had mentally regrouped and led the mule to a small ridge that seemed to parallel the ridge with the trail. It was far enough away that he felt comfortable that he could see anyone or anything on the trail. He would tie Dixie here in a small patch of dense spruce and go farther down the ridge to a spot where he believed he could easily see the whole valley and certainly anything going up or down the trail, then return for the mule when he knew that everything was safe.

Working his way down the ridge to the spot he had identified, he saw distant dots way out on the prairie; it was the group he was following. He immediately sat down and pulled out his telescope and lengthened it to full draw. Chance could just barely make out the group at that distance as he slowly counted in his mind. He could make out the two Frenchmen, then five Indians, and last, the slumped figure that had to be the woman. He froze. Had he miscounted? Hadn't there been six Indians instead of five? His body was on full alert now, and he was scared that he had walked right into a trap. Maybe they knew that someone was following them and the ostrich canteen was proof of it.

When he thought of the ostrich canteen, his mind wanted to go to when he'd won it, out-shooting over fifty men in a contest of skill, but now wasn't the time to let his mind wander. For several minutes he scanned the trail on the far ridge and then examined the canyon between him and the ridge, he saw nothing. He watched the small group disappear on the horizon in the direction of a rock face that rose steeply against the gentle valley.

The slight movement beneath a clump of ponderosa pine caught Chance's eye. At first he couldn't tell what it was, but then he recognized the gentle movement of a horse's tail flicking as the muscled back quarters shifted position. It was a well-chosen spot, mostly concealed in the thick branches of the trees and a low juniper bush, but the movement of the white tail was difficult to hide. He knew that he was very close to an Indian, but he didn't know if his enemy was above or below him.

He slowly turned and studied his back trail, there was nothing. Next he examined the area around him, searching for something that was out of place, again, he found nothing. He thought about his options. A small trickle of sweat rolled down from his neck into a small open pocket of air in his shirt. He could sneak further down the hill and hopefully surprise the Indian, but he saw little chance of that. The second choice was to sneak back up the trail he had just come down and hope the Indian didn't spot him, but who knew how close he was. The third choice was to patiently wait and not give up his location, which is the one he chose.

The horse was no farther than fifty yards away, and Chance had a good view of most of the terrain below as he tucked himself up beside the wet sagebrush leaves of a large bush. It was fall, and normally a person could pick things out better this time of year, but this wasn't the case here. No matter how hard he looked he couldn't see anything out of place, and no Indian. As he sat there, he hoped and prayed that he wouldn't be forced to shoot his Hawkens and possibly alert the rest of this group. His buckskins and undergarments were damp from the climb and wet snow, and he could feel the cold slowly trickling in as the temperature dropped. All of a sudden he could feel a gentle breeze blowing on the back of his neck. The breeze could take his scent down the slope, and Chance knew that Indians had a keen sense of smell. Everything left an odor, and his bath every two weeks didn't make him immune to it.

As Chance contemplated the direction of the breeze, he saw the Indian's head, shoulders, and top of his musket as he made his way up the hill at a forty-five degree angle towards his horse. The Indian had chosen the same great vantage point as Chance had, and only the gentle twitch of a tail had saved Chance from stumbling into the Indian's hidden position. The Indian was a big man wrapped in furs and decorated with war paint. Chance thought about shooting him with his rifle, an easy shot as he worked his way up between bushes. If the rest of the Indians heard the shot, it would probably bring more trouble than it was worth, and they would probably trail him back to his brothers and their cabin. He carefully leveled the bead of his rifle on the heart of the Indian; if the Indian were to smell him, it would be his last breath. The Indian walked into the opening that led to the horse and stopped several yards from where he was tied.

Suddenly the Indian turned and stared up the ridge, as if something might be wrong. It was at that moment that his horse raised his tail and relieved himself in a steaming pile. What timing, thought Chance as the Indian's expression and focus changed and he walked around the fresh horse pile and over to untie his horse. This Indian just looked plain mean with a two-inch scar just below his left eye and a bloody scalp tied to the horse's side as he led him out from behind the trees. That was way too close, Chance realized as the Indian began leading his paint horse down through the rocks and trees towards the huge rock face where the rest of his group had disappeared.

Chance let a full thirty minutes elapse before he turned and led Dixie back up the ridge, keeping out of the open and close to the tall juniper bushes that dotted the hillside. He took another look at the wound and was pleased to see how well it appeared to be healing. It had not been anywhere near as bad as the steady stream of bloody drops his imagination had made it out to be. One thing for sure about a horse or mule is they can lose a lot of blood and still keep going.

Most of the day had been used trailing the group of Indians and Frenchmen, and now it was only hours until dark and the sky was filling with large black clouds. He felt a snowflake hit his hand, and then another as the wind began to pick up. It was several hours back to the old barn and about six or more hours to his cabin. Chance felt good about the condition of the mule, but he didn't want to lose her after all this. Crossing the open hillside that lay in front of him before dark would certainly be dangerous if someone were watching. As he stood there holding the lead rope, the wind picked up even more and the heavy snowflakes began to come down sideways. Someone would have a hard time seeing him in the dimming light and heavy snow, but if they did he would certainly be leading them back to his cabin. He didn't know how bad the storm would be, so the safe thing might be to go back to the old barn and wait out the storm with a warm fire and grass for the mule.

With that he pulled back the makeshift rein and the two of them headed back to the barn. It was just at dark when they arrived and Chance quickly watered the mule, and then stripped the saddle and gear. He hung the mule's blanket over a board and set it close enough to the old coals of the fire from the night before that he was sure it would dry by morning. It didn't take him long to find another dry, old bird's nest tucked on top of one of the barn's timbers to make a fire in the same location. Somehow he felt protected in this place with the small fire lighting some of the interior of the barn.

He was still short on wood for the night, so he took his Hawkens and hatchet and went outside towards a snag he had eyed on his earlier trip. If a man traveled much in cold weather, he soon developed a sense to mentally remember the location of potential firewood, and usually a snag contained dry wood, no matter the weather. He walked over to the snag and within a few minutes had chopped it down and was dragging it into the barn. There would be enough wood here to go through the night if used correctly. Cutting the small snag into three equal chunks, and after the fire became coals, he started feeding the two ends of the logs into the fire from both directions. The third length was put on top of the first two. He had done this hundreds of times, saving huge amounts of needed energy.

Walking over to his saddle, Chance positioned it at the head of the corral where he had slept the night before, and readjusted the dry grass. Normally he would have slept on the mule's blanket, but it was wet from rain and sweat, and the dry grass and buffalo blanket would work just as well to insulate him against the cold. He walked back outside and drank some water from the ice-lined creek, then headed back into the barn where he took some biscuits and jerky from his saddlebags for dinner. He had not planned to be gone for more than a couple of nights, and his stock of food was running low. Hopefully the storm would relent and allow him reasonable travel in the morning, but from the howling outside the barn and the snowflakes blowing through the hole in the roof, he wasn't sure. As he lay down on the bed of grass, he wondered if the pinecone thrower, who had warned him and probably saved his life, was hiding nearby, and if so, where?

Several times during the night, he awoke to a noise outside, and each time he stayed awake for twenty or more minutes before dismissing it as only the sound of the wind. In some odd way he liked this place, its setting and view of the meadow below. Whoever built it here had searched for a while for a special place and knew this country pretty well. The thing he didn't like was the creepy feeling of being watched, something he had no evidence of. But now at least he felt that whatever was watching him meant him no harm.

He awoke in the morning when the mule moved slightly in her stall. The storm had blown over, and now an almost eerie peacefulness filled the air. Stoking the coals of the fire, soon it was burning again as he stretched and looked out in all directions through the holes in the walls. He could clearly see the deep, untracked snow, and again, he felt a strange comfort with this place he hadn't felt before. Last night as he lay in bed, he had decided to light out for Meeteetse Creek; that way he could alert the small town of what he had seen, and hopefully there would be enough men to safely go after the group of Indians.

It had been almost two years since they had traveled through Meeteetse Creek, and at that time there had been at least fifteen people living there. The town was located in a small, open river bottom that allowed for good views in all directions; it would be difficult for a large group of Indians to sneak up on them. He wondered if the woman the Indians had captured was from the town or maybe a single wagon that had fallen behind a wagon train and suffered a terrible fate. Someone needed to make them aware of the existence of this band of Indians who had teamed up with the Frenchmen. He opened the large, heavy barn door and pulled it back into the barn. There was a good two feet of fresh, powdery snow covering everything.

There was no way for Chance to be sure, but he believed it was at least forty miles to the small town from here and there was no way he was going to make it there through this heavy snow and the huge drifts the open prairie would offer. He had seen the snow drifts on open ground back home on the farm and he knew just how difficult the travel would be and how deadly the deep snow could get. He would be lucky to find a way back through the drifts to his cabin, much less the distance to town. The memory of his neighbor back in Iowa who had gotten disoriented in a terrible, blinding blizzard wandered through his thoughts. After a week of searching, they had found his body three quarters buried in a snowdrift not more than a hundred yards from their front door.

Blinding snow could confuse and easily make a man lose his bearings in open country, and Chance had a healthy respect for what could happen. He ate his last biscuit and a small piece of jerky for breakfast and brushed the mule out with his old chunk of comb. Dixie seemed ready to go as he saddled her up and tied his heavy buffalo hide in front of his saddle. He shook his head at the poor quality of his makeshift reins and gently placed the bit into the mule's mouth using his thumb between her gums. Earlier he had set the bit close to the fire for a few minutes, and Dixie barely resisted the insertion of the warm bit.

Chance felt guilty as he walked over to the fire and kicked enough dirt on it to put it out. His mind kept going to the mystery woman and how she was probably someone's wife or daughter. Chance felt terrible that he wasn't somehow warning the people of Meeteetse Creek of the whole thing, but he knew that trying to make it to town in this snow would be suicide. He was also worried how Dixie would do in the deep snow, wondering if she could bust through the snowdrifts that sooner or later they would encounter no matter which direction they went. He wished he had worn spurs, but in his haste, he had forgotten them.

He led the mule through the barn door and then closed it tightly. Without the protection of the barn, his night would have been miserable at best. He had his Hawkens in his scabbard, as much for protection from the blowing snow as anything, but he knew he could pull it at a moment's notice if he detected any threat. He led her to the creek where they both drank heartily before he put one foot in the stirrup and sprung onto the large hand mule.

As they followed the trail for the first half an hour, the snow seemed a consistent two feet deep. It was when they went down into a ravine that they hit their first real challenge. A thick lip of snow covered the creek's icy edge and the mule could not see her footing. After several attempts, much snorting and some heavy coaxing, the mule gingerly stepped out on the ice until one foot broke through to the shallow creek bed. Chance praised the big mule, then encouraged her through the rest of the creek and up through the two-and-a-half-foot drift that guarded the creek's far bank. Once through, she stepped out like she was proud of herself, and Chance's confidence that they might actually make it home increased.

The going was slow and Chance tried to keep to areas of shallow snow, but that worked only so well. The fact that the mule was tall and strong helped a lot as she learned to crash into the banks of snow, sometimes several times, before making her way through. On the second large snowdrift, Dixie unexpectedly jumped high into the air as she launched herself into the drift, sending Chance flying off into the snow. Chance was a good rider, but for some reason he hadn't seen that one coming. At first he was mad, but then he laughed as he gathered himself up and brushed the snow off. It was then that he saw Dixie standing there looking at him with questioning eyes. The rest of the trip went as well as expected.

Several times Chance gave Dixie her head, and more times than not she found the best route through obstacles blocking their path. It was a miserably cold nine hours later that Chance saw the cabin's candle in the window as he topped the last ridge. Never had he seen a more comforting sight than that of the cabin with a trail of gray smoke rising above its chimney.

He hollered, "Red fox a riding," when he was in range of the cabin and the two dogs began barking and jumping through the deep snow to greet him, their stubby tails wagging feverishly. Vern and Virgil came hurrying out the front door as they put their coats on. Vern helped a half-frozen Chance slide from his saddle as Virgil took Dixie into the barn and unsaddled and brushed her down.

It was nearly an hour later, after Chance had devoured several bowls of hot soup and drank some hot coffee, that the three brothers sat down to talk.

Vern had a large smile on his face and seemed really excited as he sat down across from Chance. "We found another clue on the location of the gold," Vern blurted out.

Chapter 6

The snow was coming down in large flakes as Chance glanced out their only window, knowing in the back of his mind that there was no way he would be able to help the captured woman. "Did you hear me? I found another clue," Vern said again, as Virgil smiled with a nod. In a way, Chance didn't want to spoil their excitement and there would be time to tell his story, for nobody was going anywhere for a while.

"What did you find?" asked Chance, trying to show more excitement than he really felt.

"While you were gone I used a candle to heat the back of a couple of the pages of the diary, and I could read a few more pages, but one page was mighty interesting."

"So what did it say?"

"It turns out the Indian could speak a little English and he told those folks about this trail that led to the gold, but I don't understand exactly what he meant by, 'The light from the sky will burn, and the old man's face and the tree of many branches will show you the way.'"

"How do you know they are even talking about the gold?"

"I don't, but it only makes sense. What else would they be talking about?"

"The light from the sky has to be lightning, but what about this old man? And why does something need to burn?" asked Chance.

"Anyway, that is what we found, but what happened to you and that cat? Looks like Dixie got the worst of whatever happened," Virgil said in a concerned voice.

"Yeah, that cat backtracked on me and it almost killed Dixie. I ended up chasing her for a couple of days. That mountain lion was huge and followed her for near on to twenty miles before it gave up. I finally caught up to Dixie at this burned out cabin and barn. Found her eating grass in this old manger behind the barn; she was worn plum out and we ended up sleeping there."

"You found another homestead? Was there any sign of people?"

"There was a cabin but it was burned to the ground. Someone had recently put the grass in the manger, and there was another pile of this year's grass in the barn. I'm pretty sure someone has been using it on a regular basis, but they might be people we don't want to mess with."

"How's that?" asked Vern.

"Well I saw a couple of Frenchmen with a band of Blackfoot and they had a woman hostage. She didn't look like she was doing well, not well at all, they had her tied to the saddle horn and were leading her somewhere. I followed them for close to a half a day and almost ran into one of the biggest Blackfoot I have ever seen. He was watching the group's back trail, and I almost walked right into him. If it hadn't been for the flicker of his horse's tail, I think I would have."

"They had a woman? Could you see her face?"

"No, not really, it definitely was a white woman with long brown hair and all. But no, I really couldn't see her face. I got a mighty close look at the big Indian, and he sure looked like a savage you didn't want to mess with. He looked plum mean with that deep scar under his left eye and all."

"You were that close?"

"Yep, too close, if you ask me; if we had gotten in a fight or fired a shot, I don't know if I would be here right now. His band was a ways out, but I don't know how far the sound of the shot would have traveled. When I bedded down for the night in that barn on the second night, my idea was to ride to the settlement at Meeteetse Creek in the morning and see if I could get enough men to trail that group and get the woman back, but with this snow, I was lucky to even make it back here, much less Meeteetse Creek. Anyways, I am sure the pass they went over is snowed shut now until spring."

"Tell me more about the cabin and barn," said Virgil.

"Well there ain't a lot to tell. Whoever built them was good with his hands, but the strange thing was someone burned down the cabin and for some reason spared the barn. They had to have known it was there hidden back in the trees, but why they spared it, who knows?"

"So do you think it was Indians that burnt it down?"

"I'm not sure. The more I think about it, the more I think they left the barn to use later. That cabin was well-placed and hidden, and whoever built it there was no pilgrim. Someone used it, and that seems to be the only reason that makes sense with the grass in the barn and in that manger. Something is going on there, and I don't think it's good."

Chance felt the effects from the two cups of coffee his brothers had fixed for him at dinner and he sat, still dressed, on the edge of his bed as the sounds of gentle snoring began to fill the room. It had been a hard three days. Slowly he removed his shirt and felt the bulge in his shirt pocket. He had almost forgotten about the small pouch he had found. Chance took it from his pocket and set it on a high shelf; he would show it to his brothers in the morning.

For the next few days the snowstorms came and went, and there never seemed a good time to make the challenging journey to Meeteetse Creek. All three brothers wanted to save the woman, but they knew that being stranded by heavy snowdrifts might ultimately end in their own deaths. What they needed was at least a window of opportunity before they could venture out, but without the pass being open, the whole posse idea didn't make sense anyways.

* * *

It was getting late in the fall and the weather was sporadic. The nights were beginning to be icy cold and travel would be risky, but that didn't bother Chance. He walked through the door of the cabin and set a handful of cut logs down beside the stone fireplace blackened by use. "I've been thinking I need to go. I will try for town tomorrow, and hopefully it will be decent for a few days so I can make it to Meeteetse Creek. Anyways, I think it's time that our mule Dixie realizes she is still a working mule; she needs to be ridden."

"I don't know if I think much of your plan. It's a hard two days' ride at best, and what are you going to do once you get there? There is no way a posse is going over that pass you talked about for at least another month or two, so why go now?"

"I guess more than anything my conscience is bothering me. I need to do something, at least tell them about what I saw." Then Chance smiled. "Anyways, I need to buy a new canteen in town."

Both Vern and Virgil laughed at his last comment, knowing he had made up his mind. The rest of the day he carefully packed his supplies for the trip, double what he would normally take for a two-day ride. The men talked into the night about their future garden and orchard and then eventually went to bed. It was a starry night with a full moon; almost light enough to hunt by.

Within a couple hours of daylight, the sound of barking dogs ripped Chance and his brothers from their sound sleep. "What is it?" yelled Vern, as the three of them jumped from their bunks and hit the plank floor. Virgil was racing to pull his pants up over his long johns while Vern and Chance just threw their boots on.

"Whatever it is, the dogs are sure making a ruckus about it," replied Vern in a loud voice. Grabbing the two lanterns, the men made it out to the porch and shined their lights over the yard as the dogs violently barked in the direction of the barn.

"I'll bet it's that mountain lion back again, wanting another one of our sheep," yelled Virgil, as he joined them seconds later and ran towards the barn, rifle in hand. Chance and Vern were right behind him and split off to circle the corrals. Virgil, rifle at ready, opened the cracked barn door wider and let the light of the lantern shine into the room. Suddenly he heard a noise and saw a flash of motion as something jumped behind one of the piles of cut hay.

"The mountain lion is in the barn," yelled Virgil, as he raised his rifle in hopes of a quick shot. Vern and Chance came running through the barn door just as Virgil shot. The sound of the shot in closed quarters was deafening and the smoke from the black powder blocked their view.

"Did you hit him?" hollered Vern.

Chance saw movement in one of the shadows of the barn and had raised his gun to shoot again when he heard a pitiful moan. "Hold it," said Chance, "that didn't sound like any mountain lion to me." He raised the lantern and moved forward. There in the corner lay the motionless body of a young white boy, no more than nine from the looks of him, and he was bleeding badly from his side.

"Well, at least he ain't dead," said Chance, as he knelt down and felt for a pulse, then gathered the young boy in his arms and headed towards the cabin at a jog.

"I didn't mean to shoot no kid," said Virgil, "I thought he was that stinking mountain lion back for another meal."

The boy's limp arm dangled from Chance's grip as he stepped up onto the porch and then hurried to the cabin's table to get a better look. The boy was skinny and dirty, and his eyes were hollow-looking. He looked like he had seen the worst life had to offer.

"Who is he, I wonder," questioned Vern, as he held the lantern for Chance while Virgil went to get water to boil. For the next hour the men worked on cleaning and bandaging the wound.

"Well, that's about all I can do. We will just need to wait and see what happens from here on out," said Chance, as he stood straight up and washed a little of the blood off his hands in a small water basin. He turned to Vern. "Get me some more warm water so I can clean the boy. Leastwise the bullet traveled straight through his side. He'll be in a bad way for a while, but I think he will pull through. I wish he had been in better shape before he got here. He looks real weak."

Chance laid the boy down in his bed and spent the rest of the night sitting in one of the chairs, refusing to let anyone relieve him. By morning the young boy had a slight fever, and Chance was worried that things were getting worse.

"I think I need to head to town and see if there is a doctor or someone that knows more than I do about getting this boy healed," said Chance with a worried look on his face.

"It's mighty tough conditions out there and you could get caught real easy in a storm on that prairie. There ain't no shelter between us and that town to use in case you get into trouble. I really don't think trying to make a two day trip to the settlement right now is smart. If'n anyone is to go, it should be me," said Virgil, "I'm the one that shot him."

"No, I'm going to go. That darn mule of mine needs the exercise, and if any animal can get me through, she can. She's all healed up good now and ready to ride, so I'm going," Chance said firmly. "I can't be positive, but I'm pretty sure the reason he's here has something to do with that cabin and that woman I saw with the Indians. I'm getting out of here first thing in the morning, and I'm going to hope for the best."

Vern and Virgil took turns that night watching over the small boy while Chance got some sleep in Vern's bed. The next morning Vern checked the boy's fever; it was slightly worse. Chance walked over and felt the boy's forehead for a second time and then turned to his brothers.

"Make the boy comfortable and do what you can for him and I will be back as soon as I can, we owe the boy that," said Chance as he grabbed his packed saddlebags and a canvas-wrapped blanket and then walked through the door and over to the barn.

Within twenty minutes, Chance had caught and saddled the mule and was making good time across the prairie in the direction of town. The mule had a fast walk that was close to a slow horse's lope as he dodged through the sagebrush and headed towards more open grassland. The thought of running into Indians crossed his mind, but the life of the boy was by far his main concern. The sun was shining and the going was good as he tried to keep the landmarks he chose over one shoulder and stay on a straight course to a point on the horizon.

It was almost dark when he stopped, unsaddled his mule, and picketed her to a large sage bush. After running out of food the last time, he felt comforted that he had packed an extra two days' rations in his saddlebag. The site he had picked was down by a small creek. At one time several large trees had grown there, but they had long since died, leaving only the remains of several large rotting logs. At least these gave him some protection from the wind as he cooked up some meat and ate hard bread.

The mule ate peacefully as she worked the picket rope, munching on clumps of grass that stood above the couple of inches of snow that covered the ground. Chance used his horse blanket and bedroll to curl up in and his saddle for a pillow as he made himself comfortable for the night.

It was almost light the next morning when Chance awoke to the feeling of snowflakes gently landing upon his face. He rolled out of his bedroll and stood up. Within minutes he was saddled and packed and headed in the direction he believed town to be. It had been almost two years since he and his two brothers had traveled through the small settlement at Meeteetse Creek, so now its location strained his memory. He could see from the dark cotton clouds rising to the west that a storm was coming and it was a big one.

Gently nudging the mule with his spurs, he got her into a full gallop. He would try to ride ahead of the storm, and he hoped somehow the storm would miss him, but by the size of the snowflakes he realized that was unlikely. There was a large hill in front of him a little over a mile away, and he hoped he might find some sort of a shelter there before the full force of the wind and snow hit.

After about twenty minutes he pulled back on the reins and put Dixie into a slow trot, worried that with the fresh snow the chances of stepping in a ground squirrel hole had increased dramatically. This was a good mule that had gone through a lot, and the last thing he wanted to do now was to have to shoot her over a broken leg.

The wind continued to increase and the swirling flakes of snow the size of small cotton balls filled his view. No longer could he see the point on the horizon he had used to keep a straight course. He pulled his duster up tighter around his neck and hoped his wool coat and heavy clothes beneath the duster would be enough to protect him. At the last minute before he left the cabin, he had decided to bring his oversized, knee-high leather leggings, which he could wear with several pairs of wool socks.

He stopped the mule to change footwear, and then tied his boots on the back of the saddle, removing the buffalo pelt. The temperature was continuing to drop so he tied a scarf tightly around his head, covering everything but his eyes. Then Chance put his foot in the stirrup and mounted Dixie. He took a minute to secure the buffalo hide around himself and then gave the mule her head. The blowing snow kept him from seeing much farther than a few feet past the long ears of the mule. His worst nightmares were coming true.

Chance had ridden for about three hours not knowing if he were going straight or in circles, and now his fingers and the part of his face that was exposed were going numb. He thought about trying to find better shelter and start a fire, but there was only frozen grass and deepening snow wherever he looked. The wind was not letting up and icicles began to dangle from Dixie's mane and tail. Chance knew he was in trouble. Maybe building some type of snow shelter would offer him some protection, but his hands were now too frozen. If he got off the mule, he would never get back on. The extreme cold and wind were zapping his strength, and his mind began to wander. He thought of the captured lady and the sad look on her face and the small boy fighting a fever back at the cabin, and he wondered how they were doing.

The biting wind continued to blow and he was cold, so terribly cold. The mule slowed and then came to a stop. Chance knew he was freezing to death and it would only be a matter of hours before he was dead. He was miserably cold. He could no longer feel his fingers, and the biting wind was making his face go numb. No longer was he thinking clearly as the mule continued walking forward into the curtain of blinding snow. He had thought about dying before, but never once had he believed he would die this way, cold and alone. For the next hour he just held on to the saddle horn as the mule meandered through the sagebrush.

Suddenly Chance thought he heard something, and it sounded like someone calling him. It sounded like his mom calling him like she did back home just before dinner. The sound of her voice was warm and soothing and Chance began to feel warm all over, and then everything went black as he toppled from the mule and lay still in the white, puffy snow just as the storm began to subside.

Chapter 7

It was the next day, when Chance awoke in a one-room log cabin with a burning kerosene lantern suspended from the ceiling. The light from the lantern illuminated a small table and several chairs, as well as numerous boxes stacked on top of each other. In the middle of the room was a barrel cut in half, full of water. At the end of the room was a small stone fireplace with bright, warm flames that danced and added to the brightness as well as the shadows in the room. On the other side of the cabin was a bunk bed with several piles of thick blankets on each bunk.

He noticed a small pail of water beside him and he reached over and tried to pick up the ladle that sat in the bucket. It was then that he noticed the severe pain in his bandaged hands. It felt like a thousand pins being shoved into his hands and the part of his face around his eyes. He stared at his hands for a moment and then carefully, using both hands, painfully raised the ladle to his lips and took a long drink. The pain was almost intolerable, but the water tasted good on his parched cotton mouth. Then he collapsed back in his bed and closed his irritated eyes.

Chance was groggy and still somewhat asleep when he heard the door to the cabin squeak open and, through partially closed, swollen eyes, saw two large men enter the room.

"Is he awake yet, Roper?" asked the large bearded man with a checker-patterned coat. His companion wore a heavy leather coat trimmed in sheepskin and a dirty brown hat that was covered with a fine layer of white snow.

The large black man named Roper shook the snow from his hat and coat before hanging them on a couple of the wooden dowels that protruded from the log wall.

"He doesn't look awake to me, but he must have drunk some water from the looks of things." There was a small puddle of water beside the pail, and the ladle lay several feet from the bed.

"Those hands of his looked mighty painful. Glad I'm not in his shoes. I wonder where he came from. We sure are a long way from anything out here," said Jake, Roper's companion.

"I don't know, but the boss sure seems interested in him. I imagine he will be waking up here pretty soon. Heck, he's slept nearly ever since we found him, probably time for us to soak his hands again."

"Get the bandages ready. Let's get the water boiling so we can heat up the tub, and I will see if he's ready to wake up; he needs to drink more and eat something."

Roper walked over to Chance's still body and gently shook him, "Time to wake up, partner."

Chance continued to watch the stranger through the slits in his puffy eyes. He felt beat, and his face and hands made him want to scream from the pain.

"How much damage did the frostbite do," asked Roper?

"I don't really know for sure, but if I was to guess, I would say in the long run he will basically recover, but his hands will probably always be sensitive to really hard cold. The guy must have had some type of guardian angel looking over him with that mule somehow finding the bunkhouse in the pitch dark and in the middle of a blizzard and then letting us know she was there by her braying."

By his own strength, Chance gingerly sat up and looked at Jake and Roper. "Where am I?" he asked.

"You are at the Greybull Ranch. I'm Roper and this here is Jake. He's the one that found you after your mule started braying at the bunkhouse. The big question is who the hell are you, and why are you on Greybull property?"

"What do you mean Greybull property? When my brothers and I came through here two years ago the only buildings were at Meeteetse Creek. There wasn't even a road to use, and now you say this is a ranch?"

"Yep, that's what we are saying, and a mighty big ranch. Mr. Gillis McCabe owns the whole valley clear up to the Yellowstone country, has for two years, and he has over a hundred hands to prove it."

"That can't be. My brothers and I homesteaded a place two days' ride up the valley from here near on to two years ago, and we were here first." He stopped for a moment. "Leastwise we were one of the first to settle this valley, but we were surely here before this McCabe fellow."

"I guess you will need to take that up with the boss. He plans to see how you are doing later. We expect him over here soon, but for now we need to soak your hands in some warm water. It will help with the pain and healing. You are just lucky that you didn't lose their use. Jake is from Minnesota and has had his share of experiences with frostbite. It's going to take a while for the swelling in your hands and face go down and a mite longer for the redness to pass."

He paused for a minute and walked closer to Chance. "We have been talking about how painful those hands you have must be. Let's help you over to the tub and get them soaking. Remember now to keep them away from the edge of the tub, you could still damage them and lose some hide. We need to keep them bandaged for at least a week."

"I appreciate your help. I probably owe you my life."

"No, I would say you owe your life to that mule of yours. If she hadn't gotten you here when she did, I doubt you would have lasted much longer in that blizzard. I can only guess at the wind chill. Anyway, this country is big and tough, and someday the shoe might be on the other foot."

The two men helped Chance over to the tub full of warm water and carefully removed the bandages before guiding his hands into the water. "We'll let them soak for around fifteen minutes and then let them air dry before we bandage them up again," said Jake in a soft and caring voice, as Chance quietly moaned.

At that moment, several solid knocks sounded at the door and without invitation, a medium-size man in a well-tailored, heavy winter coat and large ivory hat entered the room.

"So this be the stranger that showed up on our door step." He turned and stared at Chance. "What's your name and what are you doing here?" demanded Gillis McCabe in a stern voice.

Chance looked up from the tub. He still felt terrible and weak, and his hands and face felt like someone was poking thousands of needles into his skin, but more than anything he wanted more sleep. He dug deep and answered. "Hell of a greeting, but if you must know, me and my brothers own a small spread up the valley a couple of days' ride from here."

"The hell you say. I own this entire valley all the way up to the Yellowstone country, and by next year I will have the surveyed maps to prove it. I don't recall anyone saying anything about a family or a cabin up the valley. Why should I believe you?"

"Why would I lie? There's plenty of land for everyone, and we own our spread, plain and simple," replied Chance staring straight back into Gillis's steely brown eyes. "And we intend to stay."

"Is that so?" answered Gillis.

"I didn't come here to cause any problems or start a fight. The truth is I was headed to Meeteetse Creek to see if I could find a doctor for a hurt young boy and get some help to track down a couple of Frenchmen and some Indians that captured a white woman."

"I don't know of any missing white woman around here. Did you two hear anything about a missing white woman?" Gillis said, as he turned and looked first at Roper and then at Jake.

"No, sir," replied Roper, and Jake just shook his head in agreement.

"Strange that we haven't heard of a woman going missing, there are not a lot of women around here, and we would probably know if one were missing. You plan on sticking to that story, mister?" said Gillis with an angry look.

"If you are calling me a liar, no matter how bad these hands are, you got a problem," responded Chance in a defiant voice.

"You got a lot of fight in you for a man that was almost dead yesterday. We will let this rest for now. Jake, you stay with him. Roper, I want to talk to you back at the house." Gillis turned and walked out the door with Roper following him.

"What's with him?" Chance asked Jake.

"I ain't allowed to discuss why Mr. McCabe doesn't like strangers. Its ranch policy, but he has his reasons, good ones."

"I appreciate you two saving my life, but I'm none too sure that Mr. McCabe thinks you did the right thing."

"Mr. McCabe is a good man; he's just a mite cautious. I would prefer if we just didn't talk anymore on that subject. This is a good job and there ain't many good jobs that pay well around these parts. That war took the stuffing out of everybody's living." There was a pause. "I need this job and I don't want to lose it."

"A hundred hands, you say," said Chance changing the subject.

"Yeah, he's got a little of everything. Cowboys for fencing and cattle, craftsmen that can build houses, cooks, gun slingers, blacksmith, you name it, Mr. McCabe has a lot of men. Even has a crew that runs wagons from here to Fort Laramie and back for supplies every year. Mr. McCabe is a good, fair man and he pays well. He is fencing the entire valley and plans on having one of the biggest, and probably the most private, ranches in all of the Wyoming Territory."

"So where did he get all his money?" asked Chance, as he probed further to try and figure out what was going on.

"I don't know the whole story, but he was the largest ship builder in Norfolk, Virginia, from what I heard, and he sold out just before the Civil War and headed west. He's a good man to work for, but he surely mistrusts strangers and you fit the category. Let's take your hands out of the tub and put some new bandages on."

The two men talked of how both of them had made it to Wyoming, and then Jake helped Chance back to the bed. After his hands had air-dried, Jake put clean bandages back on his hands.

Chance looked at Jake for a moment and then asked, "Do you think you could help me to the privy?"

"Sure. Let's get some clothes on you, and your boots. That privy isn't too far from the cabin," said Jake, as he held Chance's arm and helped him keep his balance as he put on his trousers. "I would imagine your feet are a wee bit tender, aren't they?"

"They're tender all right, but nothing like my hands. Most of my face and feet seemed to have come through this a fair sight better than my hands."

"You'll probably lose some skin, but I think in the long run your hands will heal and be close to normal again, excepting they will probably be a mite sensitive to the cold. It's my advice that you be real careful that they don't get cold again until they're thoroughly healed. The storm seems to have passed and the sun's out, but we are going to put this towel around them hands of yours while we are outside."

Jake steadied Chance as they walked to the door and hobbled outside. The sun felt good, but what he saw was more amazing. A huge house was being framed, bigger than anything he had ever seen during his one trip to Chicago. The house was a saltbox shape and towered at least three stories into the sky. Men were working everywhere he looked, and the sound of a large saw could be heard on the other side of the construction. He could hear the blacksmith pounding on metal, and at least thirty cabins of various sizes dotted the ground below where the big house was being built. The ranch house, cabins, and several barns stood on a plateau high above the valley and looked out over a large basin and lake.

"Wow," said Chance, "who would have believed this; all this in two years, and in the middle of nowhere!"

Jake just nodded and opened the door to the privy. "You just let out a holler when you are done and I will help you back to the cabin."

A few minutes later Jake was helping Chance return to the cabin when a team of four draft mules pulled up with a load of logs. "That's one nice load of logs," commented Chance, as Jake just smiled in agreement.

"We have ten men that their sole job is to log for the ranch and keep the sawmill busy." Chance stopped at the door and looked Jake in the eyes. "How's my mule doing?"

"She doing great, Roper rides a mule part of the time, and he has her out back in a pen with his John. They're getting along great, he kind of babies them."

For the next couple of days, Jake spent part of his day helping Chance between chores, bringing him food, and changing bandages as needed. The slight sensitivity in his feet and face was almost gone, but both were still somewhat puffy and tender. His hands were getting better by the day, but the pain at times was almost unbearable.

On the evening of the third day, Jake walked through the door of the cabin and made eye contact with Chance. "Think you are able to eat at the cook shack with some of the men tonight? I think your hands are ready to have the bandages off, and as long as you are careful, I think you will be fine without them."

"That would be great; I was starting to go stir crazy in here. I know Mr. McCabe doesn't want me meandering around the place, but I wouldn't mind seeing what's going on."

There were at least twenty different buildings either built or under construction, and Chance couldn't help noticing the guard towers located around the perimeter. "Looks like this McCabe fellow has a regular fort going on here with those towers and guards."

Jake just smiled and pointed to one of the guards. "See that rifle there? It's one of those brand new Henry rifles people say you can shoot pretty near all day and never reload. Mr. McCabe just brought a shipment in and they sure beat the stuffing out of those old Hawkens rifles. Look over at that tower those men are building. That will be the new home of Mr. McCabe's Gatling gun. It came in with the Henry rifles. Folks say you can crank it so fast that it can shoot two hundred rounds a minute, if you can believe that." The two of them talked for the next hour on numerous things from the ranch to Chance and his brothers' small homestead. As they headed out the door to the cook shack, Jake turned to Chance.

"After dinner, Mr. McCabe wants you brought to his cabin to talk. I think that might be a good thing for you."

It felt great to Chance to finally get out of the cabin with his hands not bandaged, and he enjoyed talking to the men at his table. The food was served by two Chinese men that spoke only broken English, but the men were very respectful to them and everyone was cordial.

"It's surprising to me how well-mannered everyone is. No one even seems to raise his voice much."

"That's by design. Mr. McCabe is not a man to be taken lightly and expects every man to treat each other with respect, and he doesn't tolerate less. He pays them well, and Roper enforces his rules. Every one of them is handpicked and has signed on for at least five years. A man is allowed to have his wife here and that group has cabins a little farther down the slope away from the rest. Mr. McCabe and Roper put up with no nonsense. If you are caught breaking the rules, the first time you lose a month's pay, the second time you are publicly whipped and forced to leave. He's a firm believer in discipline; there ain't no doubt about that."

"Has he had to whip many?"

"No, only one that I ever saw, but another time one cowboy that thought he was pretty tough walked up to Mr. McCabe and insulted him in front of a large group of men. Hell, I thought Roper was going to beat the man to death with his bare fists before the men could pull him off. Roper is one strong man, and I have no doubt he would have killed that cowboy if we hadn't stopped him, but we need to change the subject."

The food was great, and on the way back to the cabin Chance asked a few more questions.

"Where did Roper come from?"

"He grew up with Mr. McCabe in Virginia, but that's all I know other than they came out here together and started this place. Roper was the one that handpicked every man here including myself for Mr. McCabe. They weren't always this tough with the men, but when Mr. McCabe lost his wife everything changed."

"What happened to his wife?"

"I don't know a lot about it, but she died a little over a year ago when she was out riding. She was one beautiful southern lady with that long blonde hair of hers that glistened in the sun, but that's another thing we are told not to talk about, so that's the end of that conversation," Jake said, as he opened the door to the cabin and they both walked in.

"Mr. McCabe will send someone over for you when he is ready. In the meantime, do you think your hands could hold some cards?"

Chance often played poker with his brothers and was fairly good at it, so after an hour he was twenty dollars up on Jake. It was then that a knock came at the door and a skinny cowboy walked in and said, "Mr. McCabe is ready to see the squatter now."

"I ain't no damn squatter, and you can tell that McCabe fellow that. If he wants to talk to me, then send him over."

"I don't think that's a really good idea. Are you sure you want me to tell him that?"

"Hell, yes I do. I will be damned if I am going to be called a squatter by him or anyone else."

"Okay, I will tell him, but he's not going to like it. No sir, he's not going to like it one bit," the skinny cowboy said, as he turned and walked back through the door, closing it as he left.

"I hope you know what you are doing, partner. Mr. McCabe is a no-nonsense man and I'm not sure how he is going to take your response."

"I guess we will find out, won't we?"

About an hour later, there was another firm and deliberate knock on the door and before Jake could answer, Gillis McCabe walked through the heavy door. "So you trespass on a man's land, but you're no squatter. Why am I to believe that you happened to show up in this valley just after my scouts told me it was empty? For that matter, why am I supposed to believe you even have a cabin up the valley and you aren't here for some other reason?"

At that moment, Roper walked through the door and stood behind McCabe, who glanced back over his shoulder while Roper removed his heavy leather gloves.

"If you want to see our ranch, I am sure a man of your intelligence could tell we have been living there for at least a couple of years, and if I wasn't here to get help for the boy and that captured woman then why the hell do you think I'm here?"

There was a long pause as Gillis stared at Chance with a stoic look. "Maybe I was wrong about you," said Gillis with a sly smile. "So what's your story on this young boy?" Chance told the three of them the story of the mountain lion attacking their stock and how his brother had accidentally shot the boy in the barn.

"So where did this white boy come from?" questioned Gillis.

"We don't know. He was wounded so bad that he hasn't woken up, leastwise he hadn't woken up by the time I left looking for medicine and a doctor."

"And what's this story about a captured white woman and the Frenchmen and Indians?"

"I really don't have much to tell other than I saw them leading this tied white woman on a horse, and they went over a high mountain pass before we got that new snow."

"So what are you asking of me? Do you want me to shut down the building of my ranch and send all my men out looking for some white woman that no one seems to know is missing?"

"I know it don't sound good, but it's the truth and I swear it."

"I'm sure you do Mr....?"

"Creager, Chance Creager, and my brothers are Vern and Virgil Creager."

"I will tell you what I am going to do. There is a woman in town that was a nurse during the war, and she should know what to do for the boy. She dealt with a lot of gunshot men and I am sure she probably has some medicine that might work. Roper said you should be able to ride in another three days or so, and when you are, I will send Jake with you to town to ask around about this missing white woman. If no one knows anything about it, then I guess you drank a little too much Tennessee Honey that night."

Chance stared at Gillis but held his tongue.

"It's not my job or my men's job to play sheriff in these parts. My business is mine and yours is yours. On this ranch, I am the law and I make the rules, and even if I found you weren't lying about the woman, I wouldn't send any of my men to help; it's not my fight and I'm not going to play peacekeeper. I want you and your brothers to remember there is no place for squatters on my land. Anyway, in the spring, Roper and I and a few of the boys will check your story out, and if it's true, I will give you a fair price."

"A fair price, hell, we aren't going to sell our ranch to you or anyone else. We like how it is and we intend to keep it that way."

"Let's not get too worked up over anything until you know what I am willing to pay. I don't cheat people."

With that, Gillis turned and opened the door and left as quickly as he'd entered. The way Gillis said he didn't cheat people almost made Chance believe it was true, but he was still smarting from being called a liar and a squatter.

For the next three days, Chance, with Jake by his side, toured the grounds. Chance was amazed; it was almost like a small city with a five-foot log wall extending around the perimeter. Eight manned guard stations standing at least fifteen feet tall stood just outside the wall, giving the guards excellent views and shooting lanes in most directions. Unfortunately, when Jake wasn't available, Chance was ordered to stay in the cabin, and he begrudgingly accepted that.

Chance and Jake spent a lot of time together and for the most part enjoyed each other's company, but no matter how hard and cleverly Chance tried, Jake did not divulge any more information. Three days later he was sitting in the cabin when Jake walked through the door. "It's time. The boss wants us to ride into town and check out your story. I have your mule and my horse tied outside, and I put all your stuff together, including your musket, minus the load of shot and ball, on your mule."

"Well, my hands feel a lot better, and the swelling has sure come down. I guess I'm ready." Chance grabbed his coat and hat and walked outside to his mule. He patted her on the neck and softly spoke to her before launching himself into the saddle. The ride to town was quiet because neither man was very talkative.

"Sorry the boss wasn't a mite more friendlily. He treats men he knows real well, but he sure has a real problem with strangers."

"I understand. I am just grateful that you and Roper found me and I didn't freeze to death. It could have been worse."

It was four hours later when they rode over the last rim and spotted the small town of Meeteetse Creek nestled down by the Greybull River. The tiny town had grown by at least four buildings, and as the two rode down what a person might consider the main street, Chance saw a sign proudly promoting a small general store and saloon. The two men dismounted and led their stock over to a short hitching rail and tied up. The building was of poor construction and the boards creaked as they took the first stair up onto the porch. Immediately, a small, balding man with glasses and a dirty apron greeted them at the door.

"Greetings, Jake. Greetings, stranger, come in, come in."

The main room was divided into two smaller rooms by three or four sheets that dangled from a rope that ran the length of the room, separating the spaces into a section for the general store and one area for the bar. The bar wasn't much more than several boards on top of two empty barrels with a cabinet of bottles behind it. Jake turned to Chance. "Mind if we have a drink before we get any business done? The boss doesn't allow drinking on the ranch, it's another firing offense."

As the two men turned and walked into the bar, another shorter man was just leaving. Chance thought there was something real familiar about the man, but he couldn't place him. He knew that with his partial beard and swollen, burnt face there was little chance that the stranger would recognize him.

Minutes later, as they enjoyed a little slightly aged moonshine, the man that had been in the bar rode by on a beautiful paint horse, and Chance struggled again with placing him. Chance's thoughts were interrupted by the storekeeper asking them if they wanted another drink. Both men nodded. "I hear there's a nurse that lives in town, is that right?"

"Sure is. Her name is Lilly and she just lives two houses down. Do you need some doctoring?" Chance nodded his head. "Yep, I would appreciate it if you could get her."

By the time they had finished their second drink, an older, heavyset woman walked up to their table. "My name is Lilly Short, heard you needed some doctoring." Chance explained what had happened and the wound the small boy had gotten. Lilly told them about being a nurse during the Civil

War and how she was quite familiar with gunshot wounds. She wrote down a list of things she suggested be done and gave Chance a glass bottle of pills and a schedule on which to give them to the boy. Down deep Chance was worried that it had taken way too long for him to make it back to the cabin, but at this point, he had little choice.

"Miss Short, I will take these back to my cabin. I can't tell you how much I appreciate it. I have twenty dollars to pay you."

"Well, I would like to take your money. God knows I could use it, but the bottle is only five. I wish you luck with the boy."

"One more thing, Miss Short. Have you or anybody hereabouts heard of a white woman that went missing in the last couple of weeks?"

"I think something like that would be the talk of the town, and no one said anything, leastwise anything I heard. I doubt she was from these parts. Do you know who might have gotten her?"

"I don't, but she was with a couple Frenchmen and about five Indians, by my count, and she didn't look like she would last long in her condition. I tried to figure which way they were headed. But other than that, the odds weren't with me. That is something that has haunted me a bit. I would have liked to have been able to do more."

Jake looked at Chance, "I guess we answered the boss's question. But I guess it doesn't matter, since he already said he wouldn't have helped anyway."

Chance ordered another drink and then asked the storekeeper if there was any way to get a letter out headed back east. "Yeah, a rider comes by about every six months and he delivers and picks up mail. He's a mite expensive, but the letters seem to be going through. Sometimes your men that run that supply train for the Greybull Ranch will bring a couple of letters, but only once in a while."

"How do you know when you will get them?" asked Chance.

"Well, we don't for positive, but we got a delivery last fall and out earlier that spring."

"That's great. I was hoping I could get a letter out," said Chance, as he reached deep inside his wool vest to a hidden pocket and pulled out a small envelope. "I got a letter for my family back home. I would surely be pleased to see it delivered."

"Well if you got two dollars and everything stays the same, that should work," smiled the shopkeeper, as Chance handed him the letter. The shopkeeper looked at the letter and then smiled. "Your name must be Creager. Seems your family already thought of this. I got two letters for you from last spring."

"Where are they?" a shocked Chance shot back, as he shoved his chair backwards and stood up.

"Hold on, hold on, I got the letters right back here behind the counter on the store side. They have just been collecting dust. I wasn't sure anyone would ever claim them. No one was sure where you boys settled into," he said, as he walked to the counter and retrieved the letters, shaking them in his hand to knock the dust off while he walked back to the table.

Chance stood up as the man handed him the letters. "One's from my mom and the other one is from my baby sister, Betsy," he said, as he hurried over to the table and used his knife to open the letter from his mom first. A serious look came over his face the further he read.

"Everything all right?" asked Jake.

Chance was slow to answer, "No, no, not really. My pa passed away last year and the family is struggling to keep the farm. He grabbed his chest and just fell out of his chair. Later they lost last year's crop to drought and grasshoppers, if you can believe that."

"I'm truly sorry, I never known my pa but I can only imagine what it's like to have one and then lose him."

"No one ever said life was going to be fair," said Chance, with a stoic face as he stuffed the letter gently back into the small envelope.

"Well, hopefully the other letter will be better."

Chance had almost forgotten the other letter as he refocused and opened the slightly larger envelope. He removed a single sheet of paper and a small black and white picture showing a young bride and her husband toasting to each other. "Says here my little sister got hitched and…" Chance stopped in mid-sentence as he showed the picture, and then dropped the hand with the picture back onto the table. He continued, "Says she and her husband should have arrived at Meeteetse Creek late spring or early summer of last year."

The store clerk just stared for a moment and then spoke up, "I'm sorry but there hasn't been any strangers that were asking for you or your brothers or looked like that there picture. They must have changed their minds."

"My sister Betsy has always been as stubborn as any woman this side of the Mississippi, and if she said she was coming here, well she was coming here, hell or high water. There's got to be something wrong. Something is terribly wrong; she couldn't just vanish."

Chapter 8

Rachael Dove 1864

Raven was the nickname given to her by her late father. She was born Rachael Dove, the second daughter of five children to Lewis and Sara Dove. Her father had struggled with his small locksmith business while running their five-acre Illinois farm. Raven and her older sister, Susan, helped with everything from growing a garden to assisting with the family business. From an early age, their father had taught them the ways of the woods. They had learned the art of hunting, trapping and, often as not, it was either Susan or Raven who brought home a dinner of rabbit or squirrel. Raven's nickname came from her beautiful, black hair that shone like the feathers of the bird and hung almost to the waist of the skinny youngster.

It had been tough financially for their father and people in the valley, and, as with most families, the war had taken its toll. They had lost their older brother Patrick, who had joined the Illinois First Infantry. According to the lieutenant who'd written the short letter, he had died valiantly in battle.

It was a warm spring day, a wonderful change from a winter that had been hard and longer than most. For the past two weeks the talk of their community was the upcoming dance that the tiny town of Griggsville was sponsoring. Raven had never gone to a real dance before. To say she and her sisters were excited at the prospect would be an understatement. Two weeks earlier, she had received a letter from her uncle's family inviting her for a visit to their ranch on the outskirts of Griggsville.

Two years earlier, when she was twelve, she had made the twenty-mile journey to her uncle's place alone, only accompanied by her dad's old horse, Rex. This time it would be different; she would ride Ginger, a tall chestnut mule she had trained from a yearling. It would take her about four hours to make the trip, and she was excited. Her uncle was considered well-to-do by most, investing in numerous successful businesses throughout the area. Thirteen-year-old Elsie was their only child. Their family lived in a large estate just east of the edge of town, and the road between them, although long, was well traveled and had been considered safe by Raven's father.

The morning of her trip, she was up early packing a few needed clothes and other items in a small bundle, which she tied above her saddlebags. Inside her saddlebags she had enough food for several days, numerous other small items, and at the top, she packed her 1851 Navy Colt revolver for easy access. After breakfast, she said her goodbyes and mounted Ginger. The plan was for both families to meet up at the dance in Griggsville the following week, where Raven would then accompany her family back home. Ginger had grown into a stout mule with a robust gait, and Raven felt comfortable riding her as she molded into the saddle.

A strong bond of trust had developed between the two over the three short years of training. If Raven walked anywhere near the pasture, the mule was quick to the fence for a scratch to the ears or a gentle rub to the backside. This morning was extra beautiful with the warm sun drying the dew from the grass as Raven listened to the sound of the birds chirping high above in the trees that shaded the narrow road. She had only gone a mile when she rounded a curve and caught sight of their neighbor's black carriage in the distance. The Moser family is probably headed to town, she thought, and they would make great company on my journey. She gently squeezed her thighs together against the mule and Ginger shot forward at a lope, cutting the distance. The Mosers were surprised and pleased to see her. For the next couple of minutes, they kept up a cheerful conversation as Raven rode beside the carriage down the narrow road.

As the small party rounded a sharp bend in the road, they were startled to see four men in dirty pale blue uniforms walking towards them. Raven and the Mosers waved and hollered good morning as the men looked up and waved back. Raven was used to the clean, crisp uniforms of young soldiers going off to war, but these men looked rough and tired. One of the men wore a bloody bandage over one eye and stared as she passed. Raven just assumed they were headed to their homes, wherever they might be, but the strange look on the man's face made her uncomfortable.

A couple of hours later, Raven and the Mosers' carriage parted ways at a fork in the road. The second half of her journey was uneventful until she finally arrived in front of her uncle and aunt's large home. Elsie was waiting on the porch and bounded down the stairs yelling, "Raven is here, Raven is here," as Raven tied Ginger to the hitching rail in front of the long, white picket fence that spanned the home's front.

Moments later her uncle and aunt opened the door and there were hugs for all. "Did you have a good trip?" asked her uncle, as he walked over to her mule and began undoing the straps that held her compacted bundle and saddlebags.

"It was great! I got to visit with some of my neighbors for the first part of the trip and that was fun."

The next few days everything went well as Raven enjoyed the change of pace. She enjoyed the constant flow of freshly baked bread and jams, sliced beef, and vegetables that seemed to accompany every dinner. On the fourth day, a rider rode up to the front of the house. He was tall and skinny with a thick, compact beard. The man was wearing a well-worn hat, and a dull metal badge was pinned to his leather vest. His face looked tired and wrinkled with large bags under his eyes. The girls had heard one of the dogs barking, but hadn't paid much attention as they visited on the large porch swing.

Raven couldn't help but notice the serious look on this man's face as he dismounted his lathered horse. Elsie quickly jumped from the swing and hurried to find her parents as the man began tying his horse to the hitching rail. He hadn't quite made it to the first porch step when Raven's Uncle George and Aunt Marlene opened the door with Elsie not far behind.

"Afternoon, George, Marlene, I need to have a word with you in private, if I may. It would be best if we left the kids out here to play," said the man in a solemn voice.

"Sure, come in, Sam. Is something wrong?"

"Who is that?" asked Raven, as she sat back in the swing with Elsie.

"That's the sheriff, but I don't know why he's here. He usually only comes by around Christmas, never seen him around here this time of year."

Something made Raven uncomfortable, like one of her six senses was screaming. After what seemed like forever, her aunt and uncle and the sheriff walked back out onto the porch. Her aunt rushed to her and cradled her in her arms. "Honey, I am so sorry."

Raven's eyes met her uncle's hardened face and she knew something horrible had happened.

"Raven, I don't know how to say this, but something terrible has happened to your family. Darling, we love you like our own daughter, and you will be living with us from now on."

"No, it can't be true. What happened? I need to go home, I need to go home now!" screamed Raven, as she started to break away from her aunt's grip and her uncle grabbed her.

"Honey, they're gone, they are with the Lord now and they are watching over you. They want you to be strong," said her uncle, as he knelt down and hugged the skinny, trembling Raven. A shower of tears ran down Raven's cheeks as her uncle tried to comfort her with his arm around her shoulder.

Later she would find out the soldiers she had seen were deserters with a price on their heads, and the murder, rape, and looting of her family and their home had been more brutal than anyone could imagine. An unarmed neighbor had seen the smoke and heard the hollering of the men and screams of the women as the deserters set the home ablaze.

Unarmed, he could only hide and watch as the men torched the house. He carefully hid in the tall grass and painfully witnessed the last part of the gruesome crime. Later he would give a full description to the local sheriff, and three days later, the four men would be captured, tried, and eventually hung outside the makeshift courthouse.

Raven and her new family went back for the funeral at the small community cemetery, but Raven chose to remember her family's cabin and home the way her memories painted it. She would never see the family farm again.

Some days the sadness was almost unbearable for Raven, but her new family worked diligently to show her the love she so desperately needed. Over time she began to adjust and found life far easier than she was used to.

Three months later at a quiet family dinner, her uncle announced that he was going to take a trip down to Independence, Missouri, to check on a likely business deal and asked if the two girls would like to join him. A scream of delight came from both girls as a stern look of concern appeared on Aunt Marlene's face. Aunt Marlene looked at Uncle George with a long, silent stare that could easily be interpreted as, "Where did that come from and why didn't we discuss it?"

"Don't worry, honey, I plan to take one of the men with me, and the road to Independence is well traveled and lined with roadhouses. It will be good for the girls to see the country and get out. You know that neither of these girls has ever been more than forty miles from here, and it's time for them to get out a bit. They need to see a little more of the world. Besides, they will be grown women, soon."

After much discussion and excitement, Marlene finally agreed, and two weeks later the group was headed for Missouri.

Their hired man, Albert, would accompany them. He had worked and lived on their farm for the past twelve years and had proved himself reliable and quick with a problem. He was a short man in his mid-forties, but he was experienced and decent with a musket. Raven could tell from the conversations with Albert that he had the utmost respect and loyalty for family. The group would be riding horses, with the exception of Raven, who had talked her Uncle George into letting her ride her mule, Ginger. In all, they would be taking three horses, Ginger, and three pack mules to carry their supplies. The trip, one way, would take up to three weeks, and that was if they averaged between twenty-five and thirty miles a day.

The first couple of days were uneventful and they made good time. They ate and slept well, staying in small towns or roadhouses along the way. On the morning of the third day, they were up early and ordered a hearty breakfast of eggs, toast, and bacon. George turned to the innkeeper and asked about having four lunches made. "Certainly," answered the smiling, overweight man as he rubbed his hands on his freshly washed apron, splattered with ancient stains that had defied his scrubbing. Minutes later, as the four got up from the table, the innkeeper brought them a clean, flour-cloth sack packed with their lunches, complete with apples and some extra jerky.

"So where might you be headed this fine day?" the innkeeper inquired, as he set the food on the table.

"We're headed to Independence on business; hear things are a really hopping there."

The innkeeper stared for a couple of seconds and then spoke, "You need to be careful on this next stretch, especially after dark. Problem is there ain't anywhere to stay for near on to seventy miles on that stretch of road, and there has been a heap of trouble between here and there. There is a bunch of low life skunks that have been robbing people and worse. The sheriff hasn't been able find them. They say there are at least six of them, maybe more, and they like to strike travelers after dark, waiting until people are asleep and then rob them blind, even killed a man awhile back."

"Any way to work around that stretch and still not lose too much time or ground?" asked George, concerned as he sipped his mug of coffee.

"Not really. It would add at least a couple of days to your trip to take the road south."

"Well I am sure we will be fine, but I appreciate the warning. We will be on the lookout, but I don't have an extra day figured in my plans."

"Then good luck to you and have a safe trip. By the way, there's an old bridge at Timber Creek about thirty miles down the road, and you should hit it about dark. Thick pasture and a good spring make that a good spot to stop. I'm not sure you want to travel any farther on that road at night."

"I guess we will see how it goes. Thanks for the information, I appreciate it," said George as he put his money down on the table, took a last sip of coffee, then pushed his chair back and stood up.

The morning air was fresh from the rain that night and the road was muddy and slick with pools of standing water. Their horses were big, strong Tennessee Walkers meant for travel, and the mules, including Ginger, were out of stout Fox Trotter mares. It wasn't long after leaving the roadhouse that the string got into a good gait as George took the lead, followed by Elsie, then Raven, and lastly Albert, bringing up the rear with the string of mules. Raven felt safe, even after listening to the innkeeper and his story of robbers. Both George and Albert rode with revolvers on their side and muskets in their scabbards, and the confidence in knowing that she also carried a Navy Colt was comforting.

It was close to four hours later when the group stopped for lunch at the edge of a small creek with ample trees to tie the stock. The day had been a little miserable between the sessions of drizzle and random downpours that challenged the waterproofing of their canvas slickers. After tying up the stock, the group took shelter under the boughs of several large cedars that provided a decent canopy. Several fallen logs lay next to the cedars and provided a fairly dry spot to sit and have lunch. The two girls drank from canteens while George opened a bottle of wine for Albert and himself.

They were almost finished with lunch when George looked over at Raven, who was intently staring past the stock.

"Raven, what do you see?" asked George, as Elsie and Albert turned to look.

"I'm not quite sure. I would swear that I saw the shape of a man over by that snag beside the road," she said pointing as she talked. "He was there a moment ago. I think he was hiding in that bush."

George stood up, hand on the butt of his revolver as he walked back over to the road and then in the direction of the snag. "Albert, stay here with the girls and I will check this out." He turned and started carefully making his way towards the snag, cautiously scanning both sides of the road for movement as he went. Walking down into the ditch beside the muddy road, he pulled back several leaf-laden branches, then turned and walked back to the small group.

"Someone was standing there, all right, but they are gone now. From the look of the track in the mud, it was a small man. There is no good purpose for a man to hide and be spying on us in this isolated stretch, so I think we best be moving on."

The group was quick to stuff the remains from lunch into their saddlebags, and within moments, they were back in the saddle and headed down the road. Raven rode her mule up beside her uncle. "Uncle George, could that be one of the robbers the innkeeper was talking about? I didn't get a good look at him."

"Don't worry, honey. Albert and I aren't going to let anything happen to our two favorite girls. He was probably just some lone stranger that lives around here and spies on travelers for kicks. We are well armed. I'm sure he won't follow."

Raven just smiled at him, not completely sure she believed what her uncle was saying. She knew her uncle was a strong, confident man and not afraid of much, but down deep she could only think of what happened to her family. As she rode, she carefully undid one of the two straps of her saddlebag on the side that contained her Colt. The more she contemplated the situation, the more she was sure that she wouldn't go down without one hell of a fight. Again the stock lined out well and their quick gait was covering ground as everyone kept an eye out for danger.

About an hour before dark, the party came to a thick-planked bridge that was a good fifty feet long, and the heavy sound of the horses' and mules' hooves made a thundering noise as they crossed. On the other side was a nice meadow filled with knee-high grass and a small spring that worked its way out of the ground before flowing into the river.

"The innkeeper said the road gets a whole lot worse past this point and is best traveled in the daylight. The stock is tired so we will stay here for the night. Albert and I will be keeping watch until morning, just in case. Tie the stock over in those trees while we take the packs off and we will picket out half of them for a while. Let's stack the sawbucks up and hang dry their blankets. With us getting here a little early, we will be able to let them eat and still keep a close eye on them before dark. Those mules can be hobbled; they won't be going anywhere without the horses."

Everyone dismounted and tied their mounts while Albert held the reins to his horse and the lead rope to the first mule. Raven was quick to tie off Ginger, then went to the last mule and undid the quick-release knot that Albert had tied. She led the mule to a tree so the men could unload the well-muscled molly.

"I want the mules on the outside and the group between us and the river. If anything is moving around out there tonight, those long ears of theirs will know first. Put the saddles close to that tree near the remains of that old campfire." The rain had stopped, so Albert strung a rope between several trees and hung the wet saddle blankets out to dry. The person who had originally picked this spot to camp had studied the ground and had taken his time to situate the fire near a large fallen log that would provide protection from both the wind and anything else that might want to enter the camp.

After everything was unloaded, George put his horse out first, accompanied by Ginger and one of the other mules. Albert helped by hobbling the mules as George tied a picket rope to his horse and a small tree. Almost instantly, all the stock had their heads buried in the lush, damp grass. One of the tied horses whinnied, and the largest mule began to paw, but stopped when Albert tossed a small stone at its feet.

George walked over to Albert and leaned against a tree as his mouth worked over a stiff stem of hardened grass. "I've got a bad feeling we might have visitors tonight, and by God, I plan to be ready."

Just before dark, the men led the last mule and horse from the meadow and tied them closest to the river. The cold drizzle had stopped and the light from the full moon shone between the passing clouds as George quietly thought of the warmth of the crackling fire that had warmed his room the night before. At least the girls would have a little cover from the weather and a small fire to keep them warm while he and Albert stood guard.

Movement in the thick layer of oak and maple leaves that covered the forest floor would make a fair amount of noise, but George was worried the rain and its softening effect might not allow them the needed warning. George had stretched a canvas manty between a couple of trees and the large log and it was doing a fair job of keeping the girls dry, while the small crackling fire added warmth.

The group had gathered almost enough wood for the night, if everything went as he planned, and he had warned the girls to keep the fire small. It would be hard for someone on the road to notice a small secluded fire back in the trees unless they knew they were there, and George was sure no one did. The tracks by the road and Raven's earlier sighting at lunchtime bothered him, but he didn't want to convey that to the others. He checked on Albert's position one last time and then went over to the girls.

"I think everything is going to be fine tonight, but just in case, I want you two to stay here, back behind the log. If you hear a shot, put the fire out immediately. Raven, hunker down with that pistol of yours and keep it ready."

Elsie looked at her father for a moment and then hugged him tightly. "Be careful, Pa. We will be all right."

At that, George picked up a wool blanket from one of the packs, turned and walked back towards a large tree that looked over the meadow, and sat down amongst some tall grass. He was already wet and a little cold; he knew the night would be long.

It had been dark for over an hour and both girls, although tired, were struggling to sleep. Finally Raven looked at Elsie. "I want to check on Ginger, I will be right back. Will you be okay?"

Elsie just nodded her head, so Raven turned and carefully walked through the trees over to Ginger, who was tied to a tree closest to the river. She reached up and petted the mule's neck and softly talked to her in a whisper. The river flowed past silently, except for the occasional sound of a fish jumping. As she petted the mule, she heard the faint sound of a horse whinnying far down the road. At first she wasn't sure that it wasn't her imagination or her mind playing tricks on her, but something didn't feel right as she turned and hurried back to Elsie.

Elsie had somehow fallen asleep in her absence and Raven shook her awake. In an excited whisper she said, "There's someone on the road, I heard their horse. I am going to tell your dad. Stay here, I'll be right back."

With that, she quietly moved between the trees, working her way to the entrance of the meadow. Within a couple of minutes, she was at the edge of the forest, and she stopped and slowly looked around, trying to remain calm as she struggled with not seeing him.

"Uncle George, Uncle George, where are you? It's Raven."

She saw a slight movement several trees over, and her uncle answered.

"Raven, I am over here, what's wrong?"

Raven quickly moved over to where she had seen the shadowy movement and met her uncle. "I went and petted Ginger before I went to bed, and I heard a faint whinny from a horse down the road. Do you think it could be them?" she asked in a scared voice.

There was a moment of silence before her uncle answered. "It's hard telling why anyone else would be out on a night like this unless they were up to no good. You need to be strong and remember God created men, but Sam Colt made them equal. Don't hesitate to use that Colt pistol of yours if you have to. Now sneak back and tell Albert to get ready. Then go back and stay with Elsie until this is over. Don't expose yourself, do you understand?"

Raven just looked at him in the dark and nodded, and then, crouching as she moved, she headed back towards Albert.

Albert heard the leaves rattle as Raven approached and quietly whispered, "I'm over here."

"They are coming," said Raven, "Uncle George said to be ready because I heard a horse whinny down on the road."

George knew the chances of the men he faced swimming the deep river were slim with the cold temperatures, and they knew that his party was composed of two men and two girls. He was sure whoever it was would be fairly confident, and it was likely that they would boldly enter the meadow with several of them flanking the camp. They were probably local men and knew this meadow well, so they would know the best approach for an attack.

In the darkness, he could hear men quietly talking as they made their way across the bridge. From the figures he could see, there were at least six of them and they appeared to be armed with muskets. He breathed heavily before letting out a curse only he could hear. As he had thought, two men were crossing into the meadow, and entering the woods. The other four men were spaced evenly across the narrow meadow and sneaking up on the remains of the girls' tiny fire. Only the smallest glow from the fire still existed, but it was enough to give away the location of the camp.

George's hand instinctively felt for his side arm, and he let his hand rest on the grip for a moment before raising his musket to aim at the closest figure as it moved across the meadow. He would probably get but one, maybe two, shots before he would have to rely on the Colt. The odds were bad and he knew he had to shoot and quickly change location, as the muzzle flash would tell everyone where he was. He pulled back the gun's hammer and carefully took aim, then squeezed the trigger. A dull thud was all that happened. "The percussion cap must have gotten damp," he said to himself in disgust, as he threw the rifle to the side and grabbed his Colt.

Hearing the misfire, three of the four men instantly dropped into the tall grass, leaving only the man furthest back still standing. George took aim and fired and the man grabbed his leg, flopping to the ground, but George didn't watch. He rolled to a new spot as several bullets tore large chunks of bark from the tree that had been his protection. These men were certainly serious and excellent shots, and having one of their own go down didn't seem to slow their progress.

George heard a shot, then the sound of several pistol exchanges from the area where he'd placed Albert. It was obvious that more than one man was now engaged in a circling attack. Rolling to another tree, he fired a shot at a dark figure in the tall grass as another shot hit a large root beside him. He thought of crawling back to the girls, but he knew if he exposed himself further he wouldn't be able to protect them. George would have to trust that Albert was holding his own.

Raven and Elsie hunkered down behind the saddles as Raven unbuckled her saddlebag and withdrew her Colt revolver. The volume of shots was increasing, and she knew it was only a matter of time before she would have to take part in the fight. She could only hope and pray that Uncle George and Albert would be able to hold these men off, but she had to be ready if that didn't happen. They had two horse blankets that they were using as pads to sleep on for the night. Raven motioned to Elsie to hide beneath one of the blankets and curl up against the saddles. Next, she put the other pad over herself to break up her outline and with her back to a tree she steadied the pistol with both hands, aimed it at the top of the saddles, and cocked the trigger.

It had been a couple of minutes since she had heard a shot from where Albert was guarding their flank, and she hoped that he had warded off the attack. Maybe it's over, she thought, but she was too afraid to move. That's when she heard quiet footsteps in the leaves. It was less than a minute before the soft sound of oak and maple leaves crunching under someone's feet seemed to reach the saddles. Raven hoped and prayed for Albert to say something, but the large silhouette that rose up above the saddle was definitely not Albert. For a second she froze, then dug deep and squeezed the trigger, sending a cloud of black smoke throughout the small enclosure.

She pulled the trigger back again and heard the cylinder click into place, but she knew the next shot would not be a surprise to the person on the other side of the saddles.

Chapter 9

It was at that moment that Raven heard heavy clumping on the thick-planked bridge. The sound was followed by a single shot, and then it seemed all hell broke loose as the sound of gunfire, men yelling, and muzzle flashes erupted across the small meadow. Raven put her hand on Elsie. "Are you all right?" she whispered.

"What's going on? Is my dad all right?" asked Elsie in a weak voice.

"I'm sure he is. Now you be quiet and get back under that blanket, and no matter what, you stay quiet." Elsie nodded, and pulled the horse pad back over her head.

Raven was confused; should she go help Albert or Uncle George? And who were the men who had joined the fight? Just then she heard the scream of a man in the distance and then more shooting. She felt like a sitting duck, but she knew from hunting back home that sitting still and being patient was the best way for her to bring home food for the family pot. Finally she decided to just sit with her gun pointed just above her saddle blanket and wait.

It was close to ten minutes later when the shooting subsided. She could hear men yelling, but the dark, moonlit meadow gave her little opportunity to figure out anything else.

Suddenly she heard a commanding voice. "You in there, this is Captain Knight. Are you all right?"

The next voice she heard was that of her uncle hollering back to come ahead. It was several minutes later when she heard her uncle call Elsie and then Raven. "Raven, are you and Elsie okay?" came a voice not ten yards away, and both Raven and Elsie jumped and headed in that direction. Beside Uncle George stood a short, uniformed officer with a handlebar mustache and long sideburns.

"I'm Captain Knight," the man said, as he silently motioned to his troops to fan out and move deeper into the forest. "Are you folks all right?"

"I think so, sir," said George. "Raven, have you seen Albert?"

"No," she said, shaking her head. "I heard him shooting and then it was quiet. I haven't seen him since the shooting started."

"I need to see about my man, Albert. Can you holler to your men that we are coming back into the forest? I don't want anyone taking a shot at us."

"Hold your fire, men," yelled the Captain as he headed into the woods.

"Albert, are you all right?" yelled George, as Raven and Elsie followed. The moon came out from behind a cloud and lit the meadow and woods behind it enough for them to see the body of Albert leaning against a large oak tree. Albert's legs were spread in front of him, and one of his hands covered his stomach, while his head leaned unnaturally to one side. The Captain turned and faced the girls.

"I need you two to go back over to the saddles and stay there until your uncle comes and gets you. This isn't something I want you to see."

"But is he all right?" asked Raven in an almost pleading voice.

Uncle George turned to her and Elsie. "Mind the Captain and wait over at the saddles." The girls turned and walked back to the saddles, as George and the Captain knelt down in front of Albert.

"He's been shot in the stomach and in the head, but he didn't go down without a fight, look over there by that stump," said the Captain pointing. Another soldier came out of the trees to where the captain had pointed and started turning the two dead men over onto their backs.

"Both of these were chest shots," said the soldier as he stood up.

"Captain?"

"Over here, Sergeant."

"What are your orders, sir?"

"Have the men drag all the bodies to the edge of meadow and set sentries out. Tie our horses close to theirs and put a guard on them for the night. Tomorrow we will see if we can hunt down the rest of these men, but for now we need to set up camp until morning."

"How did you find us? How did you know we would be attacked?" asked George.

"You can thank the innkeeper for that one. When you left he happened to go upstairs and notice a man watching your party as you left town. The man then followed you. The innkeeper knew there had been problems on that road, so when we rode into town about an hour and a half later, he told us what he had seen and we decided to ride your way. We weren't but a half mile away when we heard the shooting."

The next morning Raven woke to the sun in her eyes and the sound of the soldiers saddling their horses. Her uncle was up cooking over an open flame as the Captain sipped coffee several feet away. Elsie was still fast asleep, so Raven walked over to the fire and rubbed her hands together to warm them over the crackling flames.

"Your family was pretty lucky to have come through last night, that was one bad…"

A scream erupted from the saddle area, and everyone threw their coffee down and pulled their pistols as they ran towards the sound.

Elsie was standing in the center of the saddles staring over the pile and screaming uncontrollably. Raven was closest to her and got there first, so she grabbed Elsie and turned her towards herself.

"What's wrong?"

Elsie just pointed over the saddles, so Raven moved to the saddles and looked over as the rest of the men arrived. There, wedged between two fallen logs, was a huge man wearing a dark brown hat tightly pulled over his head. His eyes and mouth were wide open and flies buzzed around his face. Just below his chin, a bloody hole the size of a quarter penetrated his neck. The horrid expression of shock and disbelief covered his yellow-toothed, chewing tobacco-stained face.

"How did you men miss this body?" shouted the angry Captain. "I didn't want these young ladies to see this." There was a pause as two soldiers rushed to drag the body over with the rest. "I am very sorry that you had to witness this. It's hard enough for a soldier to see things like this, much less a young lady not long from childhood. Again my apologies, a lot has happened here but I need to know if you want me to bury Mr. Albert here or if you plan to take his body with you."

Uncle George replied, "I will take him with us and bury him in a Christian cemetery in the next town. He was a loyal, hardworking man, and everyone will miss him. If I could trouble you and your men to wrap and tie him in one of my canvas manties, it would be much appreciated."

The Captain tipped his hat. "Certainly sir, we will have it done before you are ready to leave. I do want you to know that we have been hunting these men for close to two years. These were bad men who wouldn't have hesitated to abuse and kill all of you."

George walked over to the fire, poured himself some coffee in a tin cup, and sat down looking at the two girls across the fire. "You two all right?" he asked, looking them in the eye. "I am sorry you had to experience this. This is a tough land, and I can't shield you from everything evil. These were bad men that needed killing, and the Army did their job. I'm so proud of both of you; you both acted as adults last night. You two just amazed me."

About an hour later they were back in the saddle, headed for the little town in front of them. Albert's horse still carried him, but now his body was tied securely to the saddle in a canvas manty. There was little talk for the first hour as they waved goodbye to the soldiers and got back on the dried mud of the road.

It was a sunny, beautiful day and normally the girls would be deep in discussion, but today little was said until six hours later when they reached the little town that was not much more than ten buildings, a small church and adjoining cemetery. The quick service was small, with only the three of them, the pastor, and a woman who worked for the church. The tiny town did have an inn, and the group appreciated a bath and a warm, dry bed for the night.

The rest of the trip was fairly uneventful. The worst thing that happened was one of the horses threw a shoe, which was quickly replaced by George and his hammer. It was a little over a week later when they saw the first sign indicating that Independence, Missouri, was within riding distance. It was a white-washed board in ill repair, and the letters were barely readable, but they did say "Independence, twenty miles" in faded black letters. They could see a small town in the distance, but all three excitedly voted to continue on to Independence.

It was nearly dark when the three and their pack string rode into town, and they were quick to find a livery stable for the stock. The blacksmith pointed out a reasonable inn for the night, and the exhausted party lasted only minutes before they were asleep.

In the morning, Raven woke first and gently shook Elsie's shoulder until she was awake.

"Come on, let's get dressed, I want to see this town." Elsie looked at

Raven with a mischievous smile, jumped from the bed, and started putting on her clothes. They were both almost dressed, Elsie in a dress and Raven in a baggy cotton shirt and pants, when they heard the sound of someone knocking followed by the firm voice of Uncle George.

"Time to wake up ladies, there's a town to be seen."

The three walked downstairs, through the hotel lobby, and out into the bright morning sunshine. The street was alive with activity, from men riding their horses to buckboards and heavy wagons making their way in both directions through the muddy dirt road in front of the poorly built hotel. There was a slight breeze, but the heavy stench of manure and urine mixed with mud and rain was enough to make a person gag. Even with the smell, the street was alive with activity, with carriages and wagons moving up and down it, their wheels sinking into the muddy roadbed. The rough, planked boardwalk was dirty and stood several feet above the street.

"We can walk down to the stables on the boardwalk, but we will need to ride from there to meet the people I need to visit with. I have an old friend named Andy Harrison that I would like to visit first. He is an attorney here in town and one of the few lawyers I know a man can trust. We have known each other from childhood, and I am looking at going into partnership with him on a large ranch in the Willamette Valley of Oregon. We have been working on this deal for a while, and I'm excited to see how it plays out. I will introduce you two to Andy, and then I need you ladies to make yourselves scarce later while we do some business."

The third building from the hotel was a saloon, and Elsie gasped at the sight of a passed out man lying just below the plank decking in the mud of the street. When the man moaned, Raven and George jumped down into the mud beside him as Elsie watched from above. They managed to lift the half-conscious man onto the decking and help him into a sitting position.

"Now let's move him over to that bench and prop him up against the building," said George. Raven used all of her strength to lift one shoulder while holding on to the man's arm. Just then, the swinging doors of the saloon opened and an overweight man in a stained apron stepped outside holding a broom.

"You won't find any money on him, if that's what you're helping that drunk for; he's just a dead-broke, worthless drunk like all the rest that this here town attracts."

"We weren't helping him for money, for God's sake, man. Don't you have any feelings in you?" retorted George angrily. "Go get me some coffee, and don't worry, I will pay you for it." "Mister, if you are you going to make it a habit to help every drunk you find in this town, you will be broke and dead before you get it done."

"I don't plan to help every drunk in this fine town of yours, just this one. Now get me the coffee I ordered."

The bartender turned with a disgusted look and returned shortly with a cup of steaming coffee. "That will be two bits," he said as he held his hand out for payment.

George reached in his pocket and tossed the man a quarter as Raven took the coffee and tried to get the man to take a sip. "Mister, you need to wake up," urged Raven as she gently patted his muddy face. Within a minute the man opened his eyes, bewildered, with a look of panic on his face.

"It's okay, mister, we are here to help you," said Raven as she smiled at the man. The sight of Raven's warm and friendly face seemed to take the bite out of waking up, and the man kind of half smiled back. The fall into the street had left him dirty and smelly. He moaned again as he turned to look around, then took his hand and touched the back of his head.

"What happened?" asked the man.

"The bartender said you were just a drunk and just ended up here," said Raven, trying to be as helpful as possible, to the annoyance of the stranger.

"That's not quite true. I got rolled last night while I was headed back to that hotel." All of a sudden he frantically began searching his inside pocket and then stopped with a pained look on his face. "They took every red cent, the bastards, didn't leave me with a dime."

"Did you get a look at them?" asked Raven.

"Nope, a man stopped me for a light last night, and the next thing I knew was you all were setting me on this bench, but I do know one thing, my head sure hurts."

"So you're not a drunk?" asked Raven, as her uncle showed his disapproval. "So, what's your name?"

"I'm Marshal Lou Dicker," said the man as he slowly opened his jacket, exposing a dull badge the color of nickel. "I definitely am not a drunk, but I do very much appreciate you people helping me. No telling how long I might have lain there before I woke up, if you hadn't come along. The truth is I stopped in this saloon yesterday about noon to see if I could get a little information on a case I am working on. I had lunch and a couple of drinks and told the barkeep that I planned to go out Oregon way and start a new life, and we talked about me needing to buy a wagon and some stock. Then I left, trying to dig up some more information to help me put a couple of things together. Anyway, my head is killing me; do you think you might be kind enough to help me back to the hotel? It's the Yellow Moon, and it's only a couple of buildings down the street."

"We would be glad to. That's the same place the girls and I are staying."

George and the girls helped the man back to the hotel and got help, and within twenty minutes they were once again headed to the stables to saddle up their mounts for the ride across town.

"What happened to that man, Pa? Are there robbers all over town? Are we safe to be out here?" asked a concerned Elsie.

"This is a rough new town and most of the people are good, hard-working folks. But whenever there is money involved, the riffraff always seem to show up right behind them. I am sure that if you were to get out away from town a little, you would find it's just like back home. I am pretty positive that marshal will be in touch with the sheriff and they will try and get to the bottom of the whole thing."

The walk to the stables took a little more than fifteen minutes, and soon they were riding down one of the main streets of town, Elsie and her uncle on their horses, and Raven on Ginger. Several cowboys whistled at Elsie as she rode her horse in a soft yellow dress. Though only thirteen, she was already filled out and looking like a woman. Raven, on the other hand, dressed more like a boy in her baggy shirt and pants with a hat pulled down over part of her face, and she seemed to care little that Elsie was getting all the attention.

"Just ignore them, honey; they are just cowboys without manners," said George. "There is a good side to this town, I guarantee it."

The office of Andy Harrison, Attorney at Law, was located on a quiet side street. The freshly white-washed building looked well-kept and somewhat important compared to a lot of the others. A white picket fence surrounded a small yard, and two hitching rails paralleled the fence. The left hitching rail had three horses standing tightly together and the smaller hitching rail was open.

"Well, there is enough room for two of us, but someone needs to tie up over there in the shade of that willow tree."

Raven quickly turned her mule and with a slight nudge of her heel, was headed towards the willow. The trunk itself was too big to get her lead jump around, but a stout, low-hanging limb would do just fine.

The door to the office was of fine oak, and the window in the door had an "open" sign in one corner. The secretary who greeted them was older and on the heavy side with a rough, pitted complexion. "Come in, come in. Are you three here to see Mr. Harrison?"

"Yes, I am George Dove, and these are my two young ladies. Is Andy in?"

"Oh, do you know Mr. Harrison?"

"Yes, we have known each other most of our lives. Would you tell him that George Dove is here?"

"I will be happy to as soon as he is through with the other gentlemen in his office. In the meantime, can I get you a glass of water or make you some coffee?"

"No thank you, I think we are all fine. Do you know how long he will be?"

"Well, they just got here about ten minutes ago, the nicest three brothers; headed west, they are, and needed to have some of their business affairs handled before they leave town. Keeps us busy being the last place to do your legal business and all."

"Uncle, if you don't mind, I will wait outside until you would like to have me come in."

"That will be fine. Just don't stray too far."

It wasn't long after that when Raven heard some laughing inside and the door open. Out walked three young men, two with beards and one clean-shaven. Her eyes immediately went to the tall, clean-shaven man, who was a good two inches taller than his companions. He was not only tall but broad shouldered, and he carried himself with a presence. For a brief moment their eyes met, and he gave Raven a warm smile, then continued down the steps and over to his horse. She watched the three ride down the street, making a right turn behind a tattered white building, and then they were gone. In that moment she felt something she hadn't felt before, but what that was she wasn't sure.

Raven entered the office, but her uncle and Elsie were still in another room talking, so she lingered at the secretary's desk. She turned and started back towards the door when she heard the secretary's voice. "Mighty handsome man, that tall one, don't you think? Heck, if I was fifteen years younger I would make a hard play for him." Raven just smiled, turned, and walked back out the main office door onto the small porch in front and then down the stairs.

After walking around for a few minutes, she went over and began petting Ginger. The mule had grown from a tall, lanky youngster into a real looker. A little less than an hour later, Uncle George and Elsie had finished their business and came out the door. "Let's mount up and head downtown and see if we can get a little shopping in for you two and your mom."

The rest of the day went well and was uneventful. Elsie bought several dresses, George bought a new pistol and a suit, and Raven bought another baggy cotton shirt. It was almost six when the three headed for the hotel. On the ride back, Uncle George turned to Raven. "You know, Raven, it wouldn't hurt for you to have a couple more dresses. You are becoming a beautiful lady, but a man would need to dig through a heap of those baggy clothes to find out. It's okay for you to look good, and I want you to have fun like other girls your age," he said with a smile and a fatherly look.

"What's wrong with these clothes?" questioned Raven.

"There's nothing wrong with your clothes. I am merely suggesting that you might like to wear a dress more often."

"A dress isn't all that comfortable to wear, especially when you're riding or hunting. I'm thinking I am quite happy with my clothes, and if I don't get any whistles like Elsie, that's all right with me."

George didn't say anything more as they rode to the hotel and tied their horses and mule to the hitching rail in front. "Why don't you ladies head up to your room. I will meet you in the lobby in ten minutes. We'll eat first, then after dinner I will take the stock down to the livery stable. I sure worked up an appetite shopping with you two!"

A little while later, George walked down the stairs to find the two girls sitting on a faded velvet couch in the lobby, Elsie in her new dress, and Raven in her new cotton shirt. "Well, are you two ready for a fabulous dinner?" George asked.

With one girl on each arm George escorted them into the dining room. A waiter in a gray suit seated them and took their order. The dining room was nice, but the tablecloth and chairs showed wear.

Marshal Dicker entered the room, and Elsie was the first to see him. He was now neatly dressed in a suit and string tie. "Wow, you really look different," said Elsie with a large smile. Turning to her dad, she asked, "Can Mr. Dicker have dinner with us?"

"That would be up to the marshal, but he is certainly welcome to join us if he chooses."

"Why, thank you for the invite. It would be a real pleasure to have dinner in the company of such beautiful young ladies." Elsie smiled and blushed at the compliment while Raven just seemed to ignore it.

The four talked on a variety of subjects before finishing dinner. George ordered a couple of whiskeys for dessert while the girls ate hot apple pie. "So, Marshal, what brings you to Independence?"

"I am on official business, and most of it I am not at liberty to discuss with anybody not associated with the case or the law enforcement community. I guess without being too rude or violating my orders, I will say there is something fishy going on here, but that's all I can say. I hope you understand."

George nodded his head as if he agreed, but his facial expression gave away his curiosity.

"I guess I can tell you a couple of things that are already known to the general public. I guess that wouldn't violate anything."

"Please do. I'm always interested in what's happening."

"I am sure you have never heard of the small town of Hackberry."

"No, I can't say I have."

"Well there wasn't anything real special about the town when they built it, back about ten years ago. A small group traveling west decided that they would settle a high-grassed valley they found north of the Oregon Trail, up towards the Yellowstone country. They built a decent-sized settlement with a small store, a blacksmith shop and a small saloon. It had enough people living there that it had the making of a good start. You got to hand it to them. They were one of the first to try and settle some pretty rough country. The Indians in those parts seemed for the most part to be friendly, and for several years the town slowly grew and prospered."

"In the spring of fifty-six, the storekeeper sent out a group of men to bring supplies back. It was almost a six-month trip back to the fort. When they got back in the early fall with the supplies, the town was abandoned. No people, no supplies, no stock, everything of any value was gone, and nothing seemed to be disturbed. There were no bullet holes, no broken glass, and no arrows in the walls, nothing that gave a clue about what happened. It was like they disappeared without a fight, and God knows these were tough settlers, not afraid to take on a new life. That's about all I think I can tell you without permission, but I think I may have my hands full with this one."

George nodded his head and took the last sip of whiskey from his glass. "It's been a pleasure, Marshal. Good luck with your investigation, and I hope we run into each other again."

"Likewise, you have a wonderful family, and I, too, enjoyed the evening and your company. Maybe our paths will cross again and we will both have more time." With that, everyone got up and headed towards the lobby of the hotel.

"I need to take the stock down to the livery stable, and I want to do that before dark. I think these streets get a little rougher after dark. Why don't you two head up to your room for the evening, and I will be back in a little while."

Elsie nodded her head in agreement, but Raven perked up. "Would you mind, Uncle, if I went with you? I would enjoy the walk back."

"Sure, I would enjoy the company. Elsie, are you all right with being alone for a while?"

Elsie just nodded, and George and Raven headed to the front door of the hotel. The sounds of the town met them as they walked through the hotel's front door. It was still busy outside as the sun began to fade into the west with a soft raspberry color. "By the look of the sky, we will have another beautiful day tomorrow. That will give you two another day to look around and shop, and then we will be headed home." The two walked down the boardwalk and headed to where they'd tied the stock. They strolled down the steps to the hitching rail they had tied to, and George's horse snorted softly as they approached.

"Where's Ginger?" Raven said in a raised, panicked voice, "I tied her right here." She quickly ran down the street and looked in the alley and then amongst the other horses standing peacefully nearby.

"Ginger wouldn't just walk away. She wouldn't leave the horses," she almost pleaded, as tears began to roll down her face in her desperation.

"Uncle George, where could she have gone?"

The family contacted the sheriff, and for the next two days put up hastily printed posters and searched the town systematically street by street, but there was no sign of Raven's mule. A crude blend of anger and fear seemed to overtake Raven as she tirelessly checked every livery stable and stock pen in town with no results. After two long, hard days of looking, George and the girls revisited the sheriff's office, which was located close to the center of town. The door to the office was open, letting a gentle breeze clean the air as the three entered his office.

The sheriff was sitting at his desk and slid his chair back when he saw them enter. "By the look on your face, you didn't find her."

"No, sheriff, we didn't, but I wanted to be sure you had our address, as well as the list of towns we will be passing through on our way home. We will check in with the telegram stations as we travel, and if you find the mule, I will send a man back to get her. This mule means more to this girl than you will ever know, and I will happily pay a fine reward for her return."

"I wish I could say this kind of thing doesn't happen here often, but we have probably lost somewhere around fifty prime head of stock over the last seven years since I have been sheriff. With the amount of coming and going around here, with the wagon trains and such, things have gotten a whole lot worse than I would like. I have only found a few of the stock that came up missing, and we hanged most of the men that stole them, but there must be more to it, more organized, or we would have found a lot more head."

Raven just stood there listening to the conversation with a stoic face that hid all her emotions, except the tears that moistened her eyes. The only thing that she'd felt was truly hers was gone.

Chapter 10

Three Years Later, Spring of 1867

The large wagon wheels kicked up a constant cloud of chalky, white dust off the hardened ground as it followed the wheel ruts in front of it. Over the last two and a half months, Raven had gotten used to the feeling of being dirty and breathing the oftentimes choking air. Two of the wagon's hired guards rode twenty yards behind her, bringing up the rear of the train. The ranch her uncle had bought and put together was thriving, and last fall her Uncle George and Aunt Marlene had decided to finally move to the Willamette Valley and take charge of the huge spread.

The previous fall the family had traveled to Independence and spent the winter in a comfortable rented home on the edge of town. Uncle George had money, something that was in short supply to most, and the spacious home lacked none of the comforts of her aunt and uncle's mansion. Their large custom wagon held only the needed comforts and supplies for the trip, as the rest of their belongings would be brought later through a freight company.

This was a much smaller wagon train than most, one advertised to make the journey to Oregon in record time. The majority of the trip would be on the normal Oregon Trail route, but the wagon master and his outfit knew several shortcuts with good grass and water that a smaller wagon train could utilize. They were one of sixteen wagons in the train, which was considered by most to be too small to travel in dangerous Indian country. Along with the people in the wagon train, they also had an escort of ten seasoned fighting men with soldiering backgrounds and equipped with good muskets and pistols.

This was a special wagon train, selectively put together by the wagon master, and to join, a wagon owner had to pay five times the normal rate. This seemed reasonable when you looked at the weeks of travel that they would save going smaller and using trails known only to this experienced leader. Each patron had to have enough money to pay for the trip, which included buying well-built wagons made in the East. It was clearly pointed out that Captain Bleeker would not allow oxen, as they were too slow, and each wagon would need an experienced teamster. If the family couldn't produce one, the captain would arrange for one of his men to drive their wagon. Each family that wanted to join the wagon train was thoroughly interviewed and handpicked using rigid criteria, and several families were turned down.

Raven and Elsie had gone with their uncle and aunt to the first interview at a small office at the edge of town, and it had taken almost an hour. The wagon master asked questions about horse skills, ability to shoot, and knowledge of driving a team, as well as how big their families were, and how many people and what ages would be going. Each family had to have a team of six stout horses or mules built to work, as well as two head of good riding stock. Captain Bleeker discussed the wagonload of oats that would be brought to keep the stock's strength up. He didn't seem to miss a thing. Uncle George felt that the wagon master had been very meticulous in his planning because every detail had been discussed until everything was well answered.

The men Captain Bleeker had hired to escort the wagons were tough and strong-looking but clean shaven and polite to talk to. The escorts quit shaving after they left Independence, and the beard just added to the toughness that was shared by all of them. These were the type of men that other men gave a wide berth as they walked down the street, and their personalities were similar to their appearance. The casual good morning or a slight wave was ever present, but there was no small talk or socializing of any kind with the clients, and the wagon master enforced the professionalism he demanded. Several of the men carried sawed-off shotguns in addition to their muskets and a bunch of them seemed to only speak French.

The Dove family quickly made several close friends amongst the other travelers, and if everyone wasn't too tired, about once a week they would find an evening to sit around the campfire and discuss their lives. Elsie had met a young man named Richard and spent a lot of time talking about Oregon and what lay in store for them. He was a bright young man; tall, lean, and well-spoken for a man-child of fourteen. Almost every night, they would get together and talk on a log or a rock not far from the wagons. Elsie seemed quite smitten.

About every third night, Pastor Roberts, a short, balding man with a huge smile, would stop in and spend some time talking with her aunt and uncle about everything from the trip to the weather. He was always a complete gentleman, a little on the heavy side from doing more preaching than hard work, and his laugh was intoxicating.

At night, Raven would oftentimes sneak away with her musket and do a little hunting, for rabbit, mainly. The wagon master didn't seem to like her hunting by herself and leaving the wagons, but up until now she had tolerated his comments.

As Raven walked beside their wagon, Captain Bleeker rode up from the front of the line and reined his horse to a stop. "Raven, I don't want you going out anymore and hunting after we camp. It's getting more dangerous by the day, and I don't want anything to happen to you."

Raven looked up and him and smiled. "I never go far, and we could use the fresh meat."

"You may end up meat for the Indians, if you don't follow my orders. I have spoken to your uncle and told him I don't want you wandering away anymore. Its way too dangerous, and I am responsible for your safety. Tomorrow we will be leaving the main trail and taking our first shortcut, so there won't be a good rutted trail to find your way back after dark. My advice is that you sure don't want to be out in that rattlesnake-infested sagebrush after dark," he suggested firmly, as his gray beard framed his face.

Raven just glanced back up and quietly said, "I understand." She knew there were snakes, but the truth of the matter was there weren't any more than what they'd had at home, and she sure wasn't afraid of them back there. It was almost like he was trying to scare her enough that she would follow his orders, but deep down, she felt rebellious and angry.

Captain Bleeker took a moment to stare at her with his aged, bronze face before he jerked the reins of his horse to one side and gave it a kick. The action showered Raven in dust as he galloped back to the rear of the train.

Raven was not impressed by this action, and it only reinforced her opinion of him. She had told her uncle that she really didn't like the man, but he had come down on Bleeker's side, saying it was a hard and stressful job to get these wagons to their destination, and someday she would understand.

It was shortly after midday when the train stopped on a rocky patch of trail. The word came down the line that they would be turning to the northwest, and by nightfall, they would be in good grass and near water. They would camp early, and there would even be a small lake that people of the wagon train could use for bathing and getting fresh water. Raven looked down at her arm. It was like the dust and sweat were baked on, so the idea of being able to wash the last two weeks of dirt off sounded almost too good to be true.

The sixteen wagons and their escorts turned off on a huge flat rock that showed no real signs of leading to a trail. The rock angled down gently and leveled off, and at that point, the faint marks of wagon track could be seen on the prairie floor. How Captain Bleeker knew about this route was amazing, and it piqued Raven's curiosity. The trail went over another small rise and then down into a shallow gulley before working its way back up onto the prairie. One could tell that the trail had been used before, but there was little sign of heavy travel. The train was spread widely apart to help with the dust, and a constant breeze made travel bearable.

Once on the new trail, the thick grass cut the dust down to almost nothing, and everyone appreciated the break. Four hours later, Raven heard one of Captain Bleeker's men ride up and tell her uncle that the meadow where the train would spend the night was just over the next small rise. It would be good to stop early, so she could have an opportunity to wash and rest a bit before she snuck away to see a little more of the country and try to get some fresh meat. The hunters that Captain Bleeker sent out were successful most of the time, but Raven wanted to see this desert wilderness herself and enjoy a quiet evening hunt.

The wagon train made a tight circle before the men began unhitching the stock. The grass of the meadow was nearly two feet tall, and the stock quickly buried their heads in the first lush pasture in almost two weeks. The grass was dry, but still contained most of the nutrients the animals would need, and the clear lake fed by a small meandering spring was welcome and needed to refill the wagon barrels with clean, fresh water.

Elsie and Aunt Marlene hurried to the water and were soaking their feet as they washed their arms and faces. The water was uncommonly pure for this time of year, and everyone with the exception of the guards promptly took advantage of it. It would be a good night.

It was a couple hours before sunset when a clean and fed Raven slipped over the wooden tailgate of the wagon with her musket. After watching for a few seconds, she disappeared into the tall grass, and then into the sagebrush. She stayed to a small gulley for the first hundred yards and took notice of the small hills that surrounded her for landmarks. The gulley had a narrow, dusty trail in the bottom that was used by game to come down to the shrinking lake, and the path was well worn. She saw several rabbits soon after she entered the gulley, but she knew that a shot this close would give away her location to the rest of the camp and put them all on alert. For the next twenty minutes, she carefully walked the grooved path, noticing tracks of ground squirrels, sage grouse, deer, and even an occasional pattern made by a snake. She took comfort in this environment, and thought about how much her sisters and dad would have enjoyed this walk.

Over half a mile from camp the trail rounded the ridge, and Raven was surprised to see fresh horse tracks crossing the trail from the sagebrush. These were shod horses and definitely not Indian ponies, she immediately relaxed. Running into Indians by herself this far from the camp hadn't crossed her mind but for a moment it scared her. These must be several of the hunters looking for meat, she thought, but why are they hunting so late in the evening? She smiled to herself. Maybe they were out there for the same reason she was out here, to have some quiet time and feel her surroundings.

Curiously she followed the tracks of the two riders as they rode down the gulley in a generally northerly direction. Finding horse tracks out away from the wagons still made her a little nervous. Moving silently, she cautiously scanned the ground, following the tracks through the sagebrush. She didn't want them to see her and then get another lecture from Captain Bleeker.

It wasn't long before the path broke into a dusty opening where the tracks crossed to its center. Raven knelt down and studied every direction before exposing herself and crossing into the opening. At the center, it looked like a third set of tracks had been waiting, and by the look of the torn ground, the three horses had stood together for a while. Raven stood for a minute, studying the ground, and then blended back into the sagebrush and short grass that surrounded the tracks. She thought about talking to her uncle about what she had seen, but the last time she had brought up any concerns about Captain Bleeker, he had reminded her of his stellar reputation and the many wagon trains that he had safely guided to the Oregon Territory. She had read the flattering paperwork her uncle brought home before the trip, and it was impressive to say the least.

For almost fifteen years he had guided wagons across the West with only minimal loss of human or livestock life. Finally, she turned and headed back in the direction of camp. When she got there, she quietly wrapped her musket in a small blanket before lifting it over the tailgate and placing it between two wooden boxes. Then she casually walked out and sat down beside her uncle and aunt who were engrossed in conversation with a man from one of the other wagons. She noticed Elsie and Richard sitting alone by a small fire, and she couldn't help but notice how attached they were becoming.

The next day people got up the usual two hours before light and began hitching their well-fed stock to the wagons. Every morning and night the animals received a ration of grain from the company freight wagon. Unlike most trains that had to allow for the slow pace of the cattle and a large amount of people walking, a person in this group could easily see a huge time advantage and cover a large amount of territory each day. Having teams of quality animals and no overloaded wagons allowed the train to travel an additional five to ten miles each day. In addition, Captain Bleeker's shortcuts would remove many miles and allow the troop to get to the Oregon Territory even farther ahead of a normal wagon train.

Most days Raven chose to ride one of the two horses that they had brought, as opposed to bouncing around in the wagon all day. She would have liked to have ridden off and explored as they moved, but that was strictly forbidden and one of the many rules that Captain Bleeker was constantly adding. Sometimes at night, after a hard day, he would talk to all the men of the wagon train, tell them of his concern, and ask them to be more cautious and stay closer together because of the Indian Country they were going through. But with the exception of the tracks Raven had seen, there wasn't any evidence of Indians.

At the end of the second day on the new route, Raven ate quickly and then headed to the back of the wagon. After a quick glance around, she reached up and pulled the blanket covering her gun from behind the tailgate. When she turned back around, she was face to face with the steely look of Captain Bleeker.

"Well, young lady, what do you have in mind?" he asked, with a face so stern that Raven stuttered for a moment before answering.

"Just pulling her out to clean her, lots of dust on this trail, and I want to be ready if you need any help," she answered as nonchalantly as possible.

"I am sure my men can handle anything that comes along. They really won't be requiring any help from a youngster who's wet behind the ears. Now, why don't you just pack that gun back out of the way?"

Raven felt her teeth coming together so tightly that she was sure that Captain Bleeker would notice the anger in her face. How dare that arrogant bastard talk to her as if she were a child? She wanted to smash him in the mouth with all her might, but all she could do was slowly respond, "Yes, sir. I will put it away."

The next day the country began to change, and she could see mountains in the distance, large mountains with small patches of white on their tops. Now here and there were Douglas fir trees, and sometimes a cottonwood patch along one of the small creeks they crossed. The trail had become much more varied, and Raven wondered if it skirted the bottom of the mountains she could see. She rode up at lunchtime, unsaddled the horse she had been riding, and threw the saddle into the wagon before turning her horse out amongst the herd.

Climbing into the wagon, she helped Elsie make lunch and then got comfortable as the wagons began to move again. Normally the wagon train would travel for another three and a half to four hours after lunch before making camp for the night. This had been the routine for the last week.

Elsie and Raven's wagon was next to the last wagon in the string, the heavy grain wagon pulled by six draft horses. Raven watched for a while until the herd of horses and mules was walking fairly closely to their wagon, between them and the grain wagon. Raven put her finger to her lips as she looked at Elsie, "There's probably only a couple of hours until we camp for the night, and I am going to sneak out of here pretty quick to go for a little walk."

"You'll get caught, and that Captain Bleeker will be real mad if he catches you."

"I ain't going to get caught, and nothing is going to happen," Raven responded sternly, "now are you going to help me or what?"

Elsie just nodded her head slowly in agreement before sliding up closer to Raven.

"What are you going to do?"

"Nothing, just walk. I feel so penned up on this here wagon train that I feel like some type of prisoner or something."

Raven pulled back the canvas curtain of the back of wagon slightly and after a few minutes, slipped over the wooden tailgate and onto the ground. Elsie carefully handed the musket to her, and then Raven swiftly moved between the meandering horses, softly talking to them until she worked her way to the edge of the group and was close enough to a large patch of sagebrush that with one leap she disappeared into prairie.

She sat silently in the shade of the silver branches of a sage until the dust of the wagon train disappeared over a small rise.

Raven had packed herself a small amount of food in a brown cotton pouch, the same one she'd had since coming to live with her aunt and uncle. Keeping low to the ground, blending her short stature with the taller brush of the valley, she worked her way up towards a patch of rocks that would give her a protected view of the valley. It took a good thirty minutes to reach her objective, a large overhanging rock with several evergreen trees growing beside it.

She slung the musket over her shoulder by the thin leather strap that was tied to it and began trying to find holds for her feet and hands as she climbed. Raven had reached up and gotten a solid grip of the base of a small juniper when she heard the unmistakable buzz of a rattler. She froze immediately, her body rigid, and her mind raced as to what to do. Being bitten by a snake back here away from the train would be a death sentence and she knew it. Her face was only inches from looking over the top, but she was afraid to move a muscle. The agitated buzz of the rattler was not stopping and Raven knew she had to do something.

As slowly as she could move, she lifted herself up so as to peer over the shelf. What she saw terrified her; the snake was huge and sat only a foot or so behind the shrub Raven was clinging to. It had begun to slither around the bush when suddenly it recoiled back into striking position. She let go of the bush and fell backwards just as the snake struck, falling close to eight feet down into the tight network of bushes below her. Then everything went black.

Chapter 11

When Raven woke up she saw blood on her arm and her head ached terribly. Most of the blood was dried, but a small amount still oozed from the deepest cut in the middle of her forearm. Her musket was no longer secured over her shoulder, and she had no idea where it had landed. Immediately she knew she was in trouble, but she had to try to stand and evaluate her situation. There were numerous cuts on her legs and arms, and her face was covered with a mixture of dried blood and dirt, but none seemed more than superficial as she arose. Luckily the brush had cushioned the fall and no bones appeared to be broken. It took her several minutes to find her rifle, and when she did, she saw it had broken in two. *I will carry this back to the wagon and store it*, she thought, hoping she could come up with a plausible story for her injuries. Captain Bleeker would see through anything she said, and she knew that, but what choice did she have?

She picked up the musket and walked down to the trunk of one of the trees, its branches hiding her presence and giving her a decent view. There she sat for almost twenty minutes, watching the small valley she was in, before feeling like she was ready to follow the tracks of the wagons back to camp. At first she stumbled a bit, but soon her pace was constant, and not long after, she walked out of the sagebrush into the opening that was the trail. From the look of the sun, it would be several hours until dark, so she chose a large rock to sit on to have a little water and the remaining food from her pouch.

Being short and sitting on a small rock, she created little to no profile amongst the tall sagebrush of the valley. Then she happened to look up at the crest of the small hill above her. Out rode one Indian, and then another, and then another, until she counted twelve Indians riding single file along the top. The crest of the ridge provided an excellent view of both valleys as they rode along, and Raven quietly slid from the rock into the brush with the hope she had not been spotted. Silently she watched as they passed.

There was little she could do other than continue her journey back to the safety of the wagons. Maybe Captain Bleeker had been right to order her to stay close to the train and not venture out on her own. Raven had always been terribly independent and now she questioned herself. Watching the last rider, an Indian much larger than the rest, ride out of sight in the direction of the wagon train, she didn't miss that they were carrying rifles, much like those she had seen the soldiers at the fort carry.

* * *

Captain Bleeker motioned with his arm in the air to bring everyone to a halt. The trail had worked its way up to a large flat bench with a panoramic view of the valley below. One of Captain Bleeker's men rode in from the west as George Dove realized another man was riding up from the rear of the train.

"Why are we stopping?" asked Aunt Marlene, as she worked herself up from the back of the wagon where she'd been trying to take a short nap.

"I don't know. I don't see anything alarming, but maybe Bleeker's scout saw something. Anyway, Captain Bleeker is an excellent wagon master, and he will know what to do no matter what, so don't worry."

A man that George knew only as Burton rode down the train telling every man that Captain Bleeker needed everyone together for a meeting, and quick, at the front of the train. Several of the men grabbed their muskets and headed with the rest of the group up towards the head of the train at a jog.

"What's going on?" asked one man, as he gasped for air after running up the hill to join George.

"Heck, if I know, but I am sure Bleeker will have it under control."

Captain Bleeker sat on his horse facing the group of winded men that stood before him. "I need all of you men to drop you weapons now, and that includes your knives."

"Why, what's going on?" said George, moving towards Captain Bleeker with his musket at his side. Suddenly a shot rang out, and George keeled over and rolled down the hill, coming to a stop at a thick clump of grass. Several women screamed at the sound of the shot, and Mary Beth Updike in the second wagon pulled out her rifle and took aim at the Captain, just as another man who'd ridden as their escort shot her several times with his pistol and watched her drop over the side of her wagon.

"I am not a man to explain much, and I am only going to tell you this once. You are now my prisoners, and if you don't take orders, you will be shot and left for buzzard bait. Now all of you put your hands up and order your families out of their wagons, now!" he yelled.

Most of the men threw their hands up, but at least three dove and rolled and started to run back towards their wagons. One of Bleeker's men planted his spurs into his horse and drew his pistol. He gave chase just as a woman leaned out of her wagon and let her shotgun roar, blowing the man totally out of his saddle.

Another man promptly shot into the canvas siding, and the woman fell backwards over the tailgate onto the ground. A young man in the back of the train grabbed his gun and took off running back down the trail only to be killed by the Indians who had shadowed the train earlier. One man grabbed his gun and screamed for his wife to run, as a bullet caught him in the back and he slid to the ground. At least a dozen people tried escaping into the thick sagebrush beside the trail, followed by a hailstorm of bullets. Indians and white men worked together rounding up fleeing people, and with few exceptions, they weren't taking prisoners.

Marlene grabbed a pistol and turned towards the front of the wagon just as an Indian climbed up and over the seat. The shot from her gun into the screaming Indian's chin sent him falling back into the hitching of the wagon. A second Indian shot Marlene, and she fell to the floor of the wagon as Elsie huddled between a couple of boxes crying in fear.

* * *

Raven immediately knew what had happened when she heard the distant sound of gunfire echo through the valley. She was sure the Indians had attacked, and the wagon train and its guards were fighting them off. Her only problem was that the Indians were between her and the train and she wasn't sure how she would make it back. She stopped and tried to come up with a plan. Her head ached, and the numerous small wounds on her body hurt when she moved, but she knew she had to sneak back to the train if she were going to survive. Finally she decided to climb up to the top of the ridge where the Indians had ridden and get as good a view of the situation as possible before making her way back to the wagons. The climb was steep in places. Never slowing, she worked her way to the brushy top of the ridge.

Once there, she began to work her way down the ridge crest while the sound of gunfire got louder and less frequent. By the lack of gunfire, she thought they must be running them off, as she came to a small outcropping of rock and crawled to the edge for a careful look. What she saw shook her to her very core as she watched both white men and Indians hunting the men, women, and few children that made the journey. Several hundred yards below, there was a battle going on, but it wasn't just between Indians and the wagon train; it was between Captain Bleeker, his men, and the Indians against her family and the other members of the wagon train.

She pulled herself back from the edge of the rock and sat for a minute. What was going on? Why were Captain Bleeker's men fighting alongside the Indians and killing the very people they'd been paid to protect? The sound of gunfire had slowed greatly, so she crept up over the rock and took another look. A woman was running with the large Indian she had seen earlier in hot pursuit. She watched as the Indian got within fifty yards of the woman and then pulled up his musket and fired. A cloud of smoke filled the air, but the sound of the shot took almost a full second to reach her distant location. The woman stopped and then fell down into the sagebrush. The Indian came running and ducked down into the sage in the location the woman had fallen, only to reappear with a wild, animal-type scream and a bloody scalp that he raised above his head.

What is happening? Raven screamed to herself. What could she do? Was her family okay? She had no answers, as the sporadic sound of shots continued to subside. She decided to look one more time, and this time, to her horror, an Indian was working his way up the hill in her direction. How could he have known she was there? Had he happened to see her at this great distance? She didn't know, but she would have to take off running if he got any closer, surely the Indian could out run her in her condition.

Then just barely raising her head high enough to see, she saw Richard, Elsie's boyfriend, running for his life in front of the pursuing Indian. The two of them were less than a hundred yards away. If her rifle had not been broken, she would have taken the shot. Only moments later, she heard the thump of the Indian's tomahawk and then the blood-curdling scream of the Indian celebrating his kill. She melted back into the sagebrush and crawled cross country at the same elevation to a patch of juniper trees and then headed up the ridge, keeping the wooded hillside between them.

Periodically as Raven climbed, she heard a lone, distant shot, but soon only silence came from the valley below as the adrenaline and fear that filled her body continued to help her fight her way up through the tall, grass-and-sagebrush hillside until it yielded to scattered pines and thick juniper bushes.

For the next hour she climbed, until she finally collapsed in exhaustion under a large Douglas fir tree in the grassy bed created by a deer. Raven was familiar with deer beds made in these places, and she knew they normally had an excellent view of their back trail; this one was no exception. She fell to the ground into the grass-covered bed of short, yellowed fescue and small fir needles. She could go no farther, and if they had found her trail, she wouldn't outrun them.

Why did this happen? She screamed to herself as she slugged the hard ground with her fist. Finally, she curled up in a small ball and cried until she fell asleep from exhaustion as a gentle breeze blew through the branches of the tree above her. Hurting from her fall, several times in the night she awoke from terrible nightmares of being chased by Indians and then being dragged in front of a laughing Captain Bleeker, his steely eyes piercing through her dream. And then it was morning.

Raven could feel the sun on her face and hear movement close by. Slowly she cracked her eyelid open only to see a small chipmunk jump from her pant leg and scurry up the tree. At first she hoped it had all been just a horrible nightmare, but the realization that she was shivering in the cold summer morning made everything real. She was cold and stiff. Taking her jacket with her had been a blessing, but she still hurt all over from the tumble from the rocks. She was hungry and thirsty and the small canteen she carried was almost empty.

At first she just sat there and stared back down the hill, not knowing what to do or where to go. The sudden feeling of extreme loneliness was so much stronger than anything she had ever felt. When she had lost her family on the farm, she'd had her aunt, uncle, and Elsie to be with; but now everyone was dead, everyone. Raven put her arms around her legs, tucked them tight against her body, and buried her head in her knees, crying. Her face hurt, and the dirt and dried blood from the fall washed together in streaks from her tears. She just sat looking and listening the rest of the day, then she curled up by a decomposing log and drug handfuls of old dry chunks of wood over herself in hopes of keeping warm. It was a bad night with little sleep.

The next morning Raven awoke shivering again from the morning chill. She needed water and food badly and she knew it. Still hurting all over from the fall that broke her rifle, Raven sat staring down the hill until the feeling of loss turned to anger. If she were going to survive, she would have to fend for herself and find food, water, and a weapon for protection. As much as she didn't want to, she would need to find the inner courage to go back down to the wagon train and scrounge for supplies that would keep her alive. The nearest civilization was easily a month of walking over open ground, and if her family's killers were watching, it would be easy to pick up her trail in the valley. No, she would head back down to what remained of the wagon train and try and find anything that would help her survive. Up on the wooded slopes of the ridge, she felt at least a little protected, but it was now or never as she rose to her feet and cautiously worked herself down the ridge using trees and bushes as cover.

It took close to an hour before she reached the rocky spot where she'd hidden above the valley and watched Elsie's new boyfriend be murdered by a savage. The thought made her sick, the dry heaves rattled through her before she was able to control her body. Cautiously she moved forward with only the hunting knife she carried as protection. Finding some type of weapon would probably mean her survival and was one of her first priorities.

As she worked her way down the slope, the small trees and taller brush gave way to shorter grass and sagebrush. Raven knew that a good lookout nestled high on the ridge would probably pick up her movement. There was a patch of mature sagebrush the road cut through as it emerged into the large yellow meadow of grass where she had last seen the wagons, and that was where she chose to try to cross. Taking her time she crawled between the tall sage, stopping numerous times to slowly rise above the brush for a quick look around with only her head showing.

She felt confused. Her memory told her where the wagon train had come under attack should have been in front of her in the large meadow of short grass, but there was nothing, no wagons, no bodies, no animals, and no tracks that she could see, only a calm grassy opening with a light breeze that bent the taller grass. For several minutes she looked at the hills and far mountains that she had climbed when she'd left the wagon train for bearing, and everything looked right, but there was nothing. Could she have gotten confused and somehow descended into the wrong valley? In her panic, had she gone farther up the mountain than she could have ever believed?

Finally, she stood up again and scanned her surroundings; only the sound of the breeze and a few flittering birds broke what would have otherwise been total silence. Walking to where she thought the road had been, she looked at the ground. There was an indentation, but no real marks of the hard metal edge of a wagon wheel. Standing up she looked at the hills around her, and realized she had to be in the right place. The bush and rock ledge where she had watched the massacre stood promptly on the ridgeline, and she recognized it, but where was everything else?

Raven sat down in the grass, questioning her own sanity, when her eye caught the reflection of something in the grass. She crawled over to it, not bothering to stand, and pulled a shiny shell casing from between the blades of grass. The bright shiny brass cartridge would go dark quickly if left to the weather, and this bullet smelled of fresh black powder. Several more casings were shining in the grass farther down the hill. Finally the feeling that she was going mad left her. Knowing she was in the right place helped her regain her composure as she began walking down the gentle slope of hill at the edge of the thick sagebrush and the meadow.

A large branch of sage had been thrown into the brush close to where she stood, and she took a minute to look at its dusty, ragged leaves. Someone had taken great pains to erase the deep tracks of the wagons, and Raven couldn't understand why. The farther she walked down the hill, the more items she found mixed in the grass and border of sage. A bluish green blouse almost the color of sage was wrapped around one of the bush's stems, so she reached down and picked it up. It was little, the size of a woman even smaller than herself.

The lower she went the more open it got, until she stopped where the meadow seemed to just vanish. A massive vertical cliff lay in front of her, making it impossible to reach the isolated valley below. Raven didn't like being that close to the edge, but she still couldn't see how far the cliff dropped off. Raven had never liked heights. She decided to lie down on the ground and crawl to the edge to peer over.

The edge of the rock cliff seemed to stretch as far as the eye could see in both directions, and from what she perceived, it dropped straight down for at least a hundred feet. What she saw next totally shocked her; there, at the bottom, surrounded by huge boulders, was a huge heap of mangled wood; hundreds of wagons reduced to nothing more than chunks of splintered wood, torn canvas, and broken wagon wheels. For several minutes she tried to get hold of herself, while she scanned the cliff for ways to get down to the mangled pile. Hopefully something of value had survived the fall.

Looking hard in both directions, she thought she saw a place where the rockslide jutted out into the prairie farther than the rest of the toe of the cliff. Hopefully there would be a way down there. She slid back from the edge and didn't stand until she was a good ten feet from it. The rockslide was a good half-mile back up the valley. Quickly she worked her way through the sage heading in that direction. Several times she stopped and scanned her surroundings for dust clouds, but there were none. Thirsty and hungry, the thought of finding food had her mind and stomach working overtime, as she ran along parallel to the cliff's edge, trying to stay a good twenty feet from the jagged drop off.

Suddenly Raven screamed as she slipped and fell down a steep rocky grade. In midair she turned and threw herself backwards, catching a sagebrush stem as she fell. The cliff's edge had made a ninety-degree turn and come back deeply into the hillside. Raven dangled with over a fifty-foot drop to the rocks below. With all her might, she grabbed the sagebrush branch with her other hand and pulled herself back onto the shelf from where she had fallen.

Below her was a sharp crack in the otherwise solid cliff. She examined every possible route before deciding to investigate the other side of the steep bank. It took several minutes to walk around to the other side, but once she got there, she was surprised to find a steep game trail working its way down through the large rocks. The trail was full of loose rock, gravel, and dirt; how the animals made it up or down, she wasn't sure. She firmly held on to branches to keep her balance as she descended down the narrow trail, sliding and almost falling several times before finally reaching the bottom. Taking a minute to look around, she headed through the field of boulders that covered the toe of the massive rock cliff.

Finally she made it to the huge pile of crushed wagons, and from the aged colors of the wood, she could see that this had been going on for quite some time. Whoever the mastermind was behind this hideous crime, he had picked an almost perfect place to hide it. The tall face of rock made a slight indentation back into the cliff, and this is where the culprit had chosen to conceal his act. The large field of broken wheels and the shattered wood rose high above the ground to where the last wagon was, only twenty feet below the crest of the cliff. Rotted canvas and faded rags that had once been clothing littered the ground.

Raven wanted so badly to tell someone, to scream her anger, but she knew it would only reveal that she had survived. Mangled amongst the broken wagons were chunks of twisted metal from the canvas frames and the remains of hundreds of broken boxes of various sizes mingled with the yellow grasses and wild potentilla that grew at the base.

Carefully she began climbing the pile towards the top wagons. Several times she saw white bones tightly lodged in the debris, but she kept pulling herself up the pile. She could see that there were several wagons that were almost intact on top, and she hoped that she would find something of value in at least one of them. Her mouth felt like cotton, it had been so long since she had taken a drink. Her focus shifted to one particular wagon. It had several wagons piled on top of it, but it seemed to be almost totally intact, therefore she thought it might be her best chance.

After several more minutes of climbing, she finally reached the wheel of the wagon and saw that the water barrel attached to the side was broken and splintered. Raven crawled into the back through an open tailgate held in place with one of the original chains. The wagon's sides were tall and stout and had protected the contents to a degree. Boxes, barrels, and other supplies covered the floor, torn away from the straps that had secured them. She could see a thick wool blanket lying on the floor, partially covered by boxes and clothing, so Raven began removing items to get to it. With one hard pull she yanked the blanket free, and to her horror, the white arm and head of a man appeared. Jumping back in the confined space, she tried to get a hold of herself. She recognized the thick gray mustache and white hair of Ollie Johnson, a man she had met at the start of the trip. He'd been a pleasant man with a good sense of humor, and when he laughed, his whole body would shake. She and her family had enjoyed several evenings around the campfires listening to tales of his many adventures, and now he was dead.

It took a moment to regain her composure before she could remove the rest of the items from on top of his body. She moved the final bag of beans to find a pistol gripped in his other hand. He had died fighting, and they must have pushed the wagon over the edge so as not to deal with the wounded man barricaded inside. She would have expected nothing less of the man she had briefly known. The gun was a forty-four-caliber Colt Dragoon pistol. How it had remained in his hand through the fall, she had no clue, but she almost wept at her luck in finding it.

It took her a minute to get the courage to pry the gun from the dead man's hand, and when she did, she sat back with tears in her eyes. Eventually Raven spun the oval cylinder and saw that four of the chambers were still loaded. Three of those cylinders had percussion caps still tightly seated and ready to fire. It was an expensive gun, just like the one her uncle had used to practice with her, and its blued finish and hand-carved walnut grip had a fine feel to them. For the first time since the whole attack had taken place, Raven felt she had a way to protect herself and maybe even fight back.

The small space created by the stacked wagons was tight, and to add to everything else, the decaying body of a man she'd once known and admired lay in front of her. He was in a position that she knew she would need to crawl over him to check for food and other supplies. She crept closer to the front of the wagon where, in a cracked wooden box, she found her first food: bags of beans in cotton sacks tied with a small cotton rope. There were at least six bags, and she took note of that in case she might have to return, even though the thought of climbing over the body later almost made her gag. In a large tin barrel she found hard biscuits and gobbled one down.

It was then she heard the noise; the scraping sound like someone else was climbing the pile of wagons from the other side. She had been so careful in scouting her path, and now someone, or something, knew she was there. Fear began to take over. Quickly she dumped about half of the biscuits into the large sack containing the beans and tied the top. The sounds of climbing continued, and the occasional piece of wood breaking told her she would not have to wait long to face her attacker.

Raven set the bag of food down, pulled the stiff hammer back using both thumbs, and steadied the pistol. Time seemed to stand still as the sounds continued getting closer and closer. A cold sweat crept over her body. She made up her mind that she would not be taken; she would die fighting. Being taken alive by the people who had killed her family was not an option.

The wagon was at a slight tilt upward, so whoever was outside would have to come through an opening in the boxes about three feet square towards the front of the wagon. Raven steadied the heavy gun on a box and aimed at the opening. Whoever was outside seemed to hesitate for a moment, before pushing their head through the opening.

It was not what Raven expected. She was face to face with a huge black bear. It growled as their eyes met. Raven squeezed the trigger and immediately the small space filled with thick black powder smoke that blocked her view as she worked her way back out of the wagon. Seconds later the sound of the bear crashing down amongst the wagons as it made its way to the ground could be heard, and then there was silence. Raven just stood on the tailgate of the wagon for a second, trying to absorb what just happened, then realized she had to act quickly. Anyone for miles would have heard the shot, and the steep rock wall would have amplified it even more. It was either leave now or risk capture.

Quickly and carefully Raven climbed down the pile of wagons with the pistol stuck in her belt, the cotton sack with beans and hard biscuits, and her wool blanket. She had not found water, but she would have enough food for at least a week if she rationed it. At the bottom of the cliff, she threw the sack over her shoulder and took off at a trot towards the steep trail that led to the top. The trail up was difficult, and with the sack it was all she could do to work her way back to the top before collapsing in a pile to catch her breath.

For several minutes she sat there breathing heavily and trying to figure out her next move. Then she saw it, the faint dust cloud far out on the prairie beyond the cliff. As much as she wanted it to be someone who would save her, she knew it wasn't. Jumping to her feet, she began running back towards the hillside, not taking time to crawl through the sagebrush. Within minutes she was working her way up the hill and past the first juniper bush that marked the transition from sage and grass to timber.

She stopped for a moment to catch her breath again and looked back to check if she could see any dust on the horizon, but she couldn't. Someone had heard the shot and was headed her way. If she was going to escape, she needed to be smart. Setting the sack of food down, she took her knife out, and cut two thickly leafed branches of sage. Removing the small rope from the food sack, Raven tied the two branches together with one end and tied the other to her belt. Her hasty retreat had left proof of her visit and a person trained in tracking would know what had happened. Her father had taught her much about the woods including putting food on the table for her family. Hopefully her efficiency would put a gap between her and whoever would eventually get on her trail.

Taking a different route, she made her way back up the hill and focused in on a rockslide that she hoped would allow her to lose anyone who might be tracking her. By the time she reached the top of the ridge, she was exhausted. Her stomach felt like she was going to throw up. Her lips were cracked from lack of moisture. Now she had food, but if she didn't find water soon, she would die of dehydration.

Raven crossed over the ridge and began moving perpendicular to the slope to save her energy. Touching her tongue to her cracked lips, she knew she was in trouble. It had been two days since she had water, and they had been hard days.

Crossing several small canyons, she worked her way around the ridge. As she went through a small pass, she noticed a clump of aspen in the narrow head of a draw below her. Aspen, she knew was a tree that needed a lot of water to grow, but she was concerned that if she didn't find water there, she wouldn't have the strength to climb back out the steep draw. There was no other choice as she worked her way down, often sliding, into the rocky gulley. Entering the aspen grove, she was immediately encouraged by the healthiness of the trees. In the bottom of the draw the soil was damp, but there was no water, so she began working the twenty yards up to the head of the draw, where a large rock protruded from a steep cliff. At the base, she found a seep where the water was dripping from between two rocks. She quickly opened her mouth and let the drops slowly fill her mouth. The water had the smell of sulfur and didn't taste good, but she hoped it was good enough to keep her alive.

For two days she drank the putrid-smelling water, ate hard biscuits and dried beans, and slept curled up in her wool blanket. On the third day, she filled her small canteen and climbed the steep hillside up to where she had begun and then continued on up the valley. Raven wondered if her pursuers had found her trail, and if so, how far they were behind her. She would have to make a plan, but for now she just wanted to put distance between herself and this wicked place.

For two more days Raven walked, staying to the timbered, grassy ridges. Several times she had rabbits and deer within range but passed on the shot, scared that the sound might give away her location. It was noon on the third day when the slope of the ground became gentle and she found a small, fast-moving creek with good-smelling, cold water. She dropped to the ground and drank on and off for several minutes before dumping the sulfur-smelling water from her canteen onto the ground and refilling it with the new, sweet-smelling water of the babbling creek.

After a long break, she continued on and to her surprise, found a well-worn trail working its way up the mountain. The trail had not seen much use for years, but at one time had been well traveled and the depression into the hillside was a testament to it. The wind had been a constant companion on her journey but now it had picked up. The gusts were getting stronger by the minute. If conditions worsened, she would need to find shelter soon. She stared at the trail for a moment and then started walking up the path as it made its way up the ridge. The fierce wind would help hide any tracks she was leaving. Any path this well worn had to lead somewhere.

The old trail worked its way up through the broken patches of trees into an open hillside, covered in thick fescue grass that almost looked like a rolling pasture. The trail veered from the creek, and after a couple hundred yards joined another trail that had also shown a lot of use. Like the first trail, it looked like it had not been used for years. The wind was now howling louder and blowing harder, Raven's need to find shelter was critical. The trail took her back into the small canyon where she had first found the creek. She crossed it again and came into an opening.

The first thing she saw was the stump of a large tree at the edge of the trail. She knew she had found something. Walking further into the clearing, there were more stumps. That's when she saw it, the burned remains of a cabin with some of the large lower logs still intact. Why the cabin hadn't burnt to the ground, she didn't know. Maybe a freak rainstorm had doused the flames, but there it sat, charred and black.

The remains weren't much, but they gave her hope; someone had lived there, so maybe she was closer to civilization than she thought. A huge gust of wind forced her to turn so her back was against it, and out of the corner of her eye she saw something that didn't fit with the free-flowing lines of the woods behind the cabin. She spun around and hurried towards the shape. From the outside, the aged black wood looked like a barn, as she reached what she thought was the front, opened the heavy wooden door that faced the north, and entered. Inside she immediately felt the relief from the wind and noticed the heavy craftsmanship of the logs that held the building together.

Whoever had built this barn had been an excellent builder, and with the exception of a hole in the roof at one end, the barn was in great shape. An old pile of hay was stacked in one area, and numerous horse stalls were lined up against one wall. Old tools hung from the walls, as well as traps of various sizes hanging from chains attached to nails. An ax was buried into a chopping block, and a stack of aged wood leaned against one of the two-foot-thick support posts. She had everything she needed to survive here, at least for a while.

Raven went outside, even though the wind continued to blow, and collected some rock to set around the small campfire she intended to build. After six trips, she had enough. She lined the campfire up with the hole in the ceiling, dug a shallow pit, and lined it. Next she cleared the old grass that lay everywhere on the floor away from the campfire and set some of the cleanest grass in the middle of her rock circle. Then she chopped a small log into wood shavings with the rusted ax. Minutes later, she took a flint box out and after her second try, lit the fire. The feeling of a warm fire was unbelievable and made her feel safe and secure. Curled up tightly into a ball next to the crackling flames, she slowly fed the fire with small chunks of split wood. It was a good night.

Raven woke up to a peaceful morning. The storm had blown past, and now the birds were chirping. There was also the sound of a small brook in the meadow. Examining the traps hanging on the barn walls, she was pleased that, with the exception of one large trap, the springs were still in great shape and worked well. Her father had taught her to trap at a young age, and now that knowledge would help her survive. She now had a plan. She would trap small game and dry the meat until she had enough to allow her to travel. Next she would find civilization and tell the authorities what had happened. Down deep, she was very angry and she wanted revenge, but for now it was all she could do just to survive.

For several days, she set traps and picked berries. She rationed her beans and biscuits, and cooked a stew with some of the meat from her first catch, a fat jackrabbit. She built a drying rack, and after three days, it was filled with meat drying in the hot sun. By her calculations, it would take her another week before she was ready to head east. Traveling at night for the first week, she would avoid running into anyone before turning south to pick up the main wagon trail. Raven felt good about her plan.

At night she would let her mind wander to better days, and the image of the tall handsome stranger she had met at the attorney's office often visited her dreams. She fondly remembered his chiseled body and strong face. He was a man she could only dream of.

The tenth morning, Raven got up and ate a small breakfast of squirrel and beans before going outside. Opening the heavy door of the barn, she walked out into the meadow. Today she would leave at dusk. Carefully hanging all the traps back on the walls, she returned other items to where she'd found them before packing up the dried meat.

It was dusk when she pulled her hat tightly over her head and put the heavy cotton bag of food over her shoulder. She would cross country through the trees, always heading east. Traveling was much more difficult at night, but there was a half moon and that helped a lot. The whole night she walked using the Big Dipper and the North Star to keep her direction. An hour before sunrise the temperature began to drop and Raven struggled with the bone-chilling cold. She finally decided to start a very small fire – just enough to warm her numb hands and help her stop the shaking. With some dry grass and small sticks, she quickly got a small flame started. A small fire produced little smoke. For the next hour, she warmed herself until the sun began to rise. Now that she was warm she dozed off, curled up and wrapped tightly in her blanket.

Something woke her, and as Raven struggled to focus on the object in front of her, everything went black.

Chapter 12

Raven could feel herself gently moving back and forth. One side of her head throbbed terribly, and her left eye was swollen shut. Sight was difficult through her good eye, and all she could see was the back of a large Indian on his horse, leading the dapple-gray packhorse she was on. The packhorse was totally loaded on both sides and carried a fur top pack that she straddled face down with her hands spread and tied firmly to the wooden cross of the sawbuck. How long she had been out, she didn't know, but she had wet herself, and the hair around her bruised and swollen face was filled with dirt and blood.

Her tightly fitting hat was pulled firmly down upon her head, and it irritated a large bruise on her head as the horse moved. Whoever this person was, he intended nothing good for her. The top-pack covering of furs was soft, and it made the riding at least bearable as they made their way through a scattered tree ridge littered with pine needles. Several times she lost consciousness, and when she awoke the final time, she saw a rugged ridge, a landmark she recognized. They were headed back west.

Several hours later, they broke out of the timber and headed down a steep, grassy slope to an old, rutted road and continued west. The road worked its way around several ridges and then started up a slight hill. Through a small break in the timber, she got a glimpse of a wide river below them. Within several minutes, the road worked its way close to the river's edge, buffered by intermittent trees. From what she could see, the road was about four feet above the riverbank, but almost immediately it began climbing and working its way back towards the timber. They worked their way high above the river until the steep hillside turned into a vertical cliff high above the water. Not only had they risen in elevation, but the far side of the road was now becoming very rocky and steep with large rock outcroppings towering above the trees.

Raven had no idea where they were going, but it appeared that the rough road was working its way up and onto a wide shelf bordered by the steep cliff of the river on one side and a nearly vertical cliff that lined the far side. The cliff at the base of the mountain soared almost straight up for over a hundred and fifty feet until it broke into scattered bushes and small trees desperately trying to survive on the windswept rocks. It was several more hours before sunset when they started up another hill, steeper than the rest. From Raven's angle, the road almost appeared to go straight into a solid rock wall that loomed in front of them. Rocks of various sizes lay stacked on the side of the road.

Within minutes, a narrow slit in the rocks seemed to just appear, and from what she could see from a distance, it was barely bigger than the width of a wagon. What looked like white-capped stakes stood in the grass on both sides of the entrance. As they grew closer, she saw what it really was. On both sides of the entrance, scattered amongst the thick grass, were narrow, carved poles of different heights, each with the sun-bleached remains of a human skull impaled upon it. Raven stared at the gruesome sight for a moment before becoming distracted by movement on the cliff wall; a man with a rifle was waving from a small log structure. Then she noticed another tower on the other side, and it, too, was manned by an Indian guard carefully watching the entrance.

The Indian guard barely moved only enough to give a passive wave to the men above. The horses never broke stride as they continued riding up through the hideous field of skulls. They were almost to the narrow slit in the rock. As the wind blew the tufts of tall grass back and forth amongst the gray poles and skulls, Raven closed her eyes in total terror. She knew she was going to die here.

They were through the narrow opening in the rocks when she opened her eyes and finally glanced up to see an almost straight road in front of her with numerous log buildings lining the sides. It almost looked like a small town with chickens running and pecking along the roadside as a stray dog stood and watched their progress. Raven's mind was racing with questions. Why were all these buildings out in the middle of nowhere, and who lived here? The road was now mainly a mixture of gravel and hardened clay and for the first time she heard the sound of their horses' hooves echoing off the buildings as they continued farther into the small settlement.

The buildings were of various sizes and seemed to have been well placed to take advantage of the wide, protected shelf that loomed above the valley. The shelf seemed to be no more than several hundred yards wide, and in some places it narrowed to less than sixty. The buildings appeared well built and in good repair, and several had hard-looking men sitting on their porches or standing motionless as they watched the big Indian ride in. She turned her head and was quickly reminded of her painful bruise as she strained with great difficulty to see both sides of the street.

They passed a blacksmith shop with a man hammering on a horseshoe, but the burly man with the hammer hardly gave her a second glance. Just past the shop, the Indian pulled back on his horse's leather reins and came to a stop in front of a log hitching rail. He tied the horses to the rough peeled log that was the hitching rail, then walked over to Raven's horse and cut the leather strapping holding her hands to the sawbuck pack saddle.

Reaching up, he grabbed her by her coat and threw her to the ground where she moaned from the impact. Then he grabbed the collar of her coat and began dragging her towards a large log cabin overlooking the river, without saying a word. A large older woman with graying hair and worn clothing had noticed their arrival and was quickly walking towards them when they entered the large log cabin.

With one hand, the large Indian launched Raven off the ground and onto the building's floor before turning to face the older woman outside, who had just come around the building's corner. Raven could hear a little of what they said, she was stunned by the fall and somewhat dazed. Her eyes drifted to the building's large ceiling made from wide planks carefully cut and fitted. She lay in the dirt. Near the walls there were piles of hay, with the exception of one corner that had a small fireplace built of rock and mortar. The center floor was hard dirt, and she could smell the stale soil as well as a slight odor of urine.

Raven looked back out the doorway, and for the first time she noticed how really large this Indian was. He was noticeably bigger than most and part of his face was deformed by a large scar that went from his left eye all the way down to the corner of his mouth. He and the older woman talked for a moment before the Indian walked back into the building and again grabbed Raven, and threw her onto some matted grass against the wall.

The older lady walked in behind him, knelt down between Raven and the Indian, and removed a leather string from around her neck. A lone key hung on the string, and with it she opened a rusty shackle attached to the wall and shackled Raven's ankle. The shackle was connected to a heavy chain that was spiked deeply into the thick log wall. The woman firmly looked at Raven, checking to make sure the shackle was tightly latched before standing up and facing the Indian. They looked at each other for a moment before he ducked back through the short doorway and returned to his horses. There were no words exchanged as the woman left, shutting the door creating total darkness. Raven found herself alone and scared.

It was close to an hour later when Raven opened her eyes and heard people walking outside. The heavy plank door swung open and in walked eight women in torn, faded clothes with gaunt faces. The prisoners were followed by the older woman who had put shackles on Raven and then chained her to a large log that spanned the floor six feet from the wall. In her hand, the old lady carried a small cotton sack and set it down beside the door.

Each woman went to a spot against the wall, lay down on a bed of matted hay, and took a shackle from the wall and put it on her leg. The old lady went from person to person, locking the shackles until everyone was done, and then she returned to Raven.

"There is no talking at night. Now, if you're smart you will try and get some sleep; tomorrow will be hard on you."

With that, she went outside and returned with a small cup, handing it to Raven.

"Now drink this water and hopefully you will be alive in the morning."

The sudden flood of light that occurred when the heavy plank door opened woke Raven from her much needed sleep. The old, gray-haired woman was making her rounds removing the shackles from each woman's ankle, and one by one they were standing and stretching.

"You all know the drill. Now line up to use the outhouse, and be quick about it," she grumbled, as she walked over to Raven and used her key to unlock her leg.

"Looks like Scar put you through hell. You must have really pissed him off. He's been searching for you ever since you fired that shot down on the prairie a week or so ago. Smart one, you are; he chased you longer than anyone I can recollect. Gave him a good run for his money, you did, but now you're here, and everything is different. If you try to run again, they will kill you and probably take it out on the rest of us, too. If you work hard and don't cause trouble, you might survive a while. Try to escape and I will kill you myself."

"Now go outside to that wash basin beside the wall and clean yourself. And change those pants; you stink to high heaven. There are some pants there that ain't your size, but with a bit of rope they will work. Now get out there and hurry up. Marquese will be by soon to check on me and the ladies, and I don't want any trouble, you hear?"

Raven painfully worked herself to her feet and walked outside. She hurt all over, but the thought of washing up was much appreciated. The large basin of water sat on a thick plank held above the ground by two short chunks of logs. An old manty was draped over a rope tied to a tree, and the other end was tied to the cabin. At least it gave a little privacy as Raven quickly removed her pants and washed herself with a rag. The old woman walked over to where Raven was washing.

"Don't clean yourself too well; it's the wrong thing to do here." With that, she walked back over to where the other women were and began talking to one of them. Raven had no idea what that was about, so she gently cleaned off some of the mud and blood, careful to not do a thorough job. By the time she was done, the last woman was leaving the outhouse, so she quickly opened the door and sat down. The smell was even worse than the building she had spent the night in, so she tried to hold her breath as she urinated.

As Raven walked from the outhouse, she stumbled and fell to the ground.

"You two help her back to the cabin and put her in her spot," said the older lady, pointing toward two of the other women. The two women drug her to her spot, and the old lady who was following them locked her shackle, then turned and got the small bag she had by the door and removed a chunk of bread and a small jug.

"Here's a little food and water, but tomorrow you will be expected to work like everybody else. Don't think you are anyone special; no one is in this hellhole. Oh yes, and call me Miss Martha."

With that she rose to her feet and left the room, leaving the door ajar and allowing some light to penetrate the darkness of the room. Raven ate the bread and drank the water, then slept most of the day until late afternoon when she heard the women returning. As she heard the women talking, the lady known as Miss Martha walked in, unshackled her, and helped her stand up. Raven walked to the outhouse, but had little to give, then turned and hurried as best she could back into the log building, where she went and sat down on the matted grass where she had previously lain.

A woman several years her senior was lying in the grass bed beside her, and they were the last to be shackled into their chains. There was one lone lantern in the room, and after the man known as Marquese had shackled everyone, he went and blew the small flame out.

"Are you okay?" came a quiet whisper from beside her. "My name's Betsy. Looks like Scar really beat you up; he ain't used to having to work that hard to catch someone. He's the best tracker in camp, and the camp is full of men that used to be trappers, not to mention those Indians."

"What is this place?" asked Raven.

"As far as I know its hell or the closest thing to it!"

"How did you get here?"

"It's a long story, but a little over a year ago my new husband and I were headed west. We had left a large wagon train to visit family when we were surrounded by about fifteen men, some white men, some Indians. They killed my husband and took our wagon. As you can see, they need slaves to keep this place running and to work the mines. I got pretty beat up in the attack, and when I woke up I was here. They just gunned my husband down when he protested. That's why I am surprised you are still alive and not just another skull in Scar's trophy yard. He must have taken kindly to you."

"Yeah, right," said Raven, as she gently rubbed her severely bruised face, "a real liken." With that, Raven closed her eyes, exhausted, and immediately was asleep.

The loud opening of the door and the instantly bright sliver of sunlight lit up the dark interior of the cabin as the large lady who had led her inside barked, "Get your sorry butts out of bed, you got work to do." An older man who looked part Indian and part French had begun removing the shackles from each woman's foot.

Raven looked over towards Betsy, who was sitting up and hurriedly putting on her worn socks and tattered shoes. Betsy was a pretty woman in her mid-twenties with auburn hair and a turned-up nose covered in freckles.

"Get up," was all she said, as she rose and headed to the door before turning. "Hurry up, you don't want to be last," she warned Raven.

With that, Raven gingerly got to her feet and followed the line of ladies outside. They stopped at the outhouse and then, in twos, began walking further into the encampment towards a wooden bridge that spanned an eight-foot wide creek.

"Comes right out of the mountain, that's the drinking water for the camp."

"Quiet back there, no talking. You know the rules."

They hadn't marched more than ten yards when Raven looked to the right and saw a heavy, rough sawn cross with a pitiful looking man shackled and chained to it. His head was down, his arms stretched nearly the length of the beam, and his limp body showed numerous long cuts, the kind made by a whip. Streaks of dried blood ran down his face and onto his chest, and strands of his tattered shirt gently moved in the breeze. As the women walked closer you could hear the man pathetically begging for water.

"Don't look; don't grab anyone's attention," said Betsy who marched beside her. "Don't give them any more reason to single you out; they are always watching. That's the Devil's Cross, leastwise that's what all of us call it; no one ever survives who gets strapped to it."

The small troop made their way across the planked boards of the bridge and turned right into an open, but covered area, connected to a stone building.

"What happened to him? Why are they doing that to him?" whispered Raven.

"He came in with your wagon train; it looked like he was a pastor by the white band around his neck. You can't see it now from the blood and his shirt being all torn. They had him working as a carpenter. Nice man, I even talked to him a couple of times. He tried to escape a couple of days ago, and just like all the rest, they caught him. They make examples out of those that try."

Raven couldn't stomach to look again knowing it was Pastor Roberts. The suffering man continued to beg quietly for water as the group continued marching by towards a heavy stone building.

"Here's where we work," said Betsy quietly, as she walked towards a table.

All of them, with the exception of Raven, went to their workstations and began working on their assigned tasks. "Well now, what name do you go by?" barked the large woman named Miss Martha.

"Raven."

"Okay, Raven, I want you to go over to those sacks of potatoes and start peeling them. I will tell you when to stop," she said, as she pointed to a table close to where Betsy was working.

Raven sat down on a small stool and took the short knife that was placed by the sacks and began peeling. For the next hour she kept her head down and peeled until one of the other women brought around a sack with pieces of bread. Raven had noticed her giving each person a chunk, and she hoped she would be included. She had smelled the bread being baked in the stone building and it had almost been too much for her to bear on an empty stomach.

The person giving her the bread was in her twenties and had puffy black bags under her eyes. She looked tired and dazed as she intentionally dropped a chunk of bread at Raven's feet. Raven slowly picked the bread up and hungrily tore a piece off, never taking her eyes off the woman. Eventually the girl turned and walked towards Betsy and gave her a chunk of bread before moving on to the next person.

"That's Allie. From what I hear, she has been here for a couple of years or more, and the guards abuse her periodically," whispered Betsy. "She used to be real normal like, but for the last three months something just ain't quite right with her." Betsy lowered her head and stopped talking after noticing Miss Martha glance in her direction.

Raven carefully scanned her surroundings, taking her time so as not to arouse any notice. She knew she wouldn't survive living this way and that she would either escape or die trying. She had absolutely no desire to become a plaything for the crude guards that roamed the camp.

While peeling, she glanced around and noticed several more cabins and a corral with stock in it farther down the road. Chickens wandered everywhere, pecking and scratching the ground in search of insects. Other than the fact that this was a prison, Raven couldn't understand how clean and well-built everything was. How could this be?

Of the eight women in her group, not counting Martha, four had gone into the stone building where the smell of fresh bread was coming from. Outside, one woman was stripping the hide off a whole bull elk that hung from a chain tied to one of the building's thick log beams. She was carefully cutting the meat into long strips that Raven assumed were for jerky. Another woman was doing laundry in a large steel tub and hanging clothes on a line, while another woman seemed to be making a stew in a large kettle. Everyone was working and keeping their eyes on their job.

An older man with shoulder length gray hair was leading a donkey and cart up from farther down in the road and Raven kept her one good eye on him as he made his way towards their building. The swelling had gone down enough now that she could see, but her face was still black and blue with shades of yellow, and hurt terribly. The older man with gray whiskers and a limp stopped the donkey and its cart in front of Miss Martha and began talking in a friendly tone.

Raven was too far away to listen to their conversation, but it seemed the two enjoyed each other's company, and for the first time she saw Miss Martha smile. Several minutes went by before he moved the cart over to the soup kettle and helped one of the women load it. They put bowls, a large jug of liquid, and the kettle into the cart and started back down the road. Raven picked up on how the demeanor of Miss Martha had changed when this elderly man had stopped by, so she added it to the stockpile of information she was collecting in her mind.

"Break time," yelled Miss Martha sternly, as she walked over to the water ladle and took a drink from a water barrel, "Make the most of it." Raven stood up and went over and got herself a drink from the barrel with Betsy right behind her. "Sit over there in the shade of that tree," whispered Betsy, as she kind of pointed with a nod of her head, "and keep your head down when you talk so no one can read your lips. There are women in here who would rat on you in a heartbeat if it meant extra rations."

Raven sat down on the ground in the shade of the tree with Betsy close to her.

"That's Marquese. He's been here a long time, and I think he was part of the group that originally took over the town. He and Lester are in charge of our group, and they take turns watching our cabin."

"So this town was built by miners, not these guys?"

"Pretty much, I don't know the whole story, but around ten or twelve years ago, Captain Bleeker found this place. Back then it was being run by a bunch of Irish miners and they had found a good pocket of gold. The captain and his group came in one night and killed about half of them and made the rest slaves to work the mines. The Captain is a shrewd man and he doesn't blink an eye at having someone tortured or even killed. This place is filled with old, abandoned mine shafts that go nowhere. When we go to the pond to bathe, keep an eye out and you will see a couple."

"Shhh, here comes Martha."

As Miss Martha was making her way over to the two women, her slight limp and larger-than-normal ankle were very noticeable. Just as she got even with the two women, she turned and walked over to the edge of the stone building where, for the first time, Raven saw a young boy probably eight to ten years old standing there holding a box trap, the kind meant for capture versus killing. Martha talked to him for a couple of minutes, then turned and walked to the front of the counter where she had started.

"That was close. You don't want her hearing your conversation. She has had women beat for what they talked about."

"Who's the boy?"

"I don't know much about him, he talks to Martha once in a while, but he seems to come and go as he pleases around here. They call him Link, but I haven't really ever seen him talk, probably can, but I never seen him do it if he does."

"Okay, ladies, get back to work; break is over."

With that, Raven and Betsy got up and headed back to their tasks. For the rest of the day they worked with their heads down and didn't talk, until Miss Martha finally called for dinnertime. Raven followed the other women over to the side of the stone building where a long table sat with bowls and mugs. One of the women who'd made the stew dished out an equal amount to each person as she worked her way around the table. A second, older lady followed her and handed out bread. Raven sat down and noticed she was the smallest person at the table as Betsy leaned over. "Be careful of Allie." Allie had sat down beside her after she found a seat and was looking at her out of the corner of her eye.

Raven looked at Betsy and nodded.

The servers gave Betsy her food, then Raven, and finally Allie, as they continued around the table. Raven noticed Allie focusing on her bread. As soon as the server had her back turned, Allie made her move, grabbing for Raven's bread, just as Raven put her full weight into her elbow, hitting Allie in the stomach. A loud groan came out of Allie's mouth as she slumped in her chair, gasping for breath.

"Wow, you really popped her one; be careful, there's no telling what she will do. She's a little light in the head, if you know what I mean," whispered Betsy.

Allie began slowly eating, as she scowled at Raven periodically throughout the meal. Raven hadn't made a friend, but hopefully her actions had been enough to make the others respect her and leave her alone in the future. The march back to the cabin and the lockdown was done in an orderly fashion. Raven tried to notice every little thing as it happened, still storing information that might be useful in the future.

The start of the next day was like the first as Lester unlocked the door and all the women used the privy and marched down to the cooking shed. When the group got near to the man dangling from the chains, they could see he was no longer moaning nor asking for water. As they watched, the Indian they called Scar came out of nowhere and walked up to the dying man. In one swift motion, he took his round-bladed hatchet from his belt and with one powerful back stroke severed the man's head from his body. The cut was so clean and violent that the head just dropped to the ground and rolled a couple of feet, coming to rest against a small rock. Scar reached down, took the skull by the hair, and held it up for all to see as he stared at the women who continued walking down the road towards the bridge. Raven took a quick glance back and saw Scar carrying the skull towards the front gate and his hideous trophy field.

For the next three days, the routine didn't change. They marched every morning to the cooking shed to do the cooking, cleaning, and whatever else needed doing. It was on their walk back to the cabin on the third day when Raven noticed a sunken area twenty yards off the road, bordering the cliff and overlooking the river. As they walked, she looked at Betsy and pointed.

"Don't ask you don't want to know. You will find out soon enough that there isn't anything good about that place."

As they marched along, the young boy Link crossed in front of the troop, carrying a large, dirty sack that moved as he walked. Certainly there was something alive in there, and Raven guessed it might be chickens, but she really had no idea. He didn't even look at the women as he crossed their path and headed towards the bridge. As he passed, Raven noticed the dark bruises on his small body and could only wonder how he survived in this place.

That night she quietly lay in the hay and thought of all she had heard and seen, but nothing in her mind led to an escape. From the way nature had formed this place and how the guards watched every entrance and patrolled the grounds, she could tell escaping would be a near impossibility. Finally she rolled over and wondered what her life would have been if this hadn't happened to her.

She wondered if she would someday find a tall, strong man like the one she had seen on the attorney's porch. He had been so tall and handsome, and carried himself with confidence. Down deep, it amazed her that she fanaticized about a man she had never really ever met, whose name she didn't even know, but there was little else to do if she was to keep her sanity.

The next four days were similar to the rest, with Raven trying to absorb every bit of information she could as she watched and analyzed what was going on. On the fifth day as the group walked onto the bridge, the ground began to shake violently, and Raven was thrown against the bridge's log rail, almost falling over the edge. When the shaking stopped, she was beside Betsy and one of the other women.

"What in the hell was that?" asked Raven, as she looked at Betsy with wide eyes.

"It happens here about once every six months. The whole ground shakes, but it usually doesn't last much more than a minute or so. At times it can really get to shaking. I hope none of the men in the mine died."

"There are men in a mine right now?"

"Yeah, I would guess so. We don't see them often, but I know they are there. That's who we make the food for every day, them and the guards and the women for sale."

"Quiet down now, no more talking. Now get to your feet and let's get our jobs done," barked Martha as she struggled to stand up.

"Just a little shake, nothing we aren't use to, now fall in."

For the rest of the day Raven didn't get close enough to Betsy to ask her who the women for sale were. That was the first she had heard of them, and down deep she wondered if Elsie could possibly be with them. Every day she tried to get more information that would help piece together where she was and how to get out of there, but the scraps of information came slowly at best.

That evening as they marched the women back to the cabin, Raven could feel the change of season. It was no secret that it was getting cooler every day. The lone lantern cast its light around the dimly lit room as the women entered the cabin and walked towards their respective spots. Someone had started a small fire in the potbelly stove in the corner, and the small amount of heat it put off felt good coming out of the cold.

Miss Martha was bending over Betsy's ankle, trying to chain her to the wall for the night, when Allie charged from the shadows with a large chunk of wood in her hand. She struck Martha on the back, who moaned as she fell to the ground in pain. Raven had not been chained yet, so she jumped to her feet and grabbed Allie's arm so she could not hit Martha again. For several minutes they wrestled on the ground with everyone else chained to the wall, while Martha writhed in pain on the floor. Allie was larger than Raven, and more powerful. She broke free and raised the chunk of wood, ready to swing with all her might. Raven rolled at the last minute, and the blow hit the hard dirt, dislodging the wood from her grip. Raven turned quickly and put everything she had into a punch that sent Allie stumbling back onto the floor. She then jumped on top of Allie, pinning her arm, and hit her again.

Allie's body went limp and her face rolled to one side as Raven took a couple of deep breaths before dragging Allie over to her place in the cabin. As she picked up the shackle, Raven saw a small piece of wood jammed into the lock. In the poorly lit room, it had gone unnoticed. She would remember this trick and use it, if needed. After cleaning the lock, she dragged Allie closer to her spot on the wall and shackled her using Miss Martha's key. The fight had taken everything out of her, and she crawled back to her spot and collapsed beside Betsy.

"You okay? Allie could have killed you both."

"Yeah, I am just feeling a bit beat up. How's Miss Martha?" Betsy leaned over towards Miss Martha, "You all right?"

"Yeah, yeah, I'm all right. What the hell happened?"

Betsy explained to Martha the best she could what had transpired as Raven just lay on her back and looked at the ceiling, trying to keep her own pain in check. She hadn't broken anything, but she knew she didn't have many more battles like that left in her.

The next morning came quickly, so when the door to their cabin was unlocked from the outside, Martha was slow to get up. Curiously she didn't say anything out of the ordinary about the night before. Why she didn't have the guards take Allie away and punish her was a mystery to Raven and out of character for Miss Martha.

As the troop finished using the outhouses, they lined up as they typically did. Martha was limping as they marched down the road. The women were almost to the bridge when Allie screamed and started running towards the river and the edge of the tall cliff. One of the other women tried to tackle her, but Allie's speed was surprisingly fast as she dashed between the buildings before she stopped at edge of the cliff. At that point she stared back at the women for a moment and then turned and stepped off into the air. She never screamed or yelled; she just fell out of sight onto the rocks far below.

Most just stared, but a few put their heads in their laps and moaned for the longest time before Miss Martha, in a much softer tone, ordered everyone to continue to their stations. People went to their workstations and began their labor, but nobody felt right or remained untouched by the ordeal. The look of suffering at what had just happened was on each woman's face. Martha sat on a stool by one of the tables and stared out towards the river. Her blank expression and stare said it all: this truly was hell, and Raven was in it.

That evening back in the cabin, no one spoke of what had happened, no one even whispered.

For the next few days, things went on as usual. Raven continued to study every aspect of the small settlement, including the times the guards patrolled the grounds. She was deep in thought when a voice brought her back to reality.

"You know no one has ever escaped from here. That trophy field of skulls shows you how many have tried and failed. That Indian, Scar, enjoys torturing and killing people. That preacher man that you knew, he was probably a good man but he couldn't take it any longer. He chose to try to escape and they caught him just like everyone else who has tried. Raven, this place is impossible to escape from. You just got to make the best of it. I see how you stare when the guards go by. Hell, maybe the Army or someone like that will come in here someday, but for now we just got to keep our heads down and survive."

Raven just looked back at Betsy and in a stern voice said, "I knew that man. He was the pastor on our wagon train, and he was a good man. I will never quit trying to escape; there has to be a way, and I will find it."

"Then take me with you."

"I will if I can, but we will probably die trying just like the rest of the poor bastards in Scar's cemetery. Haven't any trappers or settlers ever found this place?"

"On occasion they do. If it is a small group, the Indians usually just take care of them and bring them in over their saddles. When a larger group finds this place, they are welcomed into camp and given food and as much whiskey as they can drink. Later, the Indians kill them or capture them for slaves."

With that, Raven rolled over and hid her face in the dry grass of her bed as a few tears ran down her face, the first in quite a while.

The next couple of days went like most, and Raven saw nothing that made it seem that escape was even possible. On one side of the camp was an almost sheer cliff that rose up for over a hundred feet almost straight up, impossible for anyone to climb. On the other side was a steep cliff, made of loose rock that ran all the way down to the river. She had noticed several places where a person might work his way down through the rock for at least a ways, but even if he did make it to the river, there was open country, so the guards on their horses would easily catch them within hours.

From what she had seen, the river ran shallow, and there was no way to ride a log, and there were no canoes to steal. The guards at the gate checked everyone going in or out of the camp, and the entrance was always well-guarded. Even if she could get past the guards, the road led to some extremely tough country for a getaway. No, the escape would have to be something no one has ever thought of before and it needs to supply them with at least a two days head start.

When Raven awoke, she could hear the soft sound of rain hitting the cabin's roof as the women began getting up and Lester unlocked the door to the cabin. Marquese usually opened the door in the morning, then Miss Martha would unlock the women, but about once a week Lester would do it. Lester was a gross man, overweight and dirty, and smelled terribly even in a camp where everyone smelled bad. He chewed, and the dribble stains of tobacco were always present on the corners of his mouth. Several times Miss Martha had backed the man away when he'd tried to take advantage of the women. It had been he and another man who had taken Allie and abused her several times when Marquese wasn't in camp and not able to help.

The women had used the outhouses and were almost to the cooking shed when Link came running out from behind the building and ran right into Raven as he looked back. As the two of them stumbled to the ground, Raven looked up to see Scar standing over them. Slowly he removed his hatchet from the waistband as he stared at Link with rage in his eyes. When Scar raised the hatchet and started to swing it at Link, Raven kicked his leg with all her strength, causing the hatchet to strike harmlessly to one side as Link rolled and took off running into the trees.

There was nothing but anger and hatred in Scar's eyes as he stood up and looked for a moment at Raven through his eyes of evil as she lay on the ground. The kick had been her first instinct, and now she would pay the penalty for her spontaneous reaction. Scar stood over Raven, enjoying the moment with an evil smile on his face as he slowly lifted his hatchet for the final strike.

"Stop!" yelled a man in a loud and commanding voice. Raven turned and saw a man riding across the bridge on his horse. It was Captain Bleeker.

"Black Elk, don't kill her! Let the Pit decide her fate."

Scar, his body alive with hatred, looked up at the man on the horse. Several seconds went by before he forcefully shoved the long wooden handle of the hatchet back into his buckskin belt. As Scar turned, he lashed out with a surprisingly quick kick to Raven's thigh that violently rolled her several feet across the ground, then he walked away.

The brutal force of the blow could be heard by those close by, Raven moaned from the pain. Betsy and several of the women dropped to their knees beside Raven, trying to comfort her.

"Help her up and get to work," ordered the Captain in a hard voice.

No longer did Captain Bleeker have the trustworthy face of a wagon master; now his stoic, bronze face and his stone-cold eyes showed a totally different person.

"I probably should've let Scar kill you, as much trouble as you have been, Raven. Yes, I remember your name. You probably thought you'd almost made it before Scar caught you."

He sat back on his horse, rolled a cigarette with one hand, and sealed it with his lips as he slumped into the saddle like he wanted to be more comfortable.

"Nobody has ever escaped from here, and we certainly weren't going to let some sawed-off girl be the first. I hope Scar didn't hurt you too bad. It would be a shame if you couldn't walk well at the Gathering, I wouldn't want the competition to be unfair."

Raven just held a solid stare towards the Captain, trying not to give in to the severe pain that throbbed in her thigh.

Captain Bleeker glanced over at Marquese and then sat back on his horse and rubbed his gray beard before yanking on one of the reins of his line-back buckskin walking it up towards the gate.

With the help of Betsy and another one of the women, they moved Raven over into the shade and helped her lie down. Miss Martha sent one of the women to the creek to get some cold water on a towel and then ordered everyone else back to work. All the other women, including Betsy, were now busy at work, and Miss Martha helped make Raven more comfortable as she sat down beside her.

"You didn't have to do that today. You were lucky. When Scar starts a kill he usually finishes it. Unfortunately, I think Bleeker must want to see you suffer more in the Pit."

Chapter 13

It was several minutes later when Miss Martha got up from Raven's side and headed over to some trees where Marquese had watched the proceeding and now stood back smoking a pipe. They talked for at least ten minutes before Miss Martha returned and got Raven a cup of water from the barrel.

"You just rest for the rest of today; you have been through way too much. Hopefully the cold water is helping. Later we will wrap your leg before we walk back to the cabin. Don't show your weakness; it could cost you your life."

With Allie gone, the small group had to work a little harder to keep up, so after lunch Raven limped over to where one of the women was cutting up an elk and sat down where she could contribute.

It was almost time to march back to the cabin when Marquese walked over and talked to Miss Martha. Marquese had thick, matted gray hair and a nose that was beak shaped. His fragile-looking body was really showing his age.

"Marquese says tomorrow is bath day," said Miss Martha. With that, there was a quiet cheer and smiles swept over everyone's face. Raven saw Betsy walking nearby and motioned her over. "What's bath day?"

"Down the road there's a hot spring at the base of the mountain that they built a building over, and it has a deep pool of fresh, hot water that comes up from the ground. They let us go there every ten to fifteen days. It is the best thing that happens here. I am sure your leg will appreciate it."

"Are there a lot of hot springs here?"

"I really don't know for sure, but this is the only one I know about. The place is honeycombed with mines and caves probably created by underground water, and it would be my guess that there are probably a few more at least. It's hard to tell because they got most of the abandoned mines boarded off so the livestock don't fall in them, that and we really never get close enough to them to take a look. Besides, you don't want to stumble into the one where they keep the snakes."

"Snakes, why do they keep snakes?"

Betsy just looked at her a moment and turned, "I've got to go before Miss Martha gets on me."

Raven just sat and stared at the cliffs behind her. If only she could figure out a way to escape, but she knew that wouldn't be the way. Just as she started to turn away, something caught her eye high up above the cliff. It was white, and she was sure it was a mountain goat. She had not seen many mountain goats, but when she was with the wagon train, one of the men had pointed a couple out and tried to hunt them, but to no avail.

How that animal had gotten up on what she'd thought was a sheer cliff, she hadn't a clue. For the next hour, Raven slowly cut strips of meat off the hanging elk, never letting the white speck on the hillside move without her noticing its location. The goat seemed to be following a trail, invisible at this distance, and working its way down the mountain. Then it disappeared behind a large rock shelf. She had picked up some information that might be useful, but if there was no way to ever reach the small trail, it would be worthless to know.

The walk back to the cabin was more than difficult, so Betsy took her arm and draped it over her shoulder, trying to take as much weight off the leg as possible. It seemed like forever before the group made its way back to the cabin. The two women sat down on their beds beside each other as Miss Martha lit the kerosene lantern.

"Betsy, I want you to change beds with me for a while."

"But why?" asked Betsy.

"It is none of your business, and if you question my authority, I am sure one of the men can work that out of you, now move!"

Several minutes later, Miss Martha carefully checked all the leg irons of the women before blowing out the lantern and lying down beside Raven. Raven thought it was strange that all of a sudden Miss Martha would change places in the cabin, and she wondered if it had anything to do with what had happened that day.

As she lay in her bed of grass, her leg ached, but she thought of Elsie and wondered if she was being held or was dead. Later her mind wandered once again to the cowboy she had seen at the attorney's office and how handsome he'd been with his wide shoulders and tall, powerful body. She wondered if she would ever leave this place alive now that she had angered Scar even more than he already had been. All these things weighed heavily on her mind, until exhausted, she fell into a deep sleep.

Raven didn't know how long she had been asleep when a hand covered her mouth and someone gently shook her awake. "Be quiet, and get up. I don't want anyone to wake up," whispered a voice that Raven recognized as Miss Martha's. Raven sat up, and she could feel that her shackle had been removed.

The door was slightly ajar, and the light of a full moon had crept in through the doorway. It took a minute to adjust her eyes to the low light and then, with effort, she raised her stiff body to her feet and followed Miss Martha outside. They walked at least thirty yards before Miss Martha steered her into a dark clump of trees. Raven's mind was racing with what would happen next. She knew her leg was in no shape to run, but if she could run, where would she go?

She could see the shape of another person standing under the tree, and when he spoke she knew it was Marquese.

"Keep very quiet," he whispered in his heavy French accent. "The guards will be back past here in another twenty minutes or so."

"What's this all about?" asked Raven quietly, "Are you going to hurt me?"

"No dear, we aren't going to hurt you; on the contrary, you are in great danger and we want to help you. In less than three weeks the Gathering starts, and then the Pit fights."

"What's the Gathering?"

"When I was captured, I really got beat up; like you, I was swollen and didn't look like much, so they put me here in the women's work cabin. What I didn't know is, if I had been beautiful, they would have taken me to another cabin far different. There is another cabin down the road that is nicknamed the Queen's Cabin, and that is where they take the prettier women. These women are not mistreated or worked hard. They are kept soft and pretty, and no one is allowed to put a hand on them. They are the women of the sale."

"What sale?"

"It used to be far bigger than it is now. Men from all over the West, hard, cold men of little conscience, some from as far away as the Canadian

Territory, and even some from Mexico Territory, would make the trip for the Gathering. There is much whiskey and partying and this goes on for several weeks."

"Later in the Gathering, the pampered women are sold as servants, slaves, and even worse, to cheap mining town whorehouses. They never return. Years ago, there were twice as many women, and twice as many men coming to the Gathering, but what you need to know now is that a big part of the whole thing is the entertainment these men get from the Pit matches."

Raven stared at the two of them for a moment before speaking. "So why are you telling me this?"

"Because we don't want you to die."

"Why do you care?"

"We can't tell you right now, but we want to help you. Have you ever used a knife?"

"Some. My father and I would have competitions after dinner with all the kids, and we would throw knives a couple times a week back home. I wasn't bad, and sometimes I even won."

"When Captain Bleeker sentenced you to the Pit, he didn't do you any favors; most people don't survive the experience."

"What's the Pit? Is that the sunken triangle of logs you can kind of see from the bridge?"

"Yes, the Pit is where the Captain has his contests and what everyone comes to see. Three people are in the Pit at a time, and they are each chained to one of the three corners of the triangle. A long chain is spiked into a log just in front of each corner, and the other end is shackled to a prisoner. The chain is nine feet long, and each chain overlaps the center by a couple of feet. Each prisoner is given a weapon, usually a knife of their choosing, and then they are made to fight to the death. Half the time all three die in the Pit, but sometimes one person wins and is allowed to go back and continue working here."

"Not much of a prize for winning."

"I know it's a sick idea of sport. If possible, we want to help you survive, teach you how to work with a knife, and let you know some of the tricks of the Pit. Hopefully we will find enough time to practice and not raise suspicion as to what we are doing. Tomorrow is bath day, but we want you to lag behind with Miss Martha, and she will take a minute and show you the Pit up close, if I can distract the ladies and any guards that may be wandering by."

"You'll need to know what you are up against. We have watched the Pit fights for years, and most of the people that are forced to fight have no idea what is happening; that will be your edge. Now we need to get you back to the cabin, and if anyone asks you anything about this night, it will be in your best interest not to talk. Keep your mouth shut and maybe we can save your life."

With that, Miss Martha motioned for silence by putting her finger to her lips, turned, and led the way back to the cabin. Raven slowly sat down on the thick bed of grass as she heard the quiet click of the outside lock on the door. She stared at the pitch-black ceiling, wondering what had just happened and what she was up against.

The light of morning came too quickly for Raven as her painfully stiff leg made standing a struggle. After everyone had used the privy, Miss Martha walked up to Betsy.

"I want you to lead the ladies to work today. I am going to take it a little slower to help Raven. I want you to make sure the women go straight to work just as if I were there. Got it?"

Betsy just nodded, shocked by her newfound responsibility, and began getting the women in order to march. Raven thought to herself how much this place was run like the military and maybe Bleeker really had been a captain in the Army, a strong clue to who he really might be, which would be useful if she ever got out of here.

Miss Martha looked at Raven and whispered, "Now try to take it slow, I want the women to get out ahead of us and begin working before we reach the bridge. Then I want you to stumble and fall to the ground when I tell you, and we will both take a good look around to see if anyone is watching before we head over and look at the Pit. You understand?"

Raven just nodded her head and the two began their slow march towards the cooking shed. The rest of the women were at their workstations when Miss Martha and Raven came close to the bridge and when Miss Martha whispered, "Fall!" Raven fell to the ground on cue.

"Damn, that really did hurt."

"Quit your moaning, and let's go over closer to the Pit so I can explain a few things." They moved to within a couple yards of the edge, and Miss Martha bent down.

"Now pay attention. There is no way you can get away from the fight. The walls are four feet tall, and if you tried to get out, one of Bleeker's men would show you their boot, so don't try. It usually takes the prisoners several minutes to figure out what they can and can't do on the chain, and that is when you will be at an advantage. We have another trick up our sleeve that we plan to use, but we will talk later on that. Tomorrow I am leaving you in the cabin all day to rest; I would have done that today, but the hot water probably will do you good. From what I can see, that bruise is pretty black, it must be real painful."

"I'll live, just keep talking."

"Each contestant climbs down a ladder and is shackled to the chain on their corner log, and before anything starts, the ladder will be pulled out. For the next couple of minutes, Captain Bleeker will say the rules, but that's for show mostly; what it really amounts to is there are no rules. Then Bleeker shoots his pistol in the air and the match begins. Now let me help you back up and we'll get to the workstations. In about an hour, we will be hiking to the bathhouse and I will have a couple of the women help you."

"Can you please make Betsy one of them?"

"Yes, but it is dangerous to get to close to anyone in here. Remember, no one must know that Marquese and I are helping you."

It was closer to two hours later when Marquese walked over to Miss Martha and quietly discussed something with her, then left, his gun slung over his shoulder.

"Okay, ladies, let's form up and head to bathhouse. Betsy, you and one of the other women help Raven."

Just as Miss Martha gave the command to march, she stopped in her tracks and looked north towards the entrance gates. The sound of hooves crossing the bridge broke the silence as a man rode his horse and led another over the bridge and then up beside them. He pulled the reins of his stout buckskin to a stop, and both horses stood still, with the bloody body of a man tied to the saddle of the second horse.

The bearded man sitting on the horse locked eyes on something, and Raven turned to see Marquese coming out of the trees towards them. Raven recognized the riding man as a Frenchman that sometimes walked the road on guard duty but it was impossible to recognize the other man from the blood and the fact that his face was obscured by the side of his horse.

Marquese and the man on horseback spoke for a minute and all Raven could pick up from the conversation was that the wounded man had been attacked. He was someone she didn't know. With that, the rider gently drove his boots into his horse and they continued down the road.

Raven turned to Betsy. "What was that all about?"

"I understand a little French, but not enough to know for sure what they said; something about a large cat, but other than that I don't know." Raven thought to herself that she would ask Marquese later if she got the opportunity.

The sight of the body put a damper on the mood of the women as they formed ranks and headed down the road into an area Raven had never seen before, whispering about what might have happened to the man.

From a distance she had seen the teepees of the small camp of Blackfoot that lived in the compound, but this new site was interesting, a combination of teepees and flat-roofed log cabins. She glanced to her left, trying to absorb everything, and then to her right, where she saw a large log building with bars on its only two windows.

"What's that building?" she whispered to Betsy.

"That's where they keep the miners and other prisoners. Most of them are half starved and need medical help; pretty poor conditions for a man to survive in. It's no wonder they try to escape, but with those cliffs on both sides and trappers and Indians to track them, if they do somehow find a way out of here, they don't have much of a chance."

They continued on by a large building that Betsy whispered was a food storage building and then onto a gravel trail that meandered in front of ten to twelve wagons that sat in storage in the open grass. A goat picketed to one of their wheels was nibbling some grass.

"I can smell sulfur," said Raven.

"Yeah, the place isn't the best smelling you ever visited, but the hot water sure feels good, and a bath, even better. It's the only luxury this place has to offer, and it's none too great."

The hot springs was located in a building that appeared to be about twelve by twelve and had open windows. Inside was a large pool of water with rocks strategically placed so at least ten people could use the water at the same time. A small stream flowed out of the pool and worked its way down several feet to a small creek bed that headed towards the cliff by the river. The boards were all roughly cut and placed, and none of the craftsmanship Raven had seen throughout the rest of the camp existed here. The hot water felt like heaven on her badly bruised thigh as she lay in the water ignoring the foul smell that permeated the place.

She was totally relaxed when she felt something touch her arm.

"Raven, I saw you leave with Miss Martha last night, what's going on?" asked Betsy into Raven's ear.

"I swore I wouldn't say. I can't tell you anything." "Okay, but know one thing: if you figure a way out of this hellhole, I want to go with you no matter the odds, even if I could lose my life. If I stay much longer in this hellhole I am going to die anyway or run afoul of Bleeker or one of his men."

The next hour went by quickly, and it seemed like they had only just sat down in the hot water when Miss Martha ordered everyone to put their clothes on and get ready to head back to the cooking shed to prepare the meal for everyone's dinner. The march back was far less painful for Raven. She found a spot by an elk carcass and began cutting long, narrow strips of meat off one of the elk's hindquarters. The mature elk had a nice set of antlers, and one woman was sawing them off to later be used to make knife handles for the blacksmith shop.

After dinner was served and eaten, and cleanup was done, the group marched back to the cabin for the night. Upon entering, everyone was thrilled to see their winter buffalo hides lying on their beds of grass. The thick Buffalo hides made the nights much warmer. The hides were collected every summer, and every year about this time they were brought back in and distributed to the prisoners. Some winters had been so cold that they could only survive with a fire and a blanket, and lots of times they wore the hides during the day to keep warm.

Raven was sound asleep when she felt someone touch her arm. She looked up to Miss Martha motioning her to follow. Looking down, she noticed her shackle had already been undone. Carefully and quietly, she stood up and followed Miss Martha through the cracked door out into the dark streets lit only by the shine of a half moon.

Marquese sat under the same tree that Miss Martha had led her to before, holding a small chunk of rope in his hands.

Raven had to pay close attention as he spoke, because his thick accent was sometimes hard to understand. "This rope is nine feet long, just like what you will have in the Pit. Tie one end to your ankle, and the other I will tie to this spike in the log. Feel how long it is and know your reach. Miss Martha has tied her ankle to another log so, hopefully, you can see and feel." Miss Martha stretched the rope over to Raven, and Raven walked past her about two feet.

"Now reach out and swing your arm like you have a knife and work it back and forth until you know where the end will be."

"Marquese, will I be fighting other women?"

"You never know until the day of the competition. Captain Bleeker can be very unpredictable. A lot depends on whether he wants someone dead or how many people have not followed his orders. I have seen him put his own men in the Pit if they didn't follow an order. He is a very hard, cruel man, and not one to be messed with."

For over an hour Raven worked hard, ignoring her sore leg so she could learn how the nine feet felt and figure out how she could maneuver into the "killing space", as Marquese called it.

"That is enough for tonight; now go get some sleep. We won't work on this tomorrow to give your leg some rest, but we will work longer the following night. You have little time, and we must have you ready."

Two nights later the three met again outside in the shadows. "What happened to the man that they brought in over his saddle a couple of days ago?" asked Raven.

"From what I've heard, he was killed by a mountain lion, a big one. He and his hunting companion had separated when he heard a scream and a shot. By the time he could cover the couple hundred yards to the fellow, he was dead, tore to ribbons by the big cat, and then it disappeared. Couldn't find hardly a track, got the camp hunters a little spooked. But enough of that, we got our own problems, and we have a long ways to go and a short time to get there."

Into the late hours of the night Raven worked on the rope, trying to grasp the distance of the chain, nine feet to the inch, as she practiced her stance and thrusts.

The following night Marquese handed her a knife about twelve inches long. "Ever use one of these?"

"A Bowie knife, no, I know what they are, but I have not ever used one."

"God help us, because that is what you will probably be armed with in the Pit."

"Can you throw it? See that tree over there? Can you hit it?"

Raven took the blade in her hand and tried her best to throw it at the tree but missed. "This could be a problem," said Marquese as he gave Miss Martha a questioning glance.

"I'm fairly decent with a smaller knife, you know, the size of a throwing knife."

"Wait here. I have a smaller knife in my room; I will get it and be right back. Keep an eye out for the guards." Raven went back to thrusting and practicing the art of knowing the length of nine feet.

Minutes later Marquese returned and handed Raven a much shorter and more slender knife, which she took and sized up the weight.

"Now see if you can hit that tree. You never know how the fight will go, and being able to throw would be an advantage."

"So what do you want me to aim at?"

"Just throw at the pine tree; it's about the width of a man."

"See that light spot in the bark that is about two inches wide, that spot where it looks like someone hit it with something in the past?"

"Yes, I see it, but I'll just try and hit the tree."

With that, Raven took the end of the blade between her thumb and forefinger, turned, and flung the knife in one graceful movement. The knife hit the exact middle of the scar in the bark.

"Nice throwing! Where did you learn to throw like that?"

"My pa taught me. My brothers and sisters would have tournaments after dinner, and sometimes I won."

"That's a talent that you may need; I will do my best to try and get you a smaller knife like this one for the Pit."

It was getting late when Marquese stopped the practice session and asked Raven to come sit beside him and Miss Martha.

Miss Martha realigned herself on the logs before she spoke. "I am sure you are wondering why we are helping you. We may have found a way out for you," Martha paused, "and someone else, but you will have to win your match first for our plan to work. Marquese has heard rumors, and well, we think they may be true."

"What rumors?"

"We can't tell you yet, but we will in good time. In the next couple of weeks, men will start arriving for the Gathering and then the Pit fights will begin soon after. This is a tough time, and many mean, hard men will be drinking, fighting, and having their idea of fun. At the same time, Captain Bleeker will try to keep them in line until after the sale." He paused. "But that doesn't always happen. We can't tell you when it will be your turn; they will come for you and put you in chains about an hour before your fight. You have to be strong and believe, if you are to win. There is a chance we may make some things happen before you fight, but there is only a small chance."

"You must remember, if you fight in the Pit your only chance of escaping, or even living, is to win. We just won't know when your turn will come up, but I will try to find out the schedule; the later your match, the better. Each night it seems everyone gets drunker and more rowdy than the night before, and we want those men sleeping like babies when it's time to go. Now listen and listen good, from now on you want to look as dirty and unattractive as possible. We don't want you to draw any attention to yourself. Tomorrow we talk about the snakes." "Snakes, what about snakes?"

"We will talk tomorrow; we still have many things to tell you. Now it is time for you to get back to the cabin before we are noticed."

Chapter 14

The next night Martha had to shake Raven harder than usual to get her awake. She was suffering from lack of sleep and the energy expended to heal her injuries. The soreness was beginning to go away as she walked towards the shadows where her training usually took place. Raven followed Miss Martha behind the building into the trees where a full moon lit the area more than normal. Marquese was sitting on the log he customarily used, and upon their arrival, stood up.

"I am going to stand watch out by the road with this extra light. I don't want anyone surprising us. Miss Martha can tell you as much as I can, especially about the snakes."

Raven turned to Miss Martha, and she motioned her over to sit on the log again. Miss Martha looked down for a moment, and then began, "At the end of each triangle, where the prisoner's chain is spiked into the log, is a small triangle that is only about two and a half feet wide. Several hours before the match starts, Link will put about six rattlesnakes in each corner and cover them with a triangle-shaped board."

"Why Link?"

"He is in charge of the snakes and has been for a year or so, since the last snake man was killed. The man wasn't cautious enough when he entered the cave. One of the bigger rattlers had somehow worked its way up onto a small ledge just above the heavy wooden door that seals the cave. When he entered the shaft, the snake dropped down on him and bit him in the neck. He only made it forty feet out into the women's work area before he dropped to the ground dead. No one wanted the job after that, and since Link was in charge of live trapping small game like squirrels and mice, Captain Bleeker made him keeper of the snakes, a dubious honor at best. That's why he gets the run of the place; he sets traps all over camp for the snakes."

"So Link brings these snakes in and puts them in each corner of the Pit. What next?"

"At first, nothing but when the matches begin, Captain Bleeker normally sits on a platform above the Pit about six feet in the air. Next, each prisoner is led down the ladder into the Pit and made to go to his corner where the blacksmith puts the shackle on. Shortly after that, a man gets in the Pit with them and someone passes a tray with a dozen knives or more down to him. Each prisoner is to take one knife of his choice and then go back to his corner. That is when Captain Bleeker explains the rules."

"What are the rules?"

"They are really not much. He talks about a fight to the death and only one person will be allowed to leave when the other two opponents are dead. Basically, you fight to survive, because there really aren't any rules once the Captain shoots his pistol and the match begins, it's every man for himself. Hopefully, if you are lucky, it will be other women that they have chosen for your match and you will have a chance."

"You don't sound very positive."

"I don't want you to go into this without the right frame of mind. Let's just hope that you are one of the later matches and we can get you out of here before you have to face it. We need to train as if you are actually going to fight, and that is just what I plan to do. Now start practicing your footwork."

The next day the women assembled and began marching to the cooking shed, with Miss Martha walking beside Raven. As they started across the bridge, Raven noticed Link standing in the trees with a small bag that periodically moved like something was in the bottom. She knew better than to ask questions of Miss Martha as they marched, but she was curious about the small pouch that Link had tucked beneath his belt. She had previously spotted Link, probably once every three or four days, silently moving through the trees and had wondered where he spent his nights. Now she wondered where the snake cave was. They were almost across the bridge when they heard the sound of horse hooves behind them, Raven turned to take a look. Three strong-looking men with four pack mules were coming up the road in single file, the last one lining out the mules. The last man was overweight and had a beard stained with heavy chewing tobacco. He smiled as he rode up near enough to the women that they felt they needed to take a step away from him.

Pulling a small bottle from under his shirt, he took a swig, and then hollered at the women, slurring his speech. "Hey, you bitches, Pierre is here now, and I will come see you later." He laughed as he tugged on the lead rope of the first mule, which had slowed to stare at the movement of the women.

"Well here's the first of them," said Miss Martha in a whisper, "be extra careful from now on." After the group of men had ridden past, the women continued over the bridge and returned to their workstations. Raven found herself peeling potatoes, with Betsy working on the same pile. Betsy just stared at her for the first few minutes, and Raven could tell she wanted to talk badly, but up until now there had been no opportunity. Eventually Miss Martha walked over to talk to Marquese, who was leaning against a thick Douglas fir, smoking a pipe.

"Raven," whispered Betsy, "I know you are up to something. I see you leaving in the middle of the night. I want you to take me with you; don't forget I need to go, too."

Raven just nodded and put her finger to her lips as she noticed one of the guards that periodically walked the road stare over in her direction. Raven put her head down and whispered, "We will talk later."

That night Raven was awake when Miss Martha touched her on the shoulder and motioned for her to follow. For the first thirty minutes they worked on her footwork, as her mind began to instinctively know the length of nine feet as she lunged forward and back.

"Okay, take a break over here so we can talk quietly."

Raven caught her and then asked, "What is that pouch that Link carries under his belt?"

"Well, it really is none of our business, but from what I know it has four or five special things that Link has somehow found. The poor kid never had a fair start, growing up in this hellhole. I have always lived with the saying that life is not fair, and that kid has gotten every inch of the bad luck that is out there. It's a miracle that the kid is still alive. Thank God he isn't afraid of snakes or he would have probably died last year when we were short on food."

"The only wagon train they got didn't have much provisions and it didn't last through the winter. In one respect, we were lucky this year to capture your train. You all were carrying enough grain and other food to get us through this next winter. I know that is a terrible thing to say, but a lot of innocent prisoners will die here if there isn't anything to eat, and those are the people I see and know." She paused. "And feel for."

"How can you talk like that? He kills people, good people who the only thing they did wrong was to travel west to find a better life, and trust Captain Bleeker."

"We are not in control of anything; all we want to do here is survive."

The next day saw three more groups of men ride into the settlement with anticipation and smiles on their faces from having ended their journey. The day was quiet and Marquese never went far from the working women.

That night Marquese worked Raven harder than ever. "It's almost time, only a couple of groups have not arrived and they should be here soon. If by your bad luck you are chosen to fight first in the Pit, we can only pray that you will win. Then we will tell you our full plan. Raven, what is your full name?"

"Raven is a nickname my father gave me, but my real name is Rachael Dove."

"Raven Dove," Marquese said slowly, "do you understand that we are trusting you with our lives? If Captain Bleeker ever found out we were helping you, he would kill us immediately, or put us in the Pit. We are old and would not last long in the mines or their torture, either. What I am about to tell you could get more than us killed, but it is time."

"You know of the rattlesnakes; once in a while one of them finds its way out from its cave through passages in the rock. They usually don't go out except in the summer because it is too cool for them. Their cave is thermally active and it keeps the snakes warm. Link keeps them alive with water and food. It is only a matter of time before Link makes a mistake and is bitten by a snake. We have talked about helping Link escape when the men go down into the low valleys in the summer looking for more snakes. It is warm down there and the snakes are plentiful, and he would probably get a chance to run off, but we don't know if he could survive on his own."

"Why do you two care so much for Link?"

Marquese and Miss Martha exchanged glances until she spoke. "It's a long story, but when I first arrived here I was beaten up and scared. Marquese helped me and saved my life, and over time we fell in love. I knew my family was dead. I saw my husband's rifle on one of their packhorses while they were burning our cabin. I knew my life was gone, at least the life I had known. My father had arranged my marriage to my husband, and he was a good man, but I never really loved him, at least not like you dream of loving your husband."

"Somehow we have been able to keep our love a secret for years. I am sure some suspect it, but no one knows for sure. During that time, the Captain was gone a lot, and I think he lost track of time and just thought I must have been pregnant when they captured me or that one of the men raped me. Leastwise, no one ever asked the question."

"You mean Link is your son?"

Several large tears streamed down Miss Martha's face as she half smiled. "Yes, he is our son and he is a good boy that doesn't deserve this life of hell." Martha was silent for a moment and stared at the ground. "It is time to take you back; we will work more on things tomorrow night."

Back at the cabin, Raven stared at the ceiling. The thought of killing someone turned her stomach. She was no better than the prisoners she was to fight. How could she kill another person? The question kept floating around inside her head. For the next hour she lay there thinking and finally came to the conclusion that the only way she could ever kill someone was if they were like Captain Bleeker, a cold, hard murderer who cared little for anything besides money. The only way she could do this was trick herself into thinking that she was killing someone like Bleeker.

The squeak of the door and a burst of light awakened Raven from her sound sleep. She struggled to get up, but once on her feet the thigh felt good, better than it had for days. After she'd done her morning chores, the group marched to the cooking shed and began making breakfast for everyone in camp. Lester brought the wagon up and loaded a huge pot of stew to be taken to the cabin where all of the men and guests ate.

For lack of a better description, the wooden cart was not much more than two wooden wheels and a flat spot pulled by two handles. He would deliver this pot, and then be back for three more to go down to the miners, the ladies, and the building they used as a saloon. Lester was disgusting to look at and was always giving the women an unpleasant eye. Sometimes he would roll the tip of his tongue around his mouth in a repulsive manner. He was definitely one of the most revolting and nauseating people Raven had ever been around, and the thought of leaving, even possibly dying, was worth it if only to get away from this place and people like Lester. It was never too far from her mind what he and his accomplices had done to that poor girl Allie.

It was an hour after everyone had eaten when a small man with a thick, short beard rode up the road on a beautiful bay horse built for stout. It was the type of animal that a man would only wish for if he were in a chase. When he reached the cooking shed, he stopped and glanced over at the women.

"Any food left?" he hollered.

"Yes sir, would you care for a bowl of stew?"

"That I would, thanks."

He was a salty individual with a hard serious face. He stepped down from his stout paint horse and slid his rifle from its scabbard. Walking over to the table, he took a seat with his rifle beside him. He wore a tied-down revolver, the way professional gunmen did, and his salt and pepper hair and scars showed his age and travels. Seated with his back to the sun, his sour face and the snaky look of his eyes told you he was a man to be wary of. He took his time enjoying the stew before he stood up and reached for the reins of his ground tied horse.

"Thanks, I'll be seeing you ladies later," he said, with a slight smile as he stepped into the leather of the stirrup and mounted his horse. He nudged the horse's belly with his boot as they started walking down the road.

"Who was that?" Betsy asked one of the women who had been in camp for several years and was sitting next to Raven.

"That was Hamilton. Never heard a first name, but Hamilton is what he goes by. He is one mean man, and he mostly stays in the shadows. He is Captain Bleeker's second-in-command and he watches out for the Captain. If you challenge the Captain, you challenge Hamilton, and he has never lost a gunfight from what I have heard."

The rest of the day was fairly normal except for the steady coming and going of men walking up and down the streets. It was close to dinnertime when Betsy looked up.

"Well I'll be, would you look at this parade coming down the street."

"Quiet," ordered Miss Martha, "don't be talking unless you are spoken to, and keep your eyes on your work. Don't make eye contact with these men."

Down the road rode five men all in Mexican gear and wearing large sombreros. They were dusty, but their clothes were of exceptional quality, and it looked as if they had ridden a far piece. The men were heavily armed with pistols, rifles, and belts of ammunition crossing their chests. The last man led a string of three heavily burdened mules that were also larger and better than most. The leader rode a tall, golden Palomino that held its head high as it walked, as if it knew it was superior to the other horses.

This bronze-skinned man with boots of fine leather and a coat decorated with designs was clean shaven with a square build, and his face was seamed and lined by his years. He looked every bit a leader and a man of confidence and thought. As they rode by the women, the slightly built leader tipped his sombrero as the other men just stared forward and continued down the gravel road.

"Who in the hell was that?" asked Raven after they had passed.

"Keep your voice down. That, my dear, was Señor Ramón Gonzalez, one of the wealthiest and biggest ranchers in all of Mexico, and he is also one of the most corrupt, a man not to be taken lightly. This is becoming a very dangerous place; everyone needs to keep their eyes open and be cautious. Now get back to work; we have a lot of meals to fix, and we don't have a lot of time."

Raven helped Betsy cut up the deer the hunters had brought in.

That night, Miss Martha woke Raven as usual and led her out behind one of the buildings to their normal meeting place where Marquese sat on the log they had often talked on.

"We will not be practicing tonight. I think the matches will begin as soon as tomorrow. You will need your sleep. I think they will come for you in the afternoon; the Gathering is in full swing, and the Pit fights usually start within a day of when it starts." Marquese paused for a minute. "I am on guard tonight and tomorrow night. If we tried to escape either of these nights they would probably kill both Martha and me because they would think we helped you. The following night Lester will be on guard, and that is the night you and Link must escape. We have taken winter clothes and packed you food. I have even made you some moccasins for your journey. If everything goes well, they won't know until morning that you have gone, and by then, you should have a good head start. Remember to stick to the rocky slopes where horses cannot follow."

Miss Martha interrupted, "Raven, we did find out who fights first – it's you."

"Are you sure?"

"Yes, Marquese found out. We don't know who you will be fighting, but it will be men. Raven, you have good skills and are much smarter than these men. God and luck will protect you. He will be on your side and you will win. You have to believe that. It is becoming too dangerous for us to meet anymore. If everything goes as planned, in two nights we will come for you. Link and you will escape through a small passage in the mine Link found. That last earthquake we had must have opened it. It's very small, but you and Link will be able to crawl through it and hopefully escape."

"Since Link found it several weeks ago, he has taken salt up into the passageway and spread it outside the opening on a flat spot in hopes of bringing wild animals down the rocky slope, showing us a way up the mountain. He has not gotten very far on the trail the animals have made, but it will have to do. It should take them at least a day to figure out where you disappeared to and then get their horses down the valley and up the mountain. By then you must be far away, with few tracks to be found. We wish we could help more, but we will pray for you, your victory in the Pit, and your escape."

"Please treat Link well, he is a good boy and he needs to grow to manhood. I have heard rumors from one of the men that people are asking a lot of questions about the disappearing people and wagons, and I think Captain Bleeker might choose to abandon the camp if the Army comes looking. If he does this no one will be safe here in the future. Now listen well. On the night you escape from the cabin, I will unlock your shackle, and Marquese will sneak around and unlock the door. We will be sure to get Lester a bottle of good whiskey in the evening, so he shouldn't be any problem. I have put a letter and map in your backpack, and there is enough food for at least a week. Remember, they will be looking for you to travel east, so read the map and letter and figure out what you think will work for you two."

"Is there any way you can find out more about whom I am fighting?"

"No not really, they will bring the other two down about fifteen minutes before you three enter the Pit. There might be a chance we could tell you something then, but I am not sure that will help you."

"Now Martha needs to take you back, and God be with you."

"No not yet, I need to tell the two of you something. I want to take Betsy with us."

"That would be almost impossible. It will be hard enough to get the two of you out, much less three, and we haven't gotten any winter clothes or extra food for a third person."

"No matter if we don't have the extra food or clothes, I am not going without her. I promised her that and I am going to keep my promise."

"It is not a good decision on your part, but we will try. We hope it doesn't get you all killed."

With that, Miss Martha led Raven back to the cabin and quietly locked her shackle as Marquese set the lock on the outside of the door.

It was a cool night and Raven didn't sleep much as she tossed and turned on her bed of hay and grass, with her old buffalo hide as a blanket to keep her warm.

The next morning the women marched to the cooking shed and began preparing breakfast for all the guards, guests, and prisoners and loading them on the wagon to be taken to each cabin they used for eating. Martha looked over at Raven and hollered, "You and Betsy get a couple of pails each and go get some water on the stove to boil." She was giving Raven the opportunity to tell Betsy what they'd planned.

"Listen Betsy, after I win my Pit match, we are going to escape here. I have friends that are helping me."

"You mean Miss Martha is helping you?"

"Now be quiet and don't ask questions; just be ready when I tell you it's time to go. It will be hard and dangerous, and there is a good chance we won't make it. Hell, there is a good chance I won't even win in the Pit. Are you still sure you want to risk your life and go with us?"

"Us, who is us?"

"Link is going with us; he knows a secret way out."

"Damn tooting' I want to go! The only thing this place has to offer is death, and I would take my chances at anything versus staying here."

"Well then, you will get your chance. Just pray for me to win in the Pit; it could happen any time now."

It was several hours after lunch when Raven looked up and saw over forty men walking up the street. As they got closer, two of the guards she recognized broke from the group and walked over toward the women, focusing on Raven.

"Put your hands out in front of you," ordered the slender man who seemed to be in charge. Raven recognized him as one of the guards she had seen numerous times before. The sound of the shackles closing on her wrists told her the wait was over and soon she would experience what few people had lived through – the Pit.

As the two men escorted Raven towards the crowd of people standing near the Pit, the slender man turned and in an uncaring voice said, "Well, there is little hope for you in this. I don't know why they would match you with probably the two toughest prisoners at the Gathering. One of the men is a big, husky man that killed another miner with his bare hands, and the other one is a rogue guard that didn't follow Captain Bleeker's orders. The damn fool will pay for that, that's for sure. The Captain must really hate you to put you up against those two bastards."

The two men escorted Raven over to the edge of the Pit, and she could see her two opponents standing across from her. One had massive shoulders with thick, round arms and little fat on his body. He looked mean and mad, and he sneered at the crowd and the two guards that held each side of the chains that locked his wrists.

The other man was smaller, but well-chiseled. Raven recognized him as a man she had seen drunk and several times brawling with other men, a real troublemaker, and one who had probably pushed Captain's Bleeker's patience to its limit.

As they neared the edge of the Pit, Raven's handcuffs were removed and the guard motioned for her to climb down the ladder that stood on the edge of the log wall of the triangle. Raven recognized the blacksmith, who was waiting in the dirt of the Pit. After descending the ladder, she walked over to him and he proceeded to hammer a shackle above her ankle. After that, the two men climbed down other ladders, went to their corners, and had their shackles put on as they stared at each other and at Raven.

"Hey, little bitch, would you like a little swig of my whiskey for courage?" laughed a man behind Raven. She turned and stared at the man who had ridden in several days earlier leading a string of mules, as he drank from his bottle.

Raven nervously turned and scanned the crowd, seeing Captain Bleeker sitting in a comfortable-looking wooden chair on top of a platform six feet above the ground. He seemed to be enjoying the festivities as he scanned the crowd. Suddenly his eyes landed on Raven and their eyes met; his look was one of contempt and hatred, and he smiled for a moment, before turning and continuing to laugh and talk to his guests. Moments later, he stood up and shot his pistol in the air.

"Welcome, my friends, to the Gathering; many of you have traveled far to join us, and we appreciate your patronage." There was a cheer from the drunken crowd, and many men raised bottles and guns into the air as a wild salute. As the crowd settled down, Bleeker continued.

"We have a fine crop of women this year for sale, and tomorrow we will parade them for your inspection."

Raven scanned the area where the crowd was looking and, to her astonishment, saw Elsie all dressed up in a fancy dress with her hair all done up, in line with about twenty other women in similar attire. She was alive. A huge sigh of relief filled her for a moment, but Raven knew she had to stay focused as she turned and looked again at the crowd.

Another wild bunch of cheers went up, and laughing and talking drowned out Captain Bleeker as he tried to continue speaking. Raven saw the older Mexican known as Señor Gonzalez standing on the far side of the Pit's edge dressed in tight, tailored clothes with a pistol securely strapped to his side.

Finally the crowd calmed down enough that Captain Bleeker could continue. "Again, we welcome you, and now it is time for me to go over the rules of the Pit games. Most of you have been here before, but for our contestants, and those of you who are new, we will go over our rules again. The three prisoners in the Pit are shackled to a nine-foot chain that overlaps the center of the triangle by two feet. Now, if any of the prisoners tries to avoid the center, we will have a fun surprise for them," he laughed.

"I could give a little surprise to this little bitch right now," hollered the drunken muleskinner.

"No, we must make this a fair fight. Now let me proceed. Each prisoner will have his," he paused, "or her, choice of one knife from the tray that my man will present. There are few rules to this game. All three will fight to the death with their knives, their fists, or whatever they can until the other two are dead. No man will be allowed to climb the wall unless the other two are dead, simple, but effective. The winner will have won his freedom to return to his work here."

Raven heard the sound of someone spitting and she felt the wet spattering of chew on the back of her neck. She jerked her head around and stared at the dirty man holding a bottle of whiskey in one hand and his pistol in the other. He looked at her with a mocking smile. "You better fight good, bitch, or die," he said laughing, as he spit again, this time into the dirt. She could feel the wet, disgusting drip of juice trickling down the center of her back, and she could do nothing but bite her lip in anger.

A man with a tray of knives walked up to the miner and said something, and then he slowly took a thick-bladed Bowie knife from the tray. Next he went to the other man, who also took a larger knife, almost eight inches in length.

Lastly the man walked over to Raven. "Take only one knife," he said sternly. Raven paused for a couple of seconds before reaching for the handle of one of the larger knives. She suddenly stopped and took a far smaller, narrower knife that appeared to fit her small hand much better. At that, the man took the tray to the wall, handed it up to another man, and climbed up the ladder, pulling it up after himself.

"Not much of a pig sticker, bitch," the muleskinner joyously exclaimed as he turned to either side, looking for approval and laughs to validate his comments. "You ain't much of an opponent either. A mongrel dog could probably fight better than a little bitch like you!"

Captain Bleeker raised his arms in the air, and the crowd quieted. "When I raise my gun and fire, the match shall begin." Raven could feel the sweat rolling down her face. She knew she had no chance. The one man was twice her size, and the other man was certainly capable of killing her quickly with the larger knife. With that, Captain Bleeker squeezed the trigger and his pistol shot into the air.

Chapter 15

Instinctively the two men and Raven took a step backward. Crouching, they raised their knives and their arms. There was a moment in which each competitor glanced at the others. The big miner took off his cloth vest and wrapped his weaponless arm for additional protection. Raven could see from the look on the former Bleeker guard that the man had the same thoughts she had. Almost immediately, their chances had been reduced. Raven knew there would be nothing fair about this match and she had to fight for her life however she could. That was just what she planned to do.

"Kill the bitch first and then let's have a real fight," yelled the drunken muleskinner that stood behind Raven. She cringed at the thought of another disgusting wad of chewing tobacco splattering on the back of her neck.

Each person in the Pit moved back and forth to size up the other opponents and the length of chain that bound their ankles. Raven could see the advantage of her practices; her body seemed to know the length of her reach, but she kept her distance, looking for weakness. For over a minute, each of them moved back and forth in a sideways motion trying to find a route to attack and use his knife in a quick jab.

"Remove the boards," shouted Bleeker, to the crowd's joyous shouts of approval.

Raven saw the motion of the man in her corner pull up a long rope that was anchored from above. Inside the Pit the quiet sound of buzzing could be heard even over the noise of the crowd. Marquese had warned her about this, and now she kept one eye glancing towards the low log as snake heads popped up periodically looking around. Now the log was nothing more to the snakes than an obstacle to be crawled over. Within minutes, each corner was buzzing with the sound of rattlesnakes. The guards were extending a long stick into the small enclosures in each corner and stirring up the angry snakes that slithered back and forth, trying to avoid the stick.

This created a new level of fear as each competitor realized that no longer did they have just two opponents in the Pit. They now had to deal with these large rattlesnakes that were being provoked and angered to enter the main section of the Pit. A large rattlesnake, almost four feet long, had extended its scaled body over the log next to Raven and she knew that the snake and the men were equally dangerous. The rattler began working its way up against the four-foot wall and stopped only eighteen inches from Raven's leg, forming a tight coil as its tail buzzed a loud warning.

"Kill the b…" the rest of the words never came out of the muleskinner's mouth as Raven turned, took a step backward, and with all her strength threw her knife at the man. The knife buried itself all the way to the shaft just to the left of the man's Adam's apple. He staggered, then urgently grabbed it and yanked it from his neck while he stared at Raven with a look of disbelief. The wound gushed blood as the man just stared, then his knees buckled and he tumbled over the wall, landing right on top of the coiled rattlesnake as it struck harmlessly at Raven.

The act surprised everyone, including Raven, who had acted out of both anger and fear. The man lay on the ground, his eyes and tobacco stained mouth wide open as Raven reached down and grabbed his six-gun from his holster. In one swift movement she turned and shot the man who had once been a guard in the chest and then put two shots into the big miner as he rushed towards her. The force of the shots sent the man helplessly backward into the corner of angry snakes. One snake struck his shoulder and the fangs dug in and caught his shirt as he thrashed helplessly trying to get the biting snakes off; then he fell over and lay still.

Raven immediately dropped the gun and raised her arms in an act of surrender as several men drew their weapons and aimed them at her. The crowd was almost silent, with the exception of one man who cursed her loudly. Raven had seen this man ride into the settlement together with the man she had just killed. The anger on this man's face was visible as he pulled his weapon and walked to the edge of wall. He extended his arm, took aim at Raven's head, and cocked his pistol.

It was then that another shot rang out and the pistol was suddenly ripped from the man's hand. He grabbed his bloody hand in pain and turned to look where the shot had come from. There stood the Mexican, Señor Ramón Gonzalez, with a smoking pistol in his hands. The other five Mexicans who had ridden with him instantly made a semicircle around him, their hands ready to draw their pistols.

"Captain Bleeker, are you not a man of your word? Did you not say if the young lady wins she would be free to return to her work? Should not your guests abide by your rules?" asked the man known as Señor Ramón Gonzalez.

Captain Bleeker stood on the platform, visibly upset, his body livid with anger. For over a minute he just stood there staring, his men ready to deal with whatever happened next. Almost as quickly as his anger had come, he seemed to settle down and half smiled.

"Yes, that is what I said. Now remove the prisoner and take her back to her cabin and chain her up. She has survived this day and everyone will respect the rules."

With that, the men noisily talked amongst themselves, some with much anger in their tone. Link seemed to just appear out of the crowd, and with the aid of a long stick with a forked end, began collecting the snakes and putting them into oversized grain sacks. Raven moved as close to the center of the Pit as she could, keeping an eye out for the snakes that hadn't been caught. The blacksmith carefully descended the ladder, constantly scanning for snakes, while he hastily unshackled her ankle.

When all the snakes were removed from the Pit, Raven moved to the ladder and started up the rungs, not knowing what to expect at the top. To her surprise, as soon as she set foot on the ground, the men began to spread out and give her space. As she stood there scanning the group, she looked up into the livid face of Captain Bleeker. She knew she was a dead woman, but she hoped it wasn't until after the Gathering was over and the guests had left; maybe that would give her the needed time to escape.

She straightened up in front of the men. Some smiled in approval, some were angry for seeing their friend shot, but most just stared, wondering what had just happened. Marquese and another guard walked over to her and each grabbed an arm. They hadn't walked more than a few steps when Hamilton jumped in front of the group.

"No one makes a fool out of Captain Bleeker. When this Gathering is done, Scar and I will have our day with you; I just want you to know what's coming." Then he turned and headed back towards the crowd.

Neither man was gentle with her as they headed down the gravel road back to her cabin. At the door Marquese turned to the other man, "I can take her from here, thanks for the help; I was sure they would kill the little bitch."

"Me too, you could sure tell the Captain was pissed. I doubt she lasts long after the Gathering is done. See you later," said the man, as he turned and walked back in the direction of the group.

Marquese opened the door and gently lowered Raven to the floor. "That was amazing, girl! When I saw your opponents and the aggressive nature of the snakes, I thought there was no way. I am glad I didn't bet against you. There were great odds against you, and those that bet for you will be drinking it up and celebrating hard tonight. Sorry about the rough handle, but I have to play the part. You are amazing, Raven. Now get some sleep; you will need it."

Raven's stomach was tied in a knot to the point she felt sick. There was no way she could have eaten dinner, even if they had allowed her to. Shaking with fear, as she lay on the bed of grass with her buffalo blanket draped over her. She thought about what had happened. First she gagged and then vomited. There wasn't much in her stomach, but the motion was painful, and suddenly she collapsed in exhaustion. It was several hours after dinnertime when she awoke to the women being led back into the cabin by Miss Martha.

Strangely, Miss Martha didn't say anything to her as she locked her shackle. The lantern was on, and she could see Betsy staring in her direction. Raven knew that Betsy wanted to know what had happened, but that would have to wait. After she had locked everyone up, Raven heard Lester's voice at the door.

"I lost a bet to that damn Marquese, so I'm taking his shift; Martha, is everything good in there for the lock up?"

"Yeah, everything's fine. Go ahead and lock her up." With that, Raven heard the sound of the lock moving and closed her eyes.

Minutes later she felt a hand on her shoulder; it was Miss Martha. In a voice so quiet that Raven could barely hear, Miss Martha whispered into her ear, "That was real good today. I think you really do have the heart to make it out of here."

That night as Raven awoke several times to nightmares, the feeling of wet sticky juice being spit on her neck was always present. It was nearly morning when she felt someone unlocking her shackle. She could see it was Miss Martha, who put her finger to her lips, signaling quiet. The two women stood and tiptoed to the door and out into the open space in front of the cabin, then to the shadows of the trees. Miss Martha sat down on their normal log, and Raven sat down beside her. "That was amazing, Raven. I really thought there was no way. Enough of this talk, I have much to tell you about your escape with Link."

"Before Link was born, I lived with my husband and my two teenage children for about five years in a cabin probably twenty or so miles from here. My husband found this protected, isolated ridge where we built the cabin, but I don't think we ever really felt safe there. My husband would spend the summer getting ready for the next winter and looking for an old Indian's gold mine. Quinten would spend the winter building things for the cabin, protection, and the like. He was an ornery man, and halfway through our trip to Oregon, he'd gotten in a fight with the wagon master and we left the train on our own. Quinten decided to head north and find new country on our own, and I always followed what my husband decided."

"Several days later as we were working our way through the sagebrush we found our way down to a small creek, and there we found a very old Indian half-starved and almost dead. Well, we fed him, even though my husband felt we had no food to waste, but after a couple days he passed away. Before he did, he communicated with us using hand signals and a map. He seemed to want to repay us for our friendship, and pointed to the mountains behind us, and then gave us this map painted on a piece of deer hide."

"In the center of the deer hide was a piece of gold, good-sized and bright, and it was tied tightly to the map with a thin string. It was obvious to us that he wanted us to know there was gold in the mountains in front of us and his map would show us where. We were all pretty excited, and with some scouting it wasn't long before my husband found a truly beautiful spot isolated up on a bench on the mountain with a stream and plenty of feed for the stock."

"Well, we built the cabin and hurriedly put away the food we'd need for winter. We had already brought most of what we needed in the wagon, so we started trying to figure out the map. It took us several years, but our first breakthrough was finding what appeared to be a natural road that went up the mountain. Later, with the help of the map, we found a rock formation that looked a lot like the face of an old man staring at the sky. Then we found the tree."

"The tree?"

"Yes, a very special tree, a limber pine. Limber pines look different than all the other evergreen trees in the forest. Mother Nature gave them four times as many branches as the rest of the trees, and with their great size and powerful presence they can make trees appear as dwarfs in comparison. Anyway, there it sat on the edge of a small meadow, proudly standing like a monarch above all the rest and showing us the way to an ancient trail that led to a gold mine. I have drawn you a map, and if you can find that tree and trail, you will find a half-built cabin under an overhanging rock. My husband and son were hauling up supplies and some of our valuables when they disappeared."

"A couple of days earlier we had seen a couple of sets of horse tracks down in the prairie a few miles from the cabin. "Quinten," she paused, "Quinten Walsh, my dear dead husband, felt that we needed to have a second place to escape to if necessary." Her eyes seemed to tear up as she remembered. "We don't think Scar or his men ever found that spot on the mountain or Captain Bleeker would have mined it. If you are able to find the cabin there should be some things that you might use. It's very hidden, so use it to your advantage if you can. It may be an excellent place to hide out a while until things settle down."

In the pause, Raven spoke up, "I think I found your homestead down off the valley when I was trying to escape Captain Bleeker's men and the Indians. The barn is still there and in reasonable shape. Part of the roof at one is end is missing, but for the most part it beads water. There is nothing left of the cabin, though."

"I know; be careful if you come down the ridge and use the barn. Bleeker's men know where it is, and from time to time they use the barn, from what Marquese says. There is one thing I want you to know if you have to use the place. There is hidden passageway in the far right corner. A trapdoor with dried hay stuck to it, we did that with hot pitch. Anyway, if you follow that back, you will find a small underground room; we used it for cold storage and a possible escape route. Now don't forget we put a map in your pack. Good luck, and please take good care of Link. I think you will find he more than pulls his own weight. It's time to get you back now, let's go."

Raven was exhausted and fell asleep within minutes of lying down, the events of the day haunting her dreams. She awoke the next morning to the door being opened by Marquese, so she stumbled to her feet. "Time to get moving, ladies," said Miss Martha in a low voice, that revealed a slight head cold.

The march to the cooking shed was typical, but Raven noticed several men and guards point towards her as she marched; it was not good to stand out, and she knew it. Raven walked over to where Betsy had begun peeling potatoes and sat down by the pile of elk horns.

"Raven, cut off the elk horns from the heads and start cutting them up into eight-inch chunks for knife handles."

Raven just nodded her head and smiled. There was too much attention around her now, and she didn't want anymore.

Betsy turned to her, "Are you all right? One of the women at the privy said you fought in the Pit against two men."

"I did, but now is not the time to discuss it. All I can tell you is to be ready, and it will be soon."

Later that evening, the group formed and marched back to the cabin with Miss Martha leading the way. As she shackled Raven, their eyes met and she gave her a slight nod and continued on.

It was late that night when Raven felt a hand on her shoulder for the second time and heard another quiet whisper. "Wake up. It's time; you're leaving tonight."

The door was slightly cracked and the light of a full moon barely trickled inside, but there was enough light for her to see Miss Martha quietly unlocking her shackle. Raven looked at Miss Martha and put her hand out, pointing to the key. Miss Martha's look was one of disgust, but she begrudgingly handed it to her. Raven crawled over to Betsy, and as she started to unlock the shackle, she felt Betsy's hand brush hers.

Raven stopped and covered Betsy's hand with hers for a moment before putting her finger to her mouth and motioning for Betsy to follow her outside. The three had only gone five yards when Miss Martha stopped and spoke. "Link will be waiting for you two behind the cooking shed. There are still guards out, so you need to be very careful when you cross the street; you never know who is watching. Now stay to the shadows as much as possible."

"Who unlocked the door?"

"It was Marquese. He gave Lester a good bottle of whiskey, so when they find you gone, that worthless piece of cow dung drunk in a chair will get the blame, at least that's what we hope. He is one mean man and he doesn't deserve to live, as far as I'm concerned. He's the reason Allie is dead and I don't know how many others. Now come back into the cabin and let's get this over with; we got to make this look good and real."

"I don't know if I can do that," stammered Raven.

"Well I can," said Betsy, as she reached for the chunk of wood.

"Don't hit her too hard, Betsy, she's the reason we have this escape plan, and without her we would be nowhere."

"I won't. I will just make it look good." With that Betsy followed Miss Martha back into the cabin and moments later came back out, quietly shutting the door.

"She will be okay. I hit her just hard enough that I knocked her out. She will have one hell of a headache tomorrow, but she will be fine."

Raven just nodded as she motioned to Betsy to stay down as they crept around the building to a low-hanging tree from where they had a view down the road in both directions. They could hear noise from the saloon farther down, but no one seemed to be walking around near where they were, so Raven turned to Betsy.

"We are going to casually walk onto the street and then cross over the bridge to the cooking shed. Hopefully Link will be there waiting for us."

"What if he isn't?"

"Don't worry, he will be, Miss Martha set this up and he's her son."

Betsy just looked at Raven for a moment. "Just go. I'll be beside you," said Raven.

The two stood up and casually began walking down the road towards the bridge and the sound of the crowd that packed the saloon.

"God help us if anyone sees us."

"Don't worry, it's late, and those that aren't partying are probably asleep. I doubt the guards are real energetic this time of night. Now keep up, we are almost to the bridge."

At that moment, a man staggered into the street holding a bottle in one hand. He was close, and as he stumbled he stared in their direction, then turned and headed down the road in the opposite way.

"That was close."

Too close, if you ask me," she said as they walked across the bridge, "now head for those shadows and the cooking shed tables before we stumble upon anyone else."

The two made their way behind the tables where the stack of elk horns were kept, and knelt down and listened; there was only silence. "Now stay here for a moment while I sneak behind the building and see if I can find Link," whispered Raven.

"Okay, but don't be gone long, I'm really scared."

Raven put her hand on Betsy's. "We both are. Now stay hidden in the shadows while I find him."

In the moonlight that shone on Betsy's face, Raven could see tears on her cheek. Raven made her way to the back of the building and squatted down.

"Link, Link, are you out there?"

Link emerged from the shadows and approached her hiding place.

"Are you ready to go?"

Link just nodded.

"Good, stay here, I have to go back and get Betsy. I will be right back."

Raven worked her way back to the pile of horns where she had left Betsy, but she wasn't there. "Betsy, where are you?" Raven whispered. Out of the shadows stepped Scar, and even with the lack of good lighting, the scar on his weathered face was prominent. He stood in front of her for a moment, and then he reached across his body and pulled a Bowie knife from its sheath. Raven turned and grabbed a single side of elk horn and swung it at Scar with all her might as he charged forward. One point from the antler tore into his stomach and he staggered back in surprise. Coming out of the darkness, Betsy clubbed him with a thick chunk of wood on the back of the head.

"Quick, follow me," said Raven as she headed to the back of the building, hoping no one had heard the commotion. Raven glanced over her shoulder and saw Scar lying on the ground, the bloody antler beside him, and he wasn't moving. The two ran around the building to where Link was waiting. He motioned for them to follow as he stood up.

The three hurried through the woods on a path that Link seemed to know well. Within minutes they were at the base of the steep cliff, and in the pale moonlight Raven could see the outline of a mine with fallen trees and brush in front of it. Link dropped to the ground and began crawling under the fallen trees as the women followed. Raven noticed the grass was matted down and several of the limbs that would have stopped their progress were broken off. This certainly wasn't the first time Link had passed this way. Soon they were past the fallen logs and brush that adorned the mine entrance, and Link stood up and turned to help Raven and Betsy to their feet.

Link grabbed Raven's hand, and in turn she grabbed Betsy's as the three entered the pitch-black mine. Suddenly Link let go, and Raven hesitated not knowing what to do. Then Link knelt to the ground and began sending out sparks with a small flint. Several sparks landed on a small bundle of dry grass that Link must have placed there earlier, and soon they had a small fire. Link stood up.

Behind him lay three crudely built torches made from old clothing and pitch. He lit each of the torches and handed the other two to the women. The torches cast an eerie glow over the rough walls of the mine and the old fallen timbers that littered the mine's floor.

In front of them were three packs stuffed to the brim, winter coats, and a pair of knee high moccasins. "These for you," said Link, leaning down and handing them to Raven. "You wear now." This was the first time Raven had ever heard him speak, and it was comforting to know he could.

Raven only nodded as she took off her worn and ripped leather shoes and put on the fur-lined moccasins.

"This way," said Link quietly. The three wound around many piles of rock and debris as they made their way farther into the mountain through the mine, which rose and fell as it twisted its way deeper.

"I hope he knows where he's going," said a scared Betsy.

"Don't worry, we are going to make it, everything will be fine." Raven hoped her voice was convincing, but deep down she was scared to death of what lay ahead.

Link finally stopped at an old ladder that went through a hole in the ceiling. It wasn't a huge hole but plenty big enough for each of the three as they climbed up, shoving their packs ahead of them and then entering another chamber. Unlike the last chamber, this one was smooth, like it had been washed by time and water.

"We go up now," directed Link, pointing towards a passageway about two feet wide, but over seven feet high, that quickly rose in elevation.

Raven thought to herself that if it were steep it would be very slick or if rainwater suddenly came down it they would be in real trouble. Raven had started up the passageway last when she heard voices, angry voices of men shouting. Somehow Bleeker's men had found out about their escape, and they were in hot pursuit. The voices echoed through the mine, making them seem closer than they were.

The three frantically worked their way higher along the ancient creek bed. The width of the path varied between two and four feet, so the three could wear their packs as they hurried along, occasionally catching them on the walls' jagged rock. How could they have found out about the escape so quickly, thought Raven as she dashed along behind the other two. For the next ten minutes they raced along, following Link and breathing hard from the pace and the climb. Every so often, one of the three would bump a rock, and the sound would reverberate throughout the mine.

"Raven."

"Don't talk, the sound really carries," Raven whispered. "We don't want them to figure out what passages we've taken."

Periodically they could hear faint voices, and Raven knew the men were tracking them. They had no other choice but to keep hurrying on their path and hope and pray that Link knew where he was going. Raven's lungs were screaming for air, and she so badly wanted to stop, but she knew she couldn't. The look on Betsy's face showed that she felt the same.

Link suddenly came to a stop and pointed upward. There in the ceiling was a hole barely two feet wide. "You go there," said Link, as he took Raven's torch and buried it in the dirt to put it out. "You go now."

Raven, like Betsy, was trying to catch her breath. "Link, you go first, and then Betsy. I will follow." Link nodded and then started climbing the wall up through the hole until his feet disappeared. Then Betsy extinguished her torch and slowly made her way up to the hole, pushing her pack in front of her as she climbed through. Raven picked up her pack and extinguished her torch. The almost total darkness caught her by surprise. She cussed to herself that she had not watched for the foot and handholds the other two had used to get out of the passage.

Now she struggled with where to grab and place her feet. As she worked her way up several feet, the hole got brighter from the moonlight. She shoved her pack up through the hole and it disappeared from her sight. It was tight, but she got her arms up and out onto where Link and Betsy stood. Raven smiled to herself in relief as she started to pull her last leg through the opening. It was then that she felt it, someone's hand grabbing her foot just below the ankle and trying to pull her back down. As she turned, she could see light filling the cavity she was leaving. Men's angry voices bellowed from below her. Raven screamed for help as Link and Betsy jumped to pull her up.

"Someone's got my foot," she screamed, "Help me!"

Chapter 16

As suddenly as it had grabbed her, the hand slipped off, and Raven found herself on the ground next to the other two.

"We must run, we have to get away," screamed Betsy in terror.

Link looked at the two for a split second before stepping behind a large boulder where he picked up a large sack that buzzed angrily with the movement. He grinned mischievously as he opened the sack and poured the slithering snakes down the small hole. Several men below began to scream. Link then motioned for the women to help him as he began pushing a small boulder, just a bit bigger than the opening, towards the hole. With the help of a large stick for leverage, the three were able to move the boulder and then stack smaller rocks around it to make it almost impossible to move.

"We made it," said Betsy as she stared at the other two. "Can you believe we made it?"

Raven turned and looked at the steep cliff that rose another hundred feet above them and responded, "I don't think we're in the clear yet."

They stood on a shelf that was probably twelve by twelve feet. Raven looked at a hole in the ground that looked as if animals had dug it. Link knelt down and pulled out an empty, torn sack.

"Salt."

"Well I'll be," said Raven, looking at the hole and the obvious game trail that led away from it. "He used salt to get the animals to show him the way out. He's one smart young man. The snakes, this route, and even the boulders, Link figured out this whole thing."

Link just smiled and began putting his coat on. The women followed by putting their coats and packs on, for the wind and the early morning hour made it much colder than it had been down in the protected camp. The game trail wasn't wide, only six inches in some places, but it was consistent as it worked its way up the mountain, packed by the heavy use of mountain goats and sheep. For the next twenty minutes, they carefully followed the trail by what little moonlight there was, and shortly they came out on a larger, less steep piece of ground where they found a much older trail that was worn deep by use.

"Don't worry about your tracks here. The place we must hide them is when we get to the top of the ridge, and that is where we need to stay to the rocks, where they can't use their horses and tracking us becomes more difficult."

"How much of a head start do you think we have?"

"When they captured me, I saw a fair piece of the country riding in here, and from the look of those rocks and cliffs, I believe we got a day, maybe more, head start." Link nodded. "My worry is that they got a secret trail that I didn't see that takes them up here quicker. If that's the case, we're in big trouble."

The rest of the day, the three kept traveling up and north, hoping Bleeker's men would try to head them off by going east towards civilization. They stayed to the rock surfaces as much as possible, and when no rock was available they tried to travel on thick spruce needles, or anything that wouldn't leave a track. They had come upon several well-worn game trails, but instead of following them, they had jumped them, trying not to leave a footprint on the soft dirt.

It was early afternoon when the group finally took a break high in the rocks at a small seep with clear, cold water. The spot was secluded and between two large boulders with a level spot just big enough for the three to drink and rest. The valley below them was open and had little tree cover, so there was no way anyone could sneak up on them for hundreds of yards without being seen. It would be almost impossible to track them in this terrain, and Raven knew it.

The cool water of the seep tasted good. Raven and Betsy rinsed their faces before grabbing their packs and opening them. Raven had no idea what she would find, but right now she really hoped it was food. The top of the pack was bursting with hard bread and jerky, and all three of them ate ravenously. Raven noticed several papers tucked neatly to one side of the pack and glanced at them for a quick moment before tucking them back into her pack and continuing to eat. She would look at them when they stopped for the night.

For the next two hours the group ate, drank, and nodded off periodically, never totally asleep or awake. They were exhausted, and Raven knew that they would need to find a good, protected place for the night.

Raven stood up, the tired look on both Link and Betsy a mirror of her own. "We need to keep moving."

She didn't bother to look either of them in the eye, because she knew they were exhausted from climbing the mountain, but they needed to keep on the move. The rocky ground faded into grass and there was nowhere to walk that wouldn't leave tracks for the experienced tracker. They worked their way down the ridge and through a patch of struggling aspen, their trunks gnarled and warped by the wind and scarred by the animals.

"I want to keep as near the timber line as possible, but in the rocks, if we can. Remember to always be aware of where you are placing your feet. Tracks on soft dirt are easily seen."

They tried to move through the rocks, but it proved too slow and difficult, draining their strength, so they headed back to the timber line, continued north for another hour, and then turned west.

"Why are we going west?" asked Betsy, as she sat down, completely drained of energy.

"That should be the last direction they would think we would go. I don't know how far behind us they are, but I do know they're coming, and when they do, they will have killing on their minds."

Three hours of exhausting hiking later they came to a thick grove of lodge pole pine with a small creek running beside it. It was protected and out of the wind, something Raven knew would be important later. About twenty yards above them the timber stopped, and the bare rock and grass hillside rose up another thousand feet or so.

"We'll camp here for the night. Link, find me some dry, aged wood and Betsy, go fill your canteen and bring it back to me. We will have a fire in between these two boulders. No one will be able to see it unless they are on top of us, and then I don't think we would have a chance anyway." The other two went to get the wood and water as Raven took her knife and carefully cut and removed a small round circle of sod from the ground and set it to one side. A couple of minutes later, Betsy returned with the canteen filled with water, and Raven poured it on the sod she had removed.

"Why are you doing that?"

"Tomorrow morning when we leave I am going to make this place look like we weren't ever here. Eventually they will come by looking for us and I don't want them knowing this is where we traveled to or camped. We need to buy time."

Betsy nodded, and as she passed Link she said, "That girl sure is smart; we may make our way out of this yet."

That night as Link continually fed twigs to the small, protected fire, Raven pulled out the paper she had seen in her pack earlier and took a better look at it. There were two pages; one was a letter, and the other was a crude map. Raven chewed on a chunk of jerky as she read the letter several times before she folded it and put it back. Then she picked up the map. The quality of the paper and the pencil used to make it were poor.

From what she could tell there was a vertical, straight line intersected by lots of smaller lines and a dashed line saying "trail" behind it. Whatever this symbol was she couldn't say for sure, but she could easily make out an old man face that stared up at the sky. There were a couple of what she imagined were mountains or peaks, but overall, she really couldn't figure out much from the poor artwork and lack of detail. She wadded the paper up and threw it at her feet as Betsy jumped up and came over.

"What's wrong? What is it?"

"It's the damn map. How is anyone supposed to read it? There aren't even any landmarks. It's worthless."

Betsy grabbed the paper and sat down in such a position that the fire cast enough light on it for her to read the map.

"You're right; this is almost impossible to understand. I wonder how Miss Martha thought we could."

"Here, give it back. I am going to put it in my pack. It's just that I am so frustrated. Why couldn't she have done something I could read or understand better?"

"I'm going to go relieve myself," said Betsy as she turned and headed out towards the opening in the trees. As she squatted down in the grass, she was impressed by the millions of stars. Having been locked in the cabin every night, it had been a while since she had seen stars, and she marveled at their brightness. As Betsy began to stand, she froze in sheer panic as her eyes locked on a small light on a ridge several miles away. *Oh my God, it's them,* she thought as she turned and ran back to where Raven and Link sat by the fire.

"It's them! I can see their campfire on the ridge to the east. It sure didn't take them no day to get up here like we thought. What are we going to do now?"

"Nothing tonight, we need some sleep. But at first light we are out of here; we just have to make it as close to impossible to track us as we can."

Raven and Betsy didn't sleep well the rest of the night, always thinking about their pursuers, but Link seemed to handle the pressure and slept quietly by the small fire as the women fed sticks into the tiny flame.

Raven walked over to Link and shook him. He opened his eyes to Raven holding her finger over her lips. "Sound travels up here, so we need to use hand signals when we can. Now eat a little something, and then let's get going."

After wolfing down a chunk of hard bread and some jerky, Raven carefully scattered the ashes, replaced the round circle of sod over the location of the small fire, and seeded it with spruce needles.

"Hopefully they will miss this," whispered Raven, as she stood up and started walking through the timber towards the rocky hillside.

"We are going to climb up through those rocks for a while. Then we will drop back down to timber line where we can make better time."

The three climbed using their arms and legs to gain elevation as quickly as possible. When they reached a rock shelf, they turned and paralleled the slope for over an hour before starting back down.

"That should make it hard for them to follow," said Raven as they reached timber line. "Now we need to make up for lost time."

Hours later they stopped for lunch at a large creek that flowed from a steep rocky canyon above them, and they drank from the edge, always careful to not leave a clue that would alert their pursuers. It was a quiet lunch with no one really talking; they all knew that if they were captured again that Bleeker and his men would have no sympathy for them.

"Let's go downstream and see if we can find a log to cross. These rocks are really slick, and we don't need anyone turning an ankle."

About fifty yards down the hill, Raven saw a wide, dead fir tree laying across the stream, its roots sticking half way out of the ground. "We'll cross here. Be careful."

After an uneventful crossing, the trio walked for several yards before turning up the hill and working their way through the forest of trees and rocks. The going was rough with fallen trees everywhere when Raven climbed over a fallen log and there in front of her was a trail laden with rock, pine needles, and moss. The trail seemed to begin in the middle of the forest with no sign of it continuing past where they had found it. From what Raven could tell, it was very old and hadn't been used for years.

"Walk on the rocks and try not to create tracks. We will follow this trail for a little while; it may help us gain some elevation."

The group still had to crawl under and over numerous deadfalls, but they were certainly moving at a much faster pace than before until the trail finally broke into the open at the crest of the ridge. They could see far into the valley, but they saw no signs of other people. The views were spectacular, and the three paused to catch their breath as well as take in the amazing, beautiful countryside. Raven never lost focus. This gave her an opportunity to see the layout of the ground in front of her and plot their escape down the mountain. It bothered her that once down from the ridges, the timbered slopes turned to grass, giving men on horses an extreme advantage.

"Let's go," urged Raven, as she pushed the group to move faster as the trail went past a small meadow of thick grass.

They hadn't gone too much further when Raven stopped in shock; there in front of them was a footbridge made of stone and built into the steep hillside. This bridge had taken time and real craftsmanship to build, but why had someone done it? Here they were at the top of a mountain, and the last thing they'd expected was to find a stone bridge that looked as old and unused as the trail they'd followed.

"Keep going, they probably know this is here, and we can't waste time gawking. Now keep moving!"

Raven had not seen anything to justify their pace, but she had heard the legends about the ability of the Blackfoot to trail a person, and she wasn't going to give them anything to help the cause. The trail meandered around the ridge and then went into another draw before breaking out onto a gentle, grassy slope filled with huge boulders.

"Look, the old man's face! He's looking at the sky," Raven said in a voice louder than she would have liked.

"What are you looking at?" asked Betsy puzzled. "All I see are rocks."

"There," pointed Raven, "see those rocks? If you stare at them for a moment, they look like an old man staring at the sky, just like in the map

Miss Martha drew. That's got to be it! I think I know where we are. Let me get the map out." Raven quickly took off her pack, set it on the ground, and opened the folded paper. She looked at the adjacent mountains and then back at the map.

"We are here. We need to go back past the stone bridge. At that meadow we passed there should be a tree that Miss Martha called a limber pine, but first we need to make it look like we continued moving southwest, so they can't figure out where we went."

The three headed towards the rocks that looked like an old man's face, and then, after a little discussion, climbed until they were at a rock-filled slope.

"Now we back out of here and head towards the meadow. Work your way along using the rocks to hide your footprints. When we hit the trail, start walking backwards until we get to the meadow."

The exercise took the group almost a full hour, as it was slow and necessary to keep their weight distributed correctly. Raven led the group, and with much effort they finally reached the edge of the meadow. Stepping from the trail onto a rock, she began carefully placing her feet on other rocks as she climbed up into the meadow, followed by the others.

"There, see that tree with all the limbs? That has to be the limber pine she spoke of. The trail should be above it, off to the left somewhere. Remember to stay on rocks where you can. If she was right, there should be a cabin on a trail in here somewhere, and if there is, then maybe we can hide out for a while until they quit looking."

The other two nodded as Raven worked her way over towards the mammoth pine tree with so many branches it looked like some weird type of vertical porcupine. It took another twenty minutes to find the hidden entrance of the trail in amongst the trees and grass. Someone long ago had done a great job strategically hiding it.

The three headed up the ancient trail filled with debris, often climbing under and over fallen trees. The trail was cut at least six inches into the ground and, at one time, had been well traveled. The farther they went, the easier the trail was to follow. Finally they broke out of the trees onto the open face of a ridge where the sound of rushing water from the canyon below them echoed throughout. The trail seemed to be carved out of solid rock in places as it worked its way up the mountain, and Raven knew they were all wondering the same thing, who had built this trail? And were they alone?

Deer and bighorn sheep tracks littered the ground, and it was impossible, with the soft gravel and dirt not to leave tracks. Betsy stopped and sat down, removing pine needles from her woolen socks before putting her moccasins back on as Link and Raven looked around. They worked their way up the trail, constantly impressed with the work of these ancient men who had built it. With the exception of a few large rocks, the trail was almost in perfect shape.

The group was tired, but continued their fast pace up the trail until they broke into a meadow. At first they just stared and examined it before walking further into the grassy, open space. The meadow had numerous stumps standing in the midst of the grass, and the dirt mounds attested to the fact that many ground squirrels had made this their home.

Link suddenly pointed, and there, under a rock overhang, sat the brown logs of a cabin with a large stack of cut firewood against its side. The location was clever with the rock overhang and thick log walls protecting it. The three quickly walked up to the door, and with a little pressure, opened it. On one side of the room stood a bed and what was left of a mattress that the packrats had chewed. A small fireplace sat to the right of the front door with a pile of wood stacked beside it. A small wooden table sat against the right side of the building and numerous traps smeared in dried bear grease decorated the walls. There was a set of cabinets on one wall. Raven carefully opened it to find little besides mouse droppings and dust.

"We are going to stay here for a while and hope Bleeker's men give up searching for us. With any luck, we will make it out of here yet. We can have small fires at night when the smoke can't be seen, and we can get water from the creek but for now you might as well get comfortable. Link, would you see about those traps? We are going to need some fresh meat for our trip later, if not now."

A small, rusty hatchet stood sticking out of a twelve-inch section of log beside the stone fireplace and Raven picked it up with great satisfaction. "We can do a lot with this," she told Betsy who nodded.

"We sure can."

That night the group huddled around a small fire in the cabin, and within an hour, the cabin had warmed to a comfortable temperature. Each of them sought out a place to sleep, with Betsy taking the tattered bed. Link hadn't been sitting for more than a couple of minutes when he stood up. "Look what I found."

He held out a bow and quiver with half a dozen arrows in it. They were dusty and old, but in good shape. "Can you hit anything with that?"

Link shrugged his shoulders and answered, "Yeah, maybe."

Betsy and Raven just laughed, as they all lay down to sleep.

When Raven awoke in the morning she noticed Link was gone and the sun was already up. She realized she must have been more tired than she thought as she rubbed her face trying to wake up. It was cold but sunny, and within minutes Link came walking out of the forest on the far end of the meadow with several large blue grouse. He smiled and held them up and then looked at his bow and smiled again.

"Well, you shot some meat. That will be a welcome change for dinner."

The next week went by, and the small group stayed close to the cabin. They didn't hear or see anything of Bleeker's posse.

"Bet Bleeker's men think we fell off the face of the earth," laughed Betsy one night, as she sat on the bed. "Bet he thinks we made it back to Missouri and the whole group has quit looking."

"We will stay here another week, then I think we need to move on. It's getting mighty cold at night, and I don't want to be caught up here in deep snow with no food. That would warrant a slow death," replied Raven.

Later that day, Link brought in three six-foot wooden spears that he had made with the hatchet. They weren't perfectly straight, but he had carved a sharp end on each. Later that night, he hardened the ends in the small fire in the fireplace.

Four days later, Raven and the group awoke to a cold and cloudy day. When the group went out to the meadow, they could feel the difference in the air.

"I think it's time. Let's pack up and head out right after we eat some more of those grouse Link shot. It's probably good we go, since I think Link has shot most of the birds in this valley."

Out of habit they all sat around the fireplace, even though there was no fire, eating the last of the cold grouse before Betsy turned to Raven. "We need to split up. We can't put all of our eggs in one basket. They might find one or two of us, but someone has to make it out to tell people what Bleeker and his men are doing here. He has to be stopped."

Raven argued halfheartedly, but she knew Betsy was right. Three people's tracks were too hard to hide. The three left the meadow and headed down the ancient trail that hugged the steep canyon walls, and soon they were at the huge limber pine by the meadow. "Link needs to stay with you, Raven. He has a better chance that way, and he is too young to be by himself."

Raven nodded in agreement, and then hugged Betsy, as tears ran down both of their faces. "We have been through a lot together, and we will see each other again, I promise," said Raven. She paused. "God willing, we will make it."

Raven and Link stood there watching as Betsy turned and walked down the path to the old man rock. Then she turned back and smiled. "Remember, remember me," she implored, as she walked away.

"Will she be all right?"

"Yes, Link, she is strong and smart. She is going to make it. Now let's get moving. I want to beat that snowstorm and find some shelter farther down the mountain." The traveling was slow, and every hundred feet or so they stopped to scan the ground ahead of them for movement, but the most they saw was a doe with her fawn crossing in a small valley below them.

"Is Bleeker still looking for us?"

"That kind of man never gives up. If I were to guess, he's probably somewhere between us and the prairie. Bleeker will never stop trying." She paused. "But we fooled him once, and we will fool him again. Don't worry, Link, we will make it, and then we will go back and get your folks." Link only glanced back at her with a half-believing smile. For the next four hours they worked their way down the crest of the ridge, moving from one side to the other, always looking around.

"Where are we going?"

"I'm hoping we find your family's old barn. It's somewhere down here hidden on a ridge, but I'm not actually sure where. If we can't find it, then we will make a small hut out of branches or something. We will be fine."

They hadn't gone much farther when the first snowflake hit Raven in the face and she looked up to see snowflakes covering the sky. She could feel the temperature dropping and hoped that Link could make the journey. He was tough, but he was still just a boy of ten or so and there wasn't much size or muscle to him.

Within an hour the snow had gotten an inch deep, so they worked at being more careful placing their feet in order not to slip and fall. Normally, carrying homemade spears, they would be careful not to leave holes in the dirt, but now they used them to stabilize themselves as they made their way through the rockslides. Soon they came to a steep, rocky cliff. Raven felt cold, and she knew Link was probably colder, but he didn't complain. They stayed to the trees as much as possible, trying to hide their tracks. The snow was still very light in the thick stands of spruce and pine, so the going was good. The wind had begun to howl, and the dry snow was drifting on the open slopes.

Raven worried about Betsy, and she hoped she had found shelter somewhere in the valley. The only good thing about the blowing cold snow was that it covered their tracks almost as quickly as they made them. Raven worried that they wouldn't find shelter for the night, which caused her to question her decision to leave the warm cabin and head into the valley. But if Bleeker's men were still hunting them, this would be the perfect time to move on. At times they could only see twenty to thirty feet in front of themselves, making it frustrating to try to figure out if they were still going down the main ridge or if they had somehow ventured off onto one of the smaller ridges, it was impossible to know.

Three hours later, the slope became gentler and Raven knew they had at least made it off the sharp ridges of the mountain, but where they were she wasn't sure. On Miss Martha's map was drawn a crude location of the barn that she and her husband had built. Raven knew it was down off the valley somewhere, but in this storm it would be almost impossible to see any landmarks. It would be pure luck if they found it. They continued working themselves down through the trees, hoping they would find shelter somewhere soon because Raven couldn't feel her toes, and weary Link had a blank stare on his pale face.

Fortunately, the snowstorm had subsided, with only a few scattered flakes hitting the ground. Raven took her spear and knocked some snow off a bent branch that blocked their way. The small mountain maple sprung back into place as Raven stopped to look at a long dent in the snow. "Link, this has got to be a trail. The snow is slightly depressed in both directions by several inches where the wind hasn't blown it." In places they could see short sections of indented snow, and in other areas the wind had flattened the terrain into a smooth, even grade. "Now the only question is which way from here?"

Link looked at her as if to question what she was thinking before pointing uphill.

"I think you are right; if this were a trail from down in the valley, it would be more well-worn than a trail that was used for hunting or such. This trail was used a lot at one time, and I agree, their home was probably up on the rise somewhere in a place they felt they could protect."

The two escapees struggled up the snowy trail for another twenty minutes until Raven saw the outline of a lonely stone chimney standing strong against the blowing snow and wind.

"That's the old chimney, I remember this place," said Raven, as the two crossed over the small creek at the edge of the meadow. "Fill your canteen quickly and let's get in the barn out of this wind."

They opened the old barn door and slid inside. Raven walked around checking everything. A small used fire pit sat at one end of the barn, so Link began gathering small pieces of wood scattered around the barn floor to start a fire.

"No," said Raven, "we need to clear a new spot so we can hide it later; we can't give them clues we were here."

Raven scraped the hay from a small spot in another area of the barn, then took her knife and dug into the soil. "Leastwise it ain't frozen. Get me a little grass from that pile in the stall, it looks dry, and you light it with your flint."

Link just nodded again and gathered some dry grass from the top of the pile, handed it to Raven, and finished gathering wood for the fire. In one corner there was a large stack of wood from where a section of the roof had caved in, but for the most part it was snow laden and damp.

Within minutes they had a small, crackling fire going, one that made little smoke and one you had to sit close to in order to feel the heat. The two massaged their toes and hands next to the fire until they could feel them comfortably. Luckily neither of them had the blackened damage of frostbite. Later they ate from their packs and took turns stoking the fire as the other one rested or slept. It was late that night when Raven finally fell into a deep sleep as the wind howled outside.

The next morning she awoke to a much warmer feeling. The fire had gone out and Link slept peacefully up against her side. She hesitated to get up, not wanting to wake him. Carefully pulling herself from Link, she stood up, walked to the barn door, and cracked it open. The wind was still blowing, but the temperature had risen at least twenty degrees. The sound of snow melting and dripping off the roof was now the dominant sound. She knew that drastic changes in weather were not usual on the prairie, and she hoped that this change would help melt away any sign of their travels.

Raven walked back and started the fire again as Link continued to sleep. He looked so young, yet he'd been through so much. Removing the letter from her pack, she read what Miss Martha had written, and then she stood up and went over to the corner of the barn with her homemade spear in hand. For a couple of minutes, she carefully walked around, lightly striking the hay that littered the floor with the end of her spear.

Suddenly she stopped as her attention was heightened both by Link sitting up and by the hollow sound she'd just made. With Link watching, she hit the ground with the spear one more time, and again the hollow sound of wood met her ears. She dropped the spear, got down on her knees, and searched the ground for some type of door.

Moments later, she lifted a small trapdoor about two feet by two feet, recessed slightly into the ground. Hay, dirt, and grass had been carefully glued to the wooden top with dried pitch, so when it was closed it totally disappeared. Raven opened and closed it a couple of times; the smoothness and quietness of the latch, even after all these years, was impressive. Link had now gotten up and joined Raven as they both stared into the dark opening to a tunnel.

Chapter 17

"I wonder where it goes," said Link quietly.

"I don't know, but I guess the best way to answer that is follow the tunnel."

"How did you know it was here?"

"Your mother said to look for it if we found the barn. She always regretted not making it to the tunnel when Bleeker's men surprised them." She paused. "You need to know just how great a person your mother is; I totally misjudged her at first. If it weren't for her and Marquese, we would have never made it out of that hellhole."

A few seconds went by as Link looked at Raven, his eyes wide with a questioning expression, before she started down into the hole. A small ladder occupied one side, so Raven tugged on the wood to make sure it was solid. "Everything looks good," she said, as she descended the ladder almost a full eight feet below ground. At the bottom a tunnel led straight away towards the barn's back wall, Raven found herself crouching low as she moved through the tunnel. It was supported by finely cut logs and wasn't any bigger than about four feet wide and four feet tall. At the base of the ladder sat a small box containing eight to ten beeswax candles. She looked up at Link.

"Bring me a stick with a small flame. There are a few candles down here, and I need one to see. I will hand you the candle and you light it and hand it back."

After a minute or so Link brought a small burning piece of wood, then asked, "Can I come?"

Raven looked at Link for a moment and replied, "Sure, you are certainly part of this team. Come on down and I will light another candle for you. Then we will both have one."

Link climbed down the ladder to Raven and quickly the two of them started following the reinforced tunnel. The tunnel floor was dry, hardened clay and the two were surprised at how far it seemed to run as they remained crouched down, following the pathway.

Wherever the tunnel stopped, it would be some distance from the barn. Raven admired the skill of the builder. Finally the tunnel opened into a small room about ten feet by ten feet with a ceiling not more than six feet high, made of thick logs and reinforced in the middle by a stout post. Deer hides, tools, and traps lined the walls around two beds made of thin poles and mesh wire. On top of the tightly woven wire sat several layers of hides, including top and bottom layers of buffalo hides. A small kerosene lantern hung from a spike that had been driven into the center support post, and on the walls hung several shelves built above the floor. Numerous sized barrels were stacked on the floor in two of the room's corners.

"Let's see where this leads," said Raven, pointing to where the tunnel exited the room. "Sure is warm in here compared to outside."

Link just nodded as the two continued walking, hunched over down the tunnel shaft. About twenty yards farther, the tunnel ended in a slightly enlarged space where an old ladder stood attached to the wall.

"I guess this is where we find out where this thing ends," she said as she started climbing the ladder. The vertical tunnel ended at a small, wooden door, but when Raven pushed on it, nothing moved.

"There's a door here, but I think its frozen shut. Maybe we can get a chunk of wood or something to see if we can pry it loose."

Link turned and headed back down the tunnel. Within minutes he was back with a four-foot-long chunk of pole from the barn. "That will probably work," reasoned Raven, as she took the post and rammed it hard several times against the door above, then leaned it against the wall.

"Well, hopefully that did the trick," she said, as she once again tried to push open the door with her shoulder while she stood on the ladder. This time the door moved about six inches and she could see light, but it was a lot darker than it should have been. She had no idea where she was.

"I'm going to try to clean some of this snow out from around the door, and hopefully one of us can squeeze through. From what I can see, it looks like we are in some type of wooden shaft that has snow in it, so I really don't know if this is going to work or not."

For the next twenty minutes, Raven and Link took turns reaching through the crack to clean the snow out from around the trapdoor. Eventually they got it to open wide enough that, with the help of the post and Raven's pushing on the door, Link was able to wiggle his body through and out.

"What do you see?"

"I think I'm in a stump, a really large, tall stump."

"Just a minute, I'm coming up."

With Link's help they removed more snow, and Raven was able to climb through the wooden trapdoor out into the confined space. The tunnel entrance was completely hidden inside a large burnt stump, and from what they could see, there was no door to the outside. The two of them just stood looking at the inside of the massive, blackened stump, wondering why one would want an exit to nowhere. The stump was a good ten feet tall, and there was no way to climb out.

Then Raven noticed a tiny hole in the wood about three feet above the trapdoor. It seemed man-made; it was very narrow, only about a quarter of an inch in diameter. She reached down, picked up a twig up that had blown off one of the many trees above the stump, and stuck the three-inch-long twig into the hole until the shaft was totally buried. She would need a longer stick to clear it out.

"What's that?"

"I'm not positive, but I think I know," said Raven, as she reached down and picked up a longer stick. "Here, let me try this."

She nudged the stick through the hole until it met no more resistance, then Raven removed it and stooped down to look through it.

"Wow, someone really thought this through. We are back in the forest, but I can see the corral and the back of the barn. Quinten Walsh was quite a cautious and clever man to have figured all this out."

Link just looked at her, expressionless. Anyone giving the stump a casual view would never had noticed anything, especially not a couple of insect-sized holes.

"We better get back to the barn; we left the trapdoor open, and I don't want any visitors to discover it while we are out here."

It didn't take them long to get back inside the barn. As they closed the trapdoor, it virtually disappeared into the dirt and old grass of the barn's floor. "This trapdoor is a pretty handy thing to know about. Link if anything happens, you need to scramble down inside the tunnel and wait till the danger is over. Don't wait for me, just do it."

The gentle breeze that had started blowing earlier that morning was getting warmer, and the ground was drying out fast, becoming firm again. "If this breeze keeps up, by tomorrow we should be able to walk around and set some traps, and still not leave much sign. We need to live off the land as much as possible and save the jerky and hard bread for the journey out across the prairie."

That evening the two of them just sat in the corner of the barn waiting for the soft, moist ground outside to firm up so they wouldn't leave any tracks. "Tomorrow I think we need to try and get some more food, then make a break for it over the prairie. If we wait too much longer, we could be caught in another snowstorm and we might have to spend the winter here."

Link just nodded gently.

It was late in the afternoon when Link sat up quickly and shook Raven, who was leaning against a stall wall, sound asleep. "Listen," he said, as he pointed towards the doors to the barn. "I heard something."

"Quick, down the tunnel," said Raven as she turned, ran to the entrance and lifted the trapdoor. At that point, she turned to Link and pressed her finger over her lips. As soon as Link had climbed down the ladder and entered the tunnel, Raven quickly followed, grabbing two new candles at the base of the ladder.

"Hurry down to the room and we will wait there," she whispered.

For over an hour they sat on the edges of the two beds before Raven got up with her candle in hand and moved down the tunnel that led away from the barn. "I want to see who's here."

She raised the trapdoor quietly and stepped out with Link close behind. Within seconds, she was staring out the peephole in the stump. She turned to Link. "It's a mule with a saddle on, but I don't see any rider." For the next hour, they took turns watching the mule mill around the corrals and the barn without seeing anybody.

"I don't think there is a rider. I think that mule somehow got here on its own. Let's go back to the barn and check it out."

The two worked their way back to the barn and slowly cracked the trapdoor, looking for movement, or anything that would give away another presence. "Looks clear," said Raven as she fully opened the trapdoor and launched herself onto the barn floor with Link right behind her. They snuck to the barn doors and peered out, studying the ground for tracks. Only the tracks of the mule were visible on the dry ground.

"Looks like we got ourselves a mule to escape with," said Raven, as she grabbed a little of the year-old hay from the stall and walked it out to the corral. Raven spoke softly to the mule, as she approached, trying to reassure her that she wasn't in danger. The mule turned towards her with its long ears stretched in her direction and didn't move. Raven put one hand on the mule's shoulder, then began rubbing its neck. She placed her other hand on the tall, chestnut mule's chest as it quietly stood there, seeming to enjoy the attention as Link watched from a distance. Raven took the small amount of grass she had brought from the barn and carefully placed it in the old manger.

"What if someone comes and finds the hay?" asked Link.

"They won't. It will only take her an hour or so to eat it all and I think we can risk that to keep her around. I think the good Lord just sent us a present in chestnut-colored wrapping paper." Raven paused and turned to Link. "Just in case someone does show up, I will leave the corral gate ajar so it looks like she might have wandered in by herself. We will leave that torn-up bridle and saddle on; if someone did come, it would be a dead giveaway if she weren't wearing them. Anyway, you got to admit, that mule looks plum wore out to me, and that bloody scar on her rump and hip probably ain't good. We will need to care for her tomorrow before we leave. We will unsaddle her in the morning, and if everything goes well, hopefully she will get us out of here, but for the rest of the day we will take turns on watch. Tonight we will sleep in the tunnel; we don't need any surprises."

For the most of the afternoon, the two of them took turns staring through a crack in the barn door looking for unwelcome visitors. It was well into the afternoon when Link turned and ran towards Raven.

"There is someone coming."

Both Raven and Link dashed towards the trapdoor and quickly disappeared below the floor. They worked their way to the secret room and made themselves comfortable, with the single candle standing on a barrel in the corner. Raven sat on one of the beds, and Link sat across from her on the other. After having slept on the ground for so long, the comfort of the beds in the warm room was almost unbelievable. If it weren't for the stress of someone being in the barn above them, Raven knew she would have slept well. "When we put the candle out, we need to be sure to have a little dried grass for you to light in the morning. Let's just rest and hope they leave. We will check in the morning."

It was early morning, when Raven heard the muffled sound of a mule's brays. "Link, wake up, try and get a candle going."

From out of the darkness she heard him reply and sensed movement in the small room. A flick from Link's flint sent sparks into the small bundle of dry grass, and moments later, he used the grass to light the candle. The two just sat on their beds for the next fifteen minutes, hoping that whoever was above them would leave; and then there was silence.

"You stay here for a moment while I take a peek and see if they are gone."

A minute later she returned. "Boy that was close. I just saw a man lead the mule outside. I am going to follow him for a ways."

"No. I go," said Link, with a mature look of concern and forcefulness on his face that Raven hadn't seen before. Raven only nodded her head in agreement as Link slipped through the door of the barn and was gone.

It was almost two hours later when Raven saw Link's small silhouette sneaking through the trees as he headed back to the barn. He slid back into the barn, walked over to the post they normally leaned against, and sat down, his eyes looking at the floor. "Well, say something."

"Scar got Betsy."

Raven lowered her face into her hands and cried quietly as Link walked over beside her and put his hand on her shoulder. Raven looked up and saw Link staring at her; there were large tears streaming down over his young face, too.

It was several minutes later when Raven raised her head and spoke. "Betsy would want us to go on. Let's go down into the room and talk about a plan; we have had enough surprises and the safety of that room is what we both need tonight."

Hours later, Raven once again heard something from above and motioned to Link who was already focused on the sound. Raven knew better than to lift the trapdoor lid, but she found she could at least hear some of what was going on in the barn by listening at the door. Whoever was there had a horse or mule and a fire that popped from pitch. She listened for close to an hour, but there was no conversation, so she determined there was probably only one person.

Suddenly Link lurched over to her bed with a look of horror on his face. "I left my pouch, I left my pouch upstairs. I need to get it."

"Link, if you try and sneak up there now, whoever is up there is going to catch you, and who knows what he will do. Hopefully he is gone tomorrow and you can find it; I'm sure it's still there."

Raven had no idea if the small pouch had been found or not, but she was pretty sure it wouldn't be. The only thing in this world that Link called his own was that small pouch of trinkets he had collected. She could only hope she was right.

It was hard to tell time in the pitch-black room, but Raven finally woke up and whispered to Link, "Are you awake?"

"Yes," was all she heard as she sat up on the bed, waiting for Link to light the candle. Moments later the candle was lit, and even this small amount of light allowed her to get organized. Then she motioned for Link to stay put as she hunched down and walked back to the ladder that led to the stump. The trapdoor opened easily. She took her time staring out the peephole before sitting back and resting for a moment. It was then she noticed numerous other holes in the stump at various heights. After using another stick to force out the debris lodged in the holes, she found that she could see a far higher percentage of the ground around the barn. The stump even had a view of people coming to the barn, which she thought could be really helpful in the future. She scanned the grounds for activity, but there was none.

When she made her way back to the room, she found Link agitated and restless; he gently swayed back and forth like he was trying to lose excess energy. Raven had never seen Link like this, and she knew it had to be the pouch. "Let me go listen and see if whoever is up there is gone."

Link just nodded, as Raven crouched down and entered the tunnel that led to the barn. For several minutes she listened, but didn't hear anything, so she cracked the door. It was then she saw the back of the man as he led the mule out the barn door. She gently shut the door and took a deep breath, knowing that if she had opened it seconds earlier, they might have been found.

Raven waited a good five minutes before she tried slowly opening the door again. This time the barn was empty, so she whispered down the tunnel for Link to come up. Link raced to where he had left his pouch of trinkets and began searching. "They are not here, he took them."

Raven didn't know what to say. She approached Link, "We will get them back. I promise you, we will get them back."

Link only stared up at her for a moment before his sad eyes met the floor again. Raven knew he didn't believe her.

"When we find people to help us, we will come back here and hunt this person down and find your pouch, I swear."

Link, with a tightened lip, looked her in the eye and slowly nodded in agreement; Raven secretly hoped she could fulfill her promise.

"Why don't you go back down to the room and get our packs. Bring them up here while I clean up the mess from the mule and that campfire. I still don't want anyone figuring out we hid here." Link nodded and headed back down the tunnel as Raven started cleaning up and erasing the signs that someone had used the place. She had worked for about twenty minutes when she realized that Link hadn't returned.

Climbing down the ladder to the tunnel, she entered the hidden room. Link's backpack sat in the middle of the floor, but he was not there, so Raven raced down the tunnel towards the stump to find the trapdoor open and Link gone.

Oh my God, thought Raven as her whole body tightened up. She hurried back down the tunnel, out the barn's trapdoor, and out to the stump. The ground was dry, and she saw no immediate sign of his footsteps. Panic racked her as she thought of Link following a potential killer, or whoever this person was who had spent two nights in the barn and then left with Link's sole possession, a pouch of tiny trinkets.

Chapter 18

Chance Creager

What Chance read rocked him hard, as he sat in a makeshift bar at Meeteetse Creek. If Betsy wasn't here or at their ranch, where was she? And was she even alive?

"Jake, I want to thank you and Roper for the help. McCabe, well, I guess if it weren't for him I would be coyote pickings, but the guy sure has a personality that takes some doing to warm up to. Anyway, thank you. I need to get in the saddle and get the medicine back to that boy," he said, as he stood up and extended his hand.

"If it makes any difference, I believe you. I just think Mr. McCabe is a might bit too cautious. Look me up when you get back to these parts, and I hope for the best for the boy and your sister."

Chance kind of smiled while sucking in his lower lip as if to keep his emotions at bay. He felt fortunate to have made a friend of Jake, a man who when it came to talk, was a straight shooter. Chance walked out onto the porch and scanned the street, then went down and put the medicine and the letters into his saddlebags; he knew his brothers would want to see them. Dixie flicked her ears as Chance put his foot in the stirrup and climbed upon his mule. Within minutes they were at a full trot as they passed the last building in Meeteetse Creek and headed out onto the almost treeless prairie.

The ground was firm, so Dixie began eating up the miles as the two rode between the scattered sagebrush. It was well into evening when he stopped beside a small open creek with good, short grass, the type the mule liked, and made camp. He had bought more than enough supplies in town. The small pot of coffee he boiled tasted heaven sent as did the half a breast of chicken and a couple of slightly overripe apples from the store barrel. The sound of a lone coyote in the distance was almost comforting, as he thought of the old cabin he'd found and the mountain lion that had gotten the best of him.

He slept well on the hard ground that night and was up early the next day. After four hours of loping and trotting his tough mule, he found himself only a couple of miles from their ranch; he had made good time. A mile away he could hear the barks from Three Dot and Sadie, as he crested the ridge and rode down towards the cabin. A small stream of smoke rose above the chimney; it was good to be back. By the time he had reached the hitching rail, both Vern and Virgil had opened the door and were beside him.

"What in the Sam Hill happened to you? We expected you back three or four days ago."

"Best we go inside after I unsaddle Dixie. Then I will fill you in. How's the boy?"

"He's long gone. A day ago we checked on him in the morning and he was sleeping hard, so Virgil and I went out to work in the barn, and when we came back he was gone, clean left the place. The dogs never barked or nothing. He just seemed to vanish and he sure as heck wasn't all healed or anything. We looked for him most of yesterday, but we never even picked up a track. He is long gone and to where is anybody's guess."

"Well, I might know where he went; if I am right, that boy saved my life by throwing pinecones at me. The least I owe him is this medicine to get him well." Chance sat down on his bed and pulled the medicine out of his saddlebags. "I wonder why he came here in the first place," pondered Chance as he glanced up at the cabinet. "Oh, my Lord, did either of you move that little pouch I had up on the cabinet?"

Both Virgil and Vern shook their heads.

"He came back for his pouch, those little trinkets inside that pouch were his, I bet. They were his toys, and if I'm not missing my guess, his only toys." Chance paused for a minute and then stood up and turned his back towards his brothers. "I got some more bad news. Betsy wrote us a letter telling us that she got married."

"What's wrong with that? That's great news."

"Well, the letter also said she was coming out here and she should have arrived late spring, but no one at Meeteetse Creek has heard anything about her. I'm really worried; it seems mighty strange that she and her new husband haven't shown up by now."

Vern sat down in one of the wooden chairs as Chance turned to face them. "You know, Chance, there are a million reasons that she might not get here on time – someone got sick, they couldn't find a wagon train to join, something came up at home. All of them would take us some time to find out about. Let's write a letter home, asking if she and her new husband got started here before we get too worked up. Who knows, they could have written the letter and never left. Besides, where would we even start looking? There is a huge bunch of miles between here and Independence."

"You're probably right, I am jumping to conclusions. I need to slow down and think more rational. Tomorrow I am going to take out after that kid and see if I can find him. This is no country for a young child to be out in alone, especially a sick one."

Raven Dove

Raven ran back to the barn, gathered up her pack, and took a quick look to make sure she wasn't leaving anything out of place. Trotting out into the woods, she grabbed her spear hidden in a dark section of timber, where only one with the best of eyes could have seen it. Link's spear was still there, so she knew that he had made a split-second decision to follow the man. She circled around in the surrounding woods looking for sign, but Link had always been excellent at concealing his presence and hiding his footsteps. After thirty minutes she decided to walk the trail the man had taken with the mule to see if that led to anything. There was something very familiar to her about the mule, and in the back of her mind she couldn't shake the feeling that big mule looked like a grown-up version of the mule she'd raised. But there was no way the mule this stranger had could be Ginger. At least she didn't think it was possible.

The tracks of the man and the narrow cuts of the mule's hoof were very easy to follow as they headed north through the woods. At the Y, the man had taken the upper trail and headed northwest. For the next couple of hours she easily followed the tracks as they meandered across the slope, not dropping or raising much in elevation until the trail broke onto a large, open ridge devoid of any tree cover. Raven just stood at the edge and looked out over the ridge; she knew she couldn't follow anymore. Wherever Link had gone, he was on his own, and she had to decide what to do next.

Finding a spot under a pine tree she sat down, opened her pack, and got some jerky out. She felt extremely alone in this vast country as the constant wind blew strings of her dirty hair across her face. Raven wiped the hair back and noticed how worn and soiled her jacket was. Wouldn't it be wonderful to have a bath and wear clean clothes again? She hoped she would soon find out. Long after she had finished her lunch of several tiny strips of jerky, Raven remained under the tree trying to figure out what to do next.

She could go back to the barn, take everything she could, and head east, but if Link did come back, she would never know, and he would be without anyone. There was a possibility that Link would never return, but she hated to even consider that. Maybe if he couldn't catch up to the stranger, he would turn around and head back to the barn, and then they could make their escape across the rolling, sagebrush-filled prairie together. The thought of abandoning Link was almost more than she could bear, but she knew she had to be strong or she wouldn't survive. Someone had to find help and save everyone still in that hellhole of a slave camp, and she knew it had to be her.

Finally Raven stood up and started back down the trail. Thirty minutes later, something terrifying caught her eye. In a moist spot beside a tiny creek were large mountain lion tracks, as big as any she had ever seen. Their size jolted her senses. At first she thought of Link outside by himself and then she thought of herself and whether she would be able to fight off a cat that size with only a pointed stick. The thought almost paralyzed her. She slowly turned and scanned her surroundings before continuing on, much more cautiously than before.

That night Raven sat alone without a fire in the barn, just thinking and listening. She had only seen the one set of mountain lion tracks, but she knew the big cat had a territory to protect and would pass by this way at some time in the future. The only question was when. Eventually she came up with a plan; she would wait at the barn for the next four days, and if Link didn't come back, she would have to take off on her own to try and cross the prairie. Hopefully she would not be found by Bleeker's men or gets caught in a bad snowstorm. She would have to take the chance.

Alone she spent the night down in the hidden room, which was still stocked with an abundance of beeswax candles. Raven lit several as she studied the small enclosure that was now her temporary and private home. One of the things that surprised her was the lack of insects. The tunnel and its entrances had been made so well that they had protected the space, and with the exception of the dust, everything in the room looked like it had not deteriorated at all since Miss Martha and her husband had left. It made her feel a little warm inside that maybe someday she would be able to tell her how the tiny vault had saved her and Link's life. Soon she fell asleep.

The following day, Raven picked up Link's bow and arrows and decided to hunt around the barn to see if she could find some more food. They would certainly need it on the next part of their journey. The mountain lion was never too far from her mind as she made her way over the hill and scanned the small valley below. Her normal procedure was to walk about ten steps and crouch, listen, and watch for movement, as much for Bleeker and his men, and the mountain lion, as for the game.

She had been hunting for a little over an hour when she heard a hen turkey cluck down below her in the sagebrush. Turkey hunting was not new to her and she knew they had no sense of smell. Quietly descending the mountain, she kept behind trees and sagebrush until she was in range for a bowshot. Turkeys couldn't smell, but their hearing and keen eyesight was exceptional. She saw a dark flash of movement below her, as she silently worked herself closer. The flock was feeding and she could see close to ten bobbing heads as the birds picked berries from the sagebrush. Raven squatted; patiently waiting, and soon the birds turned and began feeding up the hill in her direction. She notched an arrow, and when a small young hen walked out into the open, she pulled back the bowstring and let the arrow fly. The shot was good, but not great, and the turkey launched itself into flight as Raven carefully watched it glide down the mountain with the other birds.

It took close to thirty minutes of searching before she found the bird dead in an open patch of grass. Quickly, she cut off the breast and legs and left the rest under a bush, hoping a coyote would find it and erase any trace that she had actually been there.

Over the next three days, Raven shot three more squirrels and a grouse and cut the meat from each one into strips that could be easily cooked or in the worst-case scenario, eaten raw. The barn had been quiet for the last two nights, and Raven was almost getting used to the total silence of the night. With the exception of an owl or a lone coyote, she had heard almost nothing after dark.

With mixed emotions, she decided to make a small fire to cook some of the meat before the trip across the prairie. The thought of leaving Link was almost unbearable, and she prayed that he would come back, but if she were to survive, with or without Link, it was what she needed to do.

It was the third night when she found herself really scared, listening to the screams of a mountain lion just north of the barn. For more than fifteen minutes, she could hear and sense the big cat's presence. Then there was silence.

The following day with her bow and quiver of arrows, Raven began searching the grounds for mountain lion tracks. There was only one, but it was massive. After spending the day hunting close to the barn with little success, when evening came she returned to the barn, carefully setting the bow and quiver down beside her spear and the post she often leaned against. Second-guessing her decision, she struggled again with the thought of leaving Link. She decided to leave some of the cooked turkey in Link's pack and hoped he would follow her to safety.

In the back of her mind she knew that was more of a pipe dream than reality. Confused and guilty she had made her decision and she hoped she was making the right one. Winter was coming, so if she stayed too much longer, she would be caught by the heavy storms that were common in those parts, and then there would be no chance of crossing the open prairie. Tomorrow she would leave, no matter what.

That night, as always, Raven shut the barn doors and wedged boards up against them. If someone really wanted to get in, he wouldn't be stopped by her efforts, but at least the boards would give her warning and hopefully enough time to prepare to fight back or hide. It was very close to dark when she removed the little circle of grass, soil and roots that hid the spot she had used for a fire. Having carefully placed the round circle of soil, grass, and roots down and out of the way, it took her only minutes before she got a fire started. The heat felt good as she rubbed her hands near the flame. Then she began to cook some of the meat on a stick and organize her few belongings for her journey in the morning.

She was almost done when she heard a quiet thump on the barn door that launched her to her feet as she grabbed her spear. The mountain lion had finally decided to test the barn, and she hoped with the fire and the spear, she would be able to keep the big cat at bay as a quiet scratching sound could be heard coming from the base of the door.

Chance Creager

Chance tied his leather bags on the back of his saddle as Dixie twitched her ears back and forth watching him pack the extra food and the medicine he had bought at Meeteetse Creek. If his guess was right, the boy would be headed back to the old barn where he had found the boy's treasures. Chance waved to his brothers as he gently nudged Dixie with his boot and headed up the small hill that hid the cabin. The sun was shining brightly, as he pushed forward wondering how the little boy was doing.

In the first four hours, Chance covered a lot of ground before stopping to have a bite to eat. Lunch consisted of some dried meat and a little Indian pemmican. He didn't take long to eat, and soon he was back in the saddle and headed cross-country towards the open ridge that hid the entrance to the trail he had found. Several hours later, he pulled the reins of the mule back and examined the open ridge in front of him where he had seen the group of men and their captive.

For the next five minutes, Chance thoroughly examined the ground up ahead until he felt comfortable enough to cross. He was almost all the way across the open ground when he saw tracks – three unshod Indian horses, and they were headed towards the same trail he had found. Chance felt a lump in his throat at the thought of them capturing the boy, especially in the shape he was in; it would be a death sentence.

Raven Dove

Raven stood there listening to the gentle scratching coming from outside the door. It was then that she heard it, a soft moan, the moan of a child. Frantically she began removing the boards that blocked the door and pulled it open to find Link crumpled up just outside, his pale face and body almost lifeless. He was too big for Raven to carry, so she began dragging him inside towards her small fire.

"Hold on, Link, you are all right now; you're with me."

With that, she quickly placed Link by the fire and added wood. Tears were streaming down Raven's face as she rubbed Link's hands. She then tried putting a small cup of water to his lips, hoping he would drink. His warm temple told her he had a fever, but how high she couldn't tell. He looked mighty sick. With the movement, Link slowly opened his eyes and half smiled as he reached into his pocket and slowly removed his pouch with pride.

"You found it! You did it, Link," but in the back of her mind Raven wasn't sure that the effort wasn't going to kill him.

He just lay there with that half smile on his pale face as Raven turned her head so that Link wouldn't see her crying. She had to get it together for him, but the emotions of the moment were too strong. She had lost her family, Betsy, and now the thought of losing Link was unthinkable. Her stomach had been in knots at the thought of losing her only friend and now he was back, but was he dying from the effort? There was nothing she could do now but have Link rest and make him more comfortable.

When she turned back, Link was looking at her and holding out his closed hand. Raven reached out and took his hand in hers as he released his tight grip and dropped something into her palm. Raven took a moment to look; it was one of his trinkets, a beautiful silver brooch with red stones decorating its perimeter.

"Here, you take."

Again a flood of emotion came over Raven as she took the small brooch, held it in her hand, and smiled back at Link with a puffy red face.

"This means more to me than you will ever know, Link. Now I want you to drink some water and rest."

Link just nodded his head, closed his eyes, and dozed off. Raven could tell he was totally worn out. Raven sat back, staring in Link's direction with the small brooch firmly cupped in her hand. She questioned herself and wondered what she could have done differently. She took the brooch and slowly tucked it into her dirty handkerchief; it was all she had to protect this very special gift.

The blow sent Raven tumbling across the dirt floor of the barn as she grabbed her side in pain. She found herself face down in the dirt, and through one eye she could see three pairs of finely painted leggings and moccasins. Defiantly she raised her head and tried to sit up, only to see the Indians standing in front of her with the immense, six-foot-six inch Scar standing in the middle. His intimidating scar and the bloody bandages that were tightly wrapped around his waist didn't appear to bother him. Smug, ugly smiles crossed their faces. Scar took another step towards Raven and slowly slid his Bowie knife from its leather sheath, never letting his eyes leave her.

"You die now."

Scar reached down, grabbed Raven by the hair with one hand, and lifted her to her knees just as a shot rang out and the room filled with black smoke. The Indian to Raven's left threw up his arms, falling violently to the ground. In that split second, Raven kicked at Scar's knee as she rolled to one side, breaking his grip. Immediately the second Indian turned and charged the stranger with his raised tomahawk, only to receive the butt of the stranger's musket hard to his face.

With a loud, bone-breaking crack, the Indian crumpled and fell to the ground as Scar's Bowie knife struck the edge of the stranger's head and knocked him to the ground. The Indian known as Black Elk to his tribe and Scar to his prisoners, stood standing in front of her as the smoke began to clear. Raven made a mad dash towards the barn door, but again Scar's massive foot launched her off the ground and sent her rolling towards the door. The white stranger that had tried to save them now lay face down in the dirt of the barn floor. Raven was out of options as she stared up at Scar's repulsive face.

The startled look on Scar's face surprised Raven as the huge Indian twisted his head to adjust his muscular body, then fell forward to his knees, never letting his eyes leave Raven's. He stared for a moment as a small spot of blood began to appear on the left side of his leather shirt. The huge Indian tried to say something, but before he could speak, he collapsed face first onto the barn floor, an arrow sticking from his back. Raven jumped to her feet to try to help Link as he staggered and dropped his bow before collapsing onto the ground.

Chapter 19

Chance Creager

Chance didn't know how much time had gone by, but when someone began gently wiping his forehead with a warm, wet cloth, he struggled to open his eyes. His head screamed from the pain and he was groggy. He could remember fighting two Indians but little else before everything went black. What had happened to the third Indian? He had no clue. He tried to move his arm but couldn't; someone had tied him securely to one of the large support poles of the barn, leaving him little to no wiggle room. The woman in front of him was young and weathered with streaks of dirt on her face.

"I'm not quite sure what to do with you. On one hand you saved both Link's and my life. On the other hand, the more I think about it, I am pretty sure you stole my mule, and where I come from we hang horse thieves," said the woman in a harsh tone.

Chance coughed and tried to clear his throat, "I ain't no damn horse thief, lady, and I would appreciate you untying me."

"If you didn't steal my mule then where the hell did you get her? And how do I know you ain't one of Bleeker's men?"

"First of all, I bought her about three years ago in Independence, Missouri, from a man named Hamilton. He worked on a ranch there that sells stock to people traveling west."

"What did he look like?" "He was medium age, graying hair and beard, with a weathered face. He was well-dressed, with pressed shirts and a gold tooth in front. Seemed like a pretty decent man."

"That doesn't sound like anyone I know."

"He did business with a neighbor lady, a widow about a mile away from where we lived at the time, and we met him there when we needed stock."

"So he just walked up to you and offered you my mule, did he?"

"Not quite. I actually bought about six different animals, including the mule, but believe me; the furthest thing from my mind was that the stock was stolen. Honest, lady, the last time I stole something was when I was five and my dad gave me one heck of a whooping for that. I haven't stolen a thing since, nor do I intend to. Are you sure that is your mule?"

"Dang right I do. You horse thieves are usually good talkers."

"So how many horse thieves do you know anyway?"

Raven paused, "Well one, counting you, but you are everything I ever thought a horse thief would be."

"And how's that?"

"None of your cotton-picking business; I ain't putting my guard down on you for a moment. I ain't so sure you aren't part of Bleeker's gang, and if you are, you would as soon slit our throats as look at us."

"Well, while you are protecting the boy…" Chance interrupted.

"His name is Link, and he's tougher than most men."

"Sorry, I didn't mean no insult. Well, while you are protecting Link, how about going out to our mule and getting that medicine I brought for him that's in my saddlebag; it may save his life."

Raven stood up, walked out the barn door, and several minutes later returned with a brown bottle. "Is this the medicine?"

"That's the stuff the lady at Meeteetse Creek sold me when I described the gunshot wound to her."

"So you shot him. Well, if it kills him, you're next, that's all I got to say. How much do I give him?"

"She wrote the directions on the bottle, but I think its two tablets every four hours, if I remember right."

"Yeah, that's what it says, this better work."

Chance just sighed as he swung his head away from Raven and talked towards the wall.

"You know I am not sure what hurts more, my head or your stupid questions. Why do you think I have that medicine? I know it had to be Link that saved my life from that band of Frenchies and Indians. Hell, the boy threw pinecones at me until I was smart enough to know there was something wrong, and then I accidentally stole his pouch. Heck, I thought this place was abandoned and whoever lived here years ago must have lost it. I surely didn't know I was stealing from some kid. I mean, man, what kind of person would do that?"

"Who knows? And that's why you shot him?"

"I didn't shoot him, my brother did. He thought Link was this mountain lion that has been hanging around our place. Damn thing killed a sheep, and my brother was way too jumpy. It all was a mistake, a terrible mistake. Who in their right mind would shoot," he paused, "a young man his age?"

"Obviously your brother would."

"Hell, lady, he thought he was shooting a mountain lion, not a young man. He feels terrible about the whole deal, and so do I. Why do you think I rode a day and a half to Meeteetse Creek to get him medicine?"

"Well, that does make a little sense. You must have been there when Bleeker's men brought Betsy through."

"Who's Betsy, and who's Bleeker?"

"Betsy was a young lady that was captured by Bleeker's men. She escaped with Link and me. Unfortunately she got caught and Link saw it, leastwise when they were taking her back. Bleeker's men are animals; they have a whole town that runs on slaves and prisoners. He kidnapped my whole wagon train and shot half the people. If I ever get out of here, I am going to bring the whole world down on their heads. I got to find someone to save those people. His gang doesn't deserve to live, and that's a fact."

"Tell me about Betsy."

"Why would it matter to you?"

"I have my reasons."

"Young, mid-twenties, auburn hair, really pretty, a real nice lady."

"Did she have a turned-up nose and freckles?"

"How did you know that?"

"I think she is my sister; she's missing. My brothers and I got a letter saying she was coming to visit us early this spring, but she never showed up, she and her new husband."

Raven hung her head. "Sounds a whole lot like the same person, I'm sorry for both of us." With that, Raven walked behind Chance and cut his rope as he stretched his arms and back.

"Well, at least that feels better."

Raven picked up the man's gun, handed it to him, and then walked over and sat down beside Link, "You try anything, anything at all, I swear I'll shoot you."

"I get it, lady, but again, I'm only here to help. Would it be too much to see if you could find a bit of snow in some shady spot so I could put some on my head?"

Raven thought about it for a minute, then got up and quickly returned with a handful of snow, which she wrapped in a piece of cloth from her pack. "Maybe this will help."

Chance held it on his bloodied head for a few minutes and then sat it down. "Boy am I tired. I can hardly keep my eyes open."

"Before you fall asleep, what name do you go by?"

"Chance, Chance Creager."

Then he closed his eyes and slumped to one side, asleep.

Raven Dove

Raven stared at the sleeping Chance Creager. There was something familiar about him, but she just couldn't put her finger on it. She really hadn't gotten a decent look at him since he'd arrived and now he lay on the floor asleep, his face still caked with blood in places, yet she knew she had seen him before. Raven turned and walked over to Link and checked his breathing; the medicine seemed to have helped and he was sleeping hard. Maybe by morning his temperature would drop.

Raven thought about dragging both Link and this man called Chance down to the hidden room, but there was no realistic way she could move that much weight, so she gave up on the idea. She heard a distant horse snicker, quietly she grabbed Chance's musket, and reloaded it before stepping out of the safety of the barn. Several hundred yards away, she found three horses tied to separate trees. She led the horses back to the corral, tied them separately, and gave them some hay from the barn that they eagerly began eating. Finally everything seemed to settle down, and the night became quiet as Raven sat down, leaned up against one of the stalls, and closed her eyes; she, too, was instantly asleep.

The next morning she awoke to Chance talking to Link as he kneeled over a small fire, fixing coffee. The smell was heavenly. It was the first time she had smelled coffee since the wagon train had been attacked. Link still looked pale and sick, but he was awake and at least talking a little, that was a good sign.

"Well, Mr. Chance, where is the nearest fort? We are going to need men and lots of them if we are going to take on Bleeker and his gang."

"That's a problem. The nearest fort is more than two hundred miles from here. By the time you got there it would be the dead of winter and you would be stuck until spring. How many men did you say that Bleeker fellow has?"

"Forty or fifty, I would guess, but I don't really know for sure. What about that Meeteetse Creek town where you got the medicine? How many people are there?"

"Probably fifteen or twenty men, but only about half of them are fighting men, and with those odds, I doubt you would get them to join you. A lot of people in these parts take care of their own, like McCabe."

"Who's McCabe?"

"Gillis McCabe came into the valley about two years ago, and from what I know, he has the only truly big ranch in these parts. I can't be sure, but my guess is he has over sixty men and they are tough men with most having fought in the War."

"Well, let's go tell him what going on and see if he will save those people."

"Gillis McCabe is all about Gillis McCabe, and there ain't no way in hell he is going to help you. When I went to get the medicine I also talked to McCabe about saving Betsy, only I didn't know it was my sister until talking to you. He flat out refused to help and basically told me it wasn't his problem. The only way McCabe is going to help you is if there is something in it for him."

"Is there anyone else?"

"Nope, that's it, leastwise until you make it to the fort."

"Well then, I'm going to that Mr. Gillis McCabe's place and convince him to help."

"You can go, but it won't do you any good. The man has no interest in helping his neighbors. Hell, I think he would appreciate someone keeping people out of here so he could gather more land. Good luck with that."

Chance stood up and looked at the three bodies still lying on the barn floor. "Guess I should do something with these bodies. It looks like we will be here for a while."

With that, Chance, with much effort, began dragging the bodies out and away from the barn and over a small rise. Before they started to rot, he was sure they would be long gone, so they wouldn't have to deal with the smell.

It was noon when Link opened his eyes and Raven noticed him moving. "Well, good morning, sleepyhead. You look a lot better today than you did yesterday; you got a bunch of your color back."

"I'm hungry."

"Well, that's because you haven't eaten for a couple of days. No doubt your stomach is asking what the heck is going on here. I have some broth I made from the turkey and squirrel meat. Hopefully that sounds good to you."

Three or four times throughout the day, Raven fed Link some more broth, and Link acted as if he were feeling a lot better. Chance came in and sat down, watching Raven as she spoon-fed Link.

"He sure has come a long way in a short time, tough kid." He paused. "I mean, one tough man!"

Raven just smiled and continued to try and get food into Link. "I am hoping by tomorrow you can take Link back to your cabin and I can light out for McCabe's place. I got to get help no matter what it takes. Bleeker got your sister, and he still has my cousin Elsie." Raven paused. "And she's the only family I have left."

"So if I understand this correctly, you want me to take Link back to the cabin, and you are headed to Gillis's ranch, after everything I told you. You put new meaning into 'stubborn'. You need to know it's a hard day-and-a-half ride north of here; they call his ranch the Greybull. Anyway, you can take Dixie or Ginger or whatever you want to call our mule. She has been there before, and I trust her instincts. She is a great mule. At least we can agree on that."

"How long would it take you and Link to make the ride to your cabin?"

"Probably six to seven hours, if everything goes well. My biggest concern is whether Link can make it. He is one strong young man, but six hours in the saddle is a long time." Link's eyes followed the conversation with a stoic look. Finally he sat up a little more and spoke up in a somewhat pitiful voice.

"I can make it. We need to save Betsy."

Raven and Chance stopped, looked at Link, and smiled. "One tough man, no doubt about it," said Chance.

"It will be dark soon, but I want to light out of here first thing tomorrow morning. I will meet you back at your cabin, hopefully with McCabe and his men. If you need to take another day for Link to get his strength up, then do it. It will take me at least two days, if not three, to get there and back. I will need you to draw out a little map, too."

"Sure thing, but I want you to take my musket with you. It would make me feel a whole lot better knowing you have some protection out on those open prairies. You never know what you might run into out there."

Raven looked up at Chance with a kind of curious look. "Been a while since anyone looked after me or even really cared, for that matter." She hesitated, "Kind of a nice feeling."

Chance seemed embarrassed by her comment as he walked towards the barn door. "Think I will check on the stock," he said. Raven just smiled to herself, then picked up her pack and walked over near Link.

It was early the next morning when Raven tied Chance's saddle bags on the back of Ginger and swung her leg over the saddle as she mounted the tall mule. She found herself excited to get on her mule after all this time and actually looked forward to the long ride.

Chance stood a few feet away with a smile on his face. "Don't worry about anything on this end. Link and I will be at the cabin. Be careful."

His words kept running through her head as she started down the trail, and as it split she took off on the trail that headed north across the prairie.

Chapter 20

The mule's trot was smooth as Raven rode the mile of trail until it disappeared into the grass and sagebrush of the prairie. Ginger gracefully meandered back and forth through the obstacles in front of her and almost always found the most direct route. Raven quickly noticed that the mule seemed to know where they were headed and she never once had to give her a nudge to pick up the pace.

The sun was beginning to set, and scattered black clouds made the sky appear darker than normal. Raven knew she should find a decent camp soon, one that would allow good grazing on a picket rope and water. A patch of tall cottonwood caught her eye on the horizon, and soon she was tying her mule to one of the smaller trees. She walked around until she saw a large, fallen log that would make a good wind break. When she got over to it, she found a small fire pit with blackened ashes. I'm not the only one who thought this would make a good camp spot, she thought, as she turned and headed back to the mule and led her over to the area.

Close to an hour before daylight, Raven was in the saddle, trotting across the prairie. About three hours later, the mule jerked to a stop. Two men on good horses stood in front of them. Raven hadn't seen them, because they had come out of a small coulee. "Hold on there, Ma'am. You're on the Greybull Ranch and we got to stop you and find out your business. I'm sorry, but it's our job."

These men looked tough and in control of the situation. She stared for a moment and let everything sink in. "I need to talk to your boss; I need to talk to Mr. Gillis McCabe."

"Why?" asked the shorter of the two cowboys in a firm authoritative voice.

"I need his help, and I need it now. Either you show me the way, or I will go by myself."

"I'm sorry, miss, but the boss doesn't like strangers much; that's why we're here. Unless there is one heck of a good reason we will need to turn you back around. That's our orders."

"I need his help. My cousin was taken by a gang, and I need to talk to Mr. McCabe."

"Mr. McCabe said that those kinds of problems aren't his and to turn anyone back that tries to come in."

"I understand," said Raven through a soft smile, but I don't know where I am. See, I was chased by…"

In that moment Raven laid her boot into Ginger's side and the two took off at a dead run, hitting one of the men's horses and launching him into the sagebrush. Immediately the other man gave chase, and Raven gave Ginger her head as they raced between the sage and over the rolling ground. Raven had caught the two men off guard, but now the second man seemed to be slowly gaining ground on his big sorrel quarter horse.

"Faster, Ginger, faster!"

All of the sudden Raven could see buildings in front of her in the distance, but she wasn't sure she could outrun the cowboy in hot pursuit. The further they went, the closer he got, as Raven veered to one side and then the other, throwing the quarter horse off stride. The tall log posts of the entrance to the ranch loomed in the distance. Raven kept working the tired mule towards the opening as she heard the sound of men at the ranch, shouting. Raven pressed her thighs harder into the mule's side as its neck began to foam from sweat. The big quarter horse was right beside her, and the cowboy reached for her reins, just as she pulled them back, causing the cowboy overshoot.

"Stop, stop right now!" yelled a finely dressed man with a heavy leather jacket trimmed in sheep fleece. The man looked to be in his thirties as he rushed from the porch of a huge white house that stood prominently on the grounds.

Raven pulled Ginger to a stop so fast that she momentarily lost her balance and fell on the man, knocking them both to the ground.

"What the hell. Never in my life have I…" the man stopped talking and looked at Raven. "You are nothing more than a girl." The thought seemed to calm the man as he turned to face at least twenty men who had gathered to do whatever was required. "Everyone, back to work, I have this situation under control."

A large Negro man grabbed one of the man's arms, as a stocky redhead lifted Raven to her feet. "Thank you, Roper, and thanks for helping her, Jake. Now what's all this about?"

"I came to ask for help from Mr. Gillis McCabe. Some men have taken my cousin Elsie and a bunch of other people, and put them in a slave camp, and..."

"Enough. I already heard a similar story from another gentleman that came through here, a Mr. Creager, if I am not mistaken, and I didn't buy into his story any more than I am going to buy into yours."

"But it's true. They took those people, and we need your help."

"You look dreadful, my dear. Jake, take her up to the house and have Lucie get her some of my wife's old clothes from her closet, and draw a bath. We will talk at dinner." With that, he quickly turned and walked away.

Raven looked down at her clothes. With the exception of her dirty new coat, everything was ripped and frayed, and she saw now why the men hadn't immediately recognized that she was a woman.

"Please follow me, madam," said the man Mr. McCabe had referred to as Jake, "I will introduce you to Lucie, Mr. McCabe's maid."

"He has a maid? Out here in the middle of nowhere, he has a maid?"

Jake just shook his head and pointed towards a side entrance to the house. "You will like Lucie, she's nice, and has a great way of looking at things."

The two walked to the back door, where Jake knocked and then slowly opened it. "Lucie, Lucie, you in here?" he said a little louder.

"Heaven's name, of course I'm in here. Where else would I be? What do you need, Jake?" Lucie was dressed in plain clothes and had a pearly white smile that stretched clear across her soft, black face.

"Well, well, what do we have here? Welcome, missy, come in, come in. Mr. McCabe wants you to draw a bath for her and find her some of his wife's old clothes. I think he wants to have dinner at the regular time, and he wants her to join him. That's all I know."

"I can handle it from here, Jake. Thanks, I will get her all fixed up."

Jake closed the door behind himself as Lucie turned and gave Raven the once over with her eyes. "My God, child, you look like you been rode hard and put to bed wet. What happened to you?"

"I was traveling to Oregon with my family and the whole wagon train was captured. This gang killed my family. I'm not sure all of them are dead, but

I know my aunt and uncle are. There is a man named Captain Bleeker that runs a prison camp up in the mountains that they use to launch ambushes against settlers and wagon trains. They kill anyone who gives them trouble, and the rest they turn into slaves for their gold mine. They are a real bad bunch, a real bad bunch."

"My lamb child, how long did they have you?"

"Four or five months, I would guess, at least it seemed that long, you kind of lose track of time. I need Mr. McCabe and his men to help me save those people and if my cousin Elsie is still alive, her, too."

"For now, let's get you all beautiful with a good bath. I will start heating the water and getting everything ready. You just sit here for a moment, and I will have Oscar get you some hot tea and some cookies I made this morning. They're gingerbread. I hope you like gingerbread cookies."

Raven could feel the saliva accumulating in her mouth as she nodded. As Lucie left, Raven scanned the room, impressed with its beauty and size. The room was filled with padded couches and chairs with string tassels. Raven soon zoomed in on a chair she thought her dirty clothes wouldn't soil. She was amazed that such a place could exist in the middle of nowhere. One day she was in a prison, threatened with death almost every day, and now she was having a bath prepared for her with hot tea and cookies coming.

Soon a well-built Negro man with graying sideburns walked into the room carrying a plate with steaming tea and a stack of cookies. Immediately Raven put her hands on her face, lowered her head and started to cry.

"Missy, are you all right?" asked the man. "Is there something else I can do?"

"No. It's just that I didn't think I would ever see," she paused. "Never mind. No, you are doing everything perfect, and thank you."

Raven sat and savored each bite of cookie and each taste and whiff of the tea. She didn't realize how much she'd missed having a home, and thoughts of Link, Betsy, and even the new stranger, Chance, filled her mind as she sat and relaxed for the first time since the day the wagon train had been captured.

"Well, that bath of yours is ready. Why don't you follow me inside here and I will show you the room? And while you are bathing, I will wash the clothes you have on. I laid out some of Mrs. McCabe's clothes for you to wear when you are finished. They're yours to keep."

Raven just stared in disbelief then followed Lucie back into a nice sized room with a big metal tub in the middle. "I put some of Mrs. McCabe's soft soap in the water for you. Hope you don't mind. I checked the water, and I think the temperature is good. There are towels on that chair. Just come on out when you're finished."

Raven quickly stripped and with a towel on, put all her clothes just outside the door in the hallway. Then she hastily returned to the tub and put her foot into the hot water. Then she lowered her whole body down into the tub, through the sudsy layer of soap into the water. It felt wonderful. She scrubbed and washed between minutes of gentle soothing until the water was cold and she felt she needed to get out.

Quickly drying herself with the towels from the large stack, she picked up the soft undergarments that lay neatly folded beside the towels. Within minutes, she was dressed, and for the first time in months Raven felt clean and wonderful. She stood in front of the mirror and noticed that her body had filled out more. For the first time in her life, she really felt attractive. The knock on the door startled her, as Lucie called out from behind the door, "Everything all right? You need anything?"

"No, I'm good. I will be out in a minute." When she was done combing her hair, Raven noticed a red ribbon still sitting on the chair and used it to tie her hair in place before opening the door and walking out into the hallway.

"My Lord, you look beautiful, girl," exclaimed Lucie, as she jumped to her feet from a chair she had been patiently sitting in.

Raven blushed. "Thank you. It's been a long time since anyone said anything nice to me like that." Lucie just smiled her broad, warm smile.

"By the way, when I went to washing your clothes, I found this brooch of yours wrapped up in your pocket. I was going to polished it up a mite and then put it back with your clothes."

"Thank you, that is so very kind of you."

"Well child, you've seen a lot in your short life. Hopefully the rest will be nothing but good."

"I hope for that, too, but I know that isn't going to happen. I still have unsettled business to deal with."

"Are you ready for dinner now? It's ready for you. Mr. McCabe has already sat down at the table."

Raven didn't know what to expect from Mr. McCabe. He obviously ruled with an iron fist and put up with no nonsense, but on the other hand, he had brought her into the house and treated her like a lady. Raven was nervous about which Gillis McCabe would be waiting for her at dinner.

The black servant rounded the corner in the hall. "Good. It looks like you are ready for dinner. I just came to get you." Raven gave a quick nod and began following the man back to the dining room.

As he opened the door and held it for her, Raven saw just how massive the dining room really was. It was at least thirty feet by thirty feet, with beautiful wallpaper. In the center was a huge table covered by a silk tablecloth with eighteen chairs standing around it.

"Have a seat here, my dear," said Gillis as he and a Negro man stood up. Gillis McCabe pointed to a seat beside his at the head of the table directly across from the large Negro man, the same one she had seen when she had first run her mule through the gates.

"I would like you to meet Roper, one of the finest cowboys I have ever known, a free man and foreman for the Greybull Ranch. He has been with me since I left Virginia years ago."

Raven put out her hand, and the two shook. "Pleased to meet you, Mr. Roper."

"It's just Roper, ma'am, and it's a pleasure meeting you, also. Welcome to the Greybull Ranch."

Raven thought about saying something about her initial welcome but changed her mind quickly, it would do no good in the long run, and she knew it.

"Well, Miss…" Gillis hesitated.

"It's Rachael Dove, but most people call me Raven."

"Well, Miss Raven Dove, I want to compliment you, you clean up very well. Nice to see there was such a beautiful young lady under all that dirt and pile of rags you rode in here with."

"Thank you that was sort of a nice thing to say. Mr. McCabe, I do appreciate all the hospitality you have shown me. Not to change the subject, but how's my mule Ginger?"

"Last time that mule rode in here the mule's name was Dixie, and a man named Chance Creager owned her," interrupted Roper.

"Yeah, it's a long story, but I raised that mule, and when I was in Independence three or four years ago she was stolen."

"By Creager?"

"Heavens no, it was actually stolen by a gang led by a man named Bleeker. Bleeker and his bunch have been robbing and stealing from wagon trains for years. Somehow three of us escaped, but they caught one of us again, Betsy."

"Then how did Chance Creager get the mule?"

"He bought it from a man named Hamilton, one of Bleeker's men, who sold him a bunch of stock before he headed west. Chance sure as heck didn't know it was stolen, leastwise that is what he says, and I believe him."

"So you know he and his brothers have a cabin somewhere near here. I think Mr. McCabe plans to visit them in the spring and make them an offer they can't refuse, them being landlocked and all, but I got to say, I think that Chance Creager is a good man, and an honest one from what I can tell. So how did you get his mule?"

"We are still working out whose mule it really is, but he helped me after I escaped from the prison camp. He killed a couple of Indians that were going to take us back and almost lost his life to a big Indian named Scar. He and Link, a child that escaped with me, are headed back to his cabin as soon as the two of them can ride. Chance gave me the mule to ride because he said the mule knew the way and he trusted her."

"Seemed to me he was more than a little fond of that mule. Surprises me he would loan her to anyone."

"It may surprise you, but that's what happened."

Gillis interrupted Roper, "So tell me more about this Bleeker fellow and his secret prison camp in the hills."

"He calls himself Captain Bleeker, and he has a gang made up of a mix of renegade trappers and Indians; a mean bunch. They sure don't think twice about killing a person. Anyway, they have figured out how to hijack wagon trains as they head west, and they take all their supplies and put most of the people into slavery to work the camp."

"A ways back I heard something about a whole town east of here vanishing, three or four years back. Every person in the town just gone, I wonder if the same guy is responsible."

"I couldn't tell you, but he killed a lot of the people on our wagon train and then hid the wagons and bodies in an isolated canyon. There was one hell of a lot of wagons in that canyon, so Bleeker must have been doing this for a while."

Gillis McCabe leaned back and quietly chewed on a piece of meat before taking his knife and fork and cutting up several more pieces. "How do you know this?"

"I saw it with my own eyes."

"So how many men does Bleeker control?"

"I don't know for sure, but I would guess between forty and sixty, counting the Indians."

"So, young lady, what do you want from me?"

"I want you to help us; I want you to take your men into their camp and save those folks. You are their only chance for survival. You have the men and, from what Chance said, the firepower."

"Tell me, how is the food? You have barely touched it."

"I appreciate your hospitality. It means a lot to me, but what I really want to know is if you will help us."

"Now, why would I help you? Do you know how much blood and guts were spilled to build this ranch? Why would I risk everything to help a bunch of settlers I don't even know? I've got no beef with this Bleeker or his gang. I sure as hell don't see myself as the sheriff of these parts. The only place I am the law is right here on this ranch and no place else."

"So you won't help us?"

"I will give you the same answer I gave that other man, Chance Creager. It is not my affair, and I am staying out of it."

Raven lowered her head and fought back the tears. She had totally believed that she could talk this man into helping her, and now, by the time she got to the Army, everything would most likely be lost.

"You were my last chance," she said, as she stood and walked from the table into the hall where Lucie stood.

"I heard. I'm sorry, Mr. McCabe is his own man, and when he makes up his mind to something, I have never seen him change it. If I were you, I would try to find another way."

"There isn't another way, but thank you, Lucie, for your kindness. If it is all right, I want to leave early, at first light. Maybe those Creager brothers can figure out something. At least they are willing to try and help."

"Mr. McCabe said to tell you to keep those clothes you are wearing; at least someone would get some use out of them.

Raven slept in a small room just outside the kitchen and close to Lucie's room. In the morning she was up early and Lucie met her in the hall with a packed bag of food for the trip.

"Thanks again, Lucie. I know it wasn't your decision."

"I hope everything turns out for the best," said Lucie, as she walked Raven out the side door and down the steps where Roper stood holding Ginger by her reins.

"Well, here's Ginger or Dixie, or whatever her name is. All I know is she is one good mule, the type with heart that you can trust. Sorry about Mr. McCabe. He has never wanted to get into other people's problems, especially strangers. I wish there was something I could do, but there ain't. Be careful on the ride back, and it was nice meeting you."

Raven tied her old clothes to the saddle bags, packed her food, and stepped into the stirrup. "Thanks, Roper. I appreciate the hospitality," as she pulled back one rein and gave the mule a nudge. As she rode through the gates, Raven glanced at her new clothes; they were beautiful and well-made, the type a real lady would wear.

A rosy cast came from the morning sun as it peeked up over the distant hills. Raven made good time across the prairie. It was a good fourteen-hour ride, from what Chance had said, and she planned to ride the whole distance that day. She kept going over in her mind what had been said at the dinner table, wondering if there was anything she could have done differently, but she could think of nothing. If she was going to save Betsy, Elsie, and the others, it would have to be just her and the Creagers.

Chapter 21

The ride back went well, with Raven and Ginger trotting most of morning. At noon Raven stopped in a small patch of cottonwood, ate lunch, and drank from a small spring. She appreciated the lunch. Lucie had fixed her a roast beef sandwich, which had been packed in a small white cotton cloth. Her mind wandered to the prison camp and what they might be doing to Betsy. They were cruel, smart men and the lack of capture of Link and herself had to have touched a nerve at the camp. Who knows what Bleeker would do once he found out Scar was dead and she and Link were truly gone. The weather was spotty at best, and the heavy snow of winter would soon hit with a vengeance. Bleeker would have to react soon, and it probably wouldn't be good.

Even with Chance, his two brothers, and herself, they were only four against at least forty, not good odds in anyone's mind. The sun was beginning to fall in the western sky, and the first snowflake hit her cheek as she rode. Hopefully she could find the cabin before the storm opened up and blinded her vision. It would be difficult enough in the dark without snow so thick that she couldn't tell what direction she was traveling in. By Chance's estimate, she had about four hours of riding left before she would find the small, secluded valley where they had built their cabin. Raven could only hope she could find it in the dark.

As she thought about Chance, there was something very familiar about him. She knew she had seen him before, but where? The thought kept crossing her mind as she rode. Where had she seen this man before? His tall, lean body, his smooth gait, and his deep strong voice were so familiar. Where had they met before?

The cry of a distant coyote broke into her thoughts. The snow was beginning to stack up on her shoulders as she rode, and she prayed Ginger would somehow find her way through this snow. Her visibility was becoming less and less and the wind seemed to be picking up. "I hope you can find your way home, girl. I don't like what this storm is threatening to do," Raven said as she leaned over the neck of her mule. "If anyone can get us back, you will."

The mule kept walking in and out of the clumps of sagebrush and Raven watched to make sure they didn't cut their own trail. Suddenly the mule stopped and pointed its ears into the blowing snow. In front of them a small herd of elk crossed and continued moving down the valley. Thank God that wasn't any of Bleeker's men, thought Raven, as she nudged the mule back into a light trot.

Several hours later, Raven could feel her toes and fingers beginning to go numb, and she hoped the faith she had in the mule was not misplaced. She wondered just how long she should keep going. Had they missed the entrance to the valley where Chance and his family had built their cabin? She doubted that if they stopped she would get a fire started in the cold dark with four inches of new snow covering the ground and no wood to keep it burning. Maybe her luck had run out. Slumping in the saddle, she tucked one hand inside her jacket, hoping to warm it long enough to ride at least a couple more miles before her hands were too cold to hold the reins.

Raven found herself nodding off, so she jerked her head up. She should have made camp hours earlier and waited out the storm with a warm fire, but now it was too late. Again she dropped her head as she started to fall asleep, but this time when she jerked her head back up she saw a light in the distance.

At first her mind questioned its existence, but Ginger had apparently seen it also and was making a beeline towards it. From what she could tell, it was a fire, a fairly large fire, and someone had built it up on a small rise so it shone over a large area of the valley. Raven's spirits jumped as Ginger picked up speed, heading towards the light. Then she saw the silhouette of a man, a tall, lean man in a heavy coat and hat; it was Chance Creager!

Ginger stopped in front of Chance, and he helped Raven down to the ground and got her close to the fire. "I think we need to warm you up a mite; pretty cold out there."

Raven staggered towards the fire with Chance helping her. "I was wondering if you were going to save me again. I hope this doesn't become some kind of habit with you."

"Just warm up a bit, the cabin is only about a mile and a half from here. My brothers will have a nice fire and hot coffee ready when we get there, you'll be fine."

Chance held Raven upright as she struggled to stand and let the campfire warm her. "Are you doing a bit better?"

Raven turned her head and smiled, "Yeah, I'm doing better. Thanks for coming out and looking for me. I was getting a mite concerned that I wouldn't find your place in this storm."

Ten minutes later, Chance helped Raven back up onto the mule. "How's that feel? Can you make it for thirty minutes or so back to the cabin?"

"Don't worry about me. I'll be fine."

Few words were spoken on the ride back. The light from the cabin's only window was a welcome sight. The dogs were barking and several of the horses whinnied as the two arrived. Chance helped Raven to the ground as the two brothers and Link met them in the dark at the hitching rail.

Link hugged Raven hard, and she could see the look of concern on Link's face. Virgil and Vern greeted Chance with handshakes that were followed by a good pat on the back. As they finished exchanging greetings, Virgil took their two mounts to the barn for a rubdown and some oats. Vern jumped up on the porch and held the door open as Chance helped Raven inside. Link stayed tightly by her side. "Well, let us get some hot coffee into you and sit you down by the fire so you can get your blood moving again," said Vern as he stopped and stared.

"What's the matter?" said Raven staring up at Vern.

"I'm sorry, ma'am, but Chance didn't tell us just how beautiful you are, and well, we don't see a lot of women, and none as pretty." He paused. "I better stop before I just dig myself a hole deep enough to reach China."

Raven blushed and her eyes began to water as she spoke, "No one has ever talked to me that way. Thank you, it means a lot. I guess I have been mostly a tomboy for the best part of my life, and then that prison camp, and well, I just haven't thought in those terms before."

"You did clean up real good. I would have never in my wildest dreams thought there been a woman as pretty as you under all that dirt and those baggy clothes," said Chance.

"I think a lot of it is the clothes I got from Mrs. McCabe."

"Mrs. McCabe gave them to you?"

"Well not her personally, her maid, Lucie, gave them to me, why?"

"Mrs. McCabe died several years back, at least according to Jake, one of the hands on the ranch. She never came back from a horseback ride, and they just found her horse near the river. They figured she drowned in the river."

"Oh, that's terrible. I didn't know, I just assumed."

"Well, enough of this. Let's get you close to that fire," said Chance.

Raven focused on Chance. A clean white bandage covered his wound, and now he was clean-shaven. Without his coat, she noticed his tall body and wide chest. There was something so familiar about this man, and she felt like she had known him for a long time.

Virgil walked through the door and crossed the room to where Raven sat in a chair in front of the crackling fire.

"Well, Raven, it's nice to finally meet you. That's quite the journey, you making it to McCabe's place and back by yourself. That's some accomplishment this time of year, if I do say so myself," said Virgil.

"She is pretty amazing, I agree," added Chance, as he put a warming rock from the fireplace at Raven's feet and gently removed her iced-over moccasins.

The group had twenty minutes of light talk, and during that whole time, Link sat tightly beside Raven. "Link, you look so much better. It seems these fellows took real good care of you."

Link nodded slowly, as he lowered his head just enough not to make eye contact with anyone.

"Raven, do you feel like talking anymore, or do you need some rest?" inquired Virgil.

"I can talk for a little while longer, but that fire is making me sleepy. I am sure you want to know what McCabe said, though."

Everyone nodded their heads and focused on Raven.

"He refused to help, didn't offer a man or gun. It was a totally wasted trip. Chance was right. He warned me. The man just doesn't give a damn about any of his neighbors or the settlers. There must be something in his past that made him such a hard man. Frankly, I have no idea what we do now."

"Well, let's visit for a few minutes, then just sleep on it tonight, and come morning we can talk some more. Link has done real well. One thing for certain is he really likes chicken soup and Three Dot."

Raven looked puzzled. "Oh, Three Dot is one of our dogs; they instantly bonded. I let Three Dot sleep beside Link for the last couple of days. Link isn't the most talkative young man I have ever been around, but he is a good boy, and we have enjoyed his stay."

"Well, tell us about your escape. How did you get out of that prison camp? We asked Link, but it didn't do us much good; he's a little short on the conversational end of things."

"Well, it was Link that found us a way out, and with the help of his mother, we somehow survived."

"His mother?"

"Yeah, Link was born in the camp. His mother is still a prisoner. She is an older lady in charge of the women in one of the cabins. Her name is Miss Martha. Without her I don't think any of us would have made it. One of the guards is sweet on her, and he helped get us our packs and supplies. It's a long story, but Link was the keeper of the snakes in a cave heated by a hot springs or vents or something, but it was enough to keep the snakes alive. His job was to feed the snakes by trapping rats and other small animals around the camp. He had free run of the old mines and caves, and when an earthquake shook the camp about four months ago, it had apparently opened a new passageway in one of the caves."

"The new opening linked a network of passageways that worked their way up to a steep, rocky cliff high above the camp. Link found the new passageway months before, but Miss Martha was the only person he'd told, and she kept it a secret. When Miss Martha was growing up, on a farm back in Ohio, they used salt all the time to move their livestock from pasture to pasture. Miss Martha thought of the idea of putting out a little salt to see if the animals would show them a way up through the rocks. Anyway, the three of us, including your sister Betsy, escaped using the trail the game made."

"How did the three of you get separated?"

"Betsy and I talked, and we knew if we were going to save those people back at camp, we had to give ourselves the best chance at doing that. We knew they were looking for us, and splitting up seemed to be the best chance for one of us to find the Army or someone to save all the rest of those people, including my cousin."

"Your cousin, your cousin was in the camp, too?"

"When Bleeker's men took control of the wagon train I thought all three of them, my aunt, uncle, and cousin, were killed, at least that's was what one of the women from the train told me. They murdered anyone who put up any resistance or didn't fit what they needed. From what I could tell, they killed more than half of our group. I didn't know my cousin made it until I saw her at the Gathering just before we escaped. They kept the women they intended to sell in a different part of the camp, away from everyone else, and we didn't have any interaction."

"Now that they captured Betsy, what do you think this Bleeker guy will do to her?"

"I really don't know, but she will be punished. To what degree, I don't know."

"Betsy is our sister and knowing she is in that hellhole with the other captives, well we just have to do something, and fast. We were hoping somehow that your visit to McCabe's place – well, never mind. We will think of something. Anyway, with all those trappers and Indians hunting you, how did you ever elude them for so long?"

"Well, again, it was Miss Martha. She made a map showing a cabin high up in the cliffs that she and her husband had built years ago. Miss Martha has been a prisoner for at least twelve years, but before that she and her husband had a home down in the valley, the one Chance found. They had another hidden cabin way up in the mountains, a small mining cabin with this amazing trail cut into solid rock in places leading to it. We would have never even guessed it was there, and I seriously don't believe anyone else would have either without a map. I hear some Indian gave them a map and they followed it to this place."

"Was it a leather map? " "I have no idea, I never saw it. I think she was going from memory. I only know that it turned out to be a very safe place, and we stayed there for about a week, hoping they would bypass us before we tried to make it down to the prairie." Raven paused. "I guess I am more tired than I first thought."

"Well, I made my bed for you, but I am worried you won't be able to stand the snoring. Vern and Virgil are terrible to sleep around."

"It couldn't be any worse than the prison cabin. Anyways, I just appreciate the warm room and the blankets. It will sure feel good to sleep in a bed."

"Would you mind talking later about that mountain cabin?" asked Virgil.

"Sure, we can talk later. I'm sorry, I shouldn't have…"

Chance interrupted. "It's okay. We will talk in the morning." Link walked over and lay down in Virgil's bed as Virgil took Three Dot outside to be with Sadie. Then Virgil sat down in the chair closest to the fire and pulled his blanket up over his shoulders. One of the few open spots on the rough spruce floor was next to Raven's bed, so Chance laid his blanket out on the floor there. Vern turned out the pale red lantern that hung in the middle of room before climbing into bed.

Chance was almost asleep when he felt a small hand on his shoulder; it was Raven. She quietly whispered, "Thank you, Chance."

Chance lay on the floor, unable to sleep, his thoughts jumping from Betsy, then to Raven's soft touch. She looked so familiar, and the sheer touch of her hand was strangely exciting him. It bothered him that he could think this way about Raven when he should be thinking of his sister, but he couldn't help it. He felt guilty and helpless, feelings he didn't often experience.

The gentle crackle of the fire woke Chance, and he saw Vern stoking the coals of the fire in the dark room. Chance rose to his feet and looked outside; it was still dark, and he felt glad the dogs hadn't detected any signs of danger close by. He walked to the stove and put some kindling in the stove box. Then Chance walked outside to the well to get some fresh water as the two dogs poked their heads out of their small doghouse made from wood and buffalo hides. The walk over to the well was quick in the cold of the morning, and soon he was back with two buckets of water.

The wonderful smell of boiling coffee met Raven's nose as she opened her eyes and realized where she was. Immediately she looked over to Virgil's bed and saw Link sleeping peacefully, then she looked at Chance making coffee on their fancy metal stove. A feeling of safety came over Raven, something she hadn't felt for quite a while. The strong, good-looking man standing at the stove making coffee seemed so calming and protective. It felt strange. For the first time in a long time, she remembered how much she appreciated the memories of her family. This was the closest she had been to that feeling since those last days on the wagon train.

Vern lit the lantern just as Chance looked over and saw Raven's eyes were open. "Well, good morning. We have a lot to do today, but before we talk we need to get a good meal in you. Did you sleep well?"

"Like a rock. Thank you for letting me sleep in your bed."

"It's a good bed. We brought it from home."

"And where might that be?"

"Iowa, good old Iowa. We have a farm and ranch there, a real pretty place that has been in the family for years." Chance paused. "Looks like the first batch of eggs are ready, and the coffee is on the table. Help yourself. After we have all eaten, we need to get an idea what we are up against: the layout of the camp, number of men, and where they are usually located."

"So you plan to attack the camp with three men?"

"Three men and you, that makes four."

"You don't understand. There were at least sixty of Bleeker's men there when we escaped, and with the Gathering there were twice that many. We would have no chance, none. It would be suicide to try. Don't you understand?"

"I totally understand, but my brothers and I couldn't live with ourselves knowing our sister is in the hands of those murderers, well, you know what they are. We will need you to draw the camp out in as much detail as you can, and when we get there, we will figure out a plan. We want to live as much as anyone, but this is something we have to do, and as you know, there ain't going to be anyone to help us."

Raven just sat there, not knowing how she wanted to respond. "Well, if you three are going to try, then I am, too, but what about Link?"

"I hadn't thought that far ahead. I guess he needs to be a part of this just as much as the rest, his mother being a prisoner and all." Chance glanced over towards Link's bed and saw Link staring at him with a look of determination.

"I guess that look on Link's face says it all; he's going. I just hope he is strong enough to do this."

For at least an hour after breakfast, Raven drew a map of the camp in as much detail as her memory and her drawing skills would allow. "It's going to be real tough getting past the front gates. They have two towers with guards, and they have a great view of the surrounding terrain. It is almost a perfect entrance with a rock cliff that works itself across the shelf the camp is on. I never got a look if there were any other passages through the rocks, but there could be – but it would be my guess that they would be guarded, too."

"Well, once we get there, we will try and figure out a plan that will work. We will travel to that barn you stayed in today, and early tomorrow, we will find an isolated spot where we can camp, a mile or so from their camp.

After that, I don't know," said Chance, as he looked into the faces of his two brothers, who both nodded their approval.

It wasn't long before everyone was packed and saddled up. Raven was riding Ginger, and Chance had saddled one of their horses for himself and one for Link.

"I left a week's food for the livestock and the dogs. Hopefully we will be back in four or five days, before they run out of food," said Vern, as Chance nodded as he pulled the rein of his horse and gave the stout gelding a nudge with his boot. The rest followed.

The darkness of early morning was lifting, and visibility was getting better as the first rays of sunlight began hitting the sky. "Sure is cold. Winter is going to be here in full force real soon," noted Vern as he rode up beside Chance.

"We just have to figure a way out for Betsy and those people, before we get snowed in and it ain't going to be an easy task, that's for sure."

There was still a good hour of light left when the five of them finally reached the old barn that had been part of the homestead of Quinten Wilson and his wife, Martha. The large, windswept chimney looked more like a grave marker, standing solidly over the burnt remains of the once solid cabin.

"Try and find posts around the corral that are still solid enough to tie to and let's feed out that last bit of grass that is in the barn."

Raven jumped in and, with Link's help, ignited a small fire where they had built their previous fires, before she started cooking dinner. "Vern and Virgil, there is a passageway and safe room under the floor. It's over in that corner there, by that post, under the hay and dirt."

Vern and Virgil walked over and, with a couple of thumps with the end of their rifles, found the entrance and opened the hatch.

"Wow, looks like these people were worried a mite about a problem coming their way."

"Unfortunately trouble caught them before they could use it. Miss Martha's husband and son were working on a trail up the mountain, but their daughter was killed when she fought back. The secret room didn't help them much, but it saved our bacon. Somehow, in a snowstorm, we stumbled upon this place when we were working our way down off the mountain. I guess having the map and having luck on our side made the difference. We also found that rock outcropping that looked like an old man staring into..."

Vern interrupted. "You know where the rock shaped like an old man is? That shows on our map."

"You have a map?"

"Yeah, Chance found it in an old chest under an abandoned wagon halfway up the mountain."

"I think I know why it was there. They were trying to build a road partway up the mountain to get supplies to their cabin."

"Did they say anything about the gold?"

"No, not really, it probably didn't seem important with all the other things we had going."

"But you found the old man rock?"

"Yes, and we found the ancient trail that was cut out of solid rock in places that takes you up to where they built that cabin. Someone long ago sure did a lot of work to build that trail, and if you didn't know that great big limber pine marked its entrance, I doubt you would ever find it."

"So that's what that straight line is with all the marks coming out from it, a limber pine with all those extra limbs. Who would have guessed?"

Raven looked at Vern. "I don't want to take the wind out of your sails, but you seem awful excited about something you will probably never see. Do you remember that in the next day or so we are going up against at least forty men, if not more, and if we can't figure out some way to slip in there and free Betsy and Elsie without someone seeing us, we are all dead?"

"Yeah, I remember, but thinking about finding a gold mine is, well, it's kind of exciting and helps a man to think about getting through this."

"I'm sorry. I shouldn't have come down so hard on you. Forgive me, I owe you and your brothers a lot and I should be thanking you, not giving you a hard time about risking your life."

The five of them ate and afterward Raven sat down beside one of the stall walls. Chance walked over and sat beside her. "You know there is a good chance that not all of us are going to make it back from this fight, so having something to look forward to, to take your mind off the danger might not be all bad."

"I know. I guess I am scared, and sometimes, well, everything comes out different than how I mean it to."

"I understand," said Chance as he reached over and put his hand on Raven's.

"Chance, your hands are all red. Did you burn them?"

"In a way, I got a little frostbite on the way to get Link's medicine. Turned into a harder ride than what I was expecting. I hit a blizzard, and if it weren't for Dixie," he paused, "or Ginger, I wouldn't have made it. If it weren't for her, I don't think we would have gotten that medicine and saved Link."

"Damn good mule, isn't she?"

"Yeah, damn good mule. Maybe somehow she will get us out of this fix," said Chance with a smile. "I just wish she was that smart."

The next morning the group was up early and had breakfast quickly. There was little talk, as each person was dealing with what lay ahead and there were a lot more questions than answers. Everyone except Link had a rifle and pistol and at least fifty rounds of ammunition, and everyone knew it was not nearly enough for the group they planned to encounter. They rode all day looking for a landmark that Raven would remember. She had been passed out most of the trip, but the image of a wide river was always in her mind. If they could find that, they would be able to locate the secluded camp.

The sun was beginning to set when Vern pointed and said excitedly, "There's the river, wide and shallow."

"Let's find a place out of the way and camp. We don't need anyone finding us before we are ready. Later tonight I will sneak down, and hopefully there will be enough moonlight for me to get the lay of the land," said Chance.

A little hollow on the side of the hill gave them everything they needed: water, seclusion, and a place a small fire wouldn't be seen. "Link, only gather dry wood; we don't need any excess smoke giving away our location, and keep it small, just big enough to heat coffee and cook on. Vern, you take first watch, and then Virgil. When I get back I will spell you, and then we can figure out our next move."

Each person took a plate of hot food as Raven dished them up, as well as some coffee to wash it down. When Raven was done, she got up and headed over to where Chance sat on an old log, and ate beside him. "I want you to be careful tomorrow. I have kind of grown accustomed to you being around." Then she just looked at the ground in front of her.

The more Chance found out about this woman, the more he cared about her. Then it struck him where he had seen her before. "You were on the steps of that attorney's office, what's-his-name's place."

"You mean Attorney Andy Harrison?"

"Yes, that's him. So you do remember?"

"How could I forget? It was the memory of this tall, lean cowboy that I thought of as a prisoner, but I didn't think you would remember a young girl with a big hat and baggy clothes."

"Hell yes, I remembered you. I remember wishing you were a mite older and wondering what you would have looked like in clothes that fit. I remember how beautiful your eyes and face were, and I thought I would never see you again."

Vern came hurriedly to where the two of them sat, "Chance, we are surrounded."

Then they heard a voice, "Drop your guns and stand up, and raise your hands where we can see them."

Chapter 22

Chance and Raven slowly rose to their feet. As Chance raised his hands, he looked at Raven. "This isn't how I planned this."

"I know, but don't make any sudden moves."

From out of the dark walked three men with their guns drawn. "Keep your hands up high," said the shorter man in a heavy sheepskin coat.

Raven could feel her stomach twisting into a knot. How had they found them? Had someone given away their position?

"Men, keep your guns ready. We don't need any of these skunks trying anything."

Raven suddenly recognized the voice. "Marshal Dicker, is that you?"

The man in the sheepskin coat kept his gun trained on Raven as he walked over to her. "Do I know you?"

"Yes, I'm Raven Dove. We met in Independence. My uncle and cousin helped you after someone rolled you. We found you in the mud in front of that saloon."

The Marshal just stared for a moment and then lowered his gun, "Raven, is it you? What in tarnation are you doing out here? Do you know how much danger you are in?"

"Marshal, it's a long story, but I know all about their camp; I escaped from there. If it wasn't for their sister, my cousin, and Link's mother, I don't think I would have had the courage to come back, but we have no choice. I figure you three are here because of the gang and the prison camp, just like us. Our wagon master, a man named Captain Bleeker and his men led our wagon train into a trap. Bleeker robbed and killed a good bunch of the settlers and took the rest prisoners for his prison camp."

"I know all about Bleeker and his partner, Hamilton. About six months ago an old teamster named Barton came into my office and spilled his guts about the whole thing. I had been investigating those disappearing wagon trains for several years. No one seemed to have clue as to what was happening, or if they did they weren't talking. I think there are quite a few people involved, but Barton pretty much opened the whole can of worms. Someone must have found out he'd been talking to us, because we found him dead in the alley the next morning."

"My deputies and I are here trying to find their camp. With Barton's help, we learned about Bleeker's trick of turning off the trail on solid rock so he left no trace. The Army is, at best, a couple of weeks behind us, and once we find the camp, we plan to ride back and meet up. They will clean out this den of rats. We were looking for Bleeker's trail when we came on yours. Who are these men you're with? I don't recognize any of them."

"They are the Creager brothers. They live in the Greybull Valley, and their sister is one of the captives." Raven pointed towards them. "This is Chance, Vern, Virgil, and the young man over there is Link. He was born in the camp."

"Well, these two are my deputies, Hollenbeck and Hood. We also have an Indian tracker, but we haven't seen him for a couple of days. He normally scouts ahead and makes contact with us in the evening at least once every couple of days. Hopefully he will be back tonight."

"Come in and set up camp with us. Bleeker's camp is less than two miles from here. Put your stock back with ours. We were just trying to figure out our next move. Bleeker and Hamilton have somewhere between forty and sixty men and almost that many Indians working for him. We were discussing how we might sneak in there and rescue Betsy and hopefully Elsie, if she is still there."

"How were four of you, or, counting the young man there, five of you, going to get past all those men? From what Barton said the camp is heavily guarded. That's why we have the Army coming. We figure they aren't giving up without one heck of a fight."

"Because we have no choice; if we don't get Betsy out, they will kill her for sure, and finding Elsie after someone bought her and took her to who-knows-where would be next to impossible."

"So you really don't know if Betsy is even alive or not?"

Raven hung her head, so Chance joined the conversation. "Marshal, that's our sister in that camp and she helped save Raven. We just have to believe they are both still alive. We are going to make a plan, and then we are going to try, no matter what happens."

Raven looked back up at the Marshal. "If Bleeker and Hamilton do to Betsy what they have done to others that met their anger, they will shackle her to what we called the Devil's Cross. It's a heavy-timbered cross that sits out in the sun, and he usually keeps them there for a number of days before Hamilton makes an example of them. The prisoners are forced to watch Hamilton use his knife, and he knows how to inflict pain."

"We certainly aren't going to commit suicide, but we are here to help. I guess with me and my men that makes eight. At least the odds are getting better."

Raven gave a weak smile. "Tonight we will come up with some ideas, and hopefully by tomorrow we will have figured out a way."

"If we do make this happen, do you have an exit strategy? Bleeker and his men are going to be on us like hornets if we pull this off."

"We know," said Raven.

For the next hour the group set up camp and made a simple, cold dinner. Everyone was quiet, trying to figure out what to do, as well as dealing with the real possibility that this could be their last meal.

The Marshal stood up and walked over to where Raven and Chance sat on a log close to Link. "Mind if we talk?"

"Sure," replied Chance.

"From what I am gathering, you really don't have a plan or a way into the compound."

Raven just shook her head in agreement.

"So how do you think we can get in there without anyone knowing?"

"It won't be we. Chance, Link and I are going, hopefully tomorrow early in the morning while it is still dark, but I haven't figured out every detail yet."

Link looked up and quietly spoke. "I might know a way, just between the rock wall that falls off into the river and the vertical riverbank there is a very narrow trail that small game uses. I don't know if a full grown man can get through on it, but I can."

"How do you know this?" asked the Marshal.

Raven jumped in. "Link had full access to the camp so he could trap small game for the snakes."

"There are snakes this high?"

"Only in the mine shaft that has some thermally heated vents from the mountain. They use the snakes for their get-together called the Gathering. Anyway, Link would know, and I trust him."

The Marshal stood up and rubbed his neck, then turned to Deputy Hood. "Would you go out and relieve Hollenbeck? He needs to get some chow in him."

"Yes sir."

Link looked at Raven and then at the Marshal. "It will work."

"If we do this, we are putting a lot of faith in a very young man. Are you sure he knows what he is talking about?"

"I have already trusted him with my life. Hopefully you and everyone else can cover our escape if we run into trouble."

"Well, that doesn't sound like much of a plan, but it might work. Tomorrow morning, how about Chance, Link, and the two of us sneak up near the camp and get the lay of the land?"

The group talked for a while longer before curling up in their wool bedrolls and settling in to get some sleep. The air was cold, everyone could feel the bite of winter starting to set in and the thought of a warm fire was on each person's mind. In the middle of the night Link got up and came over and lay down on one side of Raven, as Chance rolled over and put his back against Raven's.

The next morning, everyone began moving around. No one had slept well because of the cold, and if it hadn't been for their thick coats, no one would have slept at all. They ate jerky and hard bread, and soon Chance was leading the small group through the thick trees towards the camp. They dropped a lot in elevation as they went. Working their way down towards the river, they came upon a wide trail pounded with recent horse tracks.

Chance knelt down and looked at the tracks. "It would be my guess that there were at least twenty unshod horses that went through here in the last couple of days. Hard telling for sure, but they were certainly on the move. From what I see, we can cross the trail up here a little farther on that rock so we don't leave any tracks."

Chance continued on, moving a few steps, then looking around and listening before moving forward with the group. It was slow going, but an hour and a half later they could see one of the towers protecting the gate through the trees. "Let's move a little closer so we can see both towers," suggested Chance.

"Only looks to me as if one tower has a guard. I sure don't see anything moving in the other one," observed the Marshal.

"That's strange," said Raven. "Usually the Indians man the guard towers, and that ain't no Indian with that beard and all. I wonder what is going on. At least with the one tower unoccupied it should be easier to get to where Link says there is a trail. Let's move down there and take a look."

"This isn't the way you escaped, is it?" asked the Marshal.

"No, I guess we might have gotten out this way if the trail was enough, but they would have caught us within hours. Making them climb the mountain gave us at least a half day's head start, and we were lucky."

The group stayed low as they picked their way down through trees and sagebrush to where the natural rock wall of the camp collapsed over the steep bank of the river.

Link took the lead, and moments later he pointed, "There."

The trail was hidden by a big sage, so Chance carefully laid back a branch and looked closer. "There is a trail. It's more the size of what a rabbit would use than a man, but there is a trail. I am going to walk it a bit and make sure we can get to the other side."

Chance disappeared behind the large sage and then under a wide pine as the others knelt down and waited. Ten minutes later, Chance crawled back out from under the tree and from behind the sage. "Link was right; you can make it all the way to their camp. There's one spot where, if you slip, the fall will take you a good thirty feet to the rocks below, so we are going to have to be especially careful in the dark."

"Let's work our way back. Let's take a different route, just in case," said the Marshal. "No need to not take our time."

Chance led the way, lifting small branches and weaving and crawling between sagebrush where the cover wasn't high enough to hide their kneeling posture. They were back in the trees again and headed for a small meadow when Chance threw up his hand for them to stop and be quiet. "I heard something. It came from that small meadow. You stay here. I am going to investigate." With that, he took off crawling towards the meadow. Within minutes, he was back. "There's a man tied between a couple of trees. By the amount of blood, someone worked him over real good."

"I'm going to take a look, Chance. Why don't you scout around the meadow and make sure this isn't a trap," said the Marshal as he began crawling forward.

Chance looked at Raven. "You and Link stay hidden. I will be back as soon as I scout around a little." Raven's face showed her concern as she nodded her head in agreement.

Chance circled the meadow and found a trail used by unshod horses, then continued into the meadow. Marshal Dicker had cut the man down and drug him back into the shade of a pine tree.

"Is he alive?"

"Yeah but just barely. Those bastards worked him over pretty bad."

Marshal Dicker poured a little water onto the man's lips. His bloody face was peeled from both the sun and the gratuitous use of a knife. Dried blood covered his body, and the man quietly moaned with every slight movement.

"Little Crow, can you hear me?" The Indian face was bloody and Marshal Dicker tried to get the man to focus on him, but it was then that he realized the Indian's eyes had been removed.

"My God, those bastards cut out his eyeballs."

"Is he your missing scout?"

"His name is Little Crow, and he has worked for me a couple of years. He's a brave and smart man. It must have taken the whole bunch to surround and capture him."

Little Crow tried to raise his hand to the Marshal's face. He moaned and his hand slumped back to the ground. "omathk-attayo great spirit."

"What about omathk-attayo spirit, Little Crow?"

The man was trying to communicate, but his pain was too intense. The man crumpled in the Marshal's arms.

Link and Raven came silently into the meadow and just stared for a moment at the dead man. Link had seen too much of this. They both looked away.

"What did Little Crow mean omathk-attayo spirit?" said Chance to the Marshal.

"I'm not positive but I think that is the name the Black Feet use for big howler or mountain lion. Little Crow was certainly concerned about it. Apparently the Indians are real afraid of a big mountain lion that's around here."

"We have enough to deal with without worrying about a mountain lion," said the Marshal.

"Should we bury him?" asked Chance.

The Marshal hesitated for a moment, "No, let's put him back up against those trees and retie him in case they come back. It's not very befitting for man of his caliber but if we bury him and they come back it could cost up our lives. Take a branch and wipe out any boot prints. Then let's head back to camp."

An hour later, they quietly made eye contact with the guard and walked into their camp and sat down without saying a word.

Virgil walked over to the four. "Are you alright?"

"No, we found Little Crow, our scout, but some Indians had found him first. They have a terrible way of torturing a man. He did say something before he died. He said, "omathk-attayo spirit, apparently a big mountain lion has been giving the Indians some trouble."

Late that night, the group took their time as they headed down closer to the place where Chance had explored the trail through the rocks. A half moon dimly lit the area as the group huddled together for close to two hours in the tall sagebrush until Chance and Raven decided it was time. Raven carried a small hatchet as well as her Colt pistol as Link led the way, and Chance followed with his musket. It was almost impossible in the dark to see their footing, but they went slowly and carefully placed each step.

All of a sudden, Raven felt the loose shale slide. Her foot slipped, and she frantically reached for a branch of sage. In almost slow motion, she felt herself falling, but the falling stopped when Chance grabbed her sleeve and pulled her back up in one motion.

"That was close," she whispered as she felt a drop of sweat on her forehead.

"I only hope no one hears that sliding shale and decides to investigate."

Minutes later, they had made it to ground with solid footing and crawled up beside one of the dark cabins. Raven put her finger in front of her lips and pointed towards the next building. It took several minutes, but they crawled behind a log halfway between the buildings and took a moment to look around.

"I haven't seen a guard yet, and that bothers me," whispered Raven. "There should have been at least one walking by on the road by now."

"I guess we stay on the back side of this row of cabins," answered Chance. "Once we get past the blacksmith's building, then we have one more cabin to go. It's a big one and stands out a bit."

They continued crawling, pulled themselves up against the wall of the blacksmith shop and looked around. Just then, a chunk of splintered wood cut Raven's face, and the sound of a gunshot broke the early morning silence. Raven raised her pistol and shot back towards the street, not sure of her target. Her shot was answered by several more shots. Raven looked at Chance. "This isn't how I planned this."

The voices of men and the sound of doors swinging open became more frequent as a hail of bullets hit near where they hid and men yelled directions to each other.

"I hope the Marshal and your brothers don't get the idea they can fight their way in here. They will be cut to pieces. There's got to be at least thirty men out there by the sound of it." It was at that moment they heard more shooting, and this time it was away from them.

"Sounds like your brothers and the Marshal and his men joined the fight. Unfortunately it looks like this is going to be a bad day for all of us."

"We all knew this probably wasn't going to be a picnic. Can we crawl towards the river bank and escape that way?"

"It's almost straight down and rock lined. I heard of several prisoners trying to escape that way, and none of them survived. Just keep shooting. I will think of something."

Raven turned towards Chance and Link, "I'm not sure, but that shooting sounds like it is coming from the front gates."

The sound of gun shots intensified. "Those are Henry repeating rifles, and that is a Gatlin gun. By God, the Army must have gotten here." The sun had begun to rise, and Raven could see men running down the street in both directions. It seemed that the Gatlin gun and the Henry repeating rifles were making progress into the camp, and the sound of the fighting was getting louder.

"Quick, let's make a break for it and head for the cabin that Betsy might be in."

Chance, Raven, and Link took off running as a man appeared out of nowhere and shot in their direction. The man tried frantically to reload his musket while Raven raised her pistol and shot. A cloud of black smoke filled the air as the man crumpled face first into the dirt.

"Good shot," said Chance.

"Thanks now run!"

Raven rushed to the first building and began working her way toward the cabin compound that had once been her prison. There was still a lot of shooting, and the sound of the gunfire seemed to be progressively moving deeper into the settlement. Raven rushed to the door of the prisoners' cabin, which stood partially open. A body was lying in the opening, the body of one of the women Raven had been held captive with. She quickly peered in, and then jerked her head back, concerned that someone would be armed inside. Waiting a moment, she repeated the process, but saw no movement, only bloody bodies scattered on the dirt floor.

This time she took a moment to scan the room with her gun at the ready before entering. Raven hurriedly stepped over the body jamming the doorway and jumped to one wall. It took her eyes a moment to adjust to the light, but finally she could count six bodies lying about. She checked for a pulse as she moved from body to body, but there was none.

Then she recognized a coat. It was Marquese, and he was lying on top of one of the other bodies. A large blood stain covered the back of his coat, and when she moved him she heard a low moan. Raven quickly tried to roll the heavy body of Marquese to one side, but it was difficult. Below Marquese's stiff body lay Miss Martha, her face blood stained and bruised.

"So you made it, Raven. Did Link escape?

"Yes, Link made it. He is here with me."

Miss Martha smiled and then coughed before regaining her composure. "Thank you, Raven. Promise me you will take care of him. He's had nothing but this hell his whole life."

"I know. I will take care of him, don't worry."

"Do you know what happened to Betsy?" asked Raven.

"Some of the Indians brought her back and Scar beat her in front of everyone before chaining her to the Devil's Cross. I am sure he planned to kill her when he returned, but as of yesterday, no one had seen or heard from him."

"That's because he's dead. Link killed him."

"Link killed him. My little boy killed the toughest man in this camp. Marquese would have been proud." She coughed several more times and then continued, "Marquese tried to save me. Hell, they just started killing people after the Indians rode out. No warning, no nothing. We all heard some shots, and then a man just walked in here and started shooting us. Marquese tried to stop him, but the man shot him, too. A few of the women made it out, but I don't know what happened to them."

Raven grabbed two buffalo hides. One she rolled up and put behind Miss Martha's head, and the other one she put over her body just as Vern poked his head inside the cabin.

"Raven, are you all right?"

"Quick, come help me, Vern. Miss Martha has been shot, and she needs water. I need you and Chance to stay with her while I go look for Betsy."

"I will come, too," said Chance.

"No, I need you to help her. I know my way around, and I don't want to draw any more attention than necessary. Please, just help her. I will be back soon."

With that, Raven stood up and headed out the door, carrying her pistol at the ready. She moved stealthily between trees and buildings until she was close to where the cross stood. Several times she stepped over bodies, two of prisoners she recognized, and three of Bleeker's men.

When she could see the Devil's Cross, there, hanging from chains, was a limp body. The whine of several bullets going by her head made Raven jerk back and flatten her back against the log wall. There was no way she was going to be able to run across that road, at least not with this much shooting going on. Quickly she moved around back of the cabin and began crawling until she was able to make it to the creek bed. Sliding through the dirt down to the shallow edge of the water she carefully looked around.

She was totally out of sight with the channel of the creek bed lying a good four feet below the road. Staying low to the ground, she began crawling along the bank as she headed towards the bridge. The constant sound of shots continued as she made her way under the bridge to the bank on the other side.

Raven crept up the bank, keeping close to the bridge, until she was beside the thick, three-foot tall log that marked the bridge's entrance. She glanced over at the cross and saw a bloody Betsy, but she wasn't moving. Raven prayed that she hadn't already been executed, or killed by a random bullet. Using the timber and an abandoned wagon for cover, she feverishly crawled towards the cross. She had covered a little over five yards when she felt the sting of a bullet as it nicked her left thigh. Groaning in pain, she continued crawling.

Betsy's head hung motionless to her right. Raven made her way up to the back of the cross and touched Betsy's arm. Raven pulled the heavy hatchet from her belt, and with a solid hit, the lock exploded into two pieces as one of Betsy's arms flopped lifelessly to the ground. Raven crawled to the other side of the cross and hid behind it.

"Betsy, are you alright? Betsy?" Raven implored in a raised voice, but not loud enough to bring unwanted attention. "Betsy, talk to me," she said but there was no response.

Raven crawled closer when she saw movement to her side. It was one of Bleeker's men, and he was running straight at her with his musket pointed in their direction. In a split second Raven raised and cocked her pistol and fired at twenty feet, knocking the man backwards onto the ground. A small puff of dust rose as his musket slid across the dusty ground, coming to rest right in front of the cross where Betsy still hung by one arm. Raven stood up and with a hard chop, broke the other lock, dropping Betsy's limp body to the ground. With great effort Raven began dragging Betsy towards the trees, not knowing if she was still alive or not. Finally she made it past the tree line to a tree that provided some protection. She leaned Betsy against its trunk and looked around to see if anyone had followed. Raven knew Betsy needed water, so she turned and started crawling back towards the creek.

It was then that she heard the click of a pistol hammer being cocked and looked up to see Hamilton smiling above her. "Well, look who I have here. If it isn't my little escapee, back for some more. I really didn't think I would ever see you again, and then you drop yourself right back here at my feet! Who would have thought? If I had my druthers, I would have put you back in the Pit with all those snakes. But now, with all our newfound friends out there, I guess I will just have to…"

Out of nowhere came Chance, flying through the air, crashing into Hamilton with a thud that sent both men flying. Hamilton stumbled to his feet and threw a right cross to Chance's jaw, which threw his head back and his body crashing against a wagon. Chance and Hamilton both jumped back to their feet and Chance threw a blow to Hamilton's stomach that lifted him off the ground. He followed it with a heavy blow to Hamilton's jaw, which sent him dropping to the ground with a hard thud and a heavy moan.

Raven just looked at Chance as he knelt down beside her. Raven smiled. "You have saved me so many times that I have lost count. Betsy needs water now. Do you have any? She's in rough shape."

Chance pulled the small flask that hung over his shoulder and under his arm and squirted water onto Betsy's parched lips. "Hopefully this will help bring her around, but for now let's keep our heads down until the Army gets this job finished."

It was then that Raven saw Roper dodging his way up the street.

"Chance, that's not the Army, that's McCabe's men."

"What the hell? You're right, that's Roper leading the charge."

It was a good twenty minutes later when the final shot rang out. They waited another five minutes, listening to the shouting of men as they searched the grounds. A few of Bleeker's men had surrendered, but most lay dead throughout the compound, their bodies mingled with the bodies of the prisoners. Of the nearly fifty prisoners the camp had held, only about a third of them had survived, and they began to come out from their hiding spots once the shooting had stopped. Chance turned and saw one of McCabe's men standing beside a tree, looking around, and yelled, "Hey, do you have a doctor with you?"

"No, but we have the next best thing a battlefield-trained medic. I will go find him and bring him back."

"Thanks. Did we lose many men?"

"Not from what I've seen. This Bleeker gang sure got one heck of a whooping today. They won't be taking over any more wagon trains that is for sure. We heard there would be a pile of Indians here, but we haven't seen one."

Raven saw movement in the corner of her eye and aimed her musket at Hamilton as he struggled to sit up, his face bloodied from the fight. Just then, Roper and two of his men came running up.

"Well, this must be Hamilton, the devil's helper," said Roper.

"Pretty much, at least that's the way most know him. Have you found Captain Bleeker yet?" Raven asked, as she turned and suddenly saw the man who had worked for the Army Medical Corp running towards them. He quickly knelt down beside Betsy. Carefully he felt her pulse and checked her breathing.

"It's lucky we got here. She wouldn't have lasted much longer, but I think she'll pull through. Wish I could say the same about all those poor prison bastards, hell of a slaughter out there."

"Did you treat Miss Martha?"

"Is she the older woman over at the cabin back a ways?"

Raven nodded.

"She's in bad shape with that shot to the stomach. I did what I could for her."

Raven looked up to see Vern and Virgil as they came running over and fell to their knees beside Betsy. "Is she all right?"

The medic looked up at them. "She is really beat up, but I think she will be fine with a little care."

Chance walked over and helped Hamilton stagger to his feet, as one of McCabe's men pulled his hands behind him and tied them.

"I have to go see Miss Martha again."

"Go, Raven. We can take care of everything here," said Chance kindly. "We will take good care of Betsy."

Raven took off at a run for Miss Martha's cabin as tears streamed down her face. As she got closer, she could see a group huddled in front of the cabin. They had moved Miss Martha out into the light and Link held his mother's head in his lap, while several other men were trying to help. Raven knelt down beside Link and noticed tears rolling down his face. "Mother," he said softly.

"It's all right, Link," Miss Martha said. "I have accomplished something very special, helping you two out of this ungodly hellhole."

"Miss Martha," said Raven, "Betsy is going to live, and by helping us to escape, you probably saved the lives of a third of the prisoners. It appears that Bleeker planned to kill every prisoner before they took their loot and abandoned this place."

"Who is this man?" Miss Martha raised her trembling finger and pointed behind Raven.

Raven quickly turned and looked.

"It's Gillis McCabe."

Gillis moved up close to Link. Raven moved to one side as Gillis knelt down beside them. Raven looked at Gillis for a second.

"You were so certain that you weren't going to help us, what happened?" asked Raven.

"Your brooch."

"What about the brooch?"

"The brooch you forgot at my ranch. It was my wife's. She was wearing it the day she disappeared."

Raven instantly patted her coat pocket like she was looking for something and then seemed to realize he was right.

He pulled the brooch from his pocket and opened the cover, exposing the water damaged picture. "I know you can't see her with this water stain and all, but that was her picture. I had the brooch made special for her back in Virginia. It was the first thing I ever gave her. She never left the house without it. Lucie showed it to me after you forgot it."

"I set it next to my clothes when I took my bath and Lucie was going to clean it up. I guess if I hadn't forgotten it in my haste, you might never have seen it."

"That's probably true. Anyway, finally I came to the conclusion that there wasn't any way someone just found that brooch, that this Bleeker fellow or his men must have taken my wife." He paused. "I loved my wife, I loved her more than anything on this earth, and I damn well plan to find her and then take my revenge on this Captain Bleeker and what's left of his gang.

Raven looked back at the dying Miss Martha.

"Mr. McCabe, thank you. It tells me there is still a God out there."

"Miss Martha, may I ask you a question?"

Miss Martha coughed again, a deep, serious cough. "Yes."

"My wife disappeared from our ranch a couple of years ago, and we all thought she drowned." Gillis gently reached for Miss Martha's free hand as his eyes began to water. "Well, what I need to know is if my wife is still alive. Her name is Sandra, and she has beautiful long blonde hair and a lovely laugh," McCabe continued.

"I knew her. She spoke with a thick southern drawl."

"Yes, very. She was from southern Virginia."

Miss Martha coughed gently and then looked Gillis in the eyes, "She was here, probably for five or six months."

"Well, where is she now?"

"I'm sorry, Mr. McCabe. She was a good woman. Bleeker sold her to the Mex at the Gathering last year. I thought Bleeker was going to keep her for himself but the Mex must have offered more money than that greedy bastard could refuse. I'm sorry, I'm so sorry. She gave Link that brooch about a week before they took her. He considered it one of his most prized possessions."

With that, Miss Martha coughed up a little more blood, and Link moved to hold her head more upright.

"Miss Martha, do you know what happened to Elsie?"

"I think she was sold, but I don't know to whom. Seems to me she rode out of here four or five days ago with some men." She coughed again. "I have no idea where they were headed."

"Bleeker just went crazy after you three escaped. It was chaos here." Miss Martha suddenly spat blood all over herself. She struggled to talk, "Please, take care of Link."

Gillis McCabe interrupted, "Do you know where this Mex took her?"

Miss Martha coughed one final time before her head slumped to one side. For a split second she looked at Raven and then to Link before her hollow eyes rolled back and stared blindly up towards the sky.

Raven put her fingers on her eyelids, closed them, and gave Link a hug. "Your ma was a great lady, and I want you to know I am going to take good care of you. You will always be family to me."

A moment later, one of McCabe's men ran up. "Mr. McCabe, they captured Bleeker's main man Hamilton. They are holding him up the street by the bridge."

The man pointed back down the road as Gillis McCabe struggled to his feet, the burden of hate and pain weighed heavily on his face. He turned and slowly began walking down the road in the direction of the bridge, his head slightly down with a determined pace.

One of the men who followed him quietly spoke to another of the men, "I would hate to be that Hamilton or Bleeker guy right now, never seen Mr. McCabe so mad."

Link kneeled over Miss Martha and gave her a soft kiss on the cheek before jumping up and running after Gillis as he walked towards the bridge and the cross that had been the object of so much pain over the years.

Hamilton was standing and being restrained by Jake and Chance as Gillis walked up and stared into Hamilton's snake-like eyes. With a blow empowered by pure hatred, Gillis McCabe hit Hamilton in the stomach so hard that he tumbled back to the ground. Hamilton moaned and then gasped for breath as Gillis stood over and stared down at him. Chance reached down and helped a defiant-looking Hamilton back to his feet.

"Well, why don't you just have your piss ants shoot me or take me to the Army to hang? Let's get this damn thing done."

"Oh, Mr. Hamilton, I will deal with you in my own good time. You and your boss ripped the most precious thing in this life away from me. You have hurt and killed more people than anyone will probably ever know. No, Mr. Hamilton, I need to come up with something very special for you, the kind of death befitting a person of your character. Hell will welcome you, but I want you to suffer on your way there."

Link was standing slightly behind Gillis when he reached up and touched his arm. Gillis turned with a bit of an angry look on his face and looked down at Link. It was obvious that Link wanted to say something, but only wanted Gillis to hear. As Gillis leaned over, Link grabbed his arm and gently pulled him down where he could talk into his ear. "That's a good idea, son. Maybe that will let him share some of the terror he so routinely dealt out. Yes, Link, I like that idea."

"What idiot idea would a boy come up with?" yelled Hamilton angrily.

"It's obvious that you drastically underestimate this young man's intelligence and abilities. For the last ten years, he's seen and learned from some of the most evil men these parts have ever known." Gillis turned, "Chance, Jake, will you two bring Hamilton and follow Link and me? I think Link is right. It is only fair that he experiences the terror of his ways."

"What are you going do?" screamed a much more concerned Hamilton, as the two men forcibly dragged him.

"From what I hear, Mr. Hamilton, I am sure you will be comfortable with what we have planned. You always seemed to enjoy it when you watched others dealing with their fear."

"What are you going to do?" shouted Hamilton becoming fearful.

Link and Gillis walked to the heavy door that covered the entrance to the thermal cave.

"Well Mr. Hamilton, Link thinks tying you up and putting you inside this cave with the rattlesnakes befits your crime. We will make sure to have it totally dark, and Link will agitate the snakes enough that they will know you're there. That way, later, when they start crawling around, it will be even more entertaining for you; at least that seemed to entertain you before. I do have a question for you, Mr. Hamilton. Do you remember selling a blonde woman to a Mexican man about a year ago at your Gathering?"

"Bleeker handles the woman sales. I never liked that Mex."

"Well, Mr. Hamilton that was my wife."

"I didn't do anything to your wife and I don't know anything about the Mex."

"Well, do you know anything about what happened to a pretty young lady named Elsie?"

"No, I told you I didn't deal with the women."

"If there is nothing further you can add, then I guess it is time for you to join the snakes."

"I won't go in there. For God's sake, man, I told you what I know, now just shoot me and let's get on with it!"

"No, no, I don't think so. I want you to relate to all those people you used as entertainment," said Gillis calmly.

When Roper joined them, Chance and Jake tightly held Hamilton as beads of sweat began to cover his forehead. Gillis turned to Link. "Are there any torches or anything that he could possibly light? I don't want him finding a flint. We wouldn't want Mr. Hamilton to not play fair."

"Okay, enough is enough, stop this madness and hang me or shoot me, but don't put me in with those snakes. I hate snakes," begged Hamilton, as Link took a long stick and entered the mine.

"So do I, but unfortunately that is how this game is played, Mr. Hamilton. Roper, as soon as Link is done will you escort Mr. Hamilton into the cave and close the door?"

"No, no you can't do this," Hamilton screamed as he kicked to get free.

Several minutes later Link walked out of the cave and the three men drug Hamilton inside, tossing him onto the floor of rock and dirt. The buzz of numerous rattlesnakes could be easily heard from the darkness as the men slammed the door.

Gillis turned to Roper, "Now, have the men pile rocks over this entrance and make them big ones."

The muffled sounds of screams and pounding could be heard on the back side of the door as four of McCabe's men began carefully piling rocks over the entrance. McCabe turned to Link. "He won't hurt anyone ever again, I guarantee it."

Chapter 23

The street was littered with the bodies of prisoners, Bleeker's men, and a few unlucky gunmen who'd ridden for McCabe. Roper walked to the middle of the road and in a commanding voice shouted, "Men, fan out and search every nook and crevice. I want every person still alive out here unarmed. Check every cabin, the woods, the mine, everywhere, for survivors. There are still a bunch of Indians missing, so keep your guard up. Lark, take about five men and head up that back trail that leads to the pass and see what you find. Be back in an hour or two. Do you hear?"

"Yes, sir," they answered almost in unison.

Roper turned and led a second group over to a flat area where they began digging graves for the almost seventy dead.

Chance glanced up as a group of about nine miners walked across the bridge and up the street towards McCabe and him. "Thank God you got here when you did. We thought we were all dead men," said a tall, skinny man, the result of years of hard work and not enough food.

"Those damn men of Bleeker's just walked into the mine and started shooting. We were in the farthest shaft, and when we heard the screams and shots, we figured we better hide. We sealed off the passage with rocks and extra beams and just waited. We all thought we were goners for sure until we heard your shooting."

McCabe just nodded his head in approval at the stragglers. "Glad you made it, a lot of the rest didn't."

"Would you mind having your men help bury these people?" The miner stared at Gillis for a moment and then began to walk by. He paused in front of Chance. "The man is a little short on words, isn't he?"

Chance just smiled and nodded gently. It was about twenty minutes later when Raven joined them and walked up to Chance to hug him.

"Betsy is doing better. She is drinking water and even talking a little. Thanks, Chance. A lot of these people wouldn't have made it if it weren't for you and McCabe."

"No need to thank us. This was something we all needed to do. If it weren't for you, our sister would probably be dead or sold by now."

"Unfortunately, that seems to be what happened to Elsie. Miss Martha said she thought she was sold a few days ago."

Just then, a shot rang out, and soon three more. A couple of minutes later, one of McCabe's men led two men out into the street with their hands in the air. "Boss, these two skunks were hiding in the woods with another man. These two decided to give up after I'd had a discussion with their partner. This Henry rifle kind of changed their attitude about trying to make a run for it."

"Good job, Lark. Leave these men here and help finish searching the place. Then tell Jake to go down to their supply house and start loading the wagons with as much food and supplies as they can haul. If everything goes well, we will be headed back to the ranch tomorrow. We will separate the men and women and house most of them in the barns until spring. We have plenty of firewood, and they can help cut more if needed. I believe, after what they have been through, it will probably work for them. I want it spelled out real clear that first thing in the spring these people will need to be on their way and won't be my problem anymore. Jake, grab one of those prisoners and bring him over here."

"Yes sir, Mr. McCabe."

The dark-skinned man was dressed in a dirty, bright red coat. He was slightly overweight, had a shaggy beard, and was missing one of his front teeth. Raven saw what was happening and started walking towards Gillis McCabe. McCabe looked at the man for a moment. "Are there any more of you coyotes hiding out around here?" The man just looked at him staring defiantly.

"Roper, persuade this man we don't have time for this."

Roper walked over to the man, pulled out his Army pistol and shot the man in the foot. The man fell to the ground, screaming in agony as the other prisoner watched.

"Now sir, I will ask you one last time, is there any more of your men hiding out there?"

The man kept screaming and rolling around, holding his foot, but not answering the question.

"Roper, shoot him in the other foot."

Roper pulled his pistol from his holster again and started to aim when the man screamed, "Please, I'll talk. We were the only ones we saw. We knew you outnumbered us, so we broke and hid."

"Brave men aren't they, Roper?"

"Brave, sir, sort of brave like a scared rabbit!"

"Now, sir, I am going to ask you a few more questions." McCabe pulled a three-inch-by-three-inch picture from inside his vest and showed it to the man. "Did you ever see this woman? Look real hard, now. We wouldn't want to shoot you again for not listening."

"We, we, I mean, yes. She was here about a year ago, real attractive blonde-haired woman, blue eyes," he said in a heavy French accent.

"You are doing much better. Now, what happened to her?"

"I'm not sure. I think the Mex took her."

Gillis McCabe turned to Raven, "Do you know where this ranch is the Mex took her to?"

"No," she said staring at the man who was bleeding on the ground.

"So, what else can you tell me?"

"I don't know anything more. I wasn't here; I was on a raid. I just heard they had sold her to the Mex."

"Who is the Mex?"

"They said his name was Señor Ramón Gonzalez. Apparently he has a copper mine down in southern Colorado somewhere. He has been coming here for the last couple of years to buy women, usually blonde women, and take them back to his ranch. Will someone help me now? I am going to bleed to death."

"Not until I am done. I am sure you didn't treat these prisoners any better than I am treating you, isn't that right, sir? Now I want you to tell me where Captain Bleeker is."

"I don't know. I saw him ride out this morning but I don't know where he went."

"Roper, I'm not sure this man is telling me the truth. Can you persuade him to be more specific?"

With that, Roper grabbed the man's finger and bent it back until it broke with a snap and the man screamed again in pain.

"Am I being too hard on you?" asked McCabe sarcastically.

The man didn't answer, he just mumbled to himself as Raven walked up to Gillis. "Mind if I ask a few questions?"

"No, go right ahead."

"There was a young girl here, about fourteen, real pretty with brownish-blonde hair, named Elsie. Where is she?"

"I don't know. Really, I don't know."

"Jog his memory, Roper; the lady is waiting."

Roper hauled off and gave the man a kick to his thigh that sent him tumbling across the ground as he screamed in agony. "Now, sir, I expect you to think, and think fast. What happened to this young lady named Elsie?"

"I saw Bleeker with her a couple of days ago, but that's all I know."

"Are you sure that's all?"

"Don't tell him anymore," said the second prisoner in a firm voice.

Gillis turned, looked at the man for a moment, pulled his gun and shot the man in the stomach. "If I wanted your opinion, I would have asked."

"Now, sir, can you tell me anything more about this Mex?"

"No, no, I can't."

"How about the Indians, it was my understanding that there were a lot of Indians helping with this place. Where are they?"

"The mountain lion."

"What about the mountain lion?"

"The Indians were afraid of the mountain lion. It seemed to hunt them when they were out scouting. The damn thing killed at least eight Indians, and they began thinking it was a god, a bad omen. Several mornings ago they, all of them, just up and left. No one heard them leave, they were just gone."

"So this omathk-attayo or mountain lion hunted the Indians?"

"Oui."

Gillis paused to think for a minute, and Roper took the opportunity. "Mind if I ask him a question, boss?"

"Help yourself, Roper."

"Where is all the loot that Bleeker and you men stole from these settlers?"

"Some of the money we spend, but most of the gold, jewelry, and a lot of the money is in Bleeker's cabin in a big safe, or at least it was. The bastard always kept the lion's share of everything, he and Hamilton. They would kill you if you complained. Most of the other stuff, like the food, clothes, horse stuff, tools, we kept in those big barns down the road below the bridge."

"Do you have anything more to tell me?"

"No sir, will you help me now?" he pleaded as he held his foot.

"You and your gang took the most precious thing in my life away and have brought untold pain and suffering to many people. I think it is time you paid for your sins. Men, string him up."

The man began screaming and struggling uncontrollably as McCabe's men fought to drag him over to a large pine tree where Jake had thrown a rope over a branch. Finally, the man went totally limp as they slipped the rope around his neck.

"May God forgive you, because I sure as hell won't," said Gillis, as he turned and starting walking down the road as the man struggled, kicking his boots several feet above the ground.

"That's one tough man that's carrying a lot of pain and anger," said Chance to Raven, as the two stood and watched Gillis walk down the street.

"I know. I understand his pain. I won't rest until I find Elsie."

With that, Chance put his arm around Raven's shoulder as Link walked up and reached for Raven's hand.

"Let's go see how Betsy is doing. When the corpsman is done, I want to move her up to Hamilton's old cabin," said Raven, as the three turned and headed back down towards the bridge. When they arrived, the corpsman was working beside Betsy as Vern and Virgil stood close by. He was trying to get her to drink more water.

The corpsman heard their footsteps and turned. "Good, you're here. She is doing just fine. She has been asking for you, Raven."

Betsy lifted her hand up, and Raven took it. "We made it, Raven, we made it. I really can't believe it, but we made it." Then she raised her other hand up towards Chance. "Chance, you and Vern and Virgil, I can't believe you're here," she said, with tears streaming down her face. "I should have known you would find us."

"Your three brothers were going to storm this place by themselves if they had to. They would have done anything to save you."

Betsy smiled, "Yes, I know. They are pretty amazing and very special." She paused for a moment.

"I understand we are leaving tomorrow if we can get the all the wagons loaded."

"That's what we are hearing, too."

She looked at her three brothers and then to Raven. "Tonight I would like you to do something for me, burn the Devil's Cross to the ground. I don't want anybody to be hurt by it ever again. This is a wicked place and I want to get as far away from it as I can."

"We will be happy do that for you, Betsy. We only wish we could have done more for these poor souls."

Betsy smiled. "Saving all these people is a lot. I am so proud of you."

Everyone hugged and talked for a few more minutes, then Chance excused himself to help with the loading of the wagons, and Vern and Virgil stood ready to help take Betsy up to Hamilton's cabin.

Raven leaned down close to Betsy and whispered in her ear, "Do you remember me telling you about the man I saw in Independence, the tall, handsome man that I met on the steps of that attorney's office?"

"Yes, you told me that story at least a dozen times, and I enjoyed it every time!"

"Well, that was your brother; that was Chance. Who would have ever thought that the man I dreamed of all these months was your brother, and then he goes and saves Link and me from Scar. Life is so strange."

"From the look on Chance's face, the feeling is mutual. You are getting a good man. He was the family leader when Pa wasn't around, and he always protected me."

"I can see those qualities in him."

"What do you plan to do now? I know Bleeker killed your aunt and uncle, and well, you know. What are you thinking?" asked Betsy.

"I really don't know, except I have to find Elsie, and I want to get Link out of here. I was thinking that I will probably take him to our farm in Oregon."

"Can I go with you? I love my brothers, but I have had enough of this country and need to make a new life. There are too many terrible memories here."

"With this winter coming on strong, I think we will need to figure out where we can stay until spring. You and Link are certainly welcome to come to Oregon with me then. You two are my family now, and I promised Miss Martha that I would take care of him."

"Is she dead?"

"Her and Marquese, they killed them in the cabin. Looked like Marquese fought to protect her but…" Raven became choked up.

"It's all right, Raven, everything will be all right."

Raven looked up as the corpsman and two men carrying a stretcher were coming down the dirt street.

"We need to move her into Hamilton's cabin. I just felt a couple of snowflakes. The weather is starting to change, and I don't want her getting wet or cold. I don't know if you heard, but Mr. McCabe wants to be on the move first thing in the morning back to the Greybull. He's going to house the men and women in the barns until spring, then divide everything up and hire a guide to take these people to Oregon."

"They found a huge amount of money in Bleeker's cabin, so Mr. McCabe plans to divide it up and hire a good, honest wagon master. Mr. McCabe is well aware that, if he doesn't get these people somewhere safe and warm for the winter, with food, some won't make it. Ain't like Mr. McCabe to extend a helping hand like this; seems to go against his nature. Must be because of his wife, but whatever it is, his men seem glad he's doing it."

"Thanks. Would you take her up to Hamilton's cabin for the night? I cleaned it a number of times, and that is probably as nice as it gets, with the exception of Bleeker's cabin. I am sure Mr. McCabe will stay there for the night. Besides, he needs to keep an eye on the valuables."

Just then, Link showed up. "I am glad you're back," said Raven. "We are taking Betsy up to Hamilton's old cabin for the night. Would you like to go with us? I will be up in a little while."

As usual, Link just nodded and followed as the men carried the stretcher up the hill to the small, but well-built cabin. Tucked into the trees, the cabin, with its large fireplace, had some of the better views of the camp, and its isolated location made it quiet for a person needing some recuperative rest.

On the way, Raven saw Roper eating his dinner with Marshal Dicker on a log by one of the buildings, so she stopped. "I will catch up. I want to speak to Roper for a minute."

"Marshal, Roper, do you mind me joining you for a minute?"

"Glad to have you," said the Marshal, while Roper quietly continued eating.

"First of all, I would like to thank you, Roper."

"Just following orders."

"I take it as more than that. Anyway, how did you find us so fast? We had a heck of a head start on you."

"When you came to our ranch, you mentioned staying in an old barn with a burned out cabin. Two of the men and I found that cabin early this summer and stayed there for a couple of days scouting. We even cut some grass, just in case we ever got caught out there in one of those freak blizzards that drop through here periodically. I just put two and two together and headed there first. You were pretty easy to track from there."

"So, it was you that put the grass in the barn?"

"Yes, ma'am, it was."

Just then, Raven heard something and looked up as a rider rode up to Roper; it was Lark. "Find something?" asked Roper.

"A dead horse about eight miles up the trail looks like it must have slipped on the rocks and ice. This weren't any ordinary horse. It was big and black and fine bred, and that ain't all. We found at least thirty pounds of gold coins in some saddle bags not far from there."

"Sounds like it might have been Bleeker's horse."

"Go tell Mr. McCabe, and then get some chow," said Roper as he turned to Raven. "Excuse me ma'am, but I need to go."

Raven walked up to the cabin. The men had made the small room Betsy would stay in as comfortable as possible with a large pitcher of water and a warm fire. It wasn't long before Betsy fell into a deep sleep as Raven and Link sat down on chairs to watch over her.

Link looked over at Raven; she appeared tired and worn from the day. "What is going to happen next?"

"Well, I haven't quite figured out everything, except I know I need to find Elsie, but no matter what, you are going to be with me. I am going to watch over you the best I can; we are family."

Link just smiled and closed his eyes. An hour later, a light knock came from the door. It was Vern and Virgil.

"Thought we would give you a break and let you two get some food. They're preparing to serve supper. They have a bunch of fires for people to sit around while they eat. It helps that it isn't snowing anymore, leastwise for the moment."

"Thanks. That sounds good. I'm tired, but getting a little food into me should help all around, and I know Link has to be hungry."

On the walk down the hill, the two could see the small production line for dinner. Raven saw Chance helping to dish up plates. As they got closer, he looked up and saw them. "Well, hi there, how's Betsy?"

"She is doing as well as one could hope, a little weak and bruised. Hopefully with food and water we can bring her around. I think she will be fine by morning to ride in the back of one of those wagons on our way to your ranch."

"It's going to be great to have her around again. My brothers and I want you and Link to join us, too. The cabin will be a bit crowded, but it sure would be a heck of a lot better than McCabe's barn."

"That's a generous offer. Link and I will need a place to stay, but I need to get after it if I am going to find Elsie."

"How are you going to catch up to that bunch? Do you have at least a name?"

"No, but I will find her."

"I hear there could be at least five of them, and they probably know every trail and shortcut between here and wherever they are going. Hell, in another couple of weeks, it is going to be solid winter. There are a lot of mountains and country between here and wherever they took her. A lot of people have perished that didn't know the right route or didn't take those deep snows seriously."

"I know you are making sense, but the thought of Elsie being with those evil men, well, it's too horrible to think about."

"Here's a plate for each of you, and it's about time I got something to eat, too. So, if I'm not intruding too much, I would like to join you two."

Chance grabbed a plate, and the three of them went over to a small, crackling fire and sat down, just after three people who were sitting there got up to clean their plates and leave.

"That was good timing. The fire feels good."

The three sat down with Raven in the middle. Chance picked at his food for a moment. "Is there something wrong?" asked Raven.

"Yeah, in a way, there is," responded Chance. "I don't know where to start on this, so I guess I will just try and jump into it. However I say this, it will probably come out wrong, but I just don't want to lose you again. I lost you once, and now fate has changed everything. Here you are, older and more beautiful, and a lady, and now I don't want to lose you again. I guess I said my piece." With that, Chance stood up and started to walk back over to help with the food.

"You stop right there, mister. I have a thing or two to say myself. When I lived in this hellhole, you were the person I thought of every night. You were the person in my dreams that gave me hope that I would get through this. You ain't ever walking away from me again!"

Chance turned and walked back to Raven as she stood up. He gave her a tight hug, then a kiss. Link smiled from ear to ear.

"I guess we just need to figure things out, don't we? But for now I want to keep a close eye on Betsy. Chance, when you get done helping, come up to the cabin. I would like to finish this discussion."

Chance just smiled a huge smile. "I will," then he turned and headed back to help.

Link looked at Raven and smirked. "You like him."

Raven just smiled.

Link went to help with what he could as Raven took her time walking back up the hill to the cabin. For the first time in her life, she was happy. She had dreamed of and loved Chance from the first time she saw him, and through this terrible experience, somehow their lives had been brought together.

In the back of her mind she thought of Elsie, but for once she wanted this moment for herself, and for that she felt guilty. It was dark walking up the path, and she could see the lantern in the window as she entered the porch and opened the heavy wooden door. Both Vern and Virgil stood up to meet her.

"How is she doing?" Raven asked.

"Slept the whole time; not a peep out of her," replied Vern.

"I appreciate you two watching over her. Would you tell Link to come back up when he gets done helping with the chores?"

"Sure will. How are you doing, you two going to be okay by yourselves?"

"Yes, I'll be fine and Betsy is getting better, a good night's sleep will help a lot. By the way, did you hear McCabe is burning down the whole camp tomorrow when we leave?"

"That's probably the right thing to do so none of those lowlife coyotes ever come back. I saw the look on McCabe's face when he talked about that Señor Ramón Gonzalez, wouldn't want to be in his shoes either. Heard

McCabe is planning to get after them as soon as he gets organized," said Vern.

The two men walked out the door, and Raven could hear their heavy boots on the porch as they walked down the steps. Raven turned to the kerosene lantern on the counter beside the bed and turned the flame down to almost a flicker before closing her eyes. She lay in the chair, quietly resting and almost asleep, when a slight sound caught her attention. Her eyes shot across the open room scanning for a source, but she could see nothing. Quietly examining the dimly lit room, she still couldn't see or hear anything more. She decided it was just the normal sounds of an aging cabin and closed her eyes once again.

Soon she heard something again. It almost sounded like fabric brushing against the floor, so she slowly opened her eyes, just enough that she could see without moving. Her eye caught movement, and she focused on a rug that stretched across the floor in the middle of the room. She couldn't be sure, but in the dark room, the rug seemed to be slowly moving. She tried to breathe normally and keep calm enough to think straight, but it was difficult. She thought about getting a gun, but the pistol was on the dresser across the room.

Whatever was going on, she needed to find out quickly and make her move. Suddenly the rug began to lift off the floor. As it slowly opened, the shape of a hand moved out onto the floor. Raven's eyes were fully open as she watched someone stealthily climb out from the hidden space. She could see the man carefully lowering the door back to the floor, still crouching as he moved. Raven didn't know what to do. Should she scream? Would this person hurt Betsy? How could she defend herself from this much bigger person? All of these were questions filling her mind. Then she saw his image reflected in the lantern as the man pulled something from his belt. He had a knife!

Without a sound, the man turned and moved towards the bed and chair Raven had chosen for the night. The man moved silently, like an athlete, across the floor. Raven kept telling herself to not move until the moment was right. When the man raised his knife above her, she kicked him in the groin with all her might. Then she jumped and rolled over the bed as the man lashed out with his knife, missing her face by inches.

Like a cat, the man moved, blocking Raven's escape, as she turned to face him. He slowly moved forward, swinging his knife back and forth.

There was little room for Raven to back up, so she let out a scream, "Help, help, please help us!"

The screams were loud and panicky, but Raven knew with the sound of people talking far below, there was little chance that anyone would hear her.

"We are pretty isolated up here, Raven. Go ahead and scream, but I think your luck has finally run out."

Raven recognized the low, firm voice of Captain Bleeker immediately. "It's you." She paused. "I thought you were gone!"

"Well, you were wrong," he said, as he continued to flick his knife at her, "but you, my dear, soon will be."

Raven kept backing up into the corner, and knew she was now in a worse position than she had been before. She looked for something to strike back with, but there was only the kerosene lantern by the bed. Bleeker took another step closer putting her in reach of his knife and she now had her back against the logs of the wall. Bleeker's eyes watched her every move, like the eyes of a cat stalking its prey. Raven had no more answers and no place to run, when suddenly Betsy sat up in bed and screamed. Bleeker was only distracted for a split second, but it was long enough for Raven to reach back and throw the kerosene lantern in his direction.

Bleeker ducked, and the lantern shattered on the wall, sending kerosene throughout the room. The whole wall instantly burst into flames as Bleeker charged Raven with his knife, slashing at air. Suddenly a shot rang out and the body of Captain Bleeker fell across Raven, the knife falling harmlessly to the ground. Raven shoved the body of Captain Bleeker off herself and looked up to see Chance standing in the doorway, as Betsy continued to scream.

"Quick, help me get Betsy out of here before this whole place goes up."

With Raven's help, Chance grabbed Betsy, threw her over his shoulder, and started out through the blaze of flames. Raven watched for a second, and then began hurrying behind him. When she heard a muffled sound, she glanced down at the trapdoor, grabbed the rug, and threw the trapdoor open. There was someone down there, tied and gagged on the floor, and Raven instantly recognized that it was Elsie.

She turned and grabbed Bleeker's knife from the floor and quickly climbed down the stairs to where Elsie lay. The knife's razor-sharp edge quickly cut through the ropes. A stiff Elsie struggled to stand, but with

Raven's help she climbed up the ladder and into the room filled with flames and smoke. The flames had grown and now threatened to cut off their escape.

"Go," yelled Raven, as the two of them launched themselves through the flames and rolled out on to the porch where Chance swiftly helped them to their feet and down the stairs. Raven turned and looked back as the whole cabin burst into flames before their eyes. They then headed towards the group of people running up the hill to meet them.

Two days later

McCabe and his men led the large group on horseback, followed by men and women on foot, and finally shadowed by heavy, loaded wagons filled with supplies from the storage barns. The train made their way through the remnants of the once stout gates, leaving only the smoldering ruins and horrible memories behind.

Several miles down the river a large mountain lion scanned the valley from a high vantage point while it licked its blood stained paws. Near the big cat lay the partial remains of a decaying corpse buried under a mixture of sticks, grass and dirt.

Chance was riding his new paint horse that had once been owned by Hamilton, alongside Roper. A half days ride ahead was the cutoff trail that would take them to either the Creagers' cabin or McCabe's Greybull Ranch.

Chance heard a galloping horse and turned to see Raven riding up beside him. Roper took a look over at Chance. "I think I will check things out up ahead." With that, he gave his horse a little nudge with his spurs and galloped off, up through the grass and scattered sage.

"I was talking to Betsy, and she wants Link and me to stay the rest of the winter with you and your brothers. I hope that is alright with you. I still intend to move on to Oregon in the spring and take Link and Elsie. I don't know if Betsy told you, but she wants to come too and, well..." she paused.

"You don't say."

"What do you mean by that?"

"I guess I got a bunch on my mind today."

"Like what?"

"Well, I am thinking I need to go Oregon, too. You know to keep, my eye on my interests."

"And what interests might those be, Mr. Creager?" said Raven with a coy smile.

"Well, my interest in our mule Dixie, of course."

Raven glanced at Chance with a disgusted look.

"Sorry, I meant Ginger," said Chance with a wide smile, and they both began to laugh as light snowflakes filled the air.

I hope you have enjoyed reading *Vanishing Raven* and I look forward to hearing from you. As a new writer, the reviews and emails have been incredible and encouraging. Usually there isn't enough time in the day for all the things I need to accomplish. I juggle my time between work, riding my mules and writing on my latest book. Your encouraging emails really help me to stay on task. I personally enjoy having a physical book in my hands but those of you that use Kindle, I appreciate all the reviews of *Whispers of The Greybull* that are posted on Amazon. The next book I am working on in this series is about Gillis McCabe and mystery behind him fleeing from Virginia and the family secret that threatens his life.

Best wishes, *Stephen B. Smart*

For more on Stephen B. Smart and *Vanishing Raven*, Please visit
www.authorstephenbsmart.com

Please email the author at:
authorstephenbsmart@yahoo.com
with any comments or feedback

65510275R00157

Made in the USA
San Bernardino, CA
07 January 2018